I0723587

penalty box

LUX BRUMALIS
BOOK 1

KRIS BUTLER

Penalty Box
Lux Brumalis Book One
Kris Butler

First Edition: January 2023
Published by: Incognito Scribe Productions LLC
Kris Butler

Copyright © Kris Butler 2023
All rights reserved, including the right to reproduce, distribute, or
transmit in any form or by any means without prior permission of
the author, except in cases of a reviewer quoting brief passages in
review. For subsidiary rights, please contact Kris Butler at
authorkrisbutler@gmail.com
This book is a work of fiction. Names, characters, places and
incidents either are products of the author's imagination or are used
fictitiously. Any resemblance to actual events or locales or persons,
either living or dead, is entirely coincidental.

Proofreading: © 2023 by Owlsome Author Services
Formatting: © 2023 Incognito Scribe Productions LLC
Cover Design: © 2022 Pretty Little Design Co

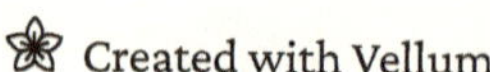 Created with Vellum

penalty BOX

KRIS BUTLER

contents

blurb

I loved two things above all others: hockey and Reese. Becoming Reese's guardian hadn't been in my plans, but I couldn't turn my sibling away when they needed me. I never anticipated how difficult juggling hockey and raising a teenager would be.

Being a woman in a male-dominated sport meant I spent the majority of my time proving I could measure up. It didn't matter that I'd won two Olympic medals or could outshoot most male players. I was a woman, and that was all that mattered.

When an ex leaked a private video, I was suspended from the league for 'morality issues.' Suddenly, I had no clue what to do with my life if it didn't include hockey. With no direction, purpose, or job prospects, I felt lost, with no clear sign of what to do next.

Visiting a friend, an opportunity for Reese emerged in Utah, and I was thrust into a world I hadn't known existed—an elite academy for winter sports. Between coaching hockey and training Reese, I met three guys who made my heart race. But after my last relationship disaster, I wasn't ready to choose a life I wasn't sure fit me anymore.

Feeling hopeful, I accepted a job coaching the male hockey team. Maybe trying something new would be what Reese and I needed. Lux Brumalis could be what got us out of the Penalty Box once and for all.

Watch out, boys; it was time you learned how to play like a girl.

My name's Henley Henshaw, but you can call me Coach.

foreword

This is a contemporary why-choose hockey romance intended for 18+ due to language and content. This book deals with some themes that might be triggering to readers. I always try to do my best to handle things with care for my characters and the reader. So please make sure to take care of yourself first.

SOME THINGS TO CONSIDER ARE THE FOLLOWING:

Family member dies from cancer
Feelings of not being good enough
Past drug use
Mild bullying of non-binary character by peers
Violation of consent (shared videos)

Mild mental/psychological abuse

This book attempts to portray hockey in its truest form, but the author has taken some liberties to make things fit within the world of the book for the story. So for any hockey purest, be kind; it was done purposefully to tell a story. This book highlights women in sports and the inequality many face. I could go on all day about this, but since you probably want to read this book and not listen to my soapbox, turn the page to start Henley's story.

introduction

The penalty box or sin bin is the area in ice hockey where a player sits to serve the time of a given penalty, for an offense not severe enough to merit outright expulsion from the contest. Teams are generally not allowed to replace players who have been sent to the penalty box.

This book is dedicated to women who fight against the parameters the world places on them and succeed anyway.

Keep fighting; we're all right here with you!

CHAPTER 1

Henley

THE ELEVATOR DOOR SHUT, closing me in silence as the words of the past hour ran circles around my head.

Suspended. Unwholesome. Placed on leave.

I didn't know which one hurt the worst as they pierced my soul, ripping me open from the inside. I'd placed my trust in the league and my boyfriend, but it turned out to be for nothing. They'd turned on me when I needed them, leaving me to pick up the pieces. I tried to hold back the tears that wanted to fall, but the second I was alone, they erupted out of me, my lungs gasping for breath.

I doubled over, sliding down the elevator wall until I was in a crouch. I clung to the bar at the back, the only thing keeping me up. What was I going to do now? How would I take care of Reese if I was unemployed? I'd spent my whole life playing hockey. I wasn't sure I knew how to do anything else.

The elevator began to descend, so I gulped in air, standing as I furiously swiped at my face. Pulling out a tissue from my bag, I wiped away the remnants of mascara, using the shiny elevator surface as a mirror. By the time the doors opened, the only indicator that I'd been crying would be my red face. I wasn't even able to get away with crying without the whole world knowing.

Pulling my sunglasses out, I placed them on, feeling a little braver now that no one could see my true state. Stepping forward, I focused on putting one foot in front of the other, ignoring everything else. If I looked at any of the guards or personnel at the complex, I'd lose it.

"Have a good day, Henshaw," the clerk at the desk said. I waved jerkily as I sped by, hoping to avoid a scene. The tears threatened to spill again, anyway.

It was a stab to my heart that I hadn't been expecting. The routine and familiar faces would no longer be part of my day. It was too much, and I barely made it outside without falling over in another heap.

The cold air of the morning hit my cheeks, making my tears more noticeable as they continued to stream down my face. Pulling my keys from my bag, I marched to my car, needing to escape from the pressure to hold everything together. I clearly wasn't as strong as I'd thought, the tears refusing to stop once they'd started.

The car beeped, and I pulled open the door, practically diving into it in the next second as I sucked in a breath, my lip quivering. Walls pressed in around me and I struggled to breathe. I clawed at my hoodie, pulling it over my head in an attempt to open my airway. It felt a little better, but I still couldn't seem to suck in enough air.

There was a knock on my window, but I couldn't make myself turn. I didn't have it in me to face whoever it was. I waved them off, hoping they'd go away.

The door opened, the cold air seeping into the car and bringing goosebumps to my skin. I tightened myself into a ball, praying whoever it was would get the memo. Strong arms wrapped around me, the smell of mint and berries invading my nose as I was pressed up against a hard chest. I wanted to fight whoever this was, but I had nothing left in me. Besides, the pressure felt nice, making the walls not seem as close, so if they were going to kidnap me, at least I'd be calmer.

"Not a kidnapper," a deep voice rumbled, sending vibrations through me. My body began to switch gears, the panic and fear easing as it took stock of the man. I couldn't see his face, but everything else about him was making me stop and take notice.

Lifting my head, I met crystal blue eyes that shimmered in the early morning light. His lashes were long and dark, instantly making me envious. I couldn't look past his eyes, too transfixed by them. He stood, holding me to him outside my car, staring at me.

I felt his slow breathing and realized he was

mirroring how I should breathe. I naturally mimicked him, sucking in a long breath and slowly letting it out. After a few times, I felt myself start to relax, the panic ebbing away as my heart slowed, my body and focus returning to me. It was then I realized my body was shaking.

The dark stranger continued to hold me tightly to him, his voice making a soothing sound as he rocked back and forth. The combination felt nice, and I slowly calmed, the last of my panic falling away. He never broke eye contact, giving me his strength until mine returned.

"Thank you," I said, my voice barely a whisper.

His eyes searched my face, seeming to find what he was looking for. He placed me on my feet, his large hands gripping my elbows until I was steady.

"Don't let them take your soul."

It felt like a reprimand and an encouragement, all in the same breath. He tucked a loose strand of hair behind my ear, the rough pads of his fingertips brushing against my lobe before he pivoted and strode away. I blinked, a bit dazed with him suddenly being gone, unsure of what had happened. Turning, I watched him disappear into a large truck that was parked oddly behind me.

Had he been watching me? How did he know I needed help?

I took a step forward, my body not ready for him to

leave. My hand stretched out, reaching for the dark stranger, urging him to return. I realized I didn't even know his name as the truck pulled away; the tires screeching on the pavement as he drove off, turning out of the parking lot.

Blinking, I used my hand to block the sun as I watched the dark truck turn into traffic. As quickly as he'd stepped into my life, he was gone.

I climbed back into my car and found my sunglasses and hoodie on the passenger seat. I quickly pulled the hoodie over my head and placed the shades on my eyes. I started the car; the music played softly, so I cranked up the volume as I fastened my seatbelt and pulled out of the lot. Glancing in my rearview one last time before I exited, I said a silent goodbye to the hockey complex that had been my work and home for the past five years.

I DROVE IN A DAZE AS I THOUGHT ABOUT THE DARK STRANGER. I couldn't figure out why he seemed familiar or why he'd pulled a random stranger out of their car to comfort them. Did he get off on weeping females or something? Though that didn't feel right. He hadn't seemed like he was getting off on helping me. In fact, if I thought about it, while he seemed concerned about my well-being, he wasn't all that comfortable.

I still couldn't get his smell out of my mind. It was intoxicating, and I knew if I ever smelled it again, it would only be him I envisioned. Crystal blue eyes, dark lashes, and sharp cheekbones that would forever be cemented in my head. I knew I'd be looking at every man from here on out, searching for him in the crowd, hoping I'd see him again.

When I pulled into my apartment complex parking structure, I realized how quick the drive had been. I guess the one advantage of breaking down in the parking lot and being rescued by Mr. Dark and Sexy was I hadn't fixated on being fired.

They could call it whatever they wanted, but I'd been fired when it came down to it. Fired for being a sexual woman who'd sent her boyfriend a video—a video I thought would be safe. It enraged me that, as a woman, I was held to a different standard in the hockey industry. How many countless male hockey stars had sex tapes and sexual exploits blasted all over the news, or sexual harassment allegations for the league to sweep it under the rug?

Too many to count.

It wasn't fair. But if I focused on the fairness in the world, especially in hockey as a woman, I'd still be alone in the parking lot with traces of mascara down my face. It was useless. I needed to think differently and show the league how wrong they were; blowing up and being "emotional" would only cement their decision. It didn't matter how sexist it was. It was how the world worked, regardless of how I felt about it. So, I had to be smarter and beat them at their own game.

The problem was, I didn't know how to do that. Right now, I just felt lost and like everything was falling apart.

With a deep breath, I opened my door and began walking toward my apartment building. I took the back staircase to avoid any press. Since I couldn't guarantee I wouldn't run into anyone I knew in the building, I pulled up the hood of my hoodie, shoving my long, dark ponytail into the back. Keeping my head down, I made my way through the building, avoiding eye contact. The stairs were vacant as I made my ascent. I focused on each step in front of me, pushing everything else aside. I could do this.

When I reached the eighth floor, I was out of breath, huffing as I pushed open the door. Sweat ran down my back, but I kept my hood up and head down, too nervous about running into anybody. I had passed a few people, but I avoided making eye contact, staring at my feet as I walked. When I was a few doors from my apartment, I sighed in relief and pulled out my keys. Glancing up, I met a pair of eyes I wanted to forget.

Everything in me hardened as I stared at Dakota Hughes—left wingman of the Baltimore Barons and my ex-boyfriend.

"Henny, I'm so sorry. I didn't think it would get out. I tried to talk to the league, I did, but my agent told me it would be better if I stayed out of it."

I swiped my hand through the air, my keys jingling with the move. "Just stop, Dakota. Don't call me that ever again. I told you we were through. I'm done, Dakota. *Done*."

"Henny, come on. Don't be like that. It was an honest mistake." He crowded me as I tried to open my door. The smell of his cologne was heady and too much, making me want to puke. It stole the last remnants of the dark stranger's scent, making me sadder than I had any right to be.

I narrowed my eyes as I gritted my teeth. "I said stop. Don't come any closer, or I'll call security. I need to ensure they know not to let you up here again."

He scoffed, stepping back as if I'd slapped him. "Henny, you don't mean that."

"Oh, you'll find that I very much mean it. Let's be real, Dakota. We haven't been good for the past year. We've been holding onto a relationship that wasn't going anywhere. On top of that, I can't ever get past it to forgive you. What you did was inexcusable. You violated me..." The tears started again, and I wouldn't let him have that. I cleared my throat, pressing my fingernails into my palms. "There's no coming back from that. I've lost everything while you got a slap on the wrist. There's nothing left of our relationship. The usefulness of it has worn off. So, just leave. There's no need to make a scene."

While I'd been talking, he'd gone from contrite to mad. When I finished, the side of him I'd always hated emerged, and he looked me up and down like I was scum. I knew his ego wouldn't handle me dismissing him, so I braced myself for whatever blow he was about to bestow upon me.

"You could've had everything, Henny. A life on my arm, a career on my coattails, even." He lifted his head like he'd been doing me a favor, and I was the dumb one for turning him away. "The moment you took in your sister—"

"Sibling. You know Reese is non-binary," I hissed, tired of this argument. He refused to call Reese by the correct pronouns, proving he wasn't as accepting as he portrayed to the media.

"*Sister*," he emphasized. "The second you took *her* in, your career was over. No one wants a weirdo like her on their team, and you going to bat for her to play on the boys' team was too far. You need to remember your place in this sport, Henny. It's cute watching you play, thinking you're as good and tough as the men. I stayed because you were the sport's sweetheart, which looked good for my image." His lip turned into a sneer, and I wondered what I'd ever seen in him.

Maybe I had been deluding myself, picturing this perfect life with him. Looking at him now, I knew it had never been real. Just a version of a future I thought I'd wanted. If he couldn't accept Reese in my life, he wasn't the man for me.

I rolled my eyes, tired of wasting words on someone who'd been more worried about his own image than comforting and protecting me—the woman he proclaimed to love.

It was clear, though, Dakota Hughes only loved himself.

"Goodbye, Dakota." I opened the door, sliding through it, keeping it only open an inch. "And that sex tape... I was thinking of your rival the whole time. It was the only way I could come."

I shut the door, a satisfied smile spreading across my face as I slid to the floor. He slammed his fist against the surface, causing me to jump, but I didn't care. I heard him storm away, and for a moment, I felt like myself—strong, in control, and respected.

It only lasted a minute until the phone rang; Reese's school appeared on the caller ID, and I knew my day from hell wasn't over.

CHAPTER 2

Henley

THE SMELL of the arena hit me as I opened the doors. Usually, it was a calming balm, a welcome embrace, as I headed to the locker room. It was a little too soon to be reminded of what I'd lost today. Squaring my shoulders, I held my head up as I marched toward the director's office. The sad reality was I knew exactly where it was, having to visit numerous times since I'd become Reese's guardian.

The shouts reached me before I even opened the door, and I braced myself. I couldn't go in there being emotional, or I'd fall apart under the pressure. Taking a deep breath, I thought about the place I put things I couldn't deal with, and I shoved all my anger, fear, and hurt deep inside a box and shut the lid. It had been a technique I'd learned to use before playing, to focus only on the game in front of me. Hopefully, it would work in this situation.

Letting out a breath, I felt better, the emotions no longer weighing as heavily on me. When I felt ready, I pasted on a smile and knocked on the office door. It swung open, and the hockey coach of Temple Day stood there with a scowl. His upper lip had a sheen of sweat on it, and I wondered just what Reese had gotten into this time. He didn't say anything, motioning for me to enter.

Once I cleared the door, I found Reese sitting slumped in the chair in front of his desk. Reese barely looked up, but it was enough for me to spot the black eye. Concerned sister mode activated, I dropped down, squatting as I lifted their face.

"What happened?" I asked. Reese swallowed but didn't say anything.

"I know we had a deal, Henley, but Reese can't be on the team any longer. She—" He stopped, grunting. "*They're* causing too many problems with the other players. I need a solid team, and right now, it's divided. There's too much infighting. On top of that, Reese starts more fights than any other player. The parents are riding my ass to do something."

He sat back in his chair, rubbing his face as he leaned against the desk. Coach McHenry hadn't been happy about having Reese on the boy's team, but he'd relented when I promised to help with drills. It seemed that favor had only gone so far.

Glancing at Reese, I caught their lip quivering. The past year hadn't been easy, but we'd been making progress. But it seemed like we'd come as far as this town would let us. Squeezing their hand, I stood, not dropping it. I wanted Reese to know I wasn't mad at them. I knew what it was like to be different in this sport and how hard it was to get any recognition.

"I understand. But since I already helped with spring tryouts and the intensive training, I think I upheld my end of the deal."

The coach groaned, opening a bottle of antacids and swallowing a few. "What do you want, Henshaw?" he asked, dropping the formality of my first name.

"A letter of recommendation for wherever we end up. I don't want to fight this battle again. A letter from the coach stating Reese's skills should go a long way in proving their ability."

He stared at me, rubbing his brow as he thought. "Fine," he grumbled.

Smiling, I tugged Reese up and began to head out the door. Before I stepped out, I stopped and glanced back over my shoulder. Reese was already in the hallway, unable to hear what I had to say.

"Don't pretend this is the parents who want this, *Josh*. We both know you didn't want Reese showing up your son. Keep that in mind when you write that letter. If it isn't honest, I'll have to contact one of my connections for the paper, ESPN, and that NHL team you hope to get your son on. You might hold all the pucks in this rink, but this is a small pond, Josh. Don't forget how far my reach is. My two Olympic gold medals speak for themselves."

He gritted his teeth, but nodded. Smiling widely, I waved and shut the door. My shoulders dropped as soon as we were a few feet away. Reese snorted, and I glanced over at them.

"What?"

"That was badass."

Cracking a smile, I shook my head. It had felt nice, but I knew I had to be careful. Piss off too many men, and they labeled you as an emotional woman, or worse, a bitch.

"Do you need to grab your gear?" I asked, taking in the uniform they still wore.

Reese sighed, but nodded. Together, we walked toward the locker room. While we'd been able to get Reese on the male team, the powers that be still insisted they use the female locker room. At least in this instance, it meant we wouldn't have to deal with any of the asshole kids who went here. Not that all of them were, but there were enough that had caused nothing but problems for Reese since they switched teams.

We both knew it had nothing to do with their gender and everything to do with the fact that Reese was good. Better than most of the boys they played against. This sport had a long way to go toward equality.

I pushed open the door and walked around toward Reese's locker. A boy stood up at our approach, and I stopped, looking to Reese to ensure this wasn't one of their bullies. Without their jerseys, it was always hard for me to tell who was who.

"Cameron, what are you doing here?" Reese asked, stepping around to the locker.

"Um, I, well, I just wanted to make sure you were okay."

He looked between Reese and me, confusion on his face. I crossed my arms as I watched the interaction.

"Reese isn't to blame. Nick and his cronies ganged up on them and charged them. It was self-defense," he defended.

I held up my hand, stopping his argument for my sibling. "I'm not mad at Reese. Believe me, I know it wasn't their fault."

"I'm off the team, Cam," Reese said, glancing at the boy as they shoved padding and hockey sticks into their gear bag.

"What?" he asked, turning back to Reese.

Realizing I didn't need to be part of this conversation, I motioned to Reese that I would be outside. Leaning against the wall, I pulled out my phone to check how bad the news about me was. There were several messages from my teammates stating their anger at the league's decision. There were even a few from the media, reaching out for my story.

Clicking on my agent's number, I waited as it rang. "Henley," Carla answered quickly. I'd worked with the woman since college, and had a good relationship with her. "How are you, dear?"

Sighing, I lifted my eyes to the ceiling as I thought about the answer. "Lost. I'm not sure what to do. They said the suspension could last a year. They won't have their final decision for three months. What am I supposed to do until then?"

"Hmph, " Carla said as a few clicks began to sound on the keyboard. "I'll see what I can find. Are you willing to do *anything*? We need to remind the world you're still their sweetheart."

"I'm not sure I want to be known for that anymore. Because I'm not ashamed of the sex tape, just that I trusted Dakota to keep it to himself. I don't regret making it. I'm twenty-eight years old, for crying out loud. I'm allowed to have a sex life."

"Yes, well, the league wants all of its players to uphold a certain image."

"You mean the women's league. If I were a man, we'd be having a different conversation."

She hummed but didn't deny what I was saying. "Yes, well, we have to work with what we have, dear. And right now, you need to fix your image."

Dropping my head, I rubbed my brow, wondering if it was even worth it. I loved playing hockey, but everything else that came with it was a drag. I was so tired of being *their* puppet. Always available for them to pull out to razzle-dazzle their image when they needed to look good.

"I need some time to think. If you see any jobs, let me know. I need to figure out how to support Reese and myself. My savings will only last for so long."

"There's always that endorsement deal…" she trailed off, knowing how I felt about that particular deal. It was for a bikini company. I played hockey. It didn't make sense for me to promote a bikini when I wore pads all day long. It felt sexist and degrading, and I'd always adamantly declined it. Now, I wondered if I was in a position to do so.

"Like I said, I need some time to decompress from everything. Reese is done for the time being. Maybe we'll go away for the week and get some space."

"Okay, dearie. Keep your head high, and I'll be in touch."

Hanging up the phone, I didn't feel any better than before I'd called. The thought of going away did sound nice. Pulling out my phone, I looked through my messages and deleted most of them. I felt better just from that act alone. I came to one from an old teammate and hesitated. It was from a month ago on social media, and I felt terrible for not responding sooner.

SERA

Hey, Henley! Hope you're doing well. If you're ever in Utah, give me a ring, and we can grab dinner.

HENLEY

Hey, Sera! Sorry, I'm just now seeing this. How is Utah? I was thinking about coming for a visit.

I started to put my phone away, expecting Sera to take as long to respond as I had. When the phone beeped, I almost dropped it.

SERA

It's incredible. You should definitely come. There's a cute little resort town close by. You could do some skiing and shopping.

SERA

And I have news! I'm engaged. I'd love for you to meet my fiancé.

SERA

Please say you'll come. Let me know what dates!

HENLEY

Wow, okay, that sounds perfect. How about this weekend? Is that too soon?

SERA

Eek! That's perfect. Let me know when you're in and if you need a pickup from the airport. I'll start booking us some reservations on the slopes.

I pocketed my phone just as the door to the locker room opened. Cameron's head was bowed as he walked out with Reese.

"It's not fair," he said. "You're my best friend and the best right-winger we have."

"Our friendship won't end because I'm not here," Reese said. They spotted me and stepped closer. "I'm ready."

I wrapped my arm around Reese's shoulder and waved goodbye to Cameron. He returned it, frowning.

"Today's been a shit show. How about we grab some takeout and eat all the things we're not supposed to? And get some ice for that eye."

"What happened?" Reese asked, looking at me. We were almost the same height. Reese's short hair fell over their eyes, their wire-frame glasses big on their face. I sighed, moving a piece of hair.

"The committee has placed me on leave."

"Those fuckers," Reese cursed. I snorted, feeling better already.

"Yeah, well, to make it worse, Dakota showed up at the apartment."

"I hope he's still there so I can kick him in the gonads!"

Squeezing Reese's shoulder, I dropped my arm and opened the door outside. "Yeah, well, I might have insinuated that in the infamous tape it was his rival, Reed Cole, I was thinking about."

Reese snorted this time, almost coughing as they swallowed a laugh. "Oh man, I'm sad I missed that. I bet his face got so red. Solid burn, Sis."

"Thanks." I smiled, realizing this one felt genuine. I knew no matter what Dakota said, taking in Reese was the right decision. It had been tough, both of us adjusting to living with one another after years of being apart. But Reese could no longer stay with our mother. Not only was she abusive and refused to let Reese be Reese, but she'd also become addicted to pills. I knew I couldn't let Reese stay there when I found out. Even if it meant giving up my freedom. My sibling needed me, and I vowed to give them a better life.

We climbed into the car after tossing Reese's gear into the trunk. As we pulled out of the school parking lot, I turned, taking in Reese. "How does a week away to ski in Utah sound?"

Henley

THE SUN HEATED my skin as I adjusted the chair I was lying on. The past week in Salt Lake City had been exactly what I'd needed—sun, fun, and anonymity.

Reese and I had been skiing, had dinner with Sera and her fiancé, and even did some shopping. Today was our last full day before we headed back to Massachusetts and everything that awaited us there. Reese and I had been discussing what the future might look like, and it had become a game of imagining the most outlandish things.

"What if we lived in Australia and learned how to surf so well that we opened a surfing school?" Reese asked, looking at me under their sunglasses.

"Hmm. Australia is sure to have an awesome view. But I don't know if I want to deal with sand getting into every crevice."

Reese laughed, making me smile as I shielded my eyes and glanced over. "What if we moved to Canada and opened one of those hot bath places? Like in *Frozen*?"

"You're such a dork," Reese said, slapping my arm.

"Maybe, but it doesn't mean it wouldn't be fun," I teased.

Sitting up, I checked my skin, ensuring I wasn't getting burned. A splash at the pool had me glancing up, watching a group of guys shove one another as they played volleyball. There was one guy in particular that kept catching my eye. He had shoulder-length blond hair, light facial hair, and a muscular body that made me drool. He had to be one of the fittest guys I'd ever seen.

"You're staring," Reese teased.

Blushing, I dropped the sunglasses over my eyes and stuck my tongue out at Reese. "Shut it. I'm allowed to stare. I'm single for the first time in a while. If I want to have some fun, I can."

Reese held up their hands, smirking. "I'm not saying you can't, just that you might want to rein in your drool. It's not very attractive."

Laughing, I grabbed the towel off the chair and swatted Reese's leg with it. "I guess we should head in and get ready. Are you sure you're okay with hanging with the twins tonight?" I asked, gathering all of my things.

"Yeah. Braden and Briana are cool. We might go catch a movie or something."

"Okay, just let me know where you end up. I trust you to make smart choices."

Reese rolled their eyes, but I caught the soft smile, letting me know they sometimes appreciated my mothering. It had been an intricate balance between being the cool older sister to guardian, but it seemed like we were finally getting there.

A loud splash sounded behind me, and I turned and looked before I could stop myself. The blond guy was staring at me, a smirk on his face. It didn't feel predatory, like some men I came across; more like a mutual understanding of appreciation. It was something I could respect.

A feeling of exhilaration raced through me at the thought of what could transpire between the swim god and me if the opportunity presented itself. It tugged at my core, sending a shiver through me as goosebumps erupted across my skin.

Reese gave me a knowing look as we stepped into the elevator, but I ignored it, choosing to live in my fantasy land for a little longer.

"I'm so glad you came to visit, Henley," Sera gushed as she wrapped an arm around me. She smiled widely, her cheeks a little red from the wine we'd had at dinner. She pulled back, swaying to the music at the local bar we'd ended up in.

"Me too. I didn't realize how much I needed to get

away from everything. Can I ask you a personal question?" She nodded, her eyes big as she waited. "What's it like not playing hockey every day? Are you happy running the store?"

Sera tilted her head a little, observing me while she thought of her answer. "Hockey wasn't ever my true love. I enjoyed it, and it gave me a lot of wonderful experiences. It allowed me to travel, attend school, and meet people I wouldn't have otherwise. But it was never my end goal. So, no, I don't miss the early morning practices, feeling stiff more than I'm not, or the intense training regimen we were under. I miss the team and the friends I made. But..."

She leaned over, peering closely, tapping me on the nose. "I can still get that now, like with you visiting me. And the shop... it was always my dream. I love everything about it. Plus, it led me to Sean, and now we're going to be married, and I'm going to be a stepmom."

She swayed, her body dancing to the music, allowing me to observe her freely. Her face was so full of joy; I knew everything she said was one hundred percent accurate. It spurred hope that I could find that, even if hockey meant more to me than her.

"I feel kind of lost, but I'm hopeful I can find the happiness you have, Sera."

"Girl! You're the most driven and passionate person I know. I have no doubt that whatever you do next will be amazing. Henley Henshaw is a Goddess. This world doesn't know the gift they've been given."

She swept her arms out, giggling, and almost knocked into the people around her. Sean caught my eye a few feet over, giving me a knowing look before landing on his soon-to-be wife, his whole face lighting up. He stepped away from someone he knew at the bar, ending his conversation to collect her.

"You ready to go home, Sera?" he cooed, his voice soft. Sean was an older man in his forties, with light brown hair, clean-shaven, and very wealthy. He'd been on a corporate retreat when he met Sera, stating it was love at first sight. He moved his family to Oak Crest Peak, where Sera's shop was, and traveled back and forth to Salt Lake City for work. They were stupidly in love to the point it almost made you gag, but instead made you stare at them wistfully, proving that kind of love existed.

"You ready, Henley?" Sera asked me, her focus solely on Sean.

"Actually, I think I'll stay for a little longer. I'll see you guys at brunch tomorrow before we head out?"

Sera giggled, but nodded as Sean led her away. As I watched them leave, I leaned against the bar, a small smile pulling at my lips. Sighing, I turned back, picking up my drink. It didn't take long for the spot next to me to be filled, my smile growing wider over the rim of my glass. I'd spotted the blond Adonis the moment we'd walked in, but I wasn't sure if the heat between us was real or imagined.

Butterflies erupted in me at his nearness. Anxiety pooled a little in my gut at the notion of flirting. It had been a long time since I'd met someone who didn't know who I was, but that made this even better. I wasn't on stage, performing to give them the Henley Henshaw the world loved.

Slowly, I turned my head, catching his eyes. Emerald green orbs bore into me, and I swallowed at their intensity.

"Hi," I said, setting my glass down. My throat grew thick, and I swallowed, trying to ease my nerves.

"Hi," he said in return, picking up my hand and caressing it. He glanced down at it, slowly running the pads of his fingers across my palm. "I was hoping to run into you." His voice was smooth as silk, setting my core on fire.

"You were?" I asked, my voice hitching slightly. My body leaned closer, wanting to be as near as possible.

"I've been watching you for the past couple of days. It seemed no matter what I was supposed to be doing, you always caught my eye. I've been a horrible best man."

"Best man?" I asked, feeling dumb that I couldn't seem to get out more than two words.

"Mmhm. See that guy?" He turned, pulling me closer to his body, his clean cotton scent enveloping me as he pointed to the table he'd been at. "That's my buddy, and he's getting married. This is his bachelor party before the big day next weekend."

"Oh." I licked my lips as he turned, bringing our faces closer. He didn't move his body back. "And what duties are these you've been neglecting?" I managed to ask without losing my words.

He smirked, his eyes dropping to my lips before returning to my eyes. "Well, for starters, I'm supposed to be getting a round of drinks right now, but I can't seem to pull myself away from you."

"Oh, that's not good." I turned my head like I had any clue what I was saying. I was just happy words appeared to be coming out in sentence form.

He lifted a hand, pushing a piece of my hair back, the move sending shivers down my spine. I closed my eyes, barely keeping in the moan that wanted to escape at his light touch.

"You keep responding to me like that, and we won't make it out of this bar, *petal*."

"Petal?" I asked, my eyes blinking open. "That's not my name."

He lifted his finger to guide it across my lips. "Sometimes it's better if we remain strangers. That's if you're interested in seeing where this goes... no strings attached."

My brain stuttered. I knew what he was saying, but it wasn't something I'd ever done before. But wasn't it what I wanted? The freedom to do this? Hadn't I just been fantasizing about it earlier? He had a point that it might be better if we didn't exchange names. That way, there wouldn't be any temptation to try to find one another. I didn't know where he was from, but it wasn't Massachusetts.

"No strings," I repeated, rolling the words around on my tongue. I decided it felt free and daring, two things I wanted more of in my life.

"Yes, Petal. If you're interested?"

Nodding, I licked my lips. He seemed to be waiting for me to speak, though, not taking my nod as consent. "Yes. One night. I leave tomorrow."

"Then it's serendipitous." He smiled, and my insides quaked at what it promised. This guy was dangerous. Thankfully, only one night meant I wouldn't have to worry about catching any feelings.

"Um, do you have a room? Mine's occupied."

He seemed to ponder the question for a minute before something clicked, and he took my hand, leading me out a back door. "I know just the place."

His palm engulfed mine, holding my hand tight, making me feel calm. I didn't know why, but I trusted this man to keep me safe. The outside air hit my skin a few minutes later, the stickiness of the bar fading as the night air began to cool me.

When we stepped into a dance club a few doors down, I almost stumbled, not having expected this was where he'd take me. He led me to the dance floor, turning me around until my ass backed into him. His palms fell to my hips, and he swayed to the music. His head dropped down, his breath fanning across my neck.

"Go with the music, Petal. *Trust* me."

He began to give me soft kisses and licks as we swayed, the music feeling intoxicating as it swirled around us. We were two strangers in the crowd, but our bodies seemed to know the dance between us. His hands began to roam more as we danced together, and my head was thrown back against his chest. I looped an arm around his neck, keeping him close. He spun me out at one point, pulling me closer as my front met his.

My blond god cradled my head as he pulled me closer to him, his lips descending on mine. The moment they touched, a fire ignited in me, and my whole body came alive. My hands snaked around his neck, tugging his strands through my fingers. He had his long hair pulled back at the nape, but I tugged at it, messing up his hair as we made out on the dance floor.

One of his hands lifted my leg, and I felt him against me, a moan escaping as his hardened length rubbed against my center. I could feel myself growing wetter as I began to throb. I was so consumed by his kiss that I didn't even care that we were surrounded on the dance floor. It felt more illicit, more seductive.

His lips pulled away, and we both gulped for breath, staring intensely into one another's eyes. Something in him shifted, and I didn't know what it meant. He wasn't staring at me like before, but more intensely. He opened his mouth to say something but stopped, grunted and grabbed my hand, and pulled me off the dance floor. My head was full of desire, lost in the kiss to end all kisses. I willingly followed him, hoping it meant we'd get back to more kissing.

We climbed some steps, one of the bouncers nodding to let us through. We entered a room, and I took a second to survey it. There was a couch, mini-bar, and pool table. It was the floor-to-ceiling piece of glass that caught my attention. I dropped his hand to walk over to it. Below was the dance floor we'd just been grinding on. I turned, smirking at him.

"Wow, I wasn't expecting a... sex room?"

My blond stranger chuckled as he prowled toward me. "It's tinted. No one can see in. You can just see out. But first, I was thinking we'd test out how sturdy that pool table was."

I didn't miss the fact he ignored my sex room comment, but by the time he started to kiss me again, I didn't care. He picked me up and walked toward the table, gently placing my ass on it. My hands were in his hair again. Something I was becoming obsessed with. The strands were silky and smooth, and the knowledge that this would be my only chance spurred me on to feel them.

As I combed through his hair with my fingers, his lips stayed on mine, his deft fingers unbuttoning my shirt. He pressed me back, his lips leaving mine as his palm drifted down my body, lingering on the space between my breasts. His eyes watched as they moved up and down with my breath, almost like he was transfixed. Ready for him to touch me more, I reached back, unsnapped my bra, and let my shirt drop off my shoulders.

I sat on the table topless, feeling sexier and braver than I had in a while. This stranger made me feel alive in ways I didn't know existed.

"Fuck, you're gorgeous. I think I was wrong…" he started before shaking his head, stopping himself.

He pushed me back, my body hitting the velvet top as his mouth covered my nipple. Within seconds, I was arching off the table, my moans filling the room. The man devoured my breasts like they were the only thing that would resolve his thirst. I'd never been consumed or worshiped like this before. It was heady, and I was suddenly glad I was leaving.

If this man was around me every day, I'd fall in love with him before I knew what was happening. He had that type of magic about him.

When my jeans fell to the ground, I was so lost in sensations that I didn't notice except that I could now move more easily. He dragged my panties down, the cold air hitting all my private parts. My butt rested on the wooden ledge of the pool table, and he spread my legs wide. My hand desperately reached out to grip something, but there wasn't anything for me to hold on to.

He bent closer, taking a deep inhale of me, making me self-conscious for all of two seconds until the sexiest sound escaped him, his moan vibrating against my inner thigh.

"Shit, you smell delicious." I didn't have time to respond before he was licking up my core, his hot tongue dividing my folds as he lavished me with long licks and kisses. Bracing my heels on the lip of the table, I reached down and found his hair, giving me something to latch on to.

My head tossed back and forth, too many nerve endings lighting up to focus on one thing. My whole body felt like a live wire. It was easy to say this was the best oral sex I'd ever had. It made me wonder what else I'd been deceived about if this was what foreplay could feel like.

I itched to feel him, but every time I tried to sit up, he knocked my hands away, holding me down. When he finally let me up, I was certain I'd die of an orgasm overload. My legs shook as he carried me over to the window. He placed me down and turned me around, positioning me easily. He dipped his head and leaned in. I could smell my arousal on his lips.

He licked them before whispering, "The thought of fucking you up against the window while everyone goes about their business below has me so hard, Petal. But are you okay with it? I'd never want you to feel exposed."

Something about the way he said that had me wondering if he knew about my sex tape, but I was too gone to give it much thought. I caught his eyes, holding his green orbs.

"They can't see us?" I asked, needing clarification.

"Nope. I promise." His hands smoothed over my skin in a comforting gesture. Despite only just having met, I trusted him.

"Then show me how hard it has you, blondie."

"Blondie?" he chuckled, giving me a breathtaking smile.

I shrugged. "It's better than 'that guy.' Plus, I figured blond god was going too far."

He smirked, his eyes heating. "Let me prove to you it isn't, Petal."

Before I could respond, he pressed my palms against the glass. The sound of the condom wrapper filled the space as he rolled it on. He knocked my feet apart, spreading my legs. His palms gripped my hips as he pulled me toward him. I felt him line up with me, plunging in with one forward thrust. My body hit the glass, my nipples pressing against it.

I moaned, my legs quivering from the feeling of him in me. While I hadn't gotten a chance to look at his cock, I knew it had to be bigger than Dakota's. Hell, he was bigger than any lover of mine. I almost felt like I couldn't move for fear of breaking if I did.

Blondie didn't seem to have the same concern as he began to piston in and out of me, his grunts filling me as he thrust forward. I'd never been handled like this before—like I was both desired and revered. It was an addictive feeling.

I had to admit that Blondie fucking me against a window with people below was a whole new kink I hadn't ever thought about. It was exhilarating, and I grew wetter as he plunged into me.

"Fuck, Petal. You're so wet I can barely stay in you. You like that you can see them, don't you?"

I nodded, my words stuck on my tongue. "Give me one more orgasm, Petal. One more. You've done so well. I love how your body responds to my touch. You're addicting, Petal. If I had more time, I'd worship every inch of you for a week straight and then more. I was wrong that one night would be enough. It won't. I'll be forever ruined after this."

His words were soft but full of emotion as he thrust into me. I whimpered, not liking that he seemed upset.

"Ssh, Petal. Give in to me. Give me my orgasm."

His begging was the end of me, and I fell over the edge, my eyes closing as everything went black, fireworks exploding behind my eyes. My body quaked as my muscles tensed, and I felt him stumble, his grip tightening on me as he grunted, coming as he slapped his palm against the glass.

We stood there for a few minutes, our breathing fogging up the surface. He smoothed my hair back from my face and kissed my lips lightly, lingering for a few seconds before he withdrew. His eyes held a pain I didn't understand.

He walked to the bar and returned with wet wipes for me. Now that we weren't in the heat of the moment, I felt nervous. He didn't feel the same apparently, not caring that he was butt ass naked. It gave me the chance to finally get a peek at his cock. It swung as he walked, the length longer than I'd even expected. I gulped, shocked I'd been able to fit it in me.

Blondie chuckled, and I found him watching me. It helped dispel some of the weird tension I'd been feeling. He handed me my clothes, helping me dress before putting on his own. We didn't say anything else, both of us remembering it was one night, no strings.

He took me back down the steps, out the back door, and walked with me to the hotel we were staying in. We were quiet, but it felt nice, like nothing needed to be said at that moment. We both enjoyed our time together, and to say anything else would ruin that.

He kissed me softly at the elevator before turning and walking the other way.

"Goodbye," I whispered.

As I walked to my room, I thought about my time with him and how amazing it had been. While I knew it was a onetime thing, it felt like something significant had shifted in me, just like that moment with Mr. Dark and Sexy. These random men were showing me things Dakota had never even gotten close to, which was something to celebrate.

I stepped into the room I shared with Reese, finding them sleeping on their bed. I crept over, taking in their sleeping form. Life might be a little more uncertain, but I didn't feel as lost as I had. Reese and I would figure it out together, giving me hope for wherever that took us.

CHAPTER 4

Henley

I TOSSED the last of my clothes into the suitcase and leaned on it to get it to close. Grunting, I tugged the zipper around, jumping back when it was done. I stood with my hands on my hips, admiring my hard work as I tried to catch my breath. They should add suitcase zipping to professional athlete's training; that shit was hard.

Pushing it off the bed, I wheeled it to the door where the bellhop would collect it while we were having brunch. Brushing my hands over my dress, I turned in the mirror, ensuring there weren't any wrinkles. My body ached in some new spots, a blush rising to my cheeks as I recalled the night before with my blond god.

"You feeling okay?" Reese asked as they stepped into the room, pushing their suitcase.

"Oh, um, yeah, fine." I cleared my throat, shoving all thoughts of being properly fucked—probably for the first time in my life—against a window, aside. "How was last night?"

"It was fun. We played a pickup game of hockey

with a few of their friends. It was nice to play with people who didn't care what gender I was, just excited when I scored."

Reese shrugged as they bent down to tie their shoe. I knew they were trying to hold back their emotions and make it seem like it wasn't as big of a deal as it had meant.

When they stood, I smiled, opening the door. Reese wouldn't want me to make a thing out of this, so I wouldn't, even if I was brimming with the need to hug them.

"I kind of wish we didn't have to go back," Reese said as we walked toward the elevator. "It's been nicer here than I expected."

I wrapped my arm around Reese's shoulder, my height and heels making me a couple of inches taller than them. We stepped into the elevator, and I let out a breath I hadn't realized I'd been holding. Part of me wanted to run into Blondie again, even if it would be awkward.

But would it?

This was where I lacked experience. It had felt so natural between us. Was that only because it was meant to be one night and the secretiveness of it made it easier to be yourself?

I knew I was overthinking it, but I couldn't help it. I clearly wasn't cut out for one-night stands. At least I'd learned something new about myself. I guess that was a win.

"You're going to kill your hamster, Sis."

"Huh?" I asked, turning to look at Reese. They snickered, shaking their head as the door to the elevator opened.

"You're thinking too hard. Going to make the hamster on the wheel in your brain die of exhaustion."

"Ha, ha." I stuck out my tongue, shoving their shoulder slightly as we walked out of the elevator, laughing together.

We turned the corner and immediately found Sean, Sera, and the twins. They waved at us from the table they were seated at, and I noticed there was an extra place setting. Raising my brow at Sera, she smiled but shook her head. Some friend she was!

"Good morning," I said as we neared.

"Hey, Reese," the twins said, motioning for a chair between them. I watched as Reese eagerly joined them, talking to both. It was the happiest and most relaxed I'd seen Reese in such a long time that it made me stop and think.

"How was the rest of your evening?" Sera asked, as I sat next to her.

"Oh, you know. It was... illuminating."

This time, her eyes widened, and she nudged me to spill the beans. I took my time placing the napkin in my lap and took a sip of water.

"A secret for a secret," I whispered, leaning closer.

"Ugh, fine. You're no fun. It's supposed to be a surprise. Sean reached out to a friend, and they're meeting us for brunch."

"Why?" I asked, alarmed I was about to be ambushed.

"I'm not going to spill *all* the beans. Now, it's your turn." Sera narrowed her eyes, waiting for me to give her something.

"You know that blond hottie from the pool?" I asked. She nodded eagerly. "Well, he was there after you left, and we went to a club and danced."

I took another sip of my water, feeling a little salty about not getting her whole story, so I kept the best details to myself.

Sera pouted but didn't get to press for more as the waiter arrived to take drink orders. Once everyone had given theirs, an older man was shown to our table. He was slightly older than Sean, probably mid-fifties. He was refined, though, with dark, slicked-back hair and clean-shaven. Sean stood, shaking hands with the gentleman. He didn't smile much, and I prayed this wasn't a setup. He was attractive, but not really my type.

"Henley, this is Dmitry Aldridge. He's the director of Lux Brumalis, where the twins attend."

The name was familiar, and I remembered he was a famous ice skater with several medals. There had been something in the news last year about him, but I couldn't recall precisely what it was now. His place in the twins' life confused me even more about what he was doing here.

"It's nice to meet you," I said, holding my hand out for him to shake. I smiled, even though my insides were a jumble of nerves.

He took my hand in his, turning my palm. His hand was smooth, taking me by surprise. I was so used to hockey players, whose hands tended to be calloused and dry, that I didn't realize he was kissing it until it was over.

"It's lovely to meet you, Henley. Please excuse my interruption of your time with your friends, but when Sean told me you were here, I knew I had to meet you."

"Me?" I asked, feeling dazed and confused.

"And Reese." He dropped my hand, taking his seat. He glanced at the teenagers, and I realized the teens were sitting up straight, giving the man respect.

"Me?" Reese parroted, looking between Braden and Briana. "What did you tell him about me?"

Dmitry smiled as he placed the napkin in his lap. Before he could answer, the waiter returned with our drinks and began to take everyone's order. I glanced toward Sera, raising my eyes, but she merely shook her head, keeping all pertinent information to herself.

Once the waiter left, the table was quiet. I had a million questions, but wasn't sure where to start.

Finally, I decided on a neutral one until I knew for certain what this man was doing at our brunch.

"Forgive me if this is common knowledge, but we're from the East Coast, so I'm not familiar with what type of school Lux Brumalis is. What does it mean, as well?"

Dmitry lifted a corner of his mouth, which I was beginning to believe was his version of a smile.

"Lux Brumalis is Latin for 'wintry light' in particular, the specific quality of light at a certain time of year. It's unique and limited, something I wanted our school to represent after everything last year." He took a moment to clear his throat, sipping his coffee.

"Lux is a premier school that focuses on winter sports. The student-athletes get training by the best in their sport and have tutors to help them pass all the required college education credits. Most of our students graduate and head to top schools in their chosen field with scholarships or even join Olympic teams."

"That sounds like an amazing program. What tracks are you in, guys?" I asked the twins.

"Hockey," Braden answered, followed by Briana, who said, "Alpine Skiing."

I glanced at Reese to gauge their expression about what had been said. Reese had a thoughtful look, but I could tell they were guarding themselves against hoping this was about them. Reese had been promised too many things from people to trust them outright. I had to admit that even I was unsure what this meeting was for. Was it a setup, or had Sean and Sera pulled some strings for Reese?

"And do you like it there?" I asked just as plates were deposited in front of us. It took a few minutes before the twins could answer, but they took turns once the waiters were gone.

"It's the best school I've ever been to. Mr. Turner, my tutor, is hard, but he's helped me learn in ways I've never been able to before. On top of that, I've had Oliver Windsor as a head coach the past two years."

Shock ran through me. Oliver was an excellent hockey player. He'd been a star a few years back until he was injured. Briana shared a similar tale about her skiing, but since I wasn't as knowledgeable about who skiers were, I just nodded, assuming they were as high quality.

"Wow, that's some talent you have at the school. It sounds like it's going well." The table was quiet, and I could tell I'd struck a nerve, but no one said anything as they ate. The twins and Reese whispered back and forth while the adults ate; Sean and Dmitry talked about a few other instructors. My brain was over-loaded, so I quietly ate my food, still trying to solve the puzzle of this guest.

Sera nudged me, motioning with her eyes to

Dmitry. He was watching me, so I placed my fork down, hoping I was finally about to get some answers.

"While this is a bit informal, after watching some footage of Reese skating, I wanted to meet you and Reese personally. I know there have been difficulties at Reese's last school," he paused. I glanced over, catching Reese dropping their eyes. "While enrollment tryouts have already occurred, there might be another option to consider."

"For Reese to attend Lux?" I asked, wanting to make sure we were on the same page.

"Yes," he said, hesitating slightly, and I wondered if I was getting the whole story.

"What is this other option?"

"We have two hockey camps over the summer. If Reese were to attend, we could use that as their tryout. Perform well at the camp, and we could find space on the team in the fall."

"Which team?" I asked, knowing this was important.

"Whichever team Reese qualifies for. Our school operates on a skill system, not gender."

"How do we know that your judges wouldn't be biased?"

"I have faith in our coaches, but I'd oversee the scoring myself if that helps ease your concern."

Looking at Reese, I found them staring at me. I couldn't read the emotion on their face. "Is this something you'd be interested in?" I asked, wanting their consent before I said yes.

Reese nodded, a small smile appearing. "Yes, I think I'd like it there. I met a few of the students last night, and they were accepting of me. Plus, Braden and Briana go there."

The twins beamed, and I wondered if there was something more brewing between the three of them. Turning to Sera and Sean, I assessed them.

"You know the troubles Reese has had. So, I'm taking your word that this school would be a good fit."

"I believe it would," Sean said. "Lux has had its share of difficulties, but the coaches and students there are all committed to their sports track. I think you'll find they're like-minded individuals who only want the best. There's competition, but it's healthy, preparing them for a life as an elite athlete. They even have media training and help cultivate a social media presence. It's the best school around for winter sports."

I thought about everything he said. It sounded like the perfect place, but nothing was ever perfect. Plus, something was nagging me at the back of my mind that I couldn't place. It would have to wait, though, as everyone stared at me, waiting for an answer.

"When is camp?" I asked, turning back to Dmitry.

"At the end of the summer. It's one week." The corner of his lip lifted again, and I wondered if I was being hoodwinked. I couldn't deny that the thought of returning to this town wasn't exciting, though, and since I didn't currently have any of my own training to be at, I had nothing holding me back either.

"Okay. Reese can attend camp and see if this school is a good fit."

The teenagers cheered, their excited chatter taking over as they started to plan, and the twins fought over who Reese would room with. Sera nudged me, giving me a knowing look, but I rolled my eyes, still feeling like I'd been ambushed, even if it had been for a good reason.

Later, as the plane took off, I smiled, the knowledge that we'd be returning soon giving me something to look toward. Maybe, just maybe, I'd have another fantastic night like I'd had with Blondie.

Something in me was changing, and I had a feeling it was going to be life-altering. It was time to get out of the penalty box the world had placed me in.

CHAPTER 5

Reed

THE OXYGEN PUMP deflated and reinflated in the room, the sound as familiar to me now as my own breathing. The chair squeaked as I shifted, my large frame finding it challenging to get comfortable in these tiny chairs. My legs stretched out far in front, the toes of my expensive sneakers hidden beneath the hospital bed. Every day, I came and sat vigil even though the outcome never changed. But what was a son to do?

The hard truth was my mother was dying, and there was nothing I could do about it. No amount of money could change that fact despite my many attempts.

Cancer was a vicious bitch, taking whoever it fucking pleased.

So, I did what I could. I got her the best care to make her comfortable. The best room to offer her privacy. And I sat beside her every day, wanting her to know that, in the end, she wasn't alone.

But it didn't feel like enough. My mother was dying, and I was helpless.

I hated feeling this way.

"Mr. Cole?" the nurse queried, pulling me from my thoughts.

"Yes?" I asked, not turning to look. It was the same drill every day.

"Visiting hours are ending, sir. We'll call you if there are any changes."

Sighing, I drew my legs up and picked up her hand. Her skin was thin and cold, but I held it, letting some of my warmth seep into her. Taking a deep breath, I dropped my head back, gazing upward, hoping that some miracle would come. When nothing happened, I kissed her palm and stood. Brushing her hair out of her eyes, I took her in one more time, committing every detail to memory, expecting each visit to be my last. It was always a blessing and a curse every day when I returned. I knew we couldn't keep this up, but I refused to relent, regardless.

My mom had done everything for me to make me successful, so I'd be here for her now. I might not be able to cure her cancer, but I could do this for her.

"See you tomorrow, Mr. Cole."

Nodding, I didn't say anything else. The staff was used to my gruffness, allowing me to grieve my mother in peace. When I stepped outside, I pulled out my phone and turned it on as I headed toward my truck. The phone lit up with messages and missed calls. The world didn't stop despite my wanting it to.

Rubbing my temple, I scanned through the ones that were the most important.

Before I could even decipher them, my phone began to ring. Only three people called me, and since I had just left the private hospice center, I knew it was either my coach or my agent. I lifted the phone, not saying anything, as I pressed the key fob to unlock my truck.

"Cole?" I didn't reply, climbing into my truck, waiting him out. "Reed? Listen, I know I said you could have time, but that was two months ago. I need an answer, son."

"I'm not your son, Coach." I pressed the on button and buckled in, placing my phone on the caddy. It linked to my system, his voice filling my speakers.

"Reed, I know this is a difficult thing. I don't envy you. But I have to submit the team roster by midnight, so I need your answer. Will you be playing this season?"

I slammed my hands against the steering wheel. Tightening my grip as I stared out the windshield. It felt like an impossible choice. Training was in Vancouver, eighteen hours away from Utah. If I played, I wouldn't be near my mom in her last days. But playing hockey was the only thing that kept me sane. Without it, I was sure to wither away into a husk of a person.

No one should ever have to pick between the thing that made them who they were and the person they loved. It was unfair, and selfishly, I directed my anger toward Coach for making me choose.

"I can't abandon her. She's too unstable to move closer. I..." I sucked in a breath, pressing the palms of my hands against my eyes. The emotion consumed me, reminding me of the woman I'd pulled out of her car when she was crumbling from the inside.

Though, to say she was just *some* woman felt insignificant.

Henley Henshaw was the furthest thing from the word. Thinking of her, I felt myself calm. It was my guilty obsession, my shame, that I kept to myself. I wasn't allowed to like Henley, but she occupied my mind for some reason. That day in the parking lot was the closest I'd ever been to her, and I'd almost succumbed to the urge to kiss her.

But it hadn't been the right time. It was only pure coincidence I'd even been at that facility for some sponsorship when I'd seen her. It was a memory that haunted me, playing over and over across my mind in the sparse moment I wasn't consumed with my grief. Oddly, Henley had become my sanctuary, unbeknownst to her.

"Cole?" my coach hollered down the line, the speakers crackling violently. I jumped, falling out of my Henley haze. My warning to her replayed across my mind, offering me the answer I sought.

"Don't let them take your soul."

It felt significant and weighty that at this moment, when I was meant to decide the fate of my career, I remembered the day hers had exploded.

And yet, I had a feeling it wouldn't be the end of Henley Henshaw.

So, why was I limiting myself to the demands of an organization that only cared about my performance? They didn't care about my needs or the fact my mother was dying. It was their bottom line they were concerned about.

"I'm out," I said, my voice breaking. It was the hardest thing I'd ever said, but the instant it passed across my lips, I knew it was the right call. I felt lighter and free, a weight I hadn't been aware I carried gone. Holding my head up, I stared at the phone, projecting my assuredness this time.

"I'm out."

Coach sighed, and I knew it wasn't what he wanted to hear. But it wasn't his decision to make. It was mine, and I wasn't going to let them take *my* soul.

Bowing to their commands and leaving my mother would crush me. I might be no one without hockey, but at least I'd be able to sleep at night.

"You sure about this, Reed? Your contract ends after this year. If you don't play this season, you might be unable to find another team."

"I'm aware, and it's a risk I'm willing to take. I need to be here for my mom, Coach. Without her, I wouldn't have hockey. I can't abandon her now. I'm sorry to let you and the team down, but I have to be here for her, even if it's only another week. I won't miss her final days."

"You're a good son, Reed. As a man and father, I'm proud of you."

"Thanks, Coach. But?" I asked, giving him a watery chuckle which he returned.

"You know me too well. As a coach, we'll miss you. Hughes is going to have a field day with this."

"Yeah, well, Hughes will be happy he won't be facing me on the ice. I have a few bones to pick with him," I seethed.

"This have anything to do with Henley?" he asked.

"I don't know what you're talking about."

"Yeah, well, I might be an old man, but I got eyes, boy. Plus, the guys in the locker room talk. I've heard a few things, is all."

"There's nothing to hear. She doesn't even know who I am. But she's definitely too good for a tool like Dakota Hughes. The only thing he has going for him is his face, and I plan to knock a few teeth loose the next time I see him on the ice."

Coach laughed, lightening my mood a little. "Take care of your mother, Reed. I'll do what I can with the commissioner. Perhaps there's something I haven't looked at yet, and it doesn't have to be an all-or-nothing thing right now."

"I appreciate that, Coach, but I don't think I'll be playing this season. Either outcome, I think I need some time off. I'll take my chances next year."

He sighed, and I could almost picture him shaking his head as he rubbed his bald head. "I can respect that. Keep up your conditioning, and I'll start laying the groundwork. You're one of the best, Cole, don't forget that."

"I won't." Grinning, I felt proud of my decision. I could practically feel Coach's smile through the phone. He sighed after a few seconds.

"Alright, I gotta break the news to the team. Any chance you want to tell them?"

"Nope. Good luck." My smile grew, the feeling unnatural but nice.

"Asshole," he said, chuckling good-naturedly. "Later, Cole."

The phone clicked, his voice leaving the cab as the silence began to fill the void. Checking my mirrors, I pulled out of the parking lot, feeling better that at least something had been handled for now. It hadn't been the choice I wanted to make, but I knew it was the right one. Hockey would still be there for me later, but my mother wouldn't.

The ride home was quick, and I entered my dark apartment, feeling the unease each time I was here lately. I'd never been one for a roommate outside of college, nor had I ever had a girlfriend stay around long enough to live with. And yet, the place felt empty now.

Maybe I should get a cat? A dog would need too much attention, but a cat might be what I needed to help me not feel so alone. It wasn't a horrible idea. Maybe if my mom was feeling better tomorrow, I could ask her what she thought.

I opened the fridge and pulled out one of the pre-made salads that were part of my meal plan. Grabbing some water, I headed to the couch, where I sat and ate, flipping through the channels.

When a news story popped up about Henley, I stopped on the channel, my desperate need to know any ounce of information about her fueling me, even if it was only hearsay gossip.

"Sources report that Henley has been spotted in Utah. Do you think she's meeting with new teams? Or perhaps looking at other ventures, Steve?" the host asked the man sitting next to her.

"It could be anything when it comes to Henley Henshaw. Before she became the disgraced sweetheart of hockey, she was involved in everything from animal shelters to canned soup. If anyone can bounce back from this, it's Henshaw. I, for one, can't wait to see what she does next."

The female host smiled, but it was tight as she stared at the camera. "Well, I guess we'll all just have to wait until she surfaces. Next up is how to wear your hair, so it goes from day to night. Stay tuned."

The show went to a commercial, and I shut it off, my mind racing, wondering if she'd really been in Utah. Of all the places for her to be, it was the same state as me? Granted, Utah was massive, but it had to mean something, right?

Or maybe I was just getting deeper into my delusion and seeing connections where there weren't any. Despite knowing this, I couldn't help but picture her later as I showered, my hand wrapped around my cock, and remember how she'd felt pressed up against me. I might never have Henley, but at least now Hughes didn't either. It was a small mercy, but it was at least something.

CHAPTER 6

Henley

THE PAST MONTH had flown by despite spending most of my days migrating from the living room to the kitchen and back to the bedroom. Outside of training Reese, there wasn't much to my life. It felt odd. I wasn't sure if it was customary to feel this unfocused, since my days had been scheduled from sunrise to sunset for as long as I could remember. The concept of free time was foreign to me. Finding myself with loads of it suddenly was jolting.

Was I becoming depressed? Or was this just relaxing? Should I embrace this time with no demands and find a hobby?

I asked myself these questions every day, but I'd yet to find a good answer. Google was no help, giving me endless results for all my options. I guess I was depressed/relaxing/needing to find a hobby all rolled into one. Which was typical of me; I could never just be one thing. I was always the extreme.

While things surrounding the sex tape had died down, I still hadn't heard anything from the league. I might have to reconsider the bikini sponsorship if I didn't hear anything soon. To top it off, I was either underqualified or overqualified for every job I applied for. Playing hockey for the past ten years didn't give me much job experience. But the worst rejections were the ones that didn't want to deal with the hassle of employing "Henley Henshaw" like I was some kind of disease they were afraid of catching.

Worst of all, I missed the ice. At least I got to skate while helping Reese prepare for camp. It was the only solace I had when I thought of never skating again—at least, there was this.

We'd arrived in Oak Crest Peak last night and were squeezing in one more practice before camp started tomorrow. Dmitry had allowed us usage of the hockey arena, and I was beginning to suspect there was more to his generosity than wanting Reese to play.

Not that Reese wasn't good, just that it felt like they were bending over backward to make it happen. Maybe I was just cynical nowadays, but nothing since I'd taken guardianship had been this easy regarding Reese.

Though, since we'd left Utah at the beginning of the summer, Reese had been a new person. They were constantly chatting with the B&B twins as we'd started to refer to them. Even when I pushed Reese to do sets, they never complained. I saw a whole new side to my sibling. If this was what Utah brought out in Reese, I was all for it.

"Good. Now, do it about twenty more times," I said, grinning. Reese groaned but took off, skating up and down the ice. I leaned against my stick as I watched.

A whistle rang out from the sides, and I turned, surprised by who I found there. "Fletcher?" I screamed, skating toward him as he hopped over the boards.

"Baby Shaw." He grinned, opening his arms as I skated into them, almost knocking us both over. Though, his large frame and build kept us up. I looked up at him, surprised to see the man he'd become staring back.

"What? How?" I asked, shaking my head in disbelief.

"I'm guessing you haven't talked to Frankie in a bit?"

I grimaced, shaking my head. "No. Sadly, it's been a while. Gosh, what's it been, eight years since I last saw you?" He pushed back, giving me a once over, and if I wasn't mistaken, I caught some heat in his eyes.

"Eight years, huh? Wow! I guess I hadn't realized how long. You look good, Shaw." He smiled, his dimples showing as he stared at me.

Fletcher Cromwell was well over 6-feet tall, especially on skates. His thick, dark hair swooped over his forehead, making his hazel eyes twinkle. He had a thick beard trimmed along his jaw, making him more dashing than I recalled. He was the older brother of my college roommate, Frankie, and had always been nice to me. Back then, I was Baby Shaw, a play-off of "Baby Shark."

"Thanks, you don't look so bad yourself, Fletch. But what are you doing here?"

"I work here. I'm one of the hockey coaches for the camp."

"No way? Reese is attending."

"I know." He gave me a sideways look, and I felt like I was missing something. "I'm excited to see how they skate. Knowing you, they're bound to be a killer shark like their sister."

I blushed, liking how the compliment from him felt. "So, what are you doing here *now*?" I crossed my arms, glancing at Reese briefly before my attention was pulled back to Fletcher.

"Oliver mentioned you were using the rink this afternoon, and I didn't want to wait until tomorrow to see you. So, I thought I'd welcome you both to campus. Maybe give you a tour and take you to dinner?"

Reese skated over, panting, bending at the knees. "Twenty. Anything else?"

"Reese, this is Fletcher Cromwell. I used to room with his sister back at college. He played for—"

"The Vancouver Tigers," Reese finished, standing up with wide eyes. "Wow, it's nice to meet you. I'm Reese."

Fletcher let go of his hold on me, shaking Reese's hand. "It's an honor to meet the sibling of Baby Shaw here. I look forward to seeing what you can do. With her as a teacher, I have no doubt you'll show everyone not to underestimate a Henshaw."

Reese gulped, but nodded. "Ah, thank you. I hope I can measure up. I just love to play."

I nudged Reese, hip-checking them. "Hey, you're brilliant. Don't psych yourself out. Now, Fletcher offered to give us a tour and take us to dinner, but I know you were hoping to see B&B. Do you want to join or hang out with them?"

"Oh..." Reese took off their helmet, pushing back sweaty clumps of hair. "Wow, I'd love to, but I already promised my friends. Rain check?"

"Absolutely. I'll be one of the coaches for camp, so you'll see me around."

"Excellent. If I'm done, can I go and shower?" they asked me, lifting their eyebrows microscopically at me, which I ignored.

"Yep. I think you're ready. Text me where you're going, and keep me updated. I want you back in the room no later than 10pm. Tomorrow starts early."

"Yeah, yeah. Love ya." Reese skated off, almost tripping; they were so excited about seeing Braden and Briana again. I still wondered if there was more there, but it wasn't my place to ask. I trusted my sibling and knew if anything was going on, they'd talk to me about it.

"So, it's just us?" Fletcher asked, lifting his eyebrow playfully, making my insides dance.

"I guess so. That's not going to ruin your plans, is it?" I teased, needing to throw off my emotions.

"Nope. In fact, how about we make it interesting?" He smiled, and I knew whatever he was about to suggest, I was down for it. Fletcher had always been fun, constantly making me laugh after a tough game.

"What are you thinking?" I asked, leaning a little closer.

"How about one-on-one? First one to score three points gets to pick where we go to eat."

"Deal. Any rules?" I asked, already scheming how I could beat him.

"Keep it friendly, but otherwise, anything goes. Think you can handle it?" His eyes twinkled, and I had to remind myself not to fall under their spell.

I tied my hair up before placing my helmet on. Even though I didn't expect us to get physical, it didn't mean I was willing to risk falling and hitting my head on the ice. I might not be skating at the moment, but I wouldn't take myself out of the game before I was ready.

We both moved toward the center, slapping our sticks on the ice. He counted to three before dropping the puck, and it was on.

My quick stickhandling had me swooping in and grabbing it away as I twisted, turning almost 180 degrees. I pushed off the back of my blades, wanting to get away from him as fast as possible. My size allowed speed, and I needed to use it. It was the same thing I'd been working with Reese on earlier.

I could hear him behind me, his skates cutting against the ice as he pursued me. I flicked the puck back and forth, getting closer to the net. When I was within shooting range, I lifted my stick back and smacked the puck toward the net. It sailed cleanly into the goal, giving me the first point.

Throwing my arms up, I turned, finding Fletcher with a mystified look on his face. For a second, I worried he wouldn't be able to take me beating him, something Dakota had never dealt with well, to the point that I had to let him win or not play against one another.

Fletcher looked between me and the net, a broad smile spreading. He placed his stick in the crook of his elbow and began to clap.

"Well done. Okay, I know now not to underestimate you. You're even more killer than you were back in college."

He skated backward around me, giving me a whistle as I stood watching him. For his large size, the man managed to glide like a gazelle. It was smooth and light, belying his large frame. He scooped up the puck, giving me a nice view of his ass as he did it.

I spun quickly, returning toward the middle so he would miss my red cheeks. The game continued, and Fletcher scored the next goal, taking me by surprise when he blocked my stick and used his skate to push the puck away. I heard him laughing the whole way to the goal as I stood, staring in disbelief.

"Tied. Still feeling confident, Baby Shaw?" he teased. This time I was ready, and I shoved him before he could move his stick. The man was a brick house and didn't budge. Thankfully, I managed to pass the puck between his legs, away from him. As I skated around him, he grabbed me around the waist and lifted me up, placing me behind him.

Screaming, I laughed as he pushed me backward and took the puck, scoring his second goal.

"I'd say that was cheating, but since I did an illegal block to start, I guess I deserved it."

Fletcher didn't say anything, just lifted the puck and let it drop. Lifting my stick, I blocked him and stole the puck, spinning around quickly and dodging his arms. I barely managed to raise my stick to aim before he was upon me. We were both out of breath from skating and the jostling we'd been doing.

"Next point wins," he said, grinning. He tossed the puck high into the air, and I watched it fall. As I glanced down, I found him watching me, not the puck.

It shocked me, freezing me to the spot. The second I heard the puck hit the ice, the trance was broken, and I took off after him, managing to catch him this time.

I shoved at his shoulders, hip-checking him as I attempted to steal the puck. Our sticks battled on the ice as we went back and forth. We were close to his goal when I decided to dive for it, causing Fletcher to lift his stick so he wouldn't hit me. I slid across the ice on my knee pads, laughing the whole way. Jumping back up, I sprinted down the ice with the puck. I could hear him hot on my trail, so I risked it, lifting my stick to score from half-court.

We both stopped, our breaths heavy as we watched the puck slide across the ice. It started to slow as it neared, and I clutched his arm, waiting to see if it would go in. I screamed and jumped up and down when it looked to have gone over the line.

"I win! I win!"

"Not yet. I need to verify." He smirked, skating toward the goal to check if it had gone over the line. He bent down, peering at the puck, glancing back at me.

"Well?" I asked, beginning to skate toward him. He picked it up, tossing it into the air as he slid back toward me.

"You win, Baby Shaw. Dinner's on me." We both grinned, and I wasn't sure who the real winner in this situation was based on that smile.

"Hells yeah." I lifted my hand up for a high-five.

The moment had felt too hot, and I needed to break it. Fletcher chuckled, slapping my palm.

"Where are you staying?"

"The B&B in town. Do you know it?"

"Yeah. Nice place. The Taylors are good people. How about I pick you up there in an hour and give you that tour and dinner?"

"Sounds perfect."

We skated off the ice together, and headed toward our separate locker rooms since I was using the guest one and he had access to the staff locker room. Based on how nice the guest one was, I was curious about what amenities they had for the staff. Maybe I could get him to give me a tour this week—you know, for research purposes.

CHAPTER 7

Fletcher

I TOSSED the third shirt onto my bed, not liking any of them. I hadn't planned for this dinner to be a big deal. When I heard Henley was in town, I was excited to see an old friend and catch up. But seeing her on the ice and playing that game had changed things. I no longer saw Henley as a friend of my younger sister's, but as a woman.

Henley had always been cute, but she'd grown into a beautiful person with confidence and strength. She was protective of her sibling, able to joke around with me, and fast on her skates. She'd blown me away in all the best ways.

And now, it felt like this dinner could be the beginning of something more—hence my shirt dilemma.

Tossing another one onto the pile, I stared at my meager offerings, wishing I was a guy who cared about clothes more. I was down to a black button-down or a navy blue henley. Chuckling, I wondered if I should wear it just to tease her all night.

"Did your shirts do something to offend you?" Dax

asked, leaning against the doorframe as he ate a banana.

As usual, he was shirtless, his long blond hair down around his shoulders, while he ate something. Dax was a fitness fanatic, so he was constantly eating to maintain his macros, whatever that meant. He was a top-notch physical therapist and fitness trainer, so I guess his method was worth something. We'd been roommates for the past two years and had an easy friendship.

"They all had the audacity not to magically change into the perfect shirt," I said, deciding on the henley. It might not be what I wanted, but I could play off my strength—jokes, that was at least something.

Dax chuckled, shaking his head as he finished his snack. He stretched his arms to the top of the door, leaning forward to stretch. "You got a date?" he asked when he was done.

"Kinda. An old friend's in town, and when I saw her earlier, it was different. She's more mature and more beautiful than I remember. We're going to dinner to catch up, but I'm hoping it's more of a date."

"Good luck then. I don't envy you at all." He chuckled dryly, but it sounded off.

"Yeah, yeah. Mr. King of No-strings. You have your methods, and I have mine."

"Except one of us gets laid more frequently."

I threw a pair of socks at his head as he chuckled,

dodging them. "Yeah, well, just wait until one day you wish one of those women were more than one night," I said, pulling on a different pair of socks. I glanced up, catching him shifting on his feet, an odd look crossing his face. "You're still thinking about that woman you met at Kev's bachelor party, aren't you?"

He scoffed, tossing the socks back at me. I caught them, not dropping them as I stared him down.

"I don't know who you're talking about. I enjoy each person I'm with and then move on to the next. In fact," he stopped, pulling out his phone, "I'm meeting Chrissy in an hour." He pocketed his phone, giving me a smug look, but something was different about it.

"I don't know how you can stand those apps. The girls on there all say one thing when they mean another. It's a game I don't want to play," I said as I laced up my boots, pulled the leg of my jeans over them, and stood.

Dax shrugged, putting his hands in the pockets of his joggers. Something was bothering him, but I didn't have time to investigate. Especially if he wasn't in the sharing mood. I'd gotten to know Dax reasonably well, and he was a closed book until he was ready to open himself up. I suspected there was a story there, but it hadn't ever come up in our relationship, so I left him be.

"Camp starts tomorrow. You have sessions scheduled?"

"Not this one. I'm working with one of the seniors and have a few physical therapy clients that I'm graduating."

"Ah, right. I'll see you around then. Good luck with your date." I patted him on the shoulder as I stepped out into the hallway.

"If you need luck, you're doing it wrong, Fletch."

Reaching for him, I chopped his head as he stepped into his room, his laugh following me down the hall. I passed one of the open rooms, wondering if we'd get a new roommate this year. Our house was one of the smaller ones with four bedrooms, meant to be for a family, but when we both started work here, it was the only house available. We had a third roommate the first year, but when they left, both rooms stayed empty. With the major overhaul of staff and instructors, I wondered if we'd get any roommates this year.

Heading toward my Jeep, I noticed a skip in my step and a smile on my face that hadn't been there earlier. The urge to stop and get some flowers was strong, but the fear Henley wouldn't view this as a date had me skipping it for now.

The drive to the B&B was quick, and I parked, taking a deep breath before getting out. The chime on the door jingled when I opened it, and I spotted Rhonda Taylor sitting behind the desk. I waved to the owner as I stepped closer.

"Well, hello, Fletcher. What brings you here?" she asked, smiling kindly at me. I'd gotten to know the Taylors well while I lived in Oak Crest. Her son, Rhett, worked with Dax and many of the hockey players, making our paths cross regularly. My family also stayed here a couple of times when they'd visited, putting me on a first-name basis with Rhonda.

"I'm here to pick up a friend," I said, leaning against the desk. "How are you and Rowan doing?"

"We're good. Thanks for asking. Rowan's excited about the internship she'll be starting in the fall. Is your family visiting any time soon? I want to get some of your mom's banana bread this time."

"I'm sure they will be in a few months. I'll let her know. She'll be happy to hear that you were asking about it. She's convinced it has magic powers."

"Ooh, what has magic?" Henley asked, drawing my attention.

I turned, stopping in my tracks when I took her in. She was dressed casually in jeans and a nice shirt, affirming my choices. But she looked so different off the ice I almost didn't recognize her. My mouth finally caught up to my brain, and I remembered she'd asked a question.

"Mama June's banana bread," I said, my mouth going dry. I licked my lips, rubbing the back of my neck.

"Oh, I remember her homemade bread. Frankie used to bribe me to do her homework with it."

"That sounds like Frankie," Rhonda said, chuckling. "You two have a good evening."

"Thanks, Rhonda. Reese is out with some friends but shouldn't be out too late with camp starting tomorrow."

"I'll keep a lookout then. I had my son write down his famous protein shake recipe for me to make in the morning as well."

"Now, that's liquid gold there," I said, the feeling finally returning to my limbs.

"Excellent. I'll let Reese know, and thanks again for the dinner recommendation. Bye." Henley waved, grabbing my arm as she dragged me out of the front door.

"In a hurry, Shaw?"

"As a matter of fact, I'm starving, so yes. You don't want to see me hangry, Fletch. It's not pretty."

"I find that hard to imagine, but come on, I don't want you to Hulk out on me." I directed her to the Jeep, opening her door for her. The drive was quiet, the radio playing as Henley looked out the window at the town.

"You know, last time I was here, I didn't really take in the view. We stayed in Salt Lake and visited a few times to see my old teammate, who has a shop here. This place is gorgeous."

"It is. It has that small-town feel I love, with Salt Lake not far to satisfy anything else you might need. Working at the school is a nice gig."

"How did you end up there, if you don't mind me asking?"

"I don't mind," I said, turning into the parking lot of the pizza place Henley picked. It was a hole in the wall, but it had some of the best pizza I'd ever had. Rhonda had given a great suggestion.

We hopped out of the Jeep and headed toward the restaurant. I waited until we were seated and had ordered before I started talking.

"I was at that place in my career where everything hurt, and I wasn't finding the same drive for the game anymore. It had all become about sponsorships and popularity. When I didn't make the last Olympic team, I thought about putting up my skates for good. I didn't see the point of skating anymore when I didn't love it. The training and the toll it took on me didn't feel worth it anymore. Oliver was an assistant at the time but reached out to me when he heard I was considering retirement. We'd played together for a bit in Nashville."

"He's the senior head coach now, right?"

"Yeah. He's a good dude."

She nodded, grabbing a breadstick the second after they were dropped on the table.

"So, what about the school made you reconsider giving up skating?" she asked between bites.

I smiled, liking how at ease she was around me. I hated that about first dates, the awkwardness, and putting on a perfect front.

"I came for a camp and fell in love with the campus, staff, and the kids, if I'm honest. They reminded me why I loved hockey. The money and fame were nice for a while, but the love for the game had evaporated. I found it again, coaching them. So, for now, I'm here, hoping to help other players reach their maximum level and avoid some of the mistakes I made by mentoring them."

"Wow, I never thought about it that way. That's admirable. I have to admit, I'm a little jealous. I feel so lost without hockey at the moment. Helping Reese prepare for camp has been the only thing I had these past few months." She dropped her head, picking at the breadstick on her plate. I didn't like seeing Henley down.

"Sorry if I offend you, but Dakota is a dick and a moron."

"No offense here. I agree. He's a giant tool." She lifted her head, the corners of her mouth pulling up slightly.

"You guys still together?" I asked, the question almost getting lodged in my throat.

"Hell no. I couldn't trust him after that. He still

claims he was hacked, but I know him. He used it to give himself some publicity."

"Good riddance then," I said, reaching across and placing my palm on hers. She peered up, her blue eyes sparkling under the lights. "And for what it's worth, I'm glad you're here. Even if it's only for a couple of weeks. It's good to see you, Henley."

"Yeah, you too."

We stared at one another, something shifting in the air between us. The pizza was delivered right then, breaking the moment between us.

We both instantly began to eat, the pizza hot and cheesy as I pulled it. She took a big bite, waving at her mouth when it scalded the roof of her mouth.

"So hot," she said, whining.

"They have these things called ovens that they cook pizza in, and it makes it hot," I said, blowing on my own piece.

"Har de, har har, smartass." She blew on her piece this time before taking a bite. "So, you're over the junior hockey team?"

"Yep. I have two assistant coaches under me. Tyler Matthews and Cody Richards. They're both good dudes. I was surprised to get the position over Tyler since he's dating Oliver and has been there longer, but he'll only be here part time this year. His dad started a security firm, and he's helping him with it after everything that went down last year."

"Yeah, so everyone keeps mentioning something, but no one really says much."

"To be honest," I said, wiping my mouth, "I don't know much. I wasn't involved, so I only know what Dmitry told all the staff. A secret organization had been using the school to funnel all kinds of illegal things through the kids and staff, promising them whatever they wanted for it. Over half of the staff was fired, and a lot of kids were pulled by their parents. Enrollment is down this year. Part of why I think they're allowing these camps to be a second tryout for the school."

"Huh. I vaguely remember something about that, but I didn't realize it was Lux."

"Well, Dmitry changed the name to give it a fresh start."

"You didn't want to leave?" she asked.

"No. Despite what other people were up to, I still believe in the school and their mission. And now, it's all out in the open; we can move forward without all of that holding us back. Though, not all of the other schools have that same mindset."

"Wow, I had no idea." She bit her lip, and I realized I might've said too much, considering her sibling was currently trying out for a spot.

"Hey, I promise that it's still the best hockey school. Reese will be in good hands."

"Thanks." Henley yawned, and I could tell she was

tired as she rubbed her eyes. I was bummed the night was ending, but I didn't want to rush anything with her. It felt like something real could be between us if I played my cards right.

"Let's get you back. Tomorrow's a big day."

Henley smiled, and I paid the bill, leading her out to the Jeep. My hand naturally fell to the small of her back, and I wondered if it had ever felt more right than it did there.

"Thanks for dinner, Fletch," Henley said when I pulled up to the B&B.

"No problem. It was good to catch up. Maybe we can do it again later this week?"

"I'd like that." She smiled, leaning over, and kissed my cheek. The act took me by surprise, and I froze, blinking. By the time I could focus, she had already hopped out of the Jeep. She waved, shutting the door, and I watched her walk up the steps.

Sitting there, I wondered if I was about to be Baby Shaw's next meal. The problem was, I wasn't against it. Any time I got with Henley would be worth the pain.

CHAPTER 8

Henley

SITTING ON THE BLEACHERS, I rubbed my palms together to warm them up. Reese was on the ice with nineteen other players and four coaches. I waved at a few of the guys I recognized, happy to see them coaching. Even more surprising was that the group was a mix of male and female players. The school continued to earn my respect.

The weirdest part was sitting on the sidelines.

It was hard not to jump in and make comments, and I often had to hold my hand over my mouth to stop myself from yelling plays.

Fletcher had winked when he first spotted me, making all of me warm despite the cold temperature. I didn't know how to take Fletcher. We had a great connection, and he was very attractive. He was the type of guy I'd always wanted to date, and I wished we'd met again a few years ago before the whole Dakota debacle.

He was the settling-down type, and I didn't know if that was me at the moment—or if I was honest at all.

Plus, I didn't know how Frankie would take it. Despite all the cons against us, I couldn't take my eyes off him. He made me smile and feel completely at ease, which I knew was rare. Fletcher was a good friend, but could there be something more?

Lost in my thoughts about my doomed attraction to Fletcher, I didn't notice when Dmitry sat next to me.

"Good morning, Ms. Henshaw. Reese seems to be doing well today."

I jumped, turning toward his voice. "Dmitry! Hi! How are you? Huh? Um, yes, Reese is doing well."

He chuckled, and I turned back toward the ice now that I'd made a fool of myself. I watched the kids as they listened to the coaches, eager for every drop of instruction. Fletcher was right that this school was different. The kids back at Reese's old school weren't this focused.

"I was wondering if I could ask another favor?"

I twisted, taking him in fully. "What kind of favor?" I asked, wondering if this was where he finally asked me out or something. He had a hidden agenda; I just wasn't sure what it entailed.

"One of the coaches we had for this camp had to step away for personal reasons. Would you want to fill in? I'd cover your housing, food, and offer a generous stipend."

My brain malfunctioned. "A job? A *hockey* job?"

Dmitry nodded, giving me a minute to process

everything. For some reason, coaching had never crossed my mind as a possibility. I'd enjoyed helping Reese, and these kids seemed to be just as committed to their craft. It might not be the nightmare I assumed it was based on Reese's coaches.

Plus, Fletcher loved it, and I'd get to spend more time with him. It wasn't like I was doing anything else this week, either. I'd get to play hockey on some level —that was something.

Take that job/hobby search! Seemed I'd found something after all.

"Are you going to split the girls and boys?" I asked, wanting to know if I was going to be separated. While there were some safety issues with girls and boys playing together, it didn't have to be as divided as the league made it. Most kids played co-ed anyway since there were never enough for two teams in most leagues.

"Nope. Remember, we value skill over gender." He smiled, and I released a breath.

"When would I start?"

"You could start after lunch in an hour or tomorrow if you need to take care of some things. You're doing me a favor, so I'm flexible with your schedule."

I quickly thought through the plan I had for the week. There was a lunch date with Sera and skiing, but I could reschedule. She'd understand.

"I can start after lunch." A big smile spread across my lips. "Does this mean I get to see the staff locker rooms?" I asked excitedly, clapping my hands.

Dmitry chuckled, nodding. "Yes, absolutely. Come on. I'll give you the tour and introduce you."

Glancing at the ice for one more second, I checked on Reese before following him. He punched in a code to enter the locker room, opening the door for me.

"I'll get you your code by the end of the day. You'll also have your own locker area, where you can store anything you might need. There's a laundry service, so if you need something washed, you can fill out a slip, and the staff will deliver it to your locker before the next day."

"Wow, that's even better than the pros."

"Yes," he said, pleased. "I adopted many features from the professional leagues and major arenas, adding a few features I always wished were included. These facilities are state-of-the-art and provide the best care for our instructors and students. Whether someone is here for a year or a few months, I want them to enjoy every moment with no external stress, if possible."

"I'm impressed. You've definitely gone above and beyond what most people do."

"Thank you. I appreciate your acknowledgment of that. It hasn't always been easy, and with the ordeal with the Council..." He shook his head, dispelling the thought. "Well, it's been tough showing the Olympic committee and colleges that it's behind us."

"Changing mass opinion is difficult," I grumbled, my experience leaving a sour taste in my mouth.

Dmitry's eyes softened, and the corners of his mouth crinkled slightly. "This way to your locker." He walked around a row and showed me to an area. The "locker" was more like a wardrobe with a leather ottoman in front of it. It was bigger than my locker in the pros.

"You're going to spoil me, Dmitry."

I couldn't be certain, but I could've sworn I heard him mumble, "That's the plan."

Shaking it off, I opened the door and found a new pair of skates in my size, a custom stick, helmet, and jersey with the school logo and colors—gold, purple, and turquoise.

"Let me or my assistant know if you need anything else. I'll have a contract brought over at the end of practice with everything we discussed. I'll leave you to get acquainted."

I nodded, but was too focused on checking out the other rooms around me. I found a sauna, state-of-the-art showers with multiple shower heads and settings, massage chairs, a viewing room, and a small kitchen. There was a whole other side, but I needed to run out to my car to grab my gear. As nice as it was for them to give me things, I liked my own equipment.

When I stepped out of the locker room, I realized my mistake when it closed behind me. Oh well, I could always change in the guest locker room if there wasn't anyone around.

Hustling out to the rental, I grabbed my bag and headed back in. I peeked at the ice, watching Reese perform a quick forehand to backhand deke around a player. Pumping my arm when they faked out the player, I smiled as I returned to the locker room.

A sudden realization that I might've needed to run it by Reese hit me, but it was too late. Hopefully, they wouldn't think I was interfering or didn't believe in them making it on their own.

Thankfully, someone was leaving the locker room when I neared, and I hurriedly jogged to catch the door. I didn't recognize the person, but they gave me a nod, heading off to one of the smaller rinks, earbuds in place.

I almost died of jealousy when Fletcher told me this arena had three rinks. This place was massive, and I understood what kept him here—helping the kids, of course. Scoffing at myself, I quickly changed into my hockey gear, putting on all the pads I thought I'd need.

Once I was set, I laced up my skates and grabbed my helmet and stick, heading for the door. Exhilaration coursed through me at the knowledge I was about to hit the ice again. It confirmed that no matter what I did next, regardless of if the league ever let me back, I had to do something with hockey. I loved it too much to give it up completely.

When I returned to the rink, I found the group huddled together, helmets off, as they listened to Fletcher and one of the other coaches. Two of the other guys saw me and skated toward me.

"Henley, right?" the ginger-headed player, who I knew to be Oliver Windsor, asked.

"Yeah. Dmitry asked me to fill in," I said, worried I was about to get the runaround from these two. Most male players didn't want women on the same ice as them.

"Yeah, I know. I'm excited to watch you work. It's an honor to have you as part of our team," he said, his whole face lighting up. I stared, a bit stunned by his response.

"Uh, thanks, same, actually. And you're Tyler Matthews?" I asked, nodding toward the other guy. I gripped my stick, using it as my safety blanket. I wasn't intimidated by these men, but something about them disarmed me.

The dark blond guy smiled wide, his green eyes intense as he stared. One side of his lips lifted. "Yeah. You're Reese's sister, too, right?"

I nodded, looking between them, ready for the fight I'd been expecting. When it didn't occur, my shoulders dropped, and I began to question everything.

"Reese is great. I can tell you've worked with them."

"Thank you for respecting their choice. Few do, and it's created a few team issues."

Oliver's face screwed up, his brow creasing. "That won't happen here. Lux might have some problems they're overcoming, but we're inclusive and accepting of who people are. Hell, Ty and I are in a polyamorous relationship with six other people."

"Wait, what?" They both laughed, and my mouth dropped open. "How does that even work?"

"Easier than you'd think. Sawyer's with all of us, Ty and I are together, and Rey and Soren are together as well. There are three others, but they're only in a relationship with Sawyer. But we're a family."

"A family..." I said, trailing off. I was still trying to picture eight people together in a relationship.

"Don't think too hard about it; you'll hurt your brain. You'll probably see most of us if you're around here this week, then you can watch us and see how it works. It's not as uncommon as you think," Oliver said, chuckling.

"Yeah, okay. Well, thanks for sharing that. That's awesome you're all able to be together like that. It means a lot to me that Reese will be given a fair chance."

"Shit, we're the lucky ones. You're Henley Henshaw. It's going to be a blast teaching with you this week. And Reese is a great player. They have a good shot at making the team, if that's something they're after," Oliver said sincerely.

"Yeah, I think Reese would like that."

We all smiled, and I noticed how easy it was to talk to them about these things. It was so strange to me, but I was learning to embrace it. Everything didn't have to be a fight. In fact, this was what I'd wanted for us both, so I needed to quell my instinct to jump into a dispute around every corner.

The whistle rang out, and the kids skated off in all directions. Their belongings were tossed into piles on the bleachers as they made their way to the cafeteria. Because, of course, this arena had one on site, letting the players eat without even having to change out of too much gear.

Seriously, I was beginning to think my team was poor based on the accommodations this school had in place.

Fletcher spotted me with Oliver and Ty and skated toward us; the other coach headed with the kids. Reese spotted me, but I waved them off. I'd catch up to them in a minute. They nodded, following Braden.

"Baby Shaw, you going to show us all up this afternoon?"

"Looks that way." I smiled so wide my face began to hurt as I held Fletcher's eyes. A throat clearing had me remembering that we weren't alone.

"Well, we're going to grab some grub. I'm famished," Oliver said, patting his stomach.

"You're always hungry," Ty teased as they started to walk off.

"Hungry for you," he said, wrapping an arm around Ty.

The ease they had with one another and the openness they seemed to have here was captivating.

"I knew you wouldn't be able to resist my charm. Be honest. I'm why you're really here," Fletcher joked, taking my stick and helmet and placing it next to his on a bench. Warmth built in my chest at the gesture.

I scoffed, rolling my eyes as we started to head toward the food. "Sorry to burst your bubble, Fletch. It was the locker room."

He held his chest, faking like I'd wounded him, making me laugh in the process.

"Fair. That locker room is sexy as hell. I'm thinking of proposing. Would you come to our wedding?" he asked, with a smile as wide as the arena.

Giggling, I nodded, asking him more nonsense questions as we continued to walk.

On paper, Fletcher Cromwell had a lot of cons. But I couldn't ignore how he made me feel or how easy his company was to be around.

Fletcher in person was nothing but pros, and I knew my heart didn't stand a chance—ready to settle down or not.

CHAPTER 9

Henley

THE FIRST NIGHT after practice ended, I felt like I'd been the one to go through training. My body hurt all over, and I needed a date with an ice bath. I was glad that the kids had been receptive to me coaching. There had only been a few comments about the video from a few of the teenage boys, but they were shut down immediately by Fletcher. Thankfully, Reese had been supportive of me coaching as well, making it an easy transition to step in.

We were now halfway through the camp, and I was sad it was almost over. I'd already seen a change in Reese; their skills had improved, and they were playing with more confidence.

Oliver, Tyler, Cody, and Fletcher had all been welcoming, making me feel like an equal. Since there were five coaches, we broke off into groups of four in the afternoons to practice skills. Today, I was going over stickhandling.

"Alright, squad, I want a set of your horizontal figure eights that transition into wide horizontals. The cleanest gets to pick the next drill. And go!"

The four kids started pushing the puck around the cones, making the moves and concentrating on stick-handling. I watched them, noticing that one stood out from the others in how clean they were.

"Great job, Braden. What do you want to do next?" I asked when they'd all finished.

"Narrow to wide," he said, grinning.

"Give me ten sets," I said as they started hitting the puck in a narrow width and then broadening out to a wide one. It was an excellent skill to practice going from close to long-range shots.

Once they were done with those, I had another kid pick, and they moved on to five-point toe drag. They had a little more trouble with this one, so I demonstrated how to hold their stick and place their feet.

"You can also transition into the pulls from the drags," I said, showing them. When I finished, I glanced up, finding the whole rink watching me. "What?" I asked, looking around.

"That was the fastest I've ever seen anyone move the puck," one of the kids said, his eyes wide.

"Oh, um, yeah, well, I happen to be really good at it. I practiced these all the time. So, keep working at it if you want to get as fast."

"She's being modest. At the last Olympics, Henley beat out everyone on accuracy during the skills competition. She's a beast. Watch and learn, younglings," Fletcher said, winking at me. My cheeks heated, but I ignored him, focusing back on my pupils.

"And go!" I shouted, hoping it would distract me from my embarrassment.

I hated that the moment I got recognition for something I deserved; I felt like I wanted to crawl inside my skin and die. The world had made me fight for so long to be noticed that when I was, I didn't know how to react. A man would puff his chest out and strut around like he was the biggest thing since sliced bread. Perhaps I just needed to find a middle ground between hiding from my success and being obnoxious about it.

When my cheeks had cooled, I felt more in control, and I lifted my head, taking pride in my skills. I was just as good as these guys, maybe even better in some areas. I'd trained my whole life and played every day for the past ten years.

I might not have a Y chromosome, but I knew hockey, and I was good at it. It was time I started acting like it.

When the last whistle blew, I felt more energized than I had all week.

"Great work, squad. You guys showed a lot of improvement in a short amount of time. I can't wait to see what you can do by the end of the week. Now, go and hit the showers. You stink."

The group laughed, giving me a wave as they

skated off. I began to follow, but decided to skate off some energy instead. Putting my helmet back on, I pushed off my blades and started to skate across the ice. It felt nice to stretch my muscles and push them. When I finished a few laps, I found Fletcher waiting for me. He was leaning back against the boards, a smile on his face.

"You look so happy when you skate. I can tell you're in your element."

"Thanks. It feels good to be here."

"I'm sorry if I embarrassed you earlier. I just wanted the kids to know how lucky they are to be taught by you. You're a superstar, Henley."

My cheeks heated again, but I figured I could get away with it since I'd just skated hard.

"You don't have to apologize. I'm not used to being recognized outside of my teammates, so it felt a little weird to me, but I had a stern talking to myself, and I will work on it."

Fletcher laughed, reaching out to take my stick and lead me off the ice. "As you should. Any chance you feel up to coming over for dinner tonight? I'll get you home early. I promise." Fletcher placed his hands together pleadingly, pushing out his lip.

He was too adorable to say no to, even if I'd wanted to. Which I didn't. Once I'd hopped on the Fletcher train, I was all aboard no matter how bad of an idea it was. I was a "see it through" type of girl, if there ever was such a thing—even to my own detriment.

Okay, okay. The word I was looking for was stubborn. I was a stubborn ass when I wanted to be, and I'd decided Fletcher was something I was going to be stubborn about... wherever the chips fell.

"Well, how could I pass up an offer like that? Home by curfew! How will I control myself?" I giggled, walking into the locker room. I was surprised to find it was empty; the other coaches were nowhere to be seen. Maybe I'd been on the ice longer than I'd thought. "I just need to check in with Reese. I'm sure they have plans, but I don't want to assume."

I walked over to my locker, still amazed each time I was in here. Sitting down on the ottoman, I unlaced my skates, my feet always feeling funny after being in them for long periods. When I spent most of my day in them, it was weird to walk without them afterward. It felt like an extension of my feet was missing. They tingled like a phantom limb.

Placing them into the cubby, I tugged off my jersey and pads, placing the pads in the open spot and tossing the jersey into the hamper. Now that I was less encumbered, I grabbed my phone and sent Reese a message.

HENLEY

You with B&B twins tonight? Fletch invited me over for dinner.

REESE

Yeah, if it's cool. We're going to grab dinner in town.

REESE

And "Fletch," is it?

HENLEY

Yeah, that's fine. Be careful and let me know when you're back.

HENLEY

And I've known Fletch a long time. We're good friends.

REESE

Is that what we're calling it?

HENLEY

See you later, dork.

While what I'd said was true, I knew I was downplaying our connection. Fletch might be an old friend, but there was something new brewing between us. I just wasn't ready to tell my seventeen-year-old sibling my love life details.

"Everything good?" Fletcher asked, scaring me. I jumped, my phone falling from my hands in the process. He laughed, picking it up. He glanced down at it before handing it to me. I prayed it hadn't been on the message. I didn't want him to think I was friend-zoning him just when I'd decided to see where things led.

"Thanks," I said, taking the phone. "And yes, I'm free for dinner."

"You know, I'm feeling a little tired. Maybe we should postpone?"

"What? No!" I leaped up, grabbing his hand. "If this was about anything you might've seen on my phone, it's not what it looked like."

He lifted a brow, not saying anything, the corners of his mouth twitching the slightest. His silence made me want to fill it, so I rushed to think of what I could say to convince him.

"I like you, Fletch. You make me smile and laugh. You believe in me. That's more than Dakota ever did, and we dated for two years. I'm just... I dunno. Not sure I'm ready to jump into a relationship."

"Wow, okay. I'm not sure what you thought I saw, but that was not the answer I expected."

"Shit, I've messed everything up, haven't I?"

"No. Absolutely not. You might've stolen my thunder a little as I planned to woo you during dinner, and here you go and show me up, saying how you feel with no fear."

"Oh." I shuffled on my feet, feeling a little embarrassed I'd jumped the gun. "Well, I mean, please feel free to still woo me. That might be nice."

Fletcher laughed, pulling me closer. "If it's nice, I'm not doing it right, Baby Shaw."

Heat seared my skin, and I sucked in a breath.

Fletcher Cromwell had game, and I was suddenly very excited to see it.

"So, dinner?" I asked, my voice squeaking a little. He smirked, making my insides flutter.

"I need to run by the store, but that will give you time to shower and change if you need to."

I snorted. "That's a nice way of saying, 'Please don't smell like the bottom of my gym bag.' I might be a girl, but I sweat. So, yeah, I'll be taking a shower. Text me the address and when you're home."

"It's a date, Baby Shaw." Fletcher winked, and my pulse began to race. He'd used the D word, making it clear what this was.

"A date." I nodded, turning back to my locker so I wouldn't get any ideas about attacking his stupid bearded face right in the locker room.

Discarding the rest of my clothes, I pulled on a robe and shower shoes and grabbed the shower stuff I'd gotten for the locker room. Fletcher waved as he headed out the door, and I took a quick shower, relishing in the hot water as it massaged my sore muscles.

By the time I'd dried my hair, I'd already received a message from Fletch with his address and that he'd start dinner once I was on my way. Cursing, I grabbed all of my stuff and rushed back to the B&B, debating what to wear. Should I keep it casual? Or go with something more formal, like a dress?

Deciding to pick something in between, I pulled on a silky cami, skinny jeans, and a pair of boots. Adding a long gold necklace and earrings, I tossed my phone, chapstick, wallet, and a few condoms into my purse, because a girl should always be prepared. Zooming down the stairs, I took a turn fast, ramming right into someone.

"Oof."

Strong hands gripped me, keeping me from falling on my ass. When I looked up, I stood stunned. Crystal blue eyes that had haunted my dreams for the past month stared back at me. Now that I wasn't emotional with tears in my eyes, I could connect why the man had seemed so familiar in that parking lot.

"Reed Cole." The words tumbled out in a whisper, my shock turning into embarrassment at the fact that one of the biggest hockey stars had held me in a parking lot as I cried and snotted all over him.

His hands flexed on my forearms, his eyes scanning me from head to toe. I couldn't gauge his emotions; his face was a solid mask.

"Henley," he said, his voice deep and slightly scratchy, like he hadn't used it in a while.

"You know who I am?" I asked right as my phone started to ring.

The sound broke the spell between us, and he let me go, moving around me as he continued up the stairs. Blinking, I didn't know what had just happened.

Reed Cole was staying at the same B&B as me, and he knew my name. The phone rang again, and I remembered I was headed to a date—a date with Fletcher Cromwell.

CHAPTER 10

Reed

I STUMBLED TO MY ROOM, my whole body feeling electrified.

Henley Henshaw was *here*.

In *this* B&B.

What were the odds?

Slumping down onto the bed, I sat, trying to formulate my thoughts into a cohesive line. I fell back, staring at the ceiling when it didn't work. That moment in the parking lot had felt like forever ago, along with the conversation with my coach.

Stepping away from the league had been the right thing to do. I'd gotten two more weeks with my mom before the cancer had finally taken her. I'd always cherish the last day I had with her when it didn't feel like cancer was part of our vocabulary, and I was thankful for that.

Memories of our last conversation surfaced, and I let myself remember; feeling everything associated with it. I'd become numb the past few months, the grief so consuming at the beginning that I pushed everything away, unable to handle it. While I wasn't sure if I was ready to face that pit inside me where everything festered, it was coming regardless. Tears developed at the corners of my eyes, unencumbered, and I let them fall in the quietness of my room as I remembered.

"Reed, when I'm gone, you have to promise to not quit living. I know you don't let many people into your life, but you can't keep everyone at arm's length forever. I want to die knowing you'll try. Can you promise me that? That you won't stop living and will let someone in?"

"Mom," I sighed, rubbing my face. "That's not fair. It's not that simple to just snap my fingers and let someone in."

She grabbed my hand, squeezing. Seeing her this alert made it seem like the last month had been a figment of my imagination. Maria Cole sat upright, her cheeks pink and her eyes focused. She looked at me, her eyes creased with concern at the edges.

Dropping my head onto the bed, I counted to ten, breathing in and out slowly. When I felt calmer, I lifted my head, kissing my mom's hand.

"If I have to make it my dying wish, I will. In fact, I have a list," she said gleefully.

"Oh, now, who's getting too big for her britches?" I said, lifting my eyebrow.

The faintest giggle escaped my mom's lips, and I locked it away, wanting to always remember that sound.

"Fine, what's this list you have for me?" I grunted, staring at her.

"*Find something to focus your time on. The days after I'm gone are going to be hard, Son. You need to have something to occupy your mind so you're not locked up in your apartment alone.*"

"*I took a leave of absence from the league, Mom. I can't just go back whenever I want. I have to wait until next season.*"

"*Reed Abraham Cole. I did not raise you to only know how to do one thing. Use your brain and get creative. You could spend a year hiking the Appalachian trail, learn how to fly a plane, or mentor young kids. It doesn't matter what you do, as long as you do something. Understand?*"

I groaned, knowing she wouldn't let it go. "*Yes, I promise to find something to occupy my days. Now, is that all?*"

"*Not even close.*" *She smiled, and I softened.* "*Let someone into your life is second. You're going to need a shoulder to lean on. Whether friend or romantic, I think if you were to open your heart, the grief wouldn't feel so unbearable.*"

"*Oh, I'm going to be unbearable, am I?*" *I teased.*

"*Absolutely.*" *She nodded resolutely.* "*I'm wonderful.*"

"*Yeah, you are, Mom.*" *I stared at her, tears threatening to fall. Clearing my throat, I squeezed her hand.* "*Okay, I promise to make an effort. But the past speaks for itself; most people are only out for themselves. I don't want to be used or taken advantage of. It won't end well.*"

"*What about that girl you're always telling me*

about?" She raised her eyes this time, giving my patent look right back to me. My face began to heat, and I cleared my throat.

"There's no girl. Just someone I admire."

"Well, it seems like she might be a good place to start if you 'admire' her."

"She's busy. Our paths don't ever cross. It's not a likely situation." I swiped my arm in front of us, hoping to physically make her drop it. Henley was out of my league. I'd sully her with my darkness. She didn't deserve any of that.

"Hmm. Well, promise me that you'll be open to possibilities. Fate has a funny way of working sometimes."

"Fate isn't real, Mom. If it were, you wouldn't be dying."

"Regardless of my medical condition, fate is a real thing. You just have to believe, Reed. I'll believe for both of us until you can."

"Is that the whole list?" I asked, feeling like my insides were going to crawl outside me. I didn't like thinking about my mom dying, even though I knew it was inevitable.

"Only one more, and this is more a request for how I want to be remembered."

Nodding, I swallowed, the lump in my throat thick.

"I want you to spread my ashes in places we were happy. The mountains, the ocean, and the cabin. Some of my happiest memories are there."

"Okay, Mom. I promise."

"You're a wonderful son, Reed. I want you to know that

you've made me so proud. I know things weren't always easy, and you had some difficult times, but I see the man you've become and the work you've done to be different. It's why I want you to be able to move on once I'm gone. I don't want you to fall back into that life."

"I won't, Mom."

She patted my hand, smiling at me with love. "Good. Good. Now, shall we try finishing our puzzle?"

"Yeah, I'll pull the table over." I stood and slid the moving tray across her bed, and we began to place the pieces of the puzzle in as quietness settled around us.

The following day, I got the call that she'd died peacefully in her sleep and my whole world tumbled down around me.

THE GRIEF SLAMMED INTO ME, AND I WAS UNABLE TO STOP it. If I stayed in this room, I was liable to break something, so I stood and grabbed my bag as I headed out the door. I'd come to Oak Crest as a favor to an old friend and my agent, but I hadn't had any intention of listening to their proposal.

The memory of my mom telling me to find something to focus on was like a slap to the face—a wake-up call.

My meeting with Oliver wasn't until tomorrow morning, but he had mentioned the rink would be open all night if I wanted to make use of it. I'd initially shrugged it off. I hadn't skated for almost a month. Perhaps it was time I got back on the ice. It could be the distraction I needed tonight—especially if Henley Henshaw was staying here. I didn't trust myself if I were to bump into her again.

The drive to the school was short, and as I stepped out of the rental and looked around, I was impressed with the campus. It was nicer than most colleges. The lights were still on in the arena, so I headed there, the adrenaline already pumping through me to get on the ice. By having a mission, I could ignore the grief that had wanted to consume me.

After I signed in at the front desk, I was directed to the guest locker room. There, I changed into my gear, some calmness falling over me already at the familiar movements. I grabbed my stick and walked toward the ice, ready to hit a few hundred pucks to wear myself out.

When I walked through the door to the ice, I was surprised to find a few teenagers playing on the ice. I debated if I could still take out my aggression with them present or if it would be better to leave.

"You can have the other half," someone said, motioning to the far end of the ice. I nodded, deciding it would be more awkward to leave now.

Picking up a bucket of pucks, I placed them on the ice and threw the first one down. The familiar sounds and smells began to work as a balm, relaxing the frayed edges of myself.

Pulling my stick back, I slapped the black circle, the movement feeling good as my body stretched to give it the power I wanted. My muscles screamed out at me, but the burn was worth it. Before long, I was out of pucks, tiny black discs filling the goal and surrounding area.

Grabbing the bucket, I skated toward the goal and began to toss them into it. When someone joined me, I didn't initially look up. When they didn't leave, I glanced up, but they were focused on picking up as many as possible.

"Thanks," I mumbled, the sound rough and raw.

"No problem. You were kind of amazing to watch. You remind me a bit of my favorite player, Reed Cole. He has a wicked slapshot."

I swallowed, the compliment taking me by surprise. I didn't normally interact with fans; their admiration always felt underserved.

"Um, thanks. You play?" I asked, finding myself asking questions.

"I'd eat, sleep, breathe hockey if I could, but I seem to make most teams uncomfortable. I was kicked off my last one, so now I'm at camp, hoping to impress them enough to let me attend in the fall."

Something about how the kid talked reminded me of myself when I first started playing. I hadn't wanted to listen to the coaches, confident I knew more than they had. I wasn't the best team player back then. But I didn't think it was the same reason for this kid.

"If you love hockey that much, then you'll eventually find a team that accepts you. It took me a few to find mine."

"You play?" they asked.

I chuckled, nodding. "Yeah. Or, well, I'm not this year, but yeah, I do."

"Wow, what's it like? I mean, my sister played, but she never tells me the good stuff."

"Hmm, something tells me I should do the same."

The kid groaned but smiled. "Fine. Be that way. If you wanted to join our game, we could use another player."

I glanced at the other end of the ice, seeing their friends waiting. I stared at the bucket, debating. While I didn't feel as angry as before, I didn't know if I wanted to play with others. It would probably be better if I just stayed on my corner of the ice.

"Thanks for the invitation, but I think I'll keep hitting from here. I don't think I'd be good company."

"Okay. If you change your mind, we're going to practice for another half hour before curfew." The kid began to skate away, and I felt I needed to say something else for their kindness.

"Hey, wait! What's your name, kid?" I asked.

"Reese."

"Well, Reese. Make sure to move your weight from your back leg to the front when you hit a slap shot, and you'll be out hitting me before you know it."

"You?" they gasped.

I laughed, placing the bucket back on the ice, and tossed the first victim down. I didn't wait to hear what they said next, feeling energized to keep hitting pucks.

When I finished the bucket this time, the ice was quiet as I collected them all. I put the pucks back where I'd gotten them as I headed off the ice, feeling more like my old self than I had in a while. I didn't want to admit it, but my mom had been right.

Having something else to focus on had helped.

Maybe I needed to consider Oliver's offer a little more seriously in the morning.

CHAPTER 11

Henley

KNOCKING ON FLETCHER'S DOOR, I smoothed down my shirt, my hands shaking a little. Running into Reed had me out of sorts. My mind kept replaying our moment in the parking lot, a million questions sprouting up.

Had he known who I was at the time?

Why was he there?

Better question, why was he here?

Fletcher opened the door with a smile on his handsome face when he spotted me, stopping my onslaught of questions.

"Wow, Henley. You look amazing. Please, come in." He ushered me in, his hand dropping to my back. I stepped through the foyer, shocked at what I found.

"This is a nice place. I wasn't expecting the staff housing to be so high-class, but I guess I shouldn't be too surprised. Everything at Lux is beautiful."

"And this is one of the smaller homes. Oliver's house is a mansion with seven bedrooms, a movie room, a fitness area, and a conference room. There are eight of them that live there, though."

"Whoa, that's incredible." I took in the living room, finding it cozy and warm, making me feel at ease.

"There are four huge houses, and the rest are smaller in comparison but still decent living spaces. There are four bedrooms here, but I currently only have one roommate."

"What's it like living with someone?"

"Dax is cool. We get along well. He's a physical therapist and fitness trainer."

"I have to keep remembering that not everyone here is a hockey player. It's just all I've met so far."

Fletcher laughed, directing me into the kitchen. It had a nice island and table off to the side. This house would be a nice home for a small family. Hopping onto the counter, I smiled as I watched Fletcher work—completely at home in the kitchen. It was making him even sexier.

"To be fair, the majority of the students and coaches are hockey. It gets the biggest pull, but there are a lot of skaters in other sports, along with skiing and snowboarding."

"When you think about it, the concept of this school really is unique. I see why you like it here. If the students are anything like the ones at camp, I'm sure it's nice to coach them," I said, swinging my feet a little.

Fletcher pulled something out of the oven, sitting

it on a trivet. "Yeah. It helps keep me grounded and feels more rewarding in some ways than just playing hockey." He turned, leaning against the counter as he watched me, a contemplative look on his face.

"Yeah, I'm starting to get that. This has been a nice break from the depressive haze I'd fallen into," I joked, wanting to take some of his gaze off of me.

Instead, Fletcher peered closer as he continued to watch me. "I'm glad this has been a good thing for you, Henley. Selfishly, I've enjoyed spending time with you, but hearing you say it's been the thing you needed to remember who you are makes me even happier. You're one of the best hockey players and kindest souls I know."

"Thanks, Fletch." I smiled, my heart growing warm as my cheeks heated.

"Dinner's ready. Hope you like enchiladas," Fletcher said, breaking the moment.

"Yum." I jumped up off the counter and walked over to him, inhaling the food deeply. "It smells amazing. And I like just about any food that's been made for me."

Fletcher chuckled, scooping a portion out onto a plate. I took it from him and sat at the table, where he joined me, handing me a glass of water.

"Sorry, I didn't think to get anything to drink."

"Water's perfect. Thanks."

The conversation fell away as we began to eat. It

was odd how at ease I felt with Fletcher, but at the same time, I felt nervous when I remembered this was a date. After a few bites, I decided to say something.

"So, are you going to tell Frankie?"

"About?" he asked, his brow raising at the question.

"This." I waved my fork back and forth between us.

"Enchiladas? She already knows the recipe."

His face was smug as he watched me. Sticking out my tongue, I couldn't stop the laugh that escaped. This was what Fletcher did. He made me feel comfortable with who I was.

Come to think about it, I never had that with Dakota. I constantly felt I had to prove my worth to keep his interest. If I wasn't hockey's sweetheart, then he ignored me. Knowing what I did now, I was just a trophy to him, nothing but a piece of arm candy.

"Hey, you okay?" Fletcher asked, placing his warm hand on top of mine.

I blinked, realizing I'd spaced out for a second. "Yeah, sorry, just thinking."

"Good things?"

"Yeah, mostly. It just occurred to me how I wasn't anything but an accessory to Dakota, and you don't make me feel that way."

"Oh, so point in my corner! Okay, I can get behind this train of thought."

Smiling, I turned our hands over, pressing my

thumb across his palm. "Definitely a point in your favor. But I can't say I'm not worried either." I dropped my eyes, not wanting to see any pain. I didn't want to hurt Fletcher.

"How about we clean up dinner and move this conversation to the living room? We can talk about *all* the things."

"You're willing to talk about things?" I asked, feeling slightly shocked.

"Yeah. Why wouldn't I?" he asked, frowning.

I shook my head, dispelling the doubt. "Just hasn't been my experience. Usually, it's a teeth-pulling type of conversation."

"Well, I promise not to pull any teeth. And not to sound cliche, but I hope I'm not like other men you've dated. I want to stand out as different."

"You do, Fletch."

Smiling, we stood, rinsed our plates and put the leftovers into the fridge. Working together, it only took a few minutes to clean everything up.

"We make a good team," Fletcher said, smacking me with the towel. "Now, get your cute butt into the living room, and let's lay it all out on the table."

Giggling, I headed to the living room and sat on the blue sofa. It was comfortable, and I sank back into the cushion. I twisted my body, so I was turned sideways, one knee bent on the couch so I could face Fletcher. He sat in a similar position, his arm going to the back. His fingers naturally played with a few tendrils of my hair.

"So, what are your concerns?" he asked, his face serious as he watched me.

"Frankie, for one. Distance for another. Are we just better as friends? Am I ready for a relationship? If I am, why do I still think of—" I rushed out until he stopped me, placing a hand on my thigh.

"Stop. One at a time. First, let's deal with the Frankie issue." He pulled out his phone and hit a button. He placed it on speaker, the phone ringing loudly in the room.

"Bro! What's up?"

"Hey, Frankie. You'll never guess who's coaching at camp this week?"

"Who?" she asked. You could hear a small child in the background, sounding like she was feeding someone.

"Henley Henshaw."

"Shut up! I haven't seen Henshaw in ages. Girl's a beast. You should take her out. She could use a good dude like you, Fletch. I can't believe all the shit she's been dealing with in the media. It makes me glad I'm out."

"I'm glad you approve. I think Henley's awesome and hope I can convince her to date me." He grinned widely at me, winking. I covered my mouth, shocked he was so open with his sister with me listening.

"Ah, how cute. I get to be in the wedding! I gotta go. Tell Henley to give me a call. The gremlins are getting out of control."

"Tell my nieces I love them."

"Will do. Love ya, Bro."

"You too, Sis."

The call disconnected, and he set his phone on the coffee table. Turning back to me, he raised his eyes. "Next concern?"

"Oh, um. You really mean all of that?" I asked instead.

"Yes, Henley. I like you. Now, what was your next concern, distance?"

"Yes. What happens when I'm back in Massachusetts?"

"It's not ideal, but I know if we tried, we could make it work. We're both not foreign to the concept of dating on the road during hockey season. It would just be a little longer. But... I don't mean to be insensitive about this, but you also don't know where you'll be, right? If Reese gets into school here, where would you go? What's holding you to Massachusetts?"

I blinked, realizing he was right. "Okay, so distance might not be as big of a concern as I originally thought." I bit my lip as Fletcher smiled at me softly, his fingers still playing with my hair.

"What was next? Better off as friends?"

"Um, yeah, I think so." I didn't know how to elaborate, so I left it at that. It was a bit cowardly, but this whole conversation was so out of my comfort zone it was taking everything in me to stay present with him.

"In my personal opinion, friends make the best lovers."

My cheeks heated at the word, but I couldn't seem to argue with him. The chemistry was there between us, no matter how hard I tried to deny it. I'd already succumbed to the desire coursing through my body. In fact, our bodies had moved closer on their own. Our faces were only a few inches apart. From this distance, I could see tiny gold flecks in his hazel eyes.

"Okay, I'll trust you. But... I don't know if I want a relationship. I was with Dakota for so long that part of me just wanted to be unattached for a while. You're not the causal type of guy. I know that."

"I'm not. But if you're not ready for something serious, we can keep it casual until you are. You're the type of girl I've been looking for. I'm not going to let you go on a technicality. If we're open with one another, we can ensure we're not doing anything to hurt each other."

"Openness. It sounds like such a simple concept, but yet..." I shook my head. "It's scary. You make me feel like I could do anything. On top of that, I feel like you give me room to take what I want. It just doesn't feel real. I don't know how to trust it."

"Do you trust me?"

"Yes."

"Then just focus on that. I'm not a young frat guy or asshat focused only on his career. I'm thirty and I know what I want. Talking about the hard things isn't always pleasant, but it solves a lot of problems. If we commit to being open, I think we could do anything together, Hen."

When he said my name shortened, it had a bit of a purr to it, hinting at something darker, making my insides quiver; my clit throbbed in response. We were so close now; our breath was fanning across one another's faces.

"Now, the last one, something about thinking about someone?"

I nodded, the movement making my nose brush against his. My mouth was dry, so I swallowed, licking my lips. His eyes dropped to them, and I wondered if he would kiss me. Fletcher stared for a minute before he glanced back up, capturing my eyes.

"Tell me, Hen." His hand was no longer playing with my hair but wrapped around the back of my neck, gently massaging the muscles there.

"Reed Cole," I said without thinking.

Fletcher blinked, looking a bit stunned. "Reed Cole? You have something with him?"

"Not exactly. He comforted me once. He was there to pull me back from the edge when I got kicked out of the league. I ran into him again before I came here.

He's at the same B&B, and I don't know." I shook my head, hoping it would dislodge what I was trying to say. "He's a mystery I haven't been able to solve."

"Okay. I wasn't expecting that, but we talked about being open, so I'll fall back to that. Was there anyone else?" I bit my lip, but eventually nodded.

"I don't know his name. I met him when I was in Salt Lake at the beginning of the summer. It was one night of no strings. I'll probably never see him again, but I sometimes think about him."

Fletcher swallowed, searching my eyes before he nodded. "So, one mystery guy and one untouchable guy, I think I have pretty good odds," he joked, the sound a little strained.

"When I'm with you, I don't think about anyone else, Fletch. I want you to know that. It feels weird talking to you about those things, but... it's also nice."

He scooted closer, our noses touching as he cupped my face. "If those are the only questions, I'm going to kiss you now."

"Yes," I said, nodding.

I closed my eyes, relishing the feel of his lips pressing into mine a second later. He held us there, and I liked that he gave us time to adjust. When he moved his lips, I moved mine, pressing harder into him. My hands trailed up his chest, his broad shoulders, and into his thick hair.

Fletcher pulled me until I was in his lap. I straddled him, finding it easier to kiss him. The kiss between us turned primal as we devoured one another. The doubt that we'd be only friends vanished as desire and arousal consumed me. I couldn't think of anything but kissing Fletcher.

When he pulled back, our breaths were heavy as we panted. His lips were swollen, and I reached up to touch my own.

"Wow," I said, smiling.

"You can say that again. It's going to be hard, no pun intended, to not push this too far too soon."

I giggled and then sighed, knowing he was right, but hating it all the same.

"Yeah. I hate it, but you're right. We can make out for a little longer, though, right?"

"Yes, Hen, we can make out."

He grinned widely, tossing me back onto the sofa as I giggled. His body pressed into mine, and we spent the rest of the evening making out like teenagers. When things got too heavy, we'd stop and cool off, talk about random things, and then make out some more. My lips were bruised from kissing him so much, and my face was covered in a beard rash, but I couldn't seem to stop.

"Stay the night? Just to sleep. I can't seem to let you go just yet."

I nodded, feeling the same. "Let me check in with Reese. I want to make sure they're okay."

HENLEY

You still out with the twins?

REESE

Yeah. Sorry. Didn't realize the time. I'll leave in a few minutes.

HENLEY

If you want to stay there, I'm cool with that.

REESE

Really?

HENLEY

Yeah. Be on time to camp.

REESE

Duh. Enjoy your sleepover.

HENLEY

Brat.

REESE

It takes one to know one.

Shaking my head, I put my phone back on the table, looking at Fletcher. "Reese is going to stay with one of the twins. I'm all yours. Got anything I can wear?"

Fletcher grinned like he'd just won the lottery. Picking me up, he carried me to a room, lightly dropping me on a bed. He opened a drawer, pulled out a shirt, and handed it to me.

"Bathroom is through there."

Changing, I returned to find him under the covers,

his bare chest on display. Climbing under them, I fell into his arms as we watched senseless TV.

I fell asleep that night feeling safe and understood in a way I'd been missing. Fletcher was my comfort, and I was glad to have found him.

CHAPTER 12

Dax

THE MUSIC BLARED in the club, making my ears ring. I lifted my hand to toss back the last of my drink, the liquid mostly water at this point. The girl I'd matched with on SASA was a total snooze fest, and I debated calling it quits for the night despite it being early.

I didn't want to admit to Fletch that he was right, and I was growing tired of hooking up—especially after this summer.

The blue eyes of my petal flashed through my mind, the sounds of her orgasm replacing the music. Just who was Petal, and how had she captivated me so completely?

It was the first time in my life that I'd hated my ploy of using fake names and not giving any information. I wanted to find her just so I could hear her scream my name.

"So, what do you think? Should I cut it all off or just do a trim?" she asked, twirling her brown hair around her finger.

"Oh, um, whatever you think," I said noncommittally.

I motioned for the bartender, deciding it was time to leave. The usual solution for my boredom wasn't working, and if I stayed here, I'd end up getting blackout drunk in order to tolerate this girl's presence. The clients I had to work with tomorrow might not appreciate my hungover state, and since my job was the only thing I had going for me at the moment, I prided myself on my professionalism.

"I just remembered I didn't feed my fish. It was nice meeting you. Good luck with your hair decision."

I signed the bill and tipped the bartender at record speed, slipping off my stool as I pocketed my wallet and headed toward the door. Her mouth had fallen open at my excuse, but I hadn't cared enough to make it more believable.

The instant I was clear of the nonsense of this date, my chest felt lighter, and I breathed easier. I might have to take Fletcher up on his idea and stop having one-night stands.

The thought felt scary, my past telling me that I couldn't trust another woman not to break my heart. But yet... the thrill of a new woman each week didn't feel as exciting as it had been.

I hated to admit I missed intimacy—the knowledge one had when being part of a couple. I'd had that once, and it had been magical... until it wasn't.

But that was three years ago, before I came to Oak Crest. It felt like such a long time now. I wasn't the same person I'd been back then. I was more confident in my skill set. My career was flourishing, and I found joy in helping athletes train and recover from injuries. I woke up with a purpose each day, and it was fulfilling.

So why was this so scary?

"Headed out?" Jason asked as I passed him at the door. We'd become friends over the past year, and he hooked me up from time to time with the VIP suite when it was empty. The last time I'd used it had been with her—my petal.

"Yeah. Just not feeling it tonight."

He assessed me, his eyes squinting as he seemed to think about what he wanted to say. I waited, respecting our relationship.

"If I'm correct, you haven't been *feeling it* since that girl you took up to VIP over the summer. Whatever happened to her?"

"No clue. That's kind of the point." I narrowed my eyes, not sure I wanted advice from a bouncer.

"Humph. In theory, hooking up with someone new sounds great, but looking at you, I don't think you love it as much as you tell yourself you do."

I opened my mouth to argue, but the words stuck on my tongue, refusing to come out. Whatever I'd planned to say would've been a lie. Sighing, I hung my head, my hair falling around my face as I rubbed my forehead.

"Yeah. I'm starting to realize that as well."

"Maybe start with finding that girl from the summer."

I rolled my eyes. "No matter how hard I want that to happen, it won't. I don't know her real name or if she's even from around here. She was staying at the hotel. Most likely, she was here on vacation, and I was a fling."

"Shit, that sucks. Then, perhaps you should try going on a date with someone you wouldn't mind seeing more than once."

"Easier said than done. I wouldn't even know where to start to meet someone."

"Get off the apps, dude. Start there." This time he narrowed his eyes at me, drilling home his point.

Someone pushed by me to get through the door, so I nodded to Jason and took my leave. "I'll see you around."

"I kind of hope you don't," he said, giving me a look I hated—pity.

Shaking my head, I made my way toward my car. It was about a thirty-minute drive back to Oak Crest. Having Salt Lake so close made it easier to meet women and keep my identity secret. It was a larger pool, and I didn't have to worry about running into them at the local coffee shop this way.

I'd only driven a few minutes when my phone rang, my brother's name coming up on the car display. Sighing, I hit the screen to answer the call; the Bluetooth coming to life through the speakers.

"Dax, you haven't responded to any of my messages. Jenny thinks you're not going to come to the wedding. Tell me that's not true?"

"Why would I want to come to the wedding, Derek? Everyone will be looking at me with pity. I'd rather eat a hundred razor blades."

"Don't be like that, Dax. It's been three years. Haven't you gotten past this yet? I know you're not still pining for her. I see you on social media with a different girl all the time. It seems like you've been fine."

"Derek, I don't have to explain myself. Not to you."

"Harsh, little brother. Listen, Mom wants to get a family picture. So, if you won't do it for me, do it for Mom."

I groaned, hating that he was using our mother against me. The last place I wanted to be was the wedding of my ex-girlfriend to my brother.

"I'll think about it," I gritted out, my knuckles tightening against the steering wheel.

"I guess that's better than a no. What can I do to make it a definite yes? We can add a person if you want to bring a plus one."

I laughed, the sound hollow. "How considerate," I

mumbled. I was glad this drive was easy and one I'd done a million times, or I'd have driven into a tree with how little I was focusing on driving.

Derek sighed, the sound echoing around me. "I know I screwed up, and I've apologized a million times to you. I didn't mean to fall for Jenny, but it happened. We've always been close, Dax. I don't want to lose our relationship because of this."

"Yeah, well, it's a little late for a guilty conscience. You're my brother, and I love you, but you're asking a lot of me. Give me time to think about it, please. It's what I need."

"Okay. I'll call you back in a few weeks. I miss you, Dax. Hope you're doing well."

The phone clicked off, and I both cursed and sighed in relief. I hated how he ended conversations, always having the last word. But I couldn't deny how relieved I was to have this discussion be over.

Ten minutes later, I pulled into my driveway, my body relaxing the rest of the way at being home. I should've stayed home tonight. This week had been tough with a few of my newer clients as I pushed them to embrace a new way of doing something. But when Fletcher had messaged he was bringing a date to the house, I felt like the polite thing to do was let him have some privacy, despite how tired I was.

Now I saw how pointless it had been to go on that date. Maybe it would be the turning point I needed to change my path. I was a big believer in fate and looking at the signs the universe sent you.

I climbed out of my car and walked up to the house, noticing all the lights were out. There was a strange car parked at the curb, so it looked like his date had ended well.

It made me wonder what it would be like to have someone stay over here. I'd never brought a woman back to this house, keeping my identity hidden even more. It felt like a big step to fully let someone into my life again. I was completely me in this house. It was where I could be Dax without putting on any airs.

Walking into the kitchen, I pulled out the pitcher and poured myself a glass of water. The cold liquid felt nice as it washed down my throat. Leaning against the sink, I tilted my head back, enjoying the silence. After a few seconds of standing there, I finished my water and headed to my room, ready to go to sleep.

Between the disaster date and my brother's call, I was exhausted—emotionally and mentally. Turning the corner, I ran straight into a body I hadn't seen there.

"Oof," the feminine voice said, her hands grabbing onto me. Electricity coursed through my body at her touch, and I sucked in a breath. Stepping back, I kept hold of her, afraid she'd vanish into thin air if I let her go.

"Blondie?" she asked, her voice barely a whisper.

"Petal, how did you find me?" I asked, knowing I should be freaked out that this woman had stalked me and managed to sneak into my house, but I was so happy to see her again I didn't care. Maybe I should have, but I didn't. "Never mind," I said when she didn't respond. Dropping my mouth down to hers, I kissed her, the action feeling so effortless I knew it meant something I wasn't ready to accept.

She gasped, and I swept my tongue into her mouth as I pulled her closer to me. Her body melded to me exactly as I remembered; her curves and muscles made my hands happy as they perused her body. She moaned, the sound even more intoxicating than I recalled. I was two seconds away from pressing her against the wall, but thought better of it and began to move us backward toward my room.

She pulled away, her breath coming out in pants as she tried to find her words. "Wait. I—"

She didn't get to finish as a light turned on, shining down on us as Fletcher stepped into view.

"What the fuck, Dax?" he yelled, moving toward me. I'd never seen him angry before. Even odder, he seemed hurt. I couldn't understand why, but his anger made me move Petal behind me to protect her.

"Calm down, Fletch. There's no reason to be angry. I don't want you to scare Petal."

"Petal? Why are you kissing *my* girl? Let her go, man!"

"*Your* girl?" I asked. A sudden cold feeling washed over me, and I turned, looking at the one girl who had made me believe in soul mates again. "You didn't find me, did you?"

"No," she whimpered. "But, Dax, was it? I—"

I dropped her hands; the electric feeling no longer felt exciting but like a live wire. I stepped back, turning quickly to walk to my room.

"Um, sorry, Fletcher. I thought she was someone else."

Fletcher looked between us, some sort of understanding passing across his face. It seemed too close to pity, and I didn't want to see that look for a second time tonight. Stepping into my room, I shut the door and locked it as I slid down to the ground, my head falling between my hands.

What the hell had just happened? How was the one girl I connected with, with Fletcher? Why did it seem like every time I found someone, there was someone better for them?

If anything, the universe had shown me the signs, proving I was only destined for one-night stands.

Anything else was too messy, and I didn't do complicated.

CHAPTER 13

Henley

BLONDIE, aka Dax, walked into a room down the hall from Fletcher's, shutting the door and leaving me breathless in the hallway. Tears ran down my face as I stared at the place he'd vanished into, wishing he'd return. I had no right to feel that way, especially as Fletcher's arms wrapped around me, pulling me to his chest.

His soft gesture had the tears falling harder as I cried. I didn't even know what I was crying for, but it felt like something precious had been stolen from me.

"Shh, it's okay, Baby Shaw." His voice was deep and comforting, rumbling through his chest. He directed me back to his bedroom, the sound of the door shutting and the feel of his bed clueing me into my surroundings.

I couldn't even remember why I'd gotten out of bed, the whirlwind I'd just experienced from bumping into Blondie and his kiss having turned the last few minutes upside down. Fletcher pulled me onto the bed, wrapping his arms around me as he cuddled me to his chest. One hand rubbed my back while the other smoothed my hair down. The gesture was calming, and I soon relaxed.

When my tears began to subside, he pulled back, wiping my face. "Want to tell me about it?"

Sucking in a breath, I nodded, scooting back so I could find the words. Everything was too hazy when I was cocooned in his arms.

"Remember the guy I said I met in Salt Lake? The one I thought I'd never see again?"

Fletcher nodded, not saying anything, and I hoped it was to allow me to talk and not because it would stop whatever was developing between us before it had a chance to start. I couldn't handle losing two guys in one night.

"Well, I guess it's your roommate. Dax. I called him Blondie. We didn't, um, exactly exchange real names."

Fletcher reached out, brushing his thumb across my hand. "I'm not surprised you're the girl he hasn't been able to get out of his mind."

"Huh? What?" I blinked, sure I'd heard him wrong.

Fletcher gave me a soft smile before sighing. "You're amazing, Henley. If there was ever a girl to make Dax stop and think about a second time, it would be you. I hope that doesn't sound weird."

"It kind of does—especially coming from you."

"Yeah, I can understand that." He chuckled,

pulling me back toward him. "How about we talk with him in the morning?"

"You're not upset I kissed someone?"

He blew out a breath, rustling my hair. "It wasn't what I expected to find in the hallway, and I was shocked and a little hurt. But I know you both, and a bigger part of me knew that if you were kissing one another, it meant more than just two people I trusted deceiving me."

"I'd never!" I exclaimed, jumping back to look into his eyes. "Fletcher, I... he kissed me, and I'm sorry I didn't react quickly. I was so stunned that I was almost convinced it was a vivid hallucination I was having."

"I know, Hen." He cupped my cheek, and I leaned into it, loving the feel of his hands on me. "And while I'd love to say, okay, let's put this behind us and move on, I can't."

"But—" I started. Fletcher lifted his finger and placed it over my lips, stopping me from talking.

"I can't, because I could see how you two feel about each other. Plus, you'd just told me this evening that you weren't ready for anything serious and that there were two guys you were unsure how you felt about. So, it would be inconsiderate of me at the first step of dating if I instantly tried to lock you into something I heard you say you weren't ready for. So, let's sleep and talk with Dax in the morning. I was serious about communication being important."

"Okay, Fletch." I kissed his cheek, grateful to have this foundation with him. I'd been in relationships before, but it had always been something that occurred naturally over time. There were never any honest conversations about it; we were just together one day. Dating casually was a whole new maze for me to navigate.

We slid under the covers, and Fletch turned out the light. My mind was busy racing with questions, wondering about Dax and if he would pretend none of this happened in the morning. For some reason, that felt worse than never seeing him again.

With Fletcher's steady heartbeat under my head, I fell asleep, the worries of tomorrow fading away.

THE ALARM WENT OFF EARLIER THAN I WANTED. THE encounters from the night before began to surface again, and I rubbed my eyes, sitting up as Fletcher rolled over and shut off the sound. It was still dark outside, but that wasn't unusual for athletes. Stretching, I cracked my neck from side to side as I twisted my torso.

"Good morning, beautiful," Fletcher said, causing me to smile. I glanced over, finding him watching me.

"Good morning, handsome." He chuckled, the sound doing dangerous things to my body at this hour.

He made a deep sound in his throat, almost like a growl, and my body heated, my clit beginning to throb from the sound alone.

"Fuck. If I only had enough time to wake you up properly," he cursed. "I'm going to jump in the shower, and then we can drive to your place if you want?"

"Yeah, that works. Um, do you think Dax is awake?"

"Probably. He usually works out as early as I do. I'll hurry, and we can see if we can catch him together."

"Together."

I nodded, liking how it sounded. Fletcher walked into the bathroom, the door shutting and the water starting a few seconds later. I climbed out of bed and quickly made it, wanting to be helpful. I grabbed my clothes from the night before and put them back on. It felt a little like a walk of shame, but I pushed it aside, knowing I had nothing to be ashamed about.

The water shut off as I finger-combed my hair. When the door opened, steam billowing out, I wasn't prepared to find Fletcher standing half-naked in a towel. I froze, unable to stop my staring, watching a few beads of water trail down his chest. He had a smattering of dark chest hair across his tan skin. His armband tattoo was on full display. I licked my lips as I took in all of his dips and bulges of muscles. The man was delicious.

"Baby Shaw, if you don't stop looking at me like

you want to eat me, then we'll never make it to practice. Oliver has a meeting this morning, so I'm in charge. It wouldn't look very good for me to skip it, but I'm about half a second from doing it." His voice was strained, and I noticed that the towel he had wrapped around him was tenting.

As much as I wanted to see what lay underneath it, I knew we didn't have the time. With a sigh, I stood and walked out of the room without a word. Once I was clear of the door, anxiety filled my chest. The idea of seeing Dax excited me, but I was also worried he'd ignore me. Finding him again felt like a huge win. To have our connection thrown back at me would be a blow I wasn't sure I could manage.

The kitchen was empty as I walked in, the coffee pot filling itself. I wondered if it was on a timer or if Dax had started it before he left. It stung to think he would've left without talking, but it was a little easier to accept than being ignored. If he left, it had to mean he felt something, and we could work with that. I didn't know exactly what I wanted the solution to be, but I knew that I couldn't let him walk away without knowing how I felt about him.

Even if it meant nothing changed, it felt important for me to tell him.

"Coffee?" Fletcher asked, stepping into the kitchen, fully clothed. He walked over to a cabinet and pulled out a travel mug.

"Sure," I said, taking it from him. In quick motions, he filled our mugs, handing me sugar and pointing to cream. He watched me, and I wondered if he was memorizing how I took my coffee. He opened the fridge and stopped, looking back to the open door of Dax's before gazing back at the refrigerator.

"Here, Dax made us some protein shakes." He handed me a container, the realization that Dax had made it for me soothing some more of the hurt edges from him being gone. Fletcher grabbed a banana and a granola bar, tucking them into his bag before lifting it up on his shoulder.

With my two drinks in hand, I followed him out the door and to my car. The sun was beginning to rise, the colors beautiful as they painted the sky. Climbing into the car, I chuckled as Fletcher scooted back the passenger seat so he could fold his large body into it.

He narrowed his eyes at me, causing me to only laugh more.

"What?" I asked, feigning innocence. Fletcher ignored my question, but I caught a smile as he turned toward the window.

The drive to the B&B was easy, and we managed to make it to my room without bumping into anyone. I could hear Rhonda in the kitchen bustling around, but thankfully I'd escaped her scrutiny. Not that I thought she'd judge me, but it was better she didn't have the opportunity, in my opinion.

I led Fletcher into the room and went straight to my suitcase. Grabbing some clothes, I stepped into the bathroom and took a quick shower. It was pointless to do much since I was about to get hot and sweaty while training. Drying off, I dressed and brushed my teeth, feeling human once again.

In under fifteen minutes, we were headed back to the car, my bag in tow. We weren't as lucky this time, running into Rhonda as we left, but at least we hadn't bumped into Reed. Dealing with one potential dating crisis at a time was all I could handle.

Thankfully, we made it to the rink before the kids. I'd downed my protein shake and coffee on the way. The shake was even better than the one that Rhonda had been making for Reese all week. Dax had skills, and I hoped to learn more about him. I couldn't get him off my mind as we prepared for the morning, placing cones down on the ice and sectioning off parts.

Once the kids arrived, I fell into my role and pushed everything else to the side. We were working on blocks and footwork today. Since we were down one coach, we split into teams of ten with two coaches. Fletcher and I were paired up, and I loved how well we worked together.

During one of the drills, I felt the hairs on the back of my neck rise. I scanned the stands, but I couldn't find anyone. When it was getting close to the lunch break, I glanced at one side of the bleachers as I checked the time, stopping in my tracks at the sight of the person watching me.

Dmitry, Oliver, and Reed Cole sat on one of the bleachers, all focused on the scrimmage the kids were doing. Except for Reed. He was staring right at me. I sucked in a breath, unable to break his gaze. A whistle blew a few seconds later, and I jumped, turning toward Fletcher. He looked concerned, but focused on the kids.

"Lunch time. See you back in an hour. Good training this morning, everyone!"

The kids hooted and hollered as they clambered off the ice. Sticks, helmets, and parts of uniforms were placed on the bleachers as they made their way toward the cafeteria. I went around picking up the cones with Fletcher, placing them all back where they belonged.

The trio was standing when I skated off the ice, apparently waiting for me. Fletcher stopped, looking at the three of them.

"Hey. Did you catch the end? The kids are looking great."

"They are," Dmitry agreed. "Fletcher, this is Reed Cole. Could you show him where to get some lunch and introduce him to some of the staff?"

"Yeah, absolutely," he said to Dmitry, turning to Reed. "It's nice to meet you, Reed. I'm Fletcher—"

"Cromwell. I remember playing against you. You're

a great player. Nashville hasn't been the same since you left."

They walked off, not before I noticed them both glancing back at me before they disappeared. I began to follow when Oliver stopped me.

"Actually, Henley, we were wondering if we could meet with you during lunch?"

Dread began to crawl up my throat. Had I broken some rules? Was I not supposed to date Fletcher while working? Had they found out about my video? Had the league called?

I followed them, my nerves flaring up, wondering what crushing blow I would receive today.

CHAPTER 14

Henley

OLIVER MOTIONED for me to take a seat on a couch as he and Dmitry took the chairs across from me. It weirdly resembled a therapy session, and I snorted, my need to dispel the anxiety making me laugh at the oddest things. Clutching my hands together, I adjusted my body on the couch. I still had some pads on, so it was hard to get comfortable.

"Thanks for meeting with us, Henley. There were some things we wanted to talk to you about."

"Am I in trouble?" I blurted, unable to hold it in any longer.

Oliver's lips twisted up, his brow furrowing. "No. Why... Ah, sorry if this felt like an interrogation." He grimaced as he looked between him and Dmitry.

The older man chuckled, rubbing his hand along his chin. "Yes, apologies, Henley. We're just excited about some possibilities and didn't want to wait. Excuse our exuberance for not realizing it would appear otherwise."

"Possibilities?" I asked, relaxing slightly now that I knew I wasn't in trouble.

Another reaction I was starting to hate about myself. I was in my mid-twenties; I shouldn't fear someone telling me I was in trouble. Rationally, I knew I hadn't done anything wrong. But my recent experience with the league clouded everything, and it would be awhile before I could shake that reaction.

Oliver smiled as he leaned forward. "Henley, you've been an excellent addition to camp this week. The kids have learned a lot from you, and you have a natural ability for coaching them."

"Oh, thank you." I blushed, shuffling my skates as much as I could.

"Oliver has decided to leave us this fall, following his dream of going to pastry school," Dmitry added, watching me. I was beginning to feel like I was at a tennis match with the way my head kept swiveling between the two.

"Wow, that's amazing. Congrats," I said, not getting why I was being told this.

"Thank you. I've always loved to bake, so now I'm going to get better at the craft. Unfortunately, that means I can't be here this coming fall."

"Okay, so is Cody or Ty going to take over, or another coach?"

"Nope. Ty is going part-time as is, and Cody doesn't want the responsibility," Dmitry said, leaning closer. I had a feeling he was about to gear up for a pitch, and I wracked my brain for what it was. When it dawned on me, I sucked in a breath.

"Me?" I asked. Oliver smiled and nodded.

"I've been having meetings all week with people, but each day I saw you with the kids, I knew you were the head coach the school needed," Oliver said.

"Lux has had some image problems as of late, along with other schools and the Olympic Committee not taking us as seriously since the Council ordeal."

A pit began to form in my stomach. "If you already have an image problem, then you don't want me. I've been placed on suspension for impropriety. I'm not hockey's sweetheart anymore."

"We both know that's bullshit. The league was grasping at straws and used you as a scapegoat. I think that we could benefit one another. Show the league you don't need them and that we think you're worthy of being the coach of the senior hockey team."

"You'd be the first female coach of a senior team," Dmitry added.

"So I'm a publicity stunt, then?" I asked, the anxiety returning.

"What part of hockey isn't?" Oliver asked. "Listen, I know it feels like a ploy on our part, but that isn't why we're asking you. I truly believe you're the right coach for the job. The one who can help this school regain its place in elite hockey. The publicity is just a bonus, helping us both in the long run."

I ran the words he said over and over in my head, looking for a sign of deception. Everything felt genuine, and it would be an answer to a lot of my problems. But it still felt like I was missing something. When I remembered seeing Reed with them before this and that Fletcher was showing him around, I knew he was the missing piece.

"What about Reed Cole? Did you ask him first?"

Oliver and Dmitry shared a look before turning back to me.

"I'll be honest with you, Henley. Reed is a great player and has a lot to offer the students here. Oliver and I invited him to be a coach at the camp, but he had some personal matters to attend to and couldn't commit. He only came to do the interview as a courtesy. When he came in today, he was different, and determined. He accepted a position as an *assistant* coach for the senior team. He was never in the running to be the head coach," Dmitry said.

I blinked, trying to process what Dmitry had just said. Reed would be an assistant coach. A coach underneath *me*. That image appeared in my head, and I began to get hot under the collar, pulling it away. Another giggle escaped me, my defense mechanism for dealing with uncomfortable situations to laugh and make inappropriate jokes—even if only in my head.

"Sorry, it just all feels a little overwhelming." I

smoothed my hands down my pants, trying to weigh my options. "What about Reese? Will their admission into this school be determined based on if I'm the coach or not?"

"Of course not," Oliver said. "Reese is a fierce player and has amazing potential. We would offer them a place on the team regardless of your decision."

"Though, I did hope that their placement here would help sway you. I know you're close. But it was never an either/or thing. Reese earned everything on their own."

The fear that Reese was being used as a pawn eased as a million questions ran through my mind.

"Where would I stay? Where would Reese stay? How long is the contract? What if I get reinstated into the league? Am I allowed to date other coaches? Is there a morality clause?"

The guys chuckled as I spewed the questions at them. Dmitry held up his hand to stop my onslaught.

"Housing would be provided, and Reese could stay in the dorms. We'd have to talk with them about which one they'd feel the most comfortable staying in and make sure their roommate was open and accepting to avoid putting Reese in a dangerous situation. Everything else can be finalized once you accept. We're not a regular school, so outside of illegal things, many of your questions can be solved easily with a conversation. Several instructors work part-time or even leave during the semester as they chase their dreams."

"It's true. My girlfriend is doing workshops while she trains for the Winter Olympics," Oliver added.

That understanding eased some of my fear. I didn't know what the year held for me, but being locked into anything felt terrifying for some reason. I needed my freedom right now—dating and career.

"Right, well, can I have a day to think about it? It just feels massive, and I want to talk to a few people first before I make a decision that impacts them."

"Of course. I was hoping to announce it tomorrow at the end of camp, so if we can have a decision by lunch tomorrow, we can get everything started then," Dmitry said.

I nodded, the three of us standing as I headed out the door. They stayed back, and I made my way to the cafeteria. I knew I should eat something, but food was the last thing on my mind for once. I grabbed a packaged box and a water bottle as I walked in. Fletcher had explained how they have dietitians who work with the athletes to plan specific meals for them to meet their needs. They numbered them all, allowing the athletes to grab and go when needed.

I glanced around and spotted Reese first. I hadn't gotten a chance earlier to talk with them during camp, only able to give a passing nod as they took to the ice to warm up. Walking toward the table, I spotted

Braden and a few other kids, all laughing. Reese noticed me when I was close, looking up and catching my eyes.

"Hey, Reese, can I talk to you for a second?"

"Yeah, sure." The boys snickered, but Reese rolled their eyes. I sat down at an empty table, placing my food on the surface. I opened the package and began to eat some of the fruit and nuts while I waited. When they sat down, I debated how to broach the topic.

"I have something I need to talk to you about, but to do that, it means telling you some private news that won't be shared until tomorrow. Including your future at Lux. Are you able to keep it to yourself and handle it?"

Reese nodded, scooting closer, their brows creasing in worry.

"First of all, you've done amazing this week. I want you to be proud of that." Reese's head fell a little, and I realized they thought I was telling them they didn't make it. I quickly reached out and took their hand. "They want to offer you a place at the school in the fall."

Reese's head snapped up, a smile beginning to spread. "Really?"

"Yeah. With that, they've asked me..." I cleared my throat. "They've asked me to be the head coach."

Reese's mouth dropped open before they launched themselves at me, hugging me. "Hen, that's amazing!"

"Yeah? I wasn't sure you'd think so. I told them I needed time to think about it and talk to you."

"Me? Why?" they asked, their brows lifting in confusion.

"I didn't know if you'd be cool with your sister as your coach, for one. And two, I didn't want to steal your thunder or make you think it was all contingent on me or anything."

"I don't care if it is. I'm in. That's all that matters. This school is amazing, and I have friends for the first time here. I know I'll become a better player. Especially with you as my coach."

"You mean that?" I asked, a small tear wanting to spill down my cheek.

"Yes, Hen. What's holding you back?"

I blew out a breath, relaxing. "You were the first person I wanted to talk with. The second is Fletcher."

They raised their eyebrows suggestively, moving closer. "Ooh, *Fletcher*. How's that going?"

"Ah, good, I think. It got a little complicated just as it was getting started. My feelings are kind of all over the place, but Fletch is great."

"Then go talk with him. I'm sure he'll agree with me."

"Yeah, I need to. Okay. Thanks, kiddo."

They did another happy squeal, giving me a hug. When they pulled back, their face fell a little. "Man, now I gotta keep this a secret for a whole day?"

I chuckled, knocking their shoulder. "Yep."

Reese rolled their eyes but got up, zipping their lips. I looked around for Fletcher but didn't see him yet. I quickly ate the rest of my food, not even tasting it. By the time I finished, there were about twenty minutes left before we needed to return to the ice. Tossing my trash away, I headed out to look for Fletcher, not at all anxious about the fact he was with Reed Cole.

Nope. Not one bit.

CHAPTER 15

Fletcher

AFTER THE THIRD room and umpteenth staff introduction, it was clear that Reed wasn't paying attention. I decided I'd have a little fun with him since I'd been roped into this tour, while the girl I was developing feelings for had been carted away from me.

"And in this room is where I proposed to Henley and then made love to her on—"

"What the hell did you just say?" a deep rumble boomed out.

Smirking, I turned and faced the silent statue, crossing my arms. "It's clear you're not paying attention to what I'm saying, so I thought it would be fun to find out what you were really focused on."

"And?" he asked, quirking an eyebrow, matching my stance as he crossed his arms. His forearms bulged at the move, drawing my attention.

"Tell me... do you have the hots for Henley? Because it sounds like it from what *she's* told me."

"Which was what?" he grunted. He dropped his arms, flexing his fist. I didn't have to be an expert in body language to note *that* change.

"That you comforted her in a time of need. She..." I shook my head, stopping myself from stepping into anything I didn't need to. "You know what, that's for you two to discuss. I'm not going to get into the middle of it."

Reed's hands stilled as he observed me. "I don't know how to take you. You act possessive of her one minute and then, like you're not interested the next."

"Ah, let me clear that up for you, then. I'm very interested in Henley Henshaw."

"So... you're staking a claim?" Reed tilted his head like he was trying to figure out a complicated problem.

"If you think you can claim Henley Henshaw, then you're in for a world of disappointment. Henley's aware of my interest, and I'm aware of hers and who that includes. While I might want to take her and run away, that's not who she is. I've known her since she was eighteen. Henley is stubborn and needs to make her own choices. If I try to box her in, then I've already lost her. I saw it happen countless times with guys on campus."

"So, you're what? Just waiting to be the last man standing?"

I shrugged. "Honestly, everything's new. I'm not sure what we are or even have. I just know I like her, and she makes me smile. To me, that's something to pursue deeper, so we are."

"You're not what I expected," he finally said, looking me up and down.

I chuckled, leading him out of the training room to walk down another hallway. At this point, I'd forgotten what I'd shown him and what I hadn't. This place was too big to keep track of.

"So, are you going to be a coach for the school term?" I asked, deciding I needed to know all the facts.

"It's not official yet, but yeah, I think so."

"You're not playing this year?"

He shook his head, his lips going tight at the motion. I wanted to pry, but it was apparent he wasn't in the sharing mood. As much as I liked to be in the know, I knew it wasn't my place to question him if he didn't want to share. The boundary was clear, and I could respect it.

"What team do you coach for?" he asked a few minutes later.

"I'm the head coach for the junior level."

He gave me another nod, this one showing some respect as he met my eyes. I wanted to ask a million other questions, but I was discovering with Reed that it was better to let him share when he was ready. So, I stayed quiet, just walking down the hall that was filled with photos of students who'd gone on to do different things since graduating.

Reed stopped at one, looking the player over. "I didn't know he attended here," he said softly.

"The alumni for this place is ridiculous. I've been here for three years, and I've met more star-studded players at alumni events than I did while in the pros."

Reed's eyes widened, and he nodded, accepting what I shared. "You enjoy your job then?" he asked.

"It's the best. I get to do what I love every day without all the hubbub. The kids are focused and more serious than most professionals. It's great pay, and the amenities are some of the best. I'll probably stay another few years unless something else comes along. Like I said, the networking here is top-notch. I've seen a lot of instructors move on to amazing things they wouldn't have been offered otherwise."

"What about the stuff with the Council or whatever? I heard something about it in the news but didn't focus on it since I didn't know the school at the time."

I nodded, taking a turn, and led us back toward the cafeteria. "I wasn't part of it, but I know it affected a lot of students and staff. The fallout has been what's impacting me now. Some of the hockey programs we play against are trying to get us barred, as well as the Olympic Committee. That part has been a shit show, but otherwise, I was lucky to be excluded from it."

"Hmm," he mumbled, rubbing his jaw.

"Do you have any concerns? Like something you're worried about?" I asked, figuring I could help ease his worries or give him the info straight.

"Not really. I chose to take a year off from the

league. So if I don't do this, then I'll just be a couch potato who occasionally works out and showers."

I assessed him, his statement sticking out to me as odd. It almost sounded like the man was depressed. I didn't know him well enough to know for sure, but it made me want to do something. I wasn't sure if it was because of my own past or because he'd helped Henley when she needed someone, but I felt a strong urge to hug him. And since he was a stranger who seemed to like his personal boundaries, I opted for a metaphorical hug instead.

"Do you like Henley?" I asked.

He stopped, blinking. "Wow, I didn't expect you to come out and say it."

I chuckled, shrugging. "What's the point of being vague?"

Reed watched me for a minute before he swallowed and nodded. "Yeah. I..." He shook his head, and I held up a hand, stopping him.

"You don't have to explain anything to me. I don't know what the future holds, but I hope we can become friends since we'll both be coaching here. So, I'll offer you a piece of advice."

"You're going to actively help me get the girl you like?"

Smiling, I placed my hands on my hips. "I never said I was going to let you get her, just that I would offer you a piece of advice. I'm not taking myself out or anything."

He assessed me, respect flaring to life in his eyes. "Okay. I'm listening."

"Don't play games with Henley. Be upfront and honest. You'll get further that way. She's protective of her sibling, Reese, and is on a mission to find herself. The last part is just my observation; the others are facts."

He nodded, rubbing his jaw. Although we were around the same height, played hockey, and had dark hair, we were nothing alike. Reed was clean-shaven, had blue eyes so light they reminded me of a frozen pond, and barely spoke unless directly questioned. I didn't know what Henley saw in either of us, but it wasn't my choice to make.

"Thanks," he said.

"No problem. Now, I'm starving, and lunch is almost over. Let's grab something to eat before they close the cafeteria."

"Sure thing."

Together, we walked off toward the cafeteria. It was practically empty when we entered, with only a few staff members at the tables. Showing Reed the options, I grabbed a few boxes and took them to go. It looked like we had less time than I'd realized.

Reed followed as we made our way back toward the ice. I ate part of a wrap while walking, unsure exactly how much time I had left before I needed to be back on the ice. The kids were already there when we entered, warming up. I sat down and put my gear back on as I finished the last parts of my meal. Reed sat on a bench behind me, giving me room to maneuver, and opened his food.

"Do you need anything before I go?" I asked, turning my head toward him. I wasn't surprised to find his gaze solely on Henley as he ate.

"No. I'm good. Thanks again, Fletcher. Is it okay if I stay and watch awhile?"

"Absolutely." I nodded, picked up my stick, and headed back to the ice just as Oliver blew the whistle for the kids to huddle up.

I skated toward Henley at the back. She smiled as I neared, setting my heart off. I returned it, happy to see her. I'd missed getting to spend lunch with her.

"How did your meeting go?" I whispered, leaning against the butt of my stick.

"Weird. Good. Shocking. So many things. I want to talk to you about it after practice. It's... it's kind of a huge deal. How did the tour go?"

Her eyes flitted to where Reed was sitting, then back to me. She might have thought she was sly, but I caught it. Between Dax and Reed, I needed to figure out where I stood with her.

My knee-jerk response was to demand an answer and make her commit to me. She hadn't been wrong when she called me a relationship guy. But I knew from everything she had going on and her conflicted feelings, I'd lose her if I tried to do that.

So, I needed to take a page from a different book and find a new approach. Which meant being nice to Dax and Reed and seeing where the chips fell. I didn't really know what else to do other than to pray I was the one for her in the end.

"It went well. We're basically best buds now."

I cheesed a massive grin at her, making her laugh and settling some of my nerves. As long as I still made her laugh, I knew I had a shot.

Oliver broke us into four teams soon after, and I focused on the kids and the skills we worked on. After an hour, we teamed up again and practiced using the new defensive or offensive moves they'd learned in their huddles.

It was hard not to be distracted by Henley as she skated and showed the kids how to do something, but I reined in my need to watch her and helped my group score.

I stayed back when the practice was over, helping pick up all the cones and pucks. When Sawyer popped her head in, both Oliver and Ty gave her a kiss as she came onto the ice with Rey, her skating partner, and boyfriend. I watched the four of them, curious in a whole new way about how their relationship worked.

There weren't any signs of jealousy. They were all

happy and obviously in love as they talked and flirted with one another. When Sawyer and Rey began to perform, Ty and Oliver stood back, watching them both with admiration. I moved off the ice, my brain trying to put all this information together.

When I made it to the bleachers where my belongings were, I noticed Reed was no longer there, but Henley was waiting for me with a smile on her face. She hugged Reese before walking with me to the staff locker room. When we entered, it was quiet, so I stopped her, wanting to know what her meeting was about.

"Tell me already, Baby Shaw!" I joked, begging her with my hands.

She giggled, taking my hand and leading me to a bench. "You remember how I wasn't sure how a long-distance relationship would work?"

"Yeah." I nodded, not wanting to say anything else and stop her from talking.

"What would you say if I were to be here in Oak Crest?"

I grinned, standing as I grasped her arms. "I'd say that's amazing and some of the best news."

"Okay, well, what would you think if I were to be the head coach of the senior team?" She grimaced, confusing me. My mouth dropped open, and I scooped her up, spinning her around.

"Really?" I asked. Her eyes scanned my face, searching for something.

"You're not mad or, I don't know, jealous?"

"Jealous?" I stopped myself when I realized what she meant. "Hen, I'm so fucking proud of you. You deserve it. No, I'm not jealous. I'm in the position I want to be in. I've been working with these kids, and I'd hate to leave them as the season starts. So, no, you don't have to worry about me being upset. So, would you be *my* boss?" I asked, a wicked gleam entering my eyes.

"Maybe? I think ultimately, Dmitry is our boss."

"Too late. I already have some sexy boss/employee scenarios I want to play out."

She giggled, and I leaned in and kissed her lips. My body was begging me to take it further, but I wasn't ready to do that until I had my heart and head in the same place. Setting her down on the ground, I walked over to my locker and began changing out of my pads and skates.

It was only after I was dressed and walking out with her a few minutes later that I realized it meant she'd be working with Reed... every day.

I needed to talk to Oliver or Ty fast before I lost her.

CHAPTER 16

Henley

THE LAST DAY of camp flew by, and I stood by the other coaches as Oliver gave his final speech. Nerves filled me as I waited to see how they'd react to the news of me being the new head coach. Reese and Fletcher had been so supportive that I hoped everyone else would feel the same.

"In just a few seconds, I'm going to call you each back and go over your performance like a general manager might do one day. If you were applying for a place at Lux, you'll also find out if you've been accepted or placed on the waitlist. But..." He turned, motioning for me. Fletcher nudged me, and I skated closer to Oliver.

"Y'all have the privilege of being the first to hear that Lux will have a new head coach in the fall. I'll be around to settle everyone in, but after that, I'll be pursuing a different dream. So, to lead Lux Hockey into the next chapter of this school, the new head coach will be... Henley Henshaw."

I smiled and waved as the kids shifted their focus from Oliver to me. It was quiet for a few seconds, and I prayed they were just digesting the news. A loud clap sounded behind me, along with a holler, and the rest joined in. I relaxed, meeting their eyes. While there were a few surprised faces, most appeared genuinely excited. I'd take that as a win.

"Alright, I'm going to start with the A's. So, go to the office if your last name starts with that letter. Everyone else can change and wait in the locker room. I'll come and get the next group when we're ready. Good camp, everyone."

The kids began to hug everyone and skate off in the directions they were told to. I looked back at the guys I'd been with all week, feeling some camaraderie myself. Fletcher snagged my hand, and we followed Ty and Cody to the locker room.

"You going to stick around for Reese?" Fletcher asked.

"Since they already know they're in, I was told I didn't have to. Reese wants to have one last hurrah with the B&B twins before we head home in the morning."

"How soon until you come back?" he asked. It felt nice to be missed and have someone want me to return.

"School starts in two weeks, so before that." I chuckled. "We need to pack up a lot of things. I'm going to sublease my apartment, so we'll need to put things in storage. It's a lot." I sighed, rubbing my forehead at the thought of everything.

"Okay, what about tonight, then?" He turned me toward him, placing his hands on my hips. The padding stopped me from feeling them, but it was nice to know they were there. He wasn't ashamed of being seen with me in front of the others.

"Hmm, let's see. I had plans to eat three slices of Rhonda's carrot cake and pack. So, you know, pretty solid ones." I puckered my lips, nodding my head. Fletcher chuckled.

"Those are pretty awesome plans you have. But what if I was to offer to help you pack and then cook you dinner at my place again?"

"Well, a home-cooked meal by Fletcher Cromwell? Sign me up. Especially if you steal some cake. That shit is the da bomb."

Chuckling, Fletcher nodded and dipped down to give me a peck on the lips. "Shower and change, and we'll head over there."

Twenty minutes later, I smelled better and had my wet hair twisted up into a messy do. Fletcher rode with me to the B&B. It gave me an odd sense of what life could be like here. Fletcher was so easygoing that he made any activity a breeze. It didn't take long to have all of my belongings packed and ready to go. I peered around the room, not spotting anything else.

"Alright, I guess I'm good to go. Let's get some cake!"

Fletcher chuckled, taking my hand as we headed toward the kitchen. When we stepped in, one of the tallest guys I'd ever seen with one of the severest brows stood there with Rhonda. I glanced between them and noticed some similarities.

"Henley and Fletcher! Are you here for some cake?" Rhonda asked, stepping away from the giant toward the glass cake dish.

"Hey, Rhett," Fletcher said, acknowledging the man.

"Fletcher. How was camp?" he asked, uncrossing his arms.

"It was good. Henley's going to take Oliver's place as head coach," he said, placing his hands on my shoulders in a proud gesture. How could I not fall for this man when he was constantly building me up?

Rhett glanced at me, part of his mouth tilting up in recognition. Rhonda began to gush, putting another piece of cake into a box, making me blush.

"Oh, Henley. That's wonderful news. Does that mean that Reese got in as well?" she asked.

"Yep. We're both excited to be coming back to Oak Crest."

"Congrats. Ollie's very excited about starting pastry school. I know he was happy to find someone he felt could replace him."

"You know Oliver?" I asked.

"He's one of my roommates, and we're both dating Sawyer," he said, watching me. I wondered if he was used to people giving him a weird response to that. Since I'd already met Ty and Oliver and seen them with Sawyer, it wasn't as big of a surprise for me.

"She sounds amazing. I saw her today with her skating partner but didn't get a chance to meet her. Oliver and Tyler talked a lot about your family, though. I don't quite understand how it works, but it sounds like you all love one another a lot, and I think that's beautiful."

Rhett relaxed, giving me a nod of respect and a grunt in response. Rhonda smiled, handing me the box of cake.

"Here you go, dear. Make sure you stop by when you return and say hello."

"Thank you, Rhonda. I definitely will. You've been an amazing host."

Fletcher and I turned to leave, stopping when the doorway was blocked by a very handsome specimen.

"Reed," I said, hating how breathless I sounded.

The man in question peered around at everyone gathered in the kitchen, landing back on me. He held my gaze for a few seconds and time felt suspended. Eventually, he lifted his eyes to Rhonda.

"I was just wondering if you had a suggestion of where I could get some dinner?" he asked.

"Well, there are a few places in town, and I'll be serving lasagna tonight for the guests if you're interested," she replied.

"Or you could have dinner with Henley and me," Fletcher offered, surprising me.

I'd wanted to do the same, but since it wasn't my home, I didn't feel right inviting people over. Fletcher had removed the obstacle for me. Reed stopped, his eyes bouncing from Fletcher to me. I smiled, hoping it looked inviting.

"We have carrot cake, too," I said, raising the box.

He swallowed, then nodded. "Okay. Yeah."

My smile grew bigger at the chance to talk to the man who was a mystery to me, despite my body's insistence that it knew him. *Being held in a parking lot while crying didn't mean people knew one another!* I chastised myself, much to my brain's annoyance.

"We're headed over now. Do you want to ride with us or follow?" I asked when no one else said anything.

"I'll just follow. I need to pack my stuff to head out in the morning."

The three of us walked out the back door toward the parking lot. Reed headed toward a blue SUV, and I motioned toward the silver rental car I had.

He nodded again, getting into his car. I sat the cake box on the back floorboard and climbed into the driver's seat. I glanced over at Fletcher, lifting my eyebrow.

"Not that I'm not thankful, but just what are you up to, Fletcher Cromwell?"

He shrugged, leaning back in the seat, and slightly turned toward me. "He seemed like he could use a friend. If he's going to be a coach here, I should get to know him."

"So it's all about you, is it?" I asked, giggling. "Nothing to do with what I told you?"

"Hmm." He tapped his chin in thought. "Nope. All about me."

Rolling my eyes, I pulled out of the B&B, the SUV not far behind me. Taking several turns, we were back on campus and at Fletcher's house within a few minutes.

I parked and waited a second, taking in a deep breath. Fletcher took my hand, squeezing it. It was enough to help me get out of the car with the cake and walk toward the house. Reed took a few strides, catching up with us, his long legs making it look easy.

"Nice place," he said as Fletcher let us into the door.

"Thanks. Lux does treat their staff well. All the housing here is top-notch."

He pushed the door open, and we walked in. The house was quiet, letting me know Dax wasn't there. He'd been avoiding Fletcher and me since the whole hallway kiss. I wanted to scream at him, but didn't know what to say.

I liked him, but I also wanted Fletcher. And if I was honest, I was also harboring a big crush on Reed. The knowledge that we'd be working together this year made my girly parts scream.

"What are you making?" I asked Fletcher as I set the cake on the counter. "Do you need help?"

"I won't ever turn away help. Would either of you like a beer?"

I shook my head. I was too nervous as it was, but Reed said yes. Fletcher grabbed one for him and took one for himself. If I added alcohol, I'd end up sleeping with them both.

Now, that was an image I could get behind.

Fletcher snapped off the lid, catching my attention and stopping my imagination from going down a perverted road.

Reed took a seat at the table, watching us. Fletcher pulled things out of the fridge, and I tried to figure out what he was making.

"Cut these up, will you?" he asked, handing me some veggies. I took them and glanced around for a bowl, opening a few cabinets. I heard Fletcher setting the timer on the oven, placing something into it once it beeped. Meanwhile, I was still looking for a cutting board when a large hand lifted over my head and brought down what I'd been searching for.

"Thanks," I said, getting trapped in Reed's blue eyes.

He nodded, leaning against the counter instead of taking his place at the table. The corners of my mouth lifted as I chopped vegetables, adding them to the bowl of lettuce Fletcher sat in front of me. Reed stayed close, watching me, and I wanted to hope it was because he wanted to be near me, not that I couldn't take care of myself.

When the vegetables were done, I washed the things I'd used, setting them on a drying rack. Both guys were watching me when I turned, my cheeks heating at their attention.

"So, how long until it's done?" I asked. Fletcher looked at his watch.

"About forty-five minutes. Should we chill in the living room until then? Do either of you have any questions about Lux?"

"Only about a million," I said, grinning. The three of us settled into the living room. Reed sat in a chair, facing the couch that Fletcher and I were on.

"Um, so, what's your day-to-day like?" I asked, then grimaced. It was a lame one.

Fletcher chuckled, but reached his arm along the back of the couch, his fingertips brushing against my neck.

"Not as packed as camp, but that's a good example of what to expect. You'll have team practice twice a day, along with fitness hours. Outside of that, I spend my time hiking, skiing, and the occasional trek into Salt Lake. Life here is laid-back."

"Is there a lot of media or people knowing who you are in town? I haven't had anything yet, but I wasn't sure once the news broke if it would increase."

Fletcher shook his head. "The town respects the relationship with the school and does its best to stop any media or people trying to find a story. You've met Rhonda, and she's just one of the townsfolk. People in Oak Crest are loyal."

"I wonder where I'll be living," I mused. "It's going to be odd going from having my own place to sharing. Was it weird for you?" I asked Fletcher.

"Not really. Dax is cool." I tensed at the mention of Dax. Fletcher paused, but then kept talking. "We're both busy, so it's not like we're ever stepping on each other's toes or anything." He cleared his throat, and I wondered if the night I was pressed up against the wall crossed his mind as well. "Some of the bigger houses might have more of that. Hopefully, you won't get stuck with any of the obnoxious girls."

"Oh no, are there a lot?" I asked, worried.

"Some of them are more interested in dating than teaching. Not all of them, but enough to make you want to avoid them in large groups."

Reed listened the whole time, but never asked his own questions. When the timer beeped, we all stood and headed into the kitchen. A door I hadn't noticed before opened as we walked in. Dax stopped in the frame when he spotted me. The other two were on the other side, so it was just him and me for a moment.

The same chemistry we had from the hotel heated between us, almost sparking to life. My body urged me to go to him, my feet rocking forward.

"Petal…" he stuttered, but stopped when he heard a noise. He stepped the rest of the way into the kitchen, noticing Reed and Fletcher. "Looks like I'm here just in time. What's for dinner?" he asked, shocking me.

I guess I was about to have dinner with three guys who set my heart on fire. One I'd slept with, another I'd kissed, and a third I'd masturbated to on film. Yep, it shouldn't be awkward at all.

CHAPTER 17

Dax

THE PAST TWO days had been hell. I'd left the house early and stayed out late, hoping to avoid Fletcher and, by association, Henley.

It turned out my life was a tad bit sad and lonely when I wasn't hooking up with anyone. I'd been so bored last night that I'd ended up at the library. The library! I read a whole book before they kicked me out when they closed.

So I told myself I wouldn't hide tonight and take my chances of facing them. I'd spotted her car the instant I'd driven up the street, but seeing her as soon as I opened the door had stopped me in my tracks.

Fuck, she was so beautiful. Her eyes sparkled as she stared at me, stealing the breath right from my lungs. A rush of emotions swept over me, and I had to forcibly hold myself back from running to her and kissing her senseless again.

Remembering she had to be here for Fletch, I stepped into the room, surprised to also find a stranger in the kitchen. Something in me shifted, a feeling like I was about to enter into a dueling match for her hand or some shit. Whatever it was, it had me uttering a question I wanted to smack myself for after.

"Looks like I'm here just in time. What's for dinner?"

As soon as the words left my mouth, I internally grimaced. If I thought watching her with Fletcher was hard, them playing happy homemaker would be worse.

And yet... something kept me in the kitchen. If anything, it would be more entertaining than the library or another horrendous date from SASA.

"My famous pot pie," Fletcher said, watching me. "I'm glad you're here. I've wanted to talk to you."

"Oh?" I asked, grabbing a beer from the fridge and popping the top. "I didn't realize."

I could've sworn I heard Henley snort, but when I looked over at her, she grabbed the salad off the counter. I sat at the table in the center of the room, reaching out to introduce myself to the stranger.

"Hey, I'm Dax."

"Reed," he said, shaking my hand.

"What brings you to the house?" I asked, taking a sip. When his eyes flicked to Henley, I felt a primal growl want to rise up. Another one? Seriously, why was it that the first girl I'd liked since Jenny had two other guys sniffing around her?

"I was promised dinner," he finally said, sitting across from me.

"And we're celebrating. Reed's one of the new hockey coaches," Henley offered, setting the salad in the middle of the table. There were already plates and silverware in each spot, so she sat between us, glancing back and forth.

"Welcome to Lux, then," I said, taking another sip.

"Henley's being coy. She's going to be the head coach."

I coughed, choking on the swig of beer I'd just taken. "I'm sorry, head coach? As in at Lux?" I asked, wiping my mouth for any potential spittle.

"Yeah."

She gave me a slight grin, almost like she was hesitant or worried about what my reaction would be. I hated that she was so timid now. The week I met her, she'd been so carefree and open. I loved her energy and spontaneity.

What was worse, I knew I was to blame for her hesitancy. I hadn't reacted well when Fletcher had claimed her right after I'd just kissed her like I couldn't breathe without her.

I hated how close to being true that statement was.

"Oh, wow. Um, congratulations. You play hockey?" I asked, causing all three of them to laugh.

"Yeah. I guess we didn't really cover what we did when we met."

She bit her lip, and I wondered if she remembered

our night together. My cock stirred, recalling that night all too well. It had been on repeat most nights when I'd lain awake in bed, unable to fall asleep.

"Henley played pro for the Cambridge Cardinals and has two gold medals," Fletcher said, bringing the hot pot pie to the table. He slid a knife and a serving spoon next to it before he sat.

"No, shit. Two medals, that's impressive. I didn't realize we had a girl's hockey team, though."

The two other guys tensed, and Henley pivoted, so she was staring straight at me. "I'll be coaching the *senior* team. It's based on skill, not gender. Do you have a problem with that?"

"Fuck, sorry, I didn't mean to imply anything. I just assumed. Of course, you're fully capable of coaching the boy's team. I think it's great."

Sweat built on the back of my neck at how much I was fucking this up. I wanted to sweep this girl away from these other two neanderthals, but at the moment, I was dead last. The universe was sending me mixed signals.

That or I was screwing up my chance all on my own.

It was silent as we dished portions of food onto our plates. Steam rolled off the chicken, and I blew a breath to cool it. When Henley took a bite, she let out a sound I'd heard in my dreams a million times already—a moan.

My cock, who'd already been stirring, rose for the occasion, straining against my pants. I gripped my fork with one hand, taking a deep breath to try to calm the raging hormones that wanted to devour her instead of this meal.

I craved to be near her, to learn more about this woman, but it was a special kind of torture.

When I'd finally gotten myself under control, the rest of the table was halfway through their meal. Quickly, without even tasting it, I shoved scoops of food into my mouth and swallowed.

"Thank you for the protein shake the other morning," Henley said, catching me off guard. I stopped, my fork in my mouth as I glanced at her. She gave me a soft look, her eyes crinkling from her smile, and I remembered to finish eating and swallow.

"Don't mention it." I focused on my meal, wondering if I could shovel the rest into my mouth in two bites.

"So, you two know one another?" Reed asked, glancing between Henley and me.

"Oh, yes, well, um, remember after that day I met you in the parking lot?" she said, fumbling over her words. He nodded, his blue eyes intense on her. "Reese, my sibling, had some trouble at school, and I decided we needed to escape the city. I messaged my friend Sera who lives here, and we met up for a vacation in Salt Lake. Dax was staying at the same place.

We didn't really know who each other was, just kind of, um, had a drink and danced together." She stopped there, taking a long drink of her water, her face bright red.

"We played some pool, too," I said, taking a slower bite this time. This dinner just got a whole lot more interesting.

I didn't know it was possible, but her face managed to get even redder at my comment. If she'd been eating, I was certain she'd have choked.

"Did you say Reese was your sibling?" Reed asked.

"Yeah. Why?"

"I think I met her the other night."

"Them. Reese is nonbinary."

"Oh, sorry—them. Thanks for letting me know." Reed bowed his head. "Reese was part of what convinced me to take the job. I'd been planning on saying no up until that night."

"Really?" she asked, smiling at him in a way I didn't like. I wanted her to smile at me that way. "I'll let them know. You're kind of their favorite player."

For once, I felt left out by not being part of the hockey world. Fletcher and Reed had that in common with Henley, giving them an advantage. I didn't want to steal her from Fletcher; we were friends. But if they weren't serious, I still might have a shot.

"Thanks for dinner, but I think I should head back.

I have an early flight in the morning," Reed said, drawing me back to the conversation.

"It was nice to meet you, man," I said, reaching out to shake his hand again. "I'll see you around campus."

"Yeah, sounds good."

Fletcher walked him out, and I stood, clearing the table of dishes with Henley. We didn't talk at first, and I felt like my seconds alone with her were running out. But I couldn't seem to find the words to say.

I like you. Date me?

We had some great sex. Want more?

In the end, it was Henley who found the courage to speak up.

"You've been avoiding me," she said, staring up at me with big eyes. I wanted to give her the world when she looked at me that way. She was dangerous. But I couldn't seem to stop myself from wanting her.

"It seemed easier," I said. "I didn't want to be reminded I was second place." The honesty came out before I could stop it.

"But you're not..." she started.

"So, if I asked you to date me, you'd choose me over Fletcher?" I asked, hope brimming in me again.

Her face fell, and I knew what she would say before she said it. Though in the end, it was Fletcher who stepped in.

"I'm not asking her to date me exclusively. I don't

really know how it would work, but I'm willing to figure it out for Henley."

Henley nodded, hope filling her eyes. "Dax, I don't want to lose you."

I glanced between them, my emotions overwhelming me as they put me on the spot. It felt like everything I wanted was right in front of me, and yet, it still felt like I was getting the raw end of the deal.

Why couldn't I have the girl like me, most of all, for once? Would I forever be mitigated to the sidelines, just happy to have the plays they tossed to me when they needed a break? Was I the relief pitcher?

My hand gripped the back of the chair, my knuckles turning white. I didn't know how to do what they were asking of me. It felt like I'd lose all of my sense of self if I did. I might not have been doing much these past three years since my heart was broken, but I'd promised myself I would never be in that position again. The one where I was overlooked.

No. I couldn't do this. It sounded like the perfect plan until I really thought about it. If I said yes, then I'd be telling myself I wasn't worth anything. I already believed that most days. I couldn't consciously make this decision and prove it. It would be the death of me.

"That's not the kind of relationship I want. I'm sorry, but I can't do whatever it is you're asking. I'll be nice when I see you around campus, and we can try to be friends, but I'm afraid that's all I can agree to."

Henley's face fell, tears forming in the corners. It was almost enough to make me stop and say I'd changed my mind. When Fletcher went to her, it was the push I needed to walk out of the kitchen and away from temptation.

I closed the door to my bedroom and sat on the bed, my hands shaking as I tried to calm myself. When it didn't work, I pulled out my phone and opened the app. When I needed a confidence booster, sex always worked. It was time to get back in the game.

CHAPTER 18

Henley

DAX WALKED AWAY, and I felt like I'd just lost something significant. It had been one night between us, with no promise of anything more, but I'd been envisioning more the second he'd popped back into my life.

I thought I could have it all. I knew it wasn't fair to him, and I didn't blame him for saying no. I couldn't say I'd respond differently if he'd asked me to be one of three girls he was dating.

But it hurt. It hurt a lot.

Tears were already falling before his door sounded in the quiet house. Fletcher had come to me, offering comfort, but I didn't feel like I deserved it. This was my own mess that I'd created by being unable to choose.

Though, that didn't feel right either. It wasn't a matter of choosing. It was more about being free to explore who I was and not being limited to the version of myself that the world wanted me to be.

A strength within surged forward, reminding me of who I was. I wasn't a prop for men to tell me what was okay for me. I was the only person who got to decide who I was and what I wanted in life.

Wiping my eyes, I stepped back from Fletcher's embrace. He smiled at me, and I could tell he wanted to say something, but wasn't sure how to broach the subject.

"I'll be okay, I promise. I'll just head back and ensure I have everything for tomorrow. Maybe take a bubble bath or something."

His hand rubbed my shoulder. "Okay. Text me when you land tomorrow."

Nodding, I kissed him briefly, not wanting to fall into the trap of his lips, and headed out the door. If I was lucky, I'd be able to fall asleep and put this awful feeling behind me. I wanted to embrace the triumph I felt at being recognized for my hockey skill, not the blow of wanting too much.

Because I was tired of being told what I could and couldn't have. So, if I wanted it all, then I'd take it, no matter what any man said about it.

THE FOLLOWING DAY, REESE AND I WAITED FOR OUR FLIGHT, a coffee in our hands as we sat at the gate. It was early, but I felt oddly awake. The night before had been a turning point for me taking back part of myself. It still stung to think of Dax walking away, but I wasn't falling apart. I was here and knew deep down what I was asking wasn't too much.

"This seat taken?" a deep and familiar voice asked, surprising me. Looking up, I spotted Reed Cole standing in front of me.

"Nope." I moved my bag so he could take a seat. He nodded toward Reese, who'd barely taken their eyes off their phone for me all morning. When they spotted Reed, they sat straight up, pulling the earbuds from their ears.

"Reed Cole!"

He chuckled, sitting back in the seat. His long legs stretched out, his leg touching mine as he spread them. I caught the corner of his mouth quirk up as he rested his head on his hand.

"So, it looks like we're on the same flight?"

"Appears so."

He didn't say anything more, and I had the urge to ask him a million questions, but I knew it wasn't his style. He'd let me know something when he was ready. I didn't know him that well yet, but I was picking up on these small details.

"We didn't talk much yesterday, but I'm excited to work with you. Does it feel weird that I'll be in charge?"

Reed didn't even hesitate, shaking his head no. "Nope. I'm cool with it."

My shoulders relaxed, the tension seeping out of

me. I stayed quiet for another ten minutes before I couldn't take it anymore.

"Where are you flying to?" Our flight had a layover in Chicago before we headed to Boston. He grunted, cleared his throat, and shifted in his seat.

"Vancouver. There are some things I need to tie up before I start."

I nodded in understanding. The school term didn't start for two more weeks, meaning we had time to pack and close up our life in Massachusetts before we had to return.

The plane began boarding soon after, halting our conversation. Reed was let on straight away since he was in first class. Reese waved bye to him as he gathered his bag. He stopped after two steps, looking at me.

"I'll be seeing you soon, Henley."

It was a simple statement, but it meant so much more. It was a promise and a comfort all in one. Something was developing between us. I wasn't imagining it, and he was telling me in his Reed way that it wasn't over.

It was more reassurance than Dakota had ever given me.

"Okay," I said, smiling. "I look forward to it."

His eyes shimmered, the blue seeming to move like the ocean as he stared at me. With one nod, he turned and handed the flight attendant his boarding pass.

Reese nudged me when he was gone, and I turned, lifting my eyebrows.

"Yes?"

"I really like Reed and all, but I thought you were seeing Fletcher?" Reese's brow scrunched up in confusion, and I knew I needed to have an honest talk with them.

"Fletcher and I have talked, and we're taking things slow. I wasn't ready to jump into a relationship. Plus, I knew I had some attraction to two other people as well, not feeling like I could just say I wanted to be locked down. I'm not sure if I'll ever want to anymore, but that's a different conversation."

"Does that mean you might date Reed?"

"I don't know. There's a connection between us, but we're still strangers. He'll be a coach working with me this year. We'll have time to get to know one another and see if there's more than our heated looks."

"I heard that Oliver was in a polyamorous relationship. Is that what you're doing?"

"Polyamorous? Huh." I thought about it, wondering what it really meant. Shaking my head, I stood when our zone was called. "I think it's too soon to tell. At the moment, I'm just casually dating. That's the label I'm using. Fletcher says as long as all parties are open about their intentions, it will work out how it's meant to."

"I hope you get your happily ever after, Sis, whatever it looks like. I'm rooting for you."

"Thanks, kiddo. I've been meaning to ask you if there was anything more between you and the B&B twins?" Reese's face went red, but they shook their head.

Our tickets were scanned as we boarded the plane. We passed Reed on the way to our seats, and I smiled, waving at him. He watched me the whole time, his eyes intense on me.

It was enough to make me pull the collar of my shirt away; the heat getting to me. Stowing our bags overhead, Reese and I took our seats. It wasn't much longer before the plane took off, and we were in the sky, headed for Chicago.

REED WAS ALREADY GONE WHEN WE EXITED THE PLANE, AND I wondered if his next flight had a tight window. Reese and I made our way to our next gate, grabbing some food and snacks as we meandered through the terminal. I was glancing through a magazine when a high-pitched squeal sounded behind me.

Turning slowly, I looked for the source of such a noise. A pink and blonde body was hurling its way toward me, its arms going around me in a vise grip.

"My girls!"

Instantly, my entire body seized up at my mother's voice. I searched for Reese, finding them stock still next to me, just as surprised as I was.

"Mom, let go," I said, trying to unhook her arms from around me. I wouldn't put it past the woman to pickpocket me. That was how much I trusted my mother.

"Oh, Henley. Don't be like that." She swatted at me, laughing like my uncomfortableness with her was a huge joke.

"Reese, I see you're still trying to look like a boy," she said, dragging her overly made-up eyes over Reese.

My big-sister instinct kicked in, and I stepped in front of Reese, shielding them from our vulture of a mother. Nothing good ever came from an interaction with her, especially after she basically sold Reese to me when she couldn't deal with Reese being non-binary—that and her pill popping problem.

I discovered later she was also broke, using all of her money for pills to attract men who wanted nothing to do with her. Carole Henshaw was still under the impression that she could bag a rich man to save her from all her problems.

Though, as I took in her clothes, hair, and mani-cure, I wondered if she'd finally succeeded. I guess being childless allowed her to pursue her lifelong dream of being a trophy wife.

"Did you need something, Carole?"

She huffed at the use of her name, not liking how I was denying her Reese as well. But I didn't care what she wanted. Reese mattered more, and any interaction with this woman was always damning.

"Most girls are happy to see their mother. You act as if I'm a leper. Things are better now. I met a wonderful man who takes care of me. He wants to meet you both. Come and meet Leroy."

I glanced back at Reese, who shook their head no. Returning to our mother, I crossed my arms, doubling down on my protective stance.

"Maybe another time, Carole. We need to make our flight."

"To where? It's not like you have a job," she shouted. "And you thought you'd do better with her than I could. I know she's been kicked out of another school. Give it up, Henley. You're not a better mother than me."

We'd started to take a few steps away, but I froze, pivoting on the spot.

"Say what, now?" I hissed, every maternal instinct in me rising to the surface.

She huffed, crossing her arms and rolling her eyes this time. "I still know people. I kept tabs on you both. You've been suspended, and Reese was kicked off her team. So, tell me, how are you doing better?"

"For one, I respect Reese's decision. Something you still can't seem to grasp. For another, I have a job, and

Reese has been admitted to an elite winter sports school to play hockey. I guess you need to get better spies, *Carole*."

Her eyes widened, and she stuttered, trying to salvage the moment. "Oh, baby, that's wonderful. Does that mean you'll be back with Dakota? He's such a good man for you. I told him that he needed to forgive you. Us Henshaws have a temper, but we always come back to the fold."

Her words were likely meant to reassure me, but all they did was enrage me more. She'd been talking to Dakota. The thought infuriated me. Just how long had that been going on? Was he one of her spies?

Reese squeezed my hand, pulling me back from the moment. I glanced around, noticing a few people watching. Only one person had their phone out so far. I saw my mother's eyes move toward them, and I knew then this had all been some setup. She wanted me to explode, to cause a scene so she could use it for leverage. I didn't know what her endgame was, but I was too smart to fall for her trap.

"Goodbye, Carole."

I turned, taking Reese's hand as we swiftly walked away. My heart was pounding in my chest, my face red from anger, the heat radiating off me as we dodged people to find our gate. It was already boarding, so we got in line, neither of us letting go of the other.

If Carole was inserting herself into our life again,

there was no telling what she was after. If she had someone with money who believed her, she was more dangerous than I'd given her credit for. I didn't breathe easier until we were seated on the plane, and it was taxiing away from the gate.

It seemed more than ever that this school was our best option. Hopefully, we'd stay hidden long enough for Carole to grow bored, or things might worsen before they were better. For Reese's sake, I prayed she'd forget about us.

CHAPTER 19

Henley

OVER THE NEXT week as we packed, I tried to push Crazy Carole and her schemes out of my mind, and focus on the next chapter of our lives. I hadn't figured out yet if it was a coincidence we'd run into her or if there was something more devious at play where she'd somehow found us. Either way, I was on high alert.

Packing turned out to be easier than I'd imagined since the school provided most of our basic needs. We only had to pack clothes, essentials, and hockey gear. We shipped a few boxes of things ahead of time, so we wouldn't have to bring everything on the flight. From all my years of traveling with the league, I was a pro at packing and flying, and thankfully Reese seemed to have inherited it too.

The flight back to Utah had been uneventful, with no crazy mothers or broody guys with blue eyes, and we now stood in baggage claim, waiting for our bags to be released from the plane. When they came around, I perked up, excited to be almost done with the airport.

I wasn't excited to see anyone. Nope, not this girl.

"You going to kiss Fletcher when you see him?" Reese asked, jolting me out of my thoughts.

"What? No. Huh?" I shook my head, turning to look at them. "I'm not even thinking about Fletcher."

"Ah, okay. So you haven't been FaceTiming or texting him nonstop since we left? My bad. Must be another dude, then."

Gasping, I smacked their arm as I laughed. Pushing my hair back behind my ears, I faked innocence. "I have no clue what you're talking about."

The truth was, we *had* been texting and calling all week, and I was excited and a tad nervous to see him. It felt like something special was developing between us, and I didn't know how to deal with it. My old tendencies were screaming to lock him down, but I knew I needed to play this differently.

If I wanted things to change, I had to forge a new path. I couldn't keep falling into the same patterns and expect a different outcome. It was the definition of insanity, after all.

"There's ours," Reese said, pointing. Moving forward, we grabbed our suitcases and rolled them out. When we exited the luggage claim, I spotted a familiar head of chestnut brown hair standing above all the others.

"Fletcher!" I shouted, gaining the attention of a few people. They turned and looked, but I ignored them, my eyes only on the man smiling as he neared us. Leaving my bag with Reese, I couldn't help myself as I took off running, jumping into his arms when I got to him.

"Hey," he said, catching me with ease. "I missed you. It's good to see you, Baby Shaw."

Smiling so wide my dimples had to be showing. I bent down and pecked his lips. "I missed you, too."

"You're reminding me of a cheesy rom-com," Reese said, making Fletcher set me down. My cheeks heated, but I was too happy to care. I stuck my tongue out at them, linking my hands with Fletcher's. It felt so natural that I hadn't even thought about it.

"Remind me to tell you the same when you see Briana and Braden, punk."

Reese could deny all they wanted, but they were just as happy to see them as I'd been to see Fletcher. It seemed like Utah was a good place for us.

Fletcher led us to a car, and we loaded our luggage. We chatted excitedly as we drove through Salt Lake to our new home.

"Reese, you're rooming in Grayson Hall with Briana, correct?" Fletcher asked as we pulled onto campus.

"Yep."

Fletcher pulled up to the dormitory, and we all got out, stretching as we made our way toward the woman at the front desk.

"Welcome!" a bubbly student said as we approached. "You must be Reese." Reese had barely nodded before the student continued. "Your room is on the second floor. Here's your keycard, schedule, map, and welcome packet. I'm Georgia. Let me know if you have any questions."

She handed everything to us and went to greet the next student. Reese looked at me, eyes wide, and mouthed, "Wow," making me chuckle.

"Come on," I said, directing them toward the stairs. We lugged the luggage up, slightly out of breath when we reached the second-floor landing. "I'm suddenly feeling out of shape," I wheezed.

"You're in perfect shape," Fletcher whispered, "a shape I want to explore more."

Coughing, I cleared my throat as my face flamed. I liked it when he said things like that, but it always surprised me. One, I wasn't used to guys saying those types of things. And two, it was Fletcher. Some days, it was hard to reconcile the man who kissed me like I was his air and the brother of my college roommate.

Reese ran ahead, using their keycard to open the door. A girlish scream was released as Reese entered, and I smiled, happy that it seemed like Reese had made true friends here. Briana was talking a mile a minute when we entered, pointing out everything she wanted to do with their room.

"Henley!" Sera exclaimed when she spotted me, almost matching her soon-to-be stepdaughter.

"Hey, Sera." I hugged her once I set the suitcase down, happy to see my friend. I'd accidentally ghosted her during camp after things started to develop with Fletcher. "We need to make plans now that I'm here. Sorry about having to cancel last time."

"No worries, girl." Her eyes lifted over my head, and she smiled. "Hey, Fletcher. I didn't realize you were part of the welcoming committee."

"Oh, um, no. Just helping Hen and Reese."

"Is that so? They must be lucky then," she teased.

Rolling my eyes, I helped Reese unpack until they shooed me away, stating they had it.

"Alright, well, I guess I'll go check out my house. Text me later, Sera." I hugged Reese and waved at the others as they discussed the best places to put the TV and mini fridge.

Fletcher took my hand as we walked out of the dorm, leading me back to the car. He opened my door and leaned down, hovering over me.

"I'm going to kiss you now like I wanted to back at the airport."

His lips met mine before I could answer, devouring me and reminding me how good of a kisser he was. Fletcher's tongue swirled, his hands sliding into my hair, and I felt like I was going to lift out of the seat from the power of it. When I couldn't breathe anymore, I pulled back, gasping.

"Wow," I said breathlessly.

"I've been imagining doing that since the moment you left."

"I'm here now. So no more imagination needed."

"I like the way you think." Smiling at one another, it was only the honk of a horn from another car that broke our spell. Giggling, I scooted back into the seat and buckled up. Fletcher ran around the car and jumped in, giving me a brilliant smile.

We pulled up to a gorgeous house a few minutes later. It was a sprawling three-story with white and black accents. The driveway was long as he drove up it. I turned in my seat, trying to take in all of the views.

"You weren't kidding about these houses," I murmured, feeling a little nervous.

"It sucks you're all the way over on this side of campus, though," Fletcher said, parking the car.

"Yeah, it does," I agreed, patting his hand.

Climbing out together, we grabbed my suitcases and made our way toward the door. It felt weird just walking in, despite the fact I now lived here. But until I'd met someone inside, it felt like I needed to ring the doorbell. Pushing it, I stood back with Fletcher while we waited.

A girl with curly hair and brown skin answered the door, smiling. "You must be Henley. I'm Chloe." She reached to shake my hand, and I exhaled, feeling a little more relaxed with the friendly greeting.

"It's nice to meet you, Chloe."

"Come in. I'll show you to your room." She nodded at Fletcher but didn't say anything.

"So, what sport do you play?" she asked as she led us through the house. She pointed out a few rooms as we went through them, including a kitchen, living room, and passed three bedrooms.

"Hockey. Both of us. You?" I asked as I took in the elegance of the place.

"Snowboarding. I didn't know we had a girl's hockey team. Wicked," she said.

"I'm actually the senior coach," I said, clearing my throat. Did no one know how hockey worked?

"What? That's badass."

I relaxed, feeling better at her reaction. We kept walking through the house, and I wondered if I'd need a map to find the front door. After we climbed the stairs to the third floor, Chloe walked all the way to the end of the hall.

"You're here," she said and grimaced if I wasn't mistaken. "Your room shares a bathroom with Julie's."

"Where's your room?" I asked, hoping I'd have a friendly face close. She grimaced at the question, all hope escaping me.

"Downstairs. This floor is mostly figure skaters, and the next is skiers."

"Oh, joy," I sighed. Figure skaters and I never got along. They didn't like that I played with the guys they were after.

"If you need anything, I'll be around," she said, waving bye as she left us. I looked at Fletcher, and he shrugged, pushing open the door.

Since the rest of the house had been so tastefully decorated, I'd been expecting the same for my room. However, it seemed whoever had this bedroom last had wanted to be surrounded by the color of Pepto Bismol. It was so pink, I wondered if it could be seen from space.

"Wow," I said, blinking, praying it would change. Opening my eyes, I was saddened to find it was still the same.

"Maybe it won't be as bad in the dark," Fletcher said hopefully. He turned off the light, only to find that the color seemed to glow even more.

"I think I might have nightmares about this room." The carpet, the walls, the bed, and the furniture were all various shades of pink. It was my literal worst nightmare.

"Does this mean I get some sleepovers?" Fletcher asked. He rubbed his hands together, making me chuckle despite the horrific nature of the room.

"Maybe I can paint it?"

Sighing, I pulled my suitcase into the room and

headed for the closet. I found my other boxes inside and sighed in relief that they'd made it.

Fletcher helped me put sheets on the bed and hang up my clothes. When we were done, I laid back on the bed, staring at the ceiling.

"It's not so bad if you only stare at the ceiling."

"How about I take you to dinner?" Fletcher asked, rolling over to stare down at me.

"Sounds like a brilliant idea. Let me jump in the shower and change clothes real quick. I feel like an airport." I kissed his nose, hopping off the bed and grabbing some clean things and a towel.

Stepping into the bathroom, I was relieved when it wasn't pink. Maybe I could escape the pink after all.

Turning on the water, I stepped into the shower, pleased with the pressure and settings. This wouldn't be horrible to wake up to. Rinsing the soap off my body, I managed to keep my hair dry, feeling cleaner already. Stepping out when I was finished, I screamed when I found a girl sitting on the counter.

I clutched the towel to myself as Fletcher barged in. "What's wrong?" he asked before stopping in his tracks.

"Hey, Fletcher," the girl said, waving at him. He gulped, looking between the random girl and me.

"What are you doing in my bathroom?" I asked, ignoring the weird interaction.

"Oh, I'm Julie. I just wanted to introduce myself."

She hopped off the counter and strolled toward me. "Welcome to the Meadows. I'll leave you the list of rules on your bed. Have a good night," she chirped. She waved her fingers as she strolled out, and I stood still, wondering what the fuck I'd gotten myself into.

CHAPTER 20

Reed

STANDING on the porch of the house I'd visited a few weeks prior, I took a moment to reconcile the fact I was doing something different. The past several years had been training, hockey, and more training. I hadn't taken much time to develop relationships, choosing to keep to myself. When my mother got sick, it was the wake-up call I needed.

I'd just never imagined walking away from the league to coach teens. But from the moment I stepped foot in Oak Crest, amazing things had happened.

I ran into Henley, her mere presence reminding me that there were other things outside of my grief.

I met Reese, re-awakening my love for hockey again.

I connected with fellow hockey peers, finding the possibility of friendship outside of competitiveness and the rink.

But mostly, I felt alive in a way I'd never felt before. My grief didn't feel as big here, and it was almost like my mother was guiding me, showing me I could still live with her gone. I'd made a promise to her, but I hadn't been keeping it.

Coming here was more than just honoring her wishes, but also finding myself in the process.

The door opened abruptly, spooking me out of my reverie. The blond-haired guy, Dax, stood shirtless in the doorway. "You coming in or planning on living on the front porch?"

I fought a smile, not wanting to like this guy, but he made it difficult with his easy going nature. He had a history with Henley I wasn't sure about or where he fit into her present. I wanted to be part of her life, which meant figuring out who the other people in it were and their roles.

So far, that looked like Dax and Fletcher.

Had I intentionally asked to be housed with them? Yes. It seemed like the best option. Plus, I already knew them, and it wasn't a big house, meaning there would be fewer people to deal with. I also hoped Henley would be around a lot, putting me more in her path outside the rink.

Working with her every day was going to be bliss and torture, so I wanted a way to be around when she wasn't coaching.

Outside of the fact Dax and Fletcher had a connection to Henley, Fletcher seemed like a guy I could be friends with. I was hoping I could make a real friend for once, and it wasn't all about who was the better hockey player. Dax was still a mystery, but he intrigued me. So, for now, I'd play it loose with him and see where he fell on the friendship board.

Not responding to Dax, I picked up my bag and lifted my eyebrows. Dax smirked, but backed up and walked into the house. I followed, unsure where to go, my suitcase trailing behind me. He stopped in a hallway between two doors.

"These are the empty ones. They share a bathroom, but since no one else is moving in, you'll have it to yourself."

I peeked into both rooms and took the furthest one. Living with people was going to be a new experience to adjust to.

"Thanks," I said as I placed my hockey gear on the bed. I sat down, testing the softness of the mattress. It was decent, making me confident I'd be able to get a restful night's sleep.

"You want a tour?"

"Nah, I think I can figure it out."

"Suit yourself. I'm headed over to the gym if you want to join."

I thought about it, and while my first instinct was to say no, it would be an excellent chance to see a different part of campus, gauge this guy more on a neutral field, and release some of the tension from traveling.

"Sure. That sounds good."

He looked shocked for a second before he cleared his face. "I'm leaving in ten." He tapped the doorframe before walking away, presumably to put on a shirt.

Opening my suitcase, I dumped my clothes into the drawers and shoved my hockey gear into the closet. I'd do a more thorough unpacking later, but it worked for the moment. Pulling out a pair of athletic pants and a tank, I changed out of my jeans and hoodie, putting it back on over my shirt. Lacing up my shoes, I heard him moving out in the hallway, another door shutting before it was quiet again.

Walking toward the kitchen, I grabbed my hydro flask and filled it with water. He walked in a second later, his eyes widening when he spotted me.

"Were you expecting me to take longer?" I asked, curious about his constant shock toward me.

"Sorta. I expected you to be more of a diva, if I'm honest. And so far, you've been chill. I was dreading rooming with someone new, but I guess if you're like this, I can deal with it."

I snorted, wiping my mouth free of water. "Let me guess, you watched some YouTube videos of me?"

Dax laughed, grabbing his own bottle of water. "Guilty. I was trying to prepare myself for who I was living with."

"Understandable. I'd do the same. You can't trust those videos, though. The media wants me to play a persona. I don't like the attention, so they use that to their advantage to say I'm difficult to work with and an asshole. Really, I just like my privacy and I don't say things unless I feel it's important."

He nodded, some respect entering his eyes. "I dig that. Okay, man. Here's to a fresh start." Dax grabbed his keys and nodded for me to follow. He climbed into a car, and I took the passenger seat, fastening my seatbelt.

The drive to the hockey arena was quick. Dax pointed out a few buildings, but most I'd already seen when I'd been here for the interview.

"Do you work mostly with the hockey students?" I asked as we walked in. Dax scanned his ID, reminding me I needed to start carrying mine everywhere. It was in the packet I received when I arrived on campus; I just wasn't used to having to use one.

"About half. I generally work with the senior team and another trainer, Rhett, works with the junior team. I have a few skiers and snowboarders as well. There are ten trainers, giving us about twenty students at a time. I also have some physical therapy clients, which keeps me fairly busy."

"Wow, that's impressive. Is that what you want to do? Physical therapy?"

"I went into sports medicine, so I'm right where I want to be. I might want to work for a solo team one day, but for the time being, it's a nice gig. It's lower stress, and I still have time to do things I enjoy."

"What is there to do around here? I wouldn't think a small town would have much to offer."

He chuckled, opening the door to the locker room. "You'd be surprised, actually. Of course, all the winter sports are available—skiing, snowboarding, and pond skating. There are several hiking trails, hidden oases, quaint shops, and dining. Salt Lake isn't very far, either, with several dance clubs, music venues, and practically any entertainment you'd want."

"Good to know."

We walked through a few doors. There were a few people around, but it was mostly empty. Since it was move-in day, I had to assume the majority of people were settling in. Dax turned a corner and opened the door to the training facility. I knew there were several around campus, one dedicated for each sport, but I'd heard that the hockey one was the best.

Looking around the room at the expensive equipment that gleamed, I'd agree. Dax went over to a machine, and I headed toward a treadmill. I didn't need to work out too much today, but a leisurely jog would be nice. Placing my headphones into my ears, I tuned out the world as I began.

After five miles, I slowed down the machine, sweat pouring down my face. Glancing in the mirror, I didn't spot Dax or anyone else around. Wiping my face with a towel, I cleaned my machine before drinking my water.

When it didn't appear Dax would return in the next few seconds, I decided to check out the locker room. I could make it back to the house if needed, but it was shitty to ditch me after inviting me to join him, in my opinion.

After a few wrong turns, I found my way into the locker room. Thankfully, I hadn't needed to open it since someone was coming out. They gave me an odd look as they rushed away. Shaking my head in confusion, I decided to check out where my locker was. If I didn't find Dax, I'd see if I could find Fletcher or Oliver. If that failed, I'd walk back to the house and figure out what to do for dinner.

My locker was next to Henley's, causing my heart to speed up. I'd get to see her every day. She was going to be so close to me. I'd have to remember not to reach out and touch her at every chance. After a cursory look through the locker room, I didn't find anyone, so I headed outside. Walking toward the side of the building, I heard muffled voices. As I neared, I could make out one of them.

"I'm not playing, man. If you don't deliver, I will break something of yours. It will be so bad, there's no amount of physical therapy you can do to fix it. Understand?"

Peering around the corner, I was the one shocked this time. A vast man towered over Dax, his shirt in his grasp as he pushed him up against the side of the building. Dax glared at the man, his lips pressed tightly together.

"Go fuck yourself, Gareth. I'm not going to help you this time," Dax spat, his body vibrating with the need to punch this man.

Against my better judgment, my feet began to move before I thought through my actions. The steroid giant pulled his arm back, his meaty fist ready to slam into my new roommate's face. Despite Dax's bravado, he tensed up and closed his eyes, prepared to accept his fate.

I grabbed the man's arm just before he made contact, spinning him around so I was between him and Dax. It was stupid on my part, as the man was bigger than either of us, but it felt right in the moment.

Gareth growled, taking a step forward, his sights set on me now.

"I don't know who you are or what your purpose is here, but I'd suggest you go. I've already alerted campus security and the police. If you don't want to be arrested for assault and extortion, which I recorded on my phone, then I'd leave now while you still have the chance."

"I don't believe you," he said, taking another step forward.

Out of sheer luck, a siren rang out close by. The guy stopped, turning his head toward the sound. Cursing, he pointed at Dax. "This isn't over, Dax." After delivering his threat, he took off running around the opposite corner.

My body sagged in relief, and I turned, taking in my new roommate. "Please tell me I didn't just help you avoid a drug deal gone wrong?"

"Did you really call the cops?"

"No." I shook my head, crossing my arms and blocking his path. "Your turn to answer."

Dax sighed and leaned back against the wall. He scrubbed his hands over his face as he took a few breaths. When he dropped his hands, I saw the face of a different man. One who wasn't as cocky or self-assured.

"It's a long story. How about I buy you a drink and share it?"

I assessed him, searching his face for the truth. He seemed sincere, and I decided to go with my gut instinct that he was a good guy.

"As long as it's a place where I can grab some food. I'm starved."

He gave a weak smile and nodded. "Yeah. I know a place."

CHAPTER 21

Dax

WHEN THE GUARD had alerted me to Gareth demanding to see me, my insides froze. I'd walked away from that part of my life, and I didn't want any of it back.

I'd glanced at Reed, finding him focused on his workout, so I'd dashed out of the center without saying anything, hopeful I'd make it back before he noticed I was gone.

Unfortunately, the conversation with Gareth hadn't gone as planned.

Reed stepping in like that was a surprise, shocking me. Which was something he'd been doing since he arrived. It wasn't that I thought he was a bad dude, just that I wasn't used to people showing up for me. Outside of Fletcher, I didn't have many friends, and since the whole Henley ordeal, Fletcher and I hadn't exactly been on the best of terms.

At best, it was awkward in the house, and I knew it was my fault. I could hear their calls at night, and it gutted me. But something kept me from agreeing to their crazy scheme. I just didn't see myself being able to be second in a relationship again.

Shaking off my wayward thoughts, I shoved them away and pushed them behind all the things I didn't like to think about. At this rate, I'd need a huge boulder to keep them at bay.

Pulling out my keys, I unlocked the car, and we both climbed in. Reed was quiet, but I was beginning to suspect it was his personality. It was a little unnerving, but it was a welcome reprieve as I tried to center myself to share a part of my past that was better left there.

As with most things in Oak Crest, the pub wasn't far from campus, and we arrived within a few minutes. We made our way inside, and I nodded toward the bartender. I wasn't as frequent of a visitor here as I was in a few places in Salt Lake, but after a long day, this was the best place to grab a drink without the drive home.

I surveyed the area, not spotting anyone I was familiar with. I debated if this conversation would be better suited for the counter or a booth. In the end, I opted for a booth, my need for privacy winning out.

"I'll take a pint of the special," I said as the waitress waltzed over. She smiled, turning her attention to Reed.

"And for you?" she asked.

"I'll have the same and the menu."

"Alrighty, boys. I'll have those right to you." She smiled, spinning on her toes as she swished her hips. It wasn't doing anything for me, though, and I sighed, glancing across toward Reed. He was watching me instead of the waitress, shocking me once again.

"That guy?" he asked, raising his eyebrows when I didn't immediately start to explain.

I held up a finger, wanting to wait until the waitress returned. It had nothing to do with needing some liquid courage or delaying the inevitable a second longer.

The waitress returned and placed our pints on the table, handing the food menu to Reed. "I'll be back in a jiffy," she said, grinning widely as she went to another table.

Reed opened the menu, letting me be for the moment while he scanned the pub's offerings. There weren't many options, so I already knew what I wanted. It didn't fit into my meal plan, but opening old wounds required lots of carbs and fat.

When he closed the paper menu, I was already halfway through my beer, the white froth leaving a ring around my glass. The waitress appeared, her bubbliness becoming too much for me.

"Burger and fries," I said, taking a big swig of my beer. "And another pint."

"I'll have the same," Reed said, watching me. The

waitress said a few things, but we both ignored her, and she soon left, leaving us for a few minutes.

Sighing, I swept my hair back, buying a few more precious seconds as I collected my thoughts on where to start.

"It wasn't a drug deal like you're thinking. Let's just get that out of the way. Gareth wanted drugs, but not the get high kind, more of the performance-enhancing type." I stopped as the waitress neared with our fresh beers.

Reed took his, but didn't say anything, letting me pick the story back up once she was gone. I took another sip, but not as big this time, already feeling the effects of the first one I'd practically chugged. My hands slid up and down the cool glass, and I debated where to go next.

"Why was he threatening you?"

It was the one question I'd hoped to avoid. The one I didn't want to answer. Letting out a self-deprecating chuckle, I pushed my shoulders back and met the man head-on. It felt like the best way to deal with this, anyway. I might as well get it out of the way now.

"Because before I worked here, I made some mistakes that haunt me still to this day."

"What kind of mistakes?"

"You're really not going to let this slide, are you?"

He grunted, shaking his head. It made me respect

the man a little more. He had integrity, something I wanted more of.

"It's a sordid tale of love and betrayal," I started, pausing slightly when our food was delivered. I stared longingly at my hamburger, debating if I should eat it first. Picking up a fry, I decided to leave it for when I really needed the comfort—at the end of my story.

"My first job out of school was for this fancy gym where I did physical training and had all these celebrity clients. They also had a small clinic where I got to focus on physical therapy. I thought I had it made back then. My girlfriend and I had been dating for a year, and we'd just moved in together. I was thinking about proposing when things went awry."

Taking a bite of my food, I took a moment to savor it as the delicious flavors of the burger spread across my tongue. I wasn't as strict about my diet as I'd once been, but burgers weren't on my menu very often. Not ones that tasted like this, at least. Wiping my mouth, I sat back, ready to pull off the bandage.

"I got myself into some trouble financially because I was trying to live the same lifestyle that my clients did. I fell for some bad investments and lost a lot of money. So, when I was ready to propose, I was looking for a way to make more money to buy a ring. One trainer proposed an offer, and I was desperate and naïve enough to think I was too valuable for anything bad to happen."

Picking up a few fries, I played with them as I got my words in order. Taking another sip for good measure, I lifted my eyes to find Reed watching me. He didn't pity me, giving me the courage I needed to finish.

"With my PT connections, I could get access to medications. The first time was small, just a few pills. But as I soon learned, they wanted more. The further in I got, the more leverage they had over me. Worse, I had to work more shifts as they demanded more of me, barely leaving me any time with my girlfriend or friends. When I finally had enough money to buy the ring, I was so excited. I left work early and purchased it. I had a whole plan for how I was going to propose. But when I got to the apartment, Jenny wasn't at work like I thought she'd be. Instead..." I shook my head, gripping the table's edge as I struggled to recall one of the worst moments of my life.

"How about you take a second and eat your food before it gets cold. I appreciate you sharing all this with me, man."

Nodding, I dropped my eyes, happy for the break in telling my sob story. Lifting my burger, I began to eat it, but I couldn't taste it anymore, too focused on pushing images of my brother fucking my girlfriend out of my mind. When I finished the burger, I quickly ate the fries and washed them down with the last of the beer. I'd need water from here on out if I was going to drive home anytime soon.

Pushing my plate away, I lifted my head and met Reed's eyes again. He was turning out to be an excellent listener, not pushing me for more until I was ready to share. I wish more people were like him.

"Jenny worked with my brother. I met her through him, actually. At the time, he said he wasn't interested and thought she was the perfect girl for me. When I started working more, they spent more time together. Well, as you can probably guess, I walked in on them in a compromising position."

"How we doing, guys?" the waitress asked, stopping my tale.

"Water, please."

"Of course. Anything for you, sweetie?" she asked Reed.

He shook his head, pushing the plate toward her. "I'm good."

She batted her eyelashes, taking the plates. Despite our dismissal, I had to give it to the girl for continuing to try with us.

"I'm guessing you didn't propose?"

Snorting, I tapped the table as I shook my head. "No. I'm not proud of my reaction. Or the fact that it took me another three months to stop stealing pills." I hung my head in shame at that. I hated Jenny and my brother for so long that I lost focus on who was really to blame. "To top it off, they're getting married now. So... There's that."

"Wow, that sucks. I'm sorry, man."

My water arrived, and I began to drink it, the coolness of the liquid helping to calm me. "Once I stopped doing their bidding, they ruined me. But I didn't care at that point. I felt so lost, and I just wanted to get away. Finding this job saved me."

"If you stopped, why is that guy threatening you now?"

I shook my head. "Beats me. Gareth isn't even from around here. I haven't seen that dude in over three years. I'm not really sure what he's doing here."

"You should tell Dmitry or someone then."

"Yeah, you're probably right." Even though Dmitry was fully aware of my past, something I had to share to get the job with the blemish on my record with my PT license, it wasn't something I wanted to bring up. But I guess it was better to stop this before they ruined my life again.

In another surprising twist, I felt better sharing this with Reed. The thoughts and images didn't seem as overwhelming now that they were out there.

"Thanks for not assuming the worst of me. I don't like talking about this part of my life, but it felt nice to get it off my chest."

"You're welcome. I'm not always great at the talking part, but I'm pretty good at the listening bit."

Chuckling, I nodded. Finishing my water, I waved toward the waitress for the check. Now that things were more familiar between Reed and me, I wanted to gauge his thoughts on Henley.

"Burning question... are you after Henley?"

"After?" he asked. While his face was neutral, I noticed how his knuckles tightened around his glass.

"Yeah. Do you want to get with her?"

"Are you?"

"Deflecting with a question makes me think you are."

He sighed, letting go of his glass. "You were honest with me, so I'll be honest with you. Henley intrigues me. I've admired her from afar for years. She's gorgeous, strong, and plays hockey like the best of them. There are things in my life that make it hard to get close to people. She's one of the first people I've wanted to try with, though. I don't know what that means. Just that I'm intrigued."

I studied him, watching every piece of body language. While what he was saying was true, I had a feeling he felt more for her than curious. And even though I knew I shouldn't think about her, I couldn't help but wonder what it meant that the three guys living in our house seemed to be hung up on her.

It was going to be an interesting year, if anything.

CHAPTER 22

Henley

UNPACKING and meeting more of my houseguests had done me in. I wasn't sure about the living situation, even if it was a beautiful house. The girls had already made up their minds about me. Either because they'd found out about the sex tape or because I played hockey; the only friendly one had been Chloe.

I wanted to hate her for abandoning me to the basement, but I couldn't. If this was what she had to deal with being a snowboarder, then I understood. Hated it. But understood.

"So, Henley. We heard that Fletcher dropped you off. What's the story there?" Brynn, another figure skater, asked me.

I'd come down to the kitchen to grab some food and had been bombarded with their critical questions ever since.

"Oh, um, Fletcher and I've known one another for a while. His younger sister was my roommate in college."

"Hmm, is that all?" another female asked. I'd

already forgotten her name. It was Coco or Chanel or something like that. She picked up a carrot stick and took a giant chomp while she waited for me to answer.

I debated on how much to share. While it wasn't a secret, I didn't want the gossip mill to run about me before classes started.

"We're getting to know one another again," I said, deciding it was better to go with a version of the truth.

The three girls looked at one another, gearing up to ask me a million more personal questions, no doubt, and I knew I couldn't take it anymore. It had already been an hour of questions about why I left hockey and what it was like to date Dakota Hughes. Gag.

"Wow, is that the time? I have someplace I need to be. Thanks for the snacks. I'll see you around, I guess."

I backed out of the kitchen and hustled toward the front door. I was too nervous to run upstairs to grab anything, so I'd have to make do with the outfit I'd been wearing. It would be miserable if they cornered me like that every time I entered this house.

Once the door closed, I cursed as I realized I didn't have my keys. Hopefully, they wouldn't lock me out. Sprinting down the steps, I headed in the direction of Fletcher's house. It wasn't super close, but walking a mile was preferable to dealing with the Barbie Brigade.

I knew it wasn't fair of me to call them that. They were lovely women, and I was sure they had pleasant personalities under the hostility and judgment. But they weren't the type of girls I typically hung out with. To each their own and all that.

Walking at a brisk pace, I began to sweat across my brow. I was so focused on my thoughts and how I would stand living with these women that I jumped a mile in the air when a horn honked behind me.

Holding a hand to my chest to calm my racing heart, I lifted the other to shield my eyes so I could make out the vehicle that had spooked me. The passenger window rolled down as they slowly approached.

"Need a lift?" Reed asked, giving me a rare smile.

My body relaxed, happy to see him again. Nodding, I walked toward the back door and opened it. When I slid in, I was surprised to find Dax was the one who was driving.

"Oh, hey, Dax. How are you?" I asked. The award for the most awkward greeting goes to me.

Dax watched me in the rearview mirror, not acknowledging my greeting. My cheeks heated as I scooted back and pulled the seat belt on.

I noticed Reed nudging Dax, who finally dropped his eyes off me to look at the other man. I couldn't determine what they were doing, but Dax finally spoke after a few quiet seconds.

"Where are you headed, Henley?" It felt like he gritted out his words, and I hated how it sounded. I wanted him to call me petal again. To use that voice to seduce me instead of hate me.

"I'm not sure. I just needed to get out of my house and away from my roommates. I was going to try to make it to Fletcher's house... your house."

"Our house," Dax said, pulling the car back onto the road. I wasn't confident, but it sounded like he was smiling at that.

"Our?" I asked, still confused.

"I live there now, too," Reed said.

"Wow. Okay. That's cool."

I fiddled with my seatbelt, my hands shaking a little with nerves. Why was I suddenly so nervous? It was just Dax and Reed.

But I knew that wasn't true either. They were two men who unnerved me in the best ways. One had brought my body to pleasurable heights, worshiping me like no other. And the other sparked a longing in me that I didn't understand. Alone, they were a sight to behold. Together... well, it was downright explosive.

So, yeah. It might *only* be Dax and Reed, but that was the understatement of the year. Neither of them was anything simple.

Taking a deep breath, I pushed my shoulders back, remembering my mantra to be who I wanted to be, whatever that looked like.

"How was your flight?" I asked Reed, leaning closer. His minty scent tickled my nostrils, sending tingles through me. The smell was also comforting, reminding me of how he held me that day.

"Not too bad. How's Reese?"

"They're good. I got them settled into their dorm first. They're very excited to be back. At least they're happy with their living arrangements."

"Yours not to your liking?" Dax asked, smirking at me.

I didn't know what his deal was, but it seemed like since I hadn't wanted to date *only* him, he was intent on punishing me for it. He would have to try a lot harder if that was his plan.

"I'm sure they're all nice girls, just a bit too forward in their questions and judgments. Not to mention my room looks like cotton candy. Plus, there are all these rules as well that I don't quite understand."

"Like what?" Reed asked, shifting a little to glance at me. Before I could answer, we pulled into the driveway. It had taken about five minutes to drive here, which wasn't far in the grand scheme of things, but for walking, it might've been more like an hour. I was suddenly very grateful they'd picked me up. I didn't need to pull a muscle before school started.

Climbing out of the car, I stuck near Reed as we followed Dax in. Reed peered down at me, giving me a soft smile. It really was a good look on him. Butterflies erupted, dancing in my belly, and I ducked my head a little as we stepped into the house.

"We found something you misplaced on our way home," Dax said, pushing past Fletcher to open the fridge. He took out a jug of something, unscrewing the cap and leaning back against the counter as he drank it. His eyes never left me, zeroing in on mine with precise scrutiny. I wondered if he was undressing me with his eyes.

"Henley?" Fletcher asked, jolting me out of my stare-down with Dax.

"Hey, I hope it's okay that I'm here. I couldn't stay in that place a minute longer."

"Of course. I would've come and got you if you'd called." He walked over and hugged me, making me feel completely relaxed in his arms. "Hey, Reed. Sorry I missed you when you got here. I hope Dax showed you around?"

Dax snorted, wiping his mouth. "Yeah, dude. I took care of it."

"He did. I took the last room on the left," Reed answered, but his eyes were on me too.

I instantly felt in over my head, standing in this small kitchen with three guys' attention on me.

"Did you get anything to eat?" Fletcher asked, and I nodded, but food was the last thing on my mind.

"Yeah. Maybe we could just hang out?"

"Sure. You guys want to watch a movie or something?"

"Nah. I'm good," Dax said, walking out of the kitchen without a backward glance. I needed to build up my defenses around him. He broke them down so quickly with just a look or word. If I wanted to prove to him I wasn't ashamed of my choices, then I needed to commit to them. I couldn't let Dax's judgment be my undoing.

"What about you?" I asked, turning to Reed. "It would be nice to hang out."

"Sure. I could do a movie." His eyes seemed to warm at my statement, making me feel better.

"Well, then. It's settled. You guys pick out the movie, and I'll make some popcorn."

Fletcher shooed us into the living room, where we sat on the couch next to one another. Reed picked up the remote and found a movie page. I remembered Fletcher had said the campus had its own streaming apps with all the latest movies.

"Whoa," Reed said as he scrolled. "There's almost too many to choose. What kind of movies do you like?"

"Just about anything. How about an action one?"

Reed nodded as he scrolled to the action section. I read the titles and descriptions as he slid over them. He'd wait until I shook my head, yes or no. When I got to one that sounded interesting, I nodded enthusiastically.

"Yes, that one." I pointed, turning to make sure he knew I meant business.

"You only want to watch it because Ryan Reynolds is in it," he said, smirking at me.

I shrugged, grinning over at him. "And that's a bad thing because?"

Reed rolled his eyes but selected it, pausing it on the title screen. Fletcher walked in a second later with three popcorn bowls and water bottles.

"That smells amazing," I said, taking a bowl as he handed it to me.

"It's because of Ryan Reynolds, isn't it?" Fletcher asked as he settled down next to me, noticing our selected movie. Reed snorted and elbowed me.

"Shut up," I mumbled around a mouthful of popcorn. "He's so pretty." I giggled, already feeling better being with them both.

If only I could live with them, things would be perfect—even with Dax throwing shade every two seconds. I preferred his disdain over the girl's judgment. With Dax, I knew it was due to feeling hurt I hadn't picked him. With the girls, I wasn't as sure what their deal was, only that I didn't fit in with them.

Fletcher squeezed my thigh, winking at me as the movie began, and I sank back into the couch cushion. Reed's shoulder and thigh pressed into my right side while Fletcher pressed into my left. They both sat sprawled out, legs wide, as they focused on the TV.

Despite Ryan Reynolds being on screen, it was hard to focus on the movie with both of them so close. Images of being between them naked swirled in my mind, and I shifted, crossing my legs to get some relief. However, it was short-lived as they both took the opportunity to widen their legs, pressing into me more.

When the movie finished, I was a sweaty mess needing a session with my vibrator. Reed cleared his throat before he stood, picking up the popcorn bowls that had been discarded on the coffee table in front.

"Good night, Henley. I'll see you at the team meeting in the morning."

"Good night, Reed." I stood up suddenly, the urge to hug him coming over me. Two hours of pressing against his body made me more comfortable initiating physical contact.

My arms wrapped around his torso, my head landing on his pecs. I could hear his heart hammering beneath me as he wrapped his arms around me. Sooner than I wanted, I stepped back, not ready to let go but knowing I needed to.

"See you tomorrow," I said. He nodded, walking out of the room and leaving Fletcher and me alone for the first time all night.

"I'd ask you to stay, but I can tell you'd say no. So, can I give you a lift?"

"I'd love that. And it's not that I don't want to stay.

I just don't want to make the wrong impression on my first day. Ask me again tomorrow, though, and the answer might be different," I teased.

Fletcher chuckled, nodding his head. "Alright. Let me take a bathroom break quickly, and then I'll bring you back."

He leaned down, capturing my lips with his for a brief kiss. When he walked away, I put the pillows back on the couch and collected the water bottles. A body pressed into me from behind, their warm palms smoothing my hair over my neck.

"I've decided not to let you go, Petal. I'll keep reminding you about our night until you cave and pick me in the end."

I sucked in a breath, shaking my head. Turning around, Dax was no longer there, just his haunting words and the smell of clean cotton lingering in the air.

CHAPTER 23

Henley

SKATING ACROSS THE ICE, I focused on warming up my muscles and not the fact that a horde of high school kids was about to descend on me and my first day as their head coach.

Reed and Oliver talked casually against the boards, but I needed to clear my head before I faced the onslaught of teenagers.

At least the team meeting had gone well; the other coaches had mostly welcomed me. Only one seemed miffed he hadn't been given the promotion—Kurt. Of course, that meant he was with me and Reed, coaching the senior team.

He scowled as I passed him, so naturally, I gave him a shit-eating grin. Focusing on proving him wrong distracted me for the moment.

In the few seconds I wasn't freaking out about coaching for the first time, I kept replaying what Dax had said in my head.

There was a large part of me eager to see what he would do to try to win me, excited that he was interested in me enough to try. The smaller part of me knew it wouldn't end well if he wasn't on board with me dating multiple people at once.

I didn't want to have to choose, so if he expected me to, it would fail from the start.

So, did I play along and hope he came over to my way of thinking, just so I could be in his arms again? Or would it be wiser to cut ties now before I fell more for the rugged and seductive man?

Neither option sounded doable at the moment, leaving me stuck in this limbo where Dax was concerned.

The first sound of voices emerged from the student locker room, so I skated toward Oliver and Reed, leaving Kurt alone. I knew him from when he played with Dakota. He was a great hockey player, just his attitude had always been more on the sour side. So I guess I couldn't take it personally.

Reed nodded as I approached, helping to calm the butterflies that were currently inhabiting my stomach. Oliver gave me a massive grin as he clapped my shoulder.

"You ready, Henshaw?"

"Why do I feel more nervous coaching than I have in years playing professional hockey?" I asked, laughing.

"Because teenagers can be vicious. But these kids are good. You'll be fine. You have a lot to offer them as a player and coach. Don't forget that we asked you for a reason. You're not a stunt."

Taking a deep breath, I nodded that I heard what he was saying. They believed in my ability to do this enough to break tradition. They'd offered me this position because I was the right person for the job.

Or, that was how my brain decided to interpret it.

Reed gave me a supportive nudge, and I skated onto the ice with Oliver as the kids began gathering in the middle. I glanced around at them all, finding Reese and Braden smiling, helping to settle my nerves a little more. At least I had two people who were excited I was the coach. A few other kids from camp nodded, and I knew I was making a bigger deal of it than I needed to.

"Welcome back, Seniors! Who's ready for a new year at Lux?"

The players cheered, knocking their sticks against the ice as they hooted and shouted, "Go, Blizzards!"

"Okay, okay, settle down. I like seeing your school spirit this early. We have quite a few new faces, so I expect everyone to be welcoming and help any newbies with anything they might need. At Lux, we're a team. We win as a team and lose as a team. If you start going after your own pursuits, then you're letting everyone down, including yourself." Oliver peered around at the group, ensuring they understood what he was saying.

"Good. Now, I have a few announcements. If you

were at the end of the summer camp, then you've already heard that I'm stepping down as the head coach so I can pursue my new dream of becoming a pastry chef. I'll be around for a few weeks to get the new coach settled in, but after that, I'll be leaving you in the very capable hands of Henley Henshaw."

Oliver turned and motioned for me. A few kids clapped and cheered, but it was only slight. I smiled, skating up next to Oliver.

"Henley played in the league for the Cambridge Cardinals for several years and has won two gold medals at the Olympics. She's one of the best precision shooters and will bring your game to the next level. I'm confident with Coach Henshaw, Coach Cole, and Coach Kuga that you'll win the national championship and earn yourself some recognition for the Olympics this year."

The team looked around at one another, smiles on their faces at that proclamation. Oliver nodded to give it over to me, so I straightened.

"I look forward to getting to know you all better over the course of the semester. But for now, let's start with twenty suicides. Go!"

Most of the team looked around at one another, not moving. Reese and Braden tossed their sticks to the side and began to skate, the majority following them. A group of four stood still, not budging, and I knew these would be the assholes of the hockey team.

Oliver opened his mouth to say something, but I stopped him, placing my hand on his arm, and shook my head. I caught Reed grimacing out of the corner of my eye, his hands tightening on his stick as he held himself back. It gave me the courage I needed.

The other players were skating, their blades swishing back and forth on the ice as they went from the half-court line to the goal and back on the other side.

Taking a deep breath, I skated to the tallest of the bunch. He stood slightly in front of the others, making me believe he was their leader.

"What's your name?" I asked, meeting him eye to eye.

"Anders," he said, smirking. His eyes dropped down my body, his thumb lifting to his mouth. He probably thought it was attractive, but it was far from it. This kid was a Dakota in the making. Memories of all the years of being harassed by guys like this surged forward.

"Well, *Anders*, did you forget how to skate over the summer?"

His cronies snickered, and he glared at them, his smile dropping now that I didn't fall at his feet.

"No," he huffed, crossing his arms.

"Then it must be that you want to be moved to the junior team. I can't think of any other reason four *senior* team members would ignore a direct order from their *coach*."

A few of the guys behind Anders shuffled, so I addressed them, hoping to break some of the power this kid held over his peers.

"You have one chance to join your teammates and do ten extra suicides to earn their forgiveness. If I get back to my post and you're still here, I'll let Coach Cromwell know you're transferring teams. I'm sure plenty of kids on the junior team are looking for the opportunity to make the Olympics."

I saw a few kids gulp and nod, moving before I'd even turned. The leader, Anders, appeared to have grown madder, his face beet red. I ignored him, not giving him any more attention. There was no way I would let him bully me or take my leadership. I might have boobs and a vagina, but I was an excellent hockey player and knew how to win games. They could take it or leave it, but I wasn't going to beg them to listen to me.

Reed's eyes bored into mine, the intensity hot, and I almost stumbled as I looked into his crystal blue depths. His hands gripped his hockey stick as he watched me skate back toward him, ignoring the kids. Oliver gave me a nod of approval, patting my shoulder pad as I neared.

I didn't glance back, but focused on the kids doing as I asked. Oliver and Reed followed suit, turning and we watched the kids together. Some of them were lagging behind, while others were going strong. I was surprised to find Kurt near them, blowing his whistle for each heat.

Out of the corner of my eye, I caught Anders joining the lines, and I felt like I'd won a victory. I knew it wasn't the last battle, but it felt nice knowing I'd held my own.

This job was already teaching me things I hadn't been prepared for, like owning my skills and not apologizing for my accomplishments.

Today was a small step toward becoming the role model I wanted to be for Reese and all the other kids out there that felt like they weren't good enough because someone said so.

When the kids finished their suicides, they were breathing heavily. Blowing my whistle, I waited for them to look toward me. "Take a few minutes to get some water, and then we'll break into groups of four."

I motioned for Kurt to join me while the kids grabbed water. He slid to a stop, spraying ice over me.

"Whoops," he said, not sounding apologetic at all.

Rolling my eyes, I ignored him as I pulled out the players' names on the clipboard and split them into groups.

"Oliver, you're going to take group one. Reed, you have group two, and Kuga, you have group three. I'll take group four to start. We're going to rotate between stations to see where everyone is after the summer. Oliver, you'll be working on backward and crossover skating. Reed, you have stickhandling and passing. Kurt, you have passing and goaltending, and I'll work on shooting. Any questions?"

Oliver smiled, looking pleased with himself as he headed to the right corner. Reed gave me a nod of respect before he skated off, leaving me with Kurt. He looked like he wanted to say something, his hands twisting on this stick. When he decided not to, he skated off in a huff, going to his corner. I had a feeling things were just getting started with him.

Skating toward the center, I called the kids back and read their names for which group they were in. They were all a little quicker this time, moving to go where they were meant to. The rest of the practice flew by as we rotated groups, scoring each kid where they stood on the skill.

When class was over, I realized I was as tired as I was after any practice or game for the league. Perhaps, maybe even more. It had been a hard day, but it felt worthwhile. Fletcher was waiting with Ty when we skated off the ice. Both men smiled widely, greeting Oliver, Reed, and me enthusiastically. Kurt had left as soon as class ended, leaving us to pick up the equipment.

"How did your first class go?" Fletcher asked when I was close.

"Pretty good. There were a few obstacles, but I think I have it handled."

"She did awesomely," Oliver said before greeting Ty. "You're going to be great, Henley. I'll see you tomorrow. We're in fitness room 1."

"Thanks. See you tomorrow."

"I almost beat up a few kids and a coach," Reed growled, that same intensity I'd witnessed earlier coming through.

"Ah, Kurt, the jerk, I'm guessing?" Fletcher asked, his brow dipping.

"Aye. Kurt, about to be hurt," Reed said, his fist clenching at his side.

Fletcher and I stopped, looking at one another, turning back to Reed in shock. He blinked, noticing our surprised expressions.

"What?" he asked, taking off his pads and putting on his skate guards.

"I believe you just rhymed, man. It was odd, that's all," Fletcher said slowly.

Giggling, I nodded, unable to hold in any longer. Reed stopped, glancing up at me at the sound. A deep chuckle left him, making me chortle more.

"You should make that sound more, Hen. It's nice," he said. My cheeks heated instantly, and I focused on putting my skate guards on.

"He's not wrong," Fletcher purred, making my insides melt. "And now I have class. Fucker." He playfully punched Reed, who snorted, shaking his head. I liked seeing them get along; it made me feel like my dream to date both was more and more possible.

"Good luck," I said to Fletcher as Reed and I headed toward the locker room. "Call me later?"

"You bet." He winked before turning and skating onto the ice. Ty and Cody were already there as they set up for their students.

"You were amazing today, Hen. I hope you know that," Reed whispered.

I smiled, nodding. I was beginning to.

CHAPTER 24

Fletcher

ALL THROUGH PRACTICE, I thought about Henley. It was my first day as the junior team's head coach, and I didn't care. It was just another day for me. I was more focused on Henley and the fact she coached her first team today. That felt significant and was something I was eager to hear more about.

Ever since she'd re-entered my life, I couldn't stop thinking about her. Henley had become my focus, and I wasn't ashamed to admit that. She was special, and I was realizing just how much.

With the last blow of my whistle, I circled the guys together. Ty and Cody gathered behind them. Everyone was sweaty and red-faced, the result of a good practice. I glanced around at the kids, taking in their faces.

"Great first practice, guys. There are a few new faces and some familiar ones, but I want to welcome you all to the junior team. We'll be having our first scrimmage against the senior team at the end of the week. It will be your first chance to demonstrate your skills for the new head coach."

"What a babe," one of the kids said, causing the others to chuckle.

"Enough," I hollered, brooking no argument. The kids quieted as I stared out at the crowd. A few ducked their heads, their cheeks heating. "Coach Henshaw isn't someone for you to gawk over. She deserves your respect. If you have a problem with that, I suggest you consider your future at Lux and whether this is the right school for you. Now, head to the showers!"

They didn't waste time, skating off quieter than they'd been all day. Cody picked up the cones as Ty and I gathered the pucks. Cody waved when he was done, heading to the locker room himself. Ty and I finished shortly after and headed off. It was quiet between us as we walked.

"Something on your mind, Coach?" Ty asked. "Or *someone*, maybe?"

I chuckled, rubbing my beard. "Yeah. I guess you could say that. Speaking of... I know that your relationship with Oliver and Sawyer isn't conventional. How did you guys come to that decision?"

"Ah, well, for me, Sawyer was already with the guys when I entered the picture. She and I had a history, though, and it hadn't dwindled for me over the years. The moment I saw her again, I just knew I needed to be with her. When I learned she was dating a few of my friends, I was disappointed and worried I'd missed my chance... again. Then the guys talked with me about their arrangement. I was angry at first, thinking they were taking advantage of her. But once I saw it in action, I understood."

"What do you mean?" I asked, stopping before we reached the locker rooms.

"I could see the love between them. They all cared for her, and she them. It wasn't a sex thing or orgy like I'd thought, but genuine relationships."

"And you're with her and Oliver?"

"Yeah. I got lucky that the two people I had feelings for happened to have feelings for one another."

"And you don't get jealous?" Ty smiled, giving me a look like he understood something I didn't yet.

"Sometimes. That's human nature." He shrugged. "It's what I do with my feelings that matters. We have to communicate all the time and make sure we spend time together and apart. There are eight of us. We're a family. It could've been Sawyer and her relationship with each guy, but I don't think it would've worked. I think BOSH, as we call ourselves, works because we created a unit. It's not just about Sawyer, but also our relationships with one another. I might not be romantically involved with everyone, but I care for these guys. They're my brothers, and we must listen to one another and make choices that we can all agree on."

"That sounds nice when you put it like that."

"It is. I've wanted something like this my whole life." He smiled so big it covered his entire face. I remembered Ty from a year ago and knew everything he'd just told me had changed him. He was different—more open and carefree. "Can I ask why the sudden interest? It wouldn't have anything to do with Henley, would it?"

"Busted." I chuckled. "I like her, and we're dating. She just came out of a relationship and said she wasn't ready to commit to one person. She was interested in two other people and wanted to see what was there. I don't know where anything is headed or if we could have something similar to what you guys have created, but it felt important to have all the information. I guess I wanted to know my options and if it was possible to be happy in something different."

Ty nodded, reaching out to squeeze my forearm. "Polyamory isn't for everyone, and it's not always easy. But if you're asking now, I think you're further along in that decision than you know. If you have questions or just need someone to chat with, then I'm all ears, man."

"Thanks, Ty."

We headed into the locker room, going our separate ways. I undressed in a daze, my thoughts whirling with scenarios as I tried to determine if I could do this. When I left the arena, I still had no clear answer. It was something I needed to see before I could really decide.

But one thing I knew for sure, Henley was worth trying something new.

WHEN I RETURNED HOME, REED WAS AT THE HOUSE, BUT Dax's car was missing. Since it was just the two of us, I wondered if it would be the perfect opportunity to talk about Henley. Reed seemed to be interested in her, but as far as I knew, there hadn't been anything between them yet.

Knocking on his door, he opened it after a few seconds, standing in joggers, a tee, and bare feet. His eyebrows lifted when he spotted me.

"What's up?" he asked, sticking his hands into his pockets.

"Do you like Henley?" I blurted.

Reed froze, then blinked. The corner of his mouth turned up, and he leaned against the door. "That some sort of initiation question for this house? Dax asked me the same thing yesterday."

I paused, a laugh erupting from me. "Seems like it's on both our minds. Care to join me in the kitchen, and we can talk?"

"Sure." He nodded, motioning for me to lead the way. I walked into the kitchen, went to the fridge, and pulled out two beers. Reed snorted again, but I ignored it, trying to figure out how to talk to him about this. Perhaps I should've asked Ty how to approach someone.

"So, Henley," I said, popping the cap off my beer. "She's special."

Reed did the same to his beer, but didn't say anything. I took a seat at the table, and he soon followed. My hands grasped the bottle, the cold condensation feeling nice against my hot skin. Reed took a drink, leaning back in his chair, waiting for me.

"Have you ever heard of a polyamorous relationship?"

"Believe it or not, I have," Reed said.

"What are your thoughts on it?" I asked, curious if he'd been doing some research as well.

"I think if people are honest with one another, then it's their business."

"Have you been in one?"

"No, but I had a buddy who was in one," Reed said, setting his bottle down. "Why do you ask?"

Sighing, I rubbed my face. "When I saw Henley again for the first time in years, I was instantly attracted to her. I knew I wanted to date her and get to know who she is now. The chemistry was there, and I was excited to start something. I knew she'd gotten out of a relationship recently, so I wasn't sure where she was with things. She told me she wasn't ready to commit and wasn't even sure if she would ever settle down. She wanted to be free to pursue her options. And well, you were someone she said she had a connection with. Along with Dax."

Reed sat back, rubbing his jaw. He looked deep in thought, but stayed quiet.

"I probably shouldn't be telling you that, but I figured we should talk about what we're comfortable with since we live together."

"What about Dax?"

"He told her he would only date her. He would walk if she was going to date me too."

Reed winced, shaking his head. "Hmm."

"So, I want to know your intentions. Would you be open to an unconventional relationship if things progressed with you two?"

"Are you asking me out, Cromwell?" Reed teased, showing a different side to the stoic man.

"You wish." Blushing, I took a drink of my beer before I looked at him. He had his hand on his jaw as he thought, glancing off in a different direction.

"My life..." He shook his head, sitting up. "I'm trying to put the pieces back together. Henley is one of the few bright spots. This might sound like a cop-out, but with everything I have going on, it feels like the perfect way for me to be in her life if she wants. I'm not a whole person. I can't give her the sweet romance. But if I'm not the only one in the relationship, then maybe what I can give her would be enough. Does that sound bad?"

I thought about what he was saying. While I felt that Reed was selling himself short, I wasn't able to tell him that since we'd just met. In a way, I understood what he meant. I hadn't considered the benefits of this type of relationship for myself.

In the past, I always went full force in the beginning, wanting to prove to the girl I was dating that I was worth it, so afraid they'd discover the truth. I figured if I already had them hooked on the line, it wasn't as big of a disappointment when they discovered the truth—that I wasn't the perfect guy they saw me as.

When hockey would be busy, or I would get focused on something else, the girls would always see the truth—that I didn't measure up in the end. I never got past the two-month mark with a girl because by then, I was so worn out and exhausted from trying to prove myself worthy that I stopped trying altogether. And the girls always left, saying that I'd changed.

Maybe Reed was right... alone, I wasn't enough to keep a girl, but if there were two of us to share the role, we could work together to keep her. Henley was the girl I could spend the rest of my life with. Now, I just needed to figure out if I could see Reed, and potentially Dax, if he got his head out of his ass, in that future.

"No." I cleared my throat, shaking my head. "No, that doesn't sound bad at all. What do you say about making some dinner and getting to know one another?"

"You sure you're not trying to date me, Cromwell?" Reed teased, knocking back the rest of his beer.

"If I was into guys, you'd be at the top of the list, Cole. I just figured if we're going to try this, with the potential, at least for me, that it could be long term, I want to know the man I could be creating a family with."

"Family?" he asked, gulping a little.

"Something Ty said. That the thing he loved about their relationship wasn't just that he was with the two people he loved but that all the guys were there for one another. They're a family unit. I don't know about you, but I could use that in my life."

He stared, some emotion passing over his face before he nodded. "Yeah. That would be nice. Got any steaks?"

Chuckling, I nodded and walked over to the fridge. After marinating the steaks, we let them sit for a bit while we played a video game together, and I got to know Reed Cole a little more. I didn't know where the relationship with Henley would lead me, but at least I was more prepared now to say yes if it got there.

CHAPTER 25

Henley

THREE DAYS of the Barbie Brigade and I wanted to change my name, move states, and never set foot in another hockey arena ever again.

Okay, so maybe I was being slightly dramatic. But I was about at my wit's end with my roommates. The worst part... if I was to tell anyone what they were doing, I'd be the one who looked insane.

Brynn insisted on making food for the whole house, but never asked if anyone disliked certain things before serving. She then would proceed to sit with you while you ate it, and if you didn't immediately compliment her, she pouted and would passive-aggressively open and close all the cabinets loudly. I'd become a ninja trying to get to the kitchen to find food before she woke up, just so I could eat in peace.

Coco didn't understand the concept of boundaries and would mandate we all have a group huddle every night where we shared our day. If I wasn't being talkative enough, they'd grill me with a million questions, prying into my life. They didn't like it when I wouldn't share and made catty remarks about how I wasn't being a good Meadows roomie and how could they trust me if I wasn't willing to share?

It always ended with everyone saying nice things about each other. Which sounded nice in theory, but they all focused on physical things. Chloe had late training hours, and I was suspicious that she'd scheduled it on purpose to avoid the torture.

Julie—who I was fortunate to share a bathroom with—took insanely long showers, hogged the sink, left her beauty products everywhere, and didn't know how to hang up a wet towel. She constantly barged into my room and insisted on giving me advice on how to make myself more "feminine" and attractive to guys. At this rate, I was showering more on campus than the Meadows.

Which was a stupid name for a house, I decided. The Meadow's was a sadist's playground, and I was the masochistic who kept returning for more.

I didn't feel comfortable in my house, afraid a roommate would jump out and tell me something they thought I could improve on. I couldn't eat what I wanted when I was hungry, and showering solo had become impossible. Adding in constantly having to share my feelings left me an exhausted mess.

Living in the Meadows was akin to psychological warfare, and I was unraveling three days in. I wasn't sure how much longer I could take it.

There was one more day until the scrimmage

against the junior team, and I didn't feel confident at this point that we'd win. I'd stuck around after practice yesterday in an effort to avoid the house and watched Fletcher at work. The junior team looked so flawless I was legitimately nervous.

And today, we had conditioning first... with Dax.

I'd expected to see him on Tuesday, but he'd been needed for something else, so Rhett had filled in for him. I hadn't minded. It was easier to focus on coaching when my attention wasn't being pulled in a million directions. And Dax felt like a bomb waiting to go off any day.

Between my shitty mood, irritable state, and nerves over the game, that day could very well be today.

Lacing up my shoe, I made my way toward the fitness room. I'd learned the hard way on Tuesday that I couldn't wear what I usually wore to work out in. It didn't compute well with teenage boys that I was their coach and more than a sexual figure when I was in a crop top.

Thankfully, Reed had given me an extra hoodie, but I'd roasted the whole workout, almost passing out at one point. So, today, I wore a long-sleeved shirt that concealed my womanly curves. Hopefully, it was enough to prove my point.

Reed was waiting for me outside the fitness room,

two smoothies in his hand. His eyes lit up when he spotted me, the corner of his mouth tilting up slightly. He'd been a supportive shadow since we got here, and I was learning to lean on him. The energy between us still sparked every time we were near, but with classes starting and wanting to prove myself, I hadn't spent much time outside the rink with him.

The tension between us was building, though, and I was excited to see where it would lead.

"Thanks," I said, taking the smoothie. It was strawberry—my favorite. Reed seemed to watch and learn my favorites, unlike some of my Meadow roommates.

His fingertips brushed against my hand, sending tendrils of heat down my spine.

I lifted the straw to my mouth, attempting to hide the developing blush. His eyes followed, focusing on my lips as I sucked some of the cold liquid.

When I pulled the smoothie away, I licked my lips, catching a bit of smoothie that had lingered. Reed's hand tightened on his own cup, and I was worried it would burst open and spill to the floor. His nostrils flared, his blue eyes darkening as I sucked in a breath, wondering if this was the moment he cracked and the energy between us exploded.

I was wondering if I had a thing for explosives considering how I was with my love interests lately.

A door slammed down the hall, and voices filtered toward us. It was enough to break the spell, and we awkwardly shuffled into the fitness room a minute before the students. Kurt glared at us from across the room. He was talking with Dax, and something about that upset me. Dax and I were nothing, but with the way Kurt seemed to hate me, if Dax associated with him, it felt like he'd picked a side—one without me.

It was stupid, but I couldn't hide the hurt as I walked over to the wall to put my stuff down. Reed followed, his presence a constant comfort. From the moment we'd met, he seemed to understand my emotions in ways I hadn't, always able to anticipate them when I didn't even know what I was feeling.

"I don't like that guy," he growled, making me laugh.

"Kurt or Dax?" I asked, blanking my face as the kids entered. I leaned against the wall as I finished my smoothie.

"Kurt. Dax is cool, just a bit lost."

"Hmph," I grunted, not sure I agreed with him. Dax seemed to know exactly who he was and what he wanted—me under him and only him.

I couldn't deny the chemistry, but I wouldn't deny my heart.

I kept watching Kurt and Dax, apparently needing more pain today since I'd managed to avoid my room-mates this morning. So, it was only because I'd been watching them so closely that I noticed when things shifted between them.

One second they were laughing at something, and the next, Dax had Kurt up against the wall, his forearm across his throat as he pinned him down.

Immediately, I leaped into action. Reed beat me there, pulling them apart before anything escalated in front of the kids. Kurt's face was red, and he glared daggers at Dax. It felt pivotal at that moment for me to handle the situation, or I'd lose every inch of power I'd fought for all week.

"Kurt, take the morning off and meet us back on the ice later," I said, not offering him a choice.

"Fine," he spat, walking out the door, steam practically billowing out of his ears the whole way. The kids present were silent, watching to see what happened next.

"Get in position for warmups," I shouted, moving toward the front of the room. I fought the urge to look at Dax, afraid of what I would see there.

When I felt a body move close to me, I couldn't stop myself from looking. Dax glared at me, his eyes piercing my soul. But what I couldn't figure out was why it seemed he wasn't mad at me, but for me? Why did he care?

Turning my head, I stretched my arms across my chest, trying to get my breathing back to normal. If that was even possible with Blondie standing right next to me, but I was determined to try.

What felt like a millennium later, Dax began teaching the class, calling the kids into stretches and directing them to stations for weight training and cardio. I moved to the treadmill, needing to zone out for a while. Placing my earbuds in, I picked some music and lost myself in the run.

The machine beeped and slowed, breaking me out of my fog. I blinked, looking around at who had messed with my machine, and found Dax standing there, a severe frown on his face. Pulling out my earbuds, I slowed down with the device, realizing how out of breath and fatigued I was. Shit, how long had I been running?

"What?" I barked, the week of irritation and repressed anger having finally caught up with me. Not to mention how I hated him looking at me like I was the crazy one.

Dax crossed his arms. "You're going to hurt yourself if you keep at that rate. You didn't stretch enough or eat enough calories for the amount you're burning and will send yourself into a metabolic crisis if you're not careful. So, as the one with the degree in sports medicine, I'm cutting you off."

I sputtered, not used to someone watching me that closely or, quite frankly, caring. Not that I often ran irresponsibly—this had been an emotional accident.

Dax smirked, handing me a bottle of water and a towel. "You got a bit of sweat," he said, pointing to my face.

Huffing, I stepped off the treadmill and reached out to take the towel. My hand closed around the fluffy cotton material, but instead of Dax letting go of it, he pulled me toward him, causing me to fall into his chest. I sucked in a breath, looking around the room, afraid of what the kids were thinking of the interaction.

Thankfully, the room was empty, so I took a deep breath.

"They're all gone. Class ended thirty minutes ago. Reed was waiting for you, but I sent him away before I walked over to your machine. It's just you and me, Petal."

My heart raced for a new reason now.

Dax's hand skated down my side, leaving a trail of heat in its wake. His head bent down, and I closed my eyes, eager for his kiss.

But then I remembered where I was and what a kiss with Dax would mean. Stepping away quickly, I shook my head, using the towel I now held in my hands to wipe my face. Dax's face fell for a second before his smirk returned.

"You'll cave eventually, Petal. You're just dragging it out. Now, go drink a sports drink and eat something. Your ass is perfect as it is, don't be running it off."

I gathered my things, nodding as I hurried out of the room.

Dax wasn't a bomb. He was a minefield. And I didn't know if I had the fortitude to make it through without things blowing up in my face.

CHAPTER 26

Henley

THE SOUND of my alarm blared throughout my room, reminding me how much I hated living here. I had to set it for 4am in order to have any privacy. Today was too important to let the Barbie Brigade ruin it. Practice yesterday had been better, but I didn't feel confident that our team would win without a fight.

Stepping into the shower, I relished the feeling of the warm water. The stalls in the locker room were nice, but sharing it with mostly males meant I never felt I could fully relax. My showers had become a quick in and out. I'd missed this time to luxuriate in the warm water and privacy. Though, my thoughts didn't tend to linger like they wanted to now that I was focused on being quick.

My hands trailed over my naked body and the tension and heat between Dax and Reed yesterday surfaced. I'd been so tired after practice, I'd returned to the Meadows and crashed, missing out on that session with my vibrator.

Dax's words, the memory of his touch, the smell of his cologne, and the heat in his gaze had my body weeping for pleasure. Combined with the intensity of Reed and the sparks I constantly felt around him, it didn't take long for things to begin to slicken between my legs. Remembering how Fletcher kissed me, I was soon lost to the lustful thoughts.

Throwing my head back, I roamed my wet body, pretending my hands were someone else's. I tweaked my nipples with one, moving the other further south. When I reached my apex, I spread my pussy lips open and found my clit. The bundle of nerves throbbed as it anticipated what I would do. Slowly, I rolled the pad of my thumb around it, pressing one digit inside my hot center.

I was so wired a gasp escaped me at the release, a loud moan leaving my lips. My free hand fell to the tiles as I moved faster, not needing much to build my orgasm. Thinking of Dax pressing me against the window at the club, my legs shook as everything in me tightened, ready to fall over the edge.

Gasping, I thrust my fingers faster, my eyes beginning to see stars as I spasmed around myself, and I came with a moan. Panting, I tried to regain my balance as I recalled where I was. It had all felt so real, the memory pushing me to the breaking point.

The pounding on the door took me a few seconds to register, my heart beating almost as loud and fast. When I realized it was the door, I quickly rinsed and shut off the shower. It was coming from the adjacent door—Julie's. Wrapping a towel around my hair, I pulled on my robe as I walked toward.

"Yes?" I asked, opening the door. Instead of the petite blond I'd been expecting to come face to face with, I was greeted with a hairy chest.

Traveling up the chest, I pulled my robe tighter, not wanting a stranger to catch sight of my body. When I met the eyes of Coach Kuga, I stepped back in shock.

"Kurt? What are you doing here?"

The typical glare I found on his face when I was around stared down at me even more menacing at this early hour, if that was possible. His eyes trailed over me, seeming to go slower over my bare legs. I stepped back another step, feeling the need to have more space between us.

"I need to piss, and you've been in here moaning for an hour. Learn some decency, and don't hog the water," he shouted, stepping into the bathroom and my space.

With each step he took forward, I took one backward until I decided it was better to just turn and get the hell out of there. I was so shocked and confused at his presence in my Barbie nightmare house that I had nothing to say back.

Closing the door behind me, I locked it from my side, grateful it had locks on both. There was no way I wanted him to have access to my room when I was vulnerable. He'd never bothered me before, just another "bro dude" I was used to dealing with in hockey.

But encountering him in my bathroom felt under-handed and devious. Maybe I was making it into something bigger, my recent orgasmic vulnerable self unable to process this logically, but I had a weird feeling in my gut.

And my gut had never been wrong.

Dressing quickly, I was grateful Reese and I had breakfast planned together this morning. With both of our schedules, I hadn't gotten to see much of them. So, we'd decided to get breakfast together on Friday each week so we could catch up on how things were going.

When I had everything, I ran a brush through my hair and braided it quickly, glad I didn't need to look a certain way to coach. It was probably more preferable I didn't remind them I was a girl most days. Something about that soured my stomach, and I knew I'd need to look more closely at the thought at some point. Just not today.

Picking up my phone, I pocketed it and headed out the door. This weekend I needed to figure out a car situation. Things might be close on campus, but it wouldn't always be walking weather. I could hear a man's voice followed by giggling in Julie's room as I walked past, making me scurry even faster down the stairs. This was no longer a creeping mission but a get the heck out of here one.

The lights were still out in the main part of the house, so I sighed in relief as I neared the front door. I was half expecting Coco to jump out and ask me if I knew how awful my butt looked in these pants. I get it, lady. You didn't like me. But leave my ass alone. I had it on good authority that it was terrific.

I just wouldn't tell Dax his compliment had meant something to me.

Nope. There was no reason he needed to know.

Opening the front door, the dark sky greeted me as I stepped out into the beautiful Utah morning. I took a moment to appreciate the mountains as the moon shone on them. The sun would soon rise, coating the landscape in purples and pinks. I wasn't sure which version I liked the best—the mountains were beautiful from every angle.

Closing my eyes, I took in a deep inhale of the mountain air, pulling my hoodie a little tighter around me. When I let it out, I felt calmer and ready to leave the awful encounter in the bathroom behind me. I paused a few steps down when I spotted a familiar car in the driveway. The headlights flashed at me as the car door opened.

I continued my trek as the figure emerged out the door, my heart lurching at the sight of Fletcher. Skipping a few steps, I jumped into his arms when I was closer.

"Hey, Baby Shaw. I was hoping to catch you." He chuckled, his words having a double meaning.

"It's so good to see you, but what are you doing here?" I asked, wrapping my legs around his waist. Fletcher held me with ease as he leaned back against his car.

"I missed you. I haven't gotten to see you much this week, so I thought I'd try to catch you on your way to campus and take you to breakfast."

I kissed him, trying not to get lost in the act. "Ah, you're the best, Fletch, but I made plans with Reese. I haven't spent time with them and wanted to check in."

"Can I give you a ride to campus, then?"

"That would be perfect. Thank you."

"Anytime with you is better than no time."

"Are you sure you're not trying to butter me up so you can beat us this afternoon in the scrimmage?" I teased as he walked around toward the passenger door.

"Me? Never!" Fletcher chuckled, kissing me for a little longer before he placed me down on my feet. He opened the door for me, so I climbed in, smiling up at him.

While I buckled myself in, Fletcher ran around the car and opened his door. He started the car and pulled out of the driveway. Once on the road, he reached across and took my hand. It felt so natural, the way our fingers laced together. I stared at our hands, marveling at them.

"Since you're not free this morning, what about dinner and drinks at the Pub after the game? The loser has to buy?"

"Oh, now we're wagering on the game, are we?" I teased, giggling.

He shrugged, peeking over at me. "If you're up for the challenge, Coach."

"I could definitely use a night out after this week," I said, some of my exhaustion leaking out.

"Everything okay?" Fletcher asked, squeezing my hand in concern.

"Yeah. I think so. Things have just been harder to adjust to than I expected. I love that I'm getting to coach, but not all the kids are okay with it. I feel like I have to prove myself with every decision, down to what I'm wearing. Then, to top it off, my living situation hasn't been the greatest."

"The girls not nice?"

"Oh, they are. Almost *too* nice. I know I sound ridiculous, but they make it impossible to have alone time. They don't understand boundaries whatsoever, and assume they know what I want without asking. I've been forced to eat food I don't like just so I didn't make one of my roommates mad. To use my own shower, I have to wake up at 4am, and another girl likes to give me pointers and tips every chance. While they're just being friendly, it's driving me insane. I always thought I was nice, but maybe I'm not. I've never wanted to live with a bunch of introverted, anti-social people so badly in my entire life. And that's not even getting to the fact that my room practically glows even when I shut the lights off. It haunts me!"

I took a deep breath, my hands gripping his forearm as I regaled him with my troubles. My eyes were wide, and I felt sick to my stomach saying it out loud. It wasn't until my second deep breath that I realized we'd stopped.

Fletcher's hands cupped my face, pulling me closer until our foreheads met. His thumbs made soothing circles on my cheeks, calming me with his touch.

"Hey, it's going to be okay. You're under a lot of stress, and I know this can feel like a big deal, but don't forget that at the end of the day, it's just a game."

I nodded, closing my eyes, needing to hear his words. "Just a game." I scoffed, not fully believing his words.

"Yes, a game. Say it with me. It's just a game."

"It's just a game." I opened my eyes and found Fletcher staring deep into mine.

"It's just a game," he said, and I repeated it, believing it a little bit more.

When he was convinced, he kissed my forehead

before pulling back. "As for the roommates. If you want to give it another try, you could always talk with them."

I cringed, shaking my head. "I tried, but they said they wanted to help make me feel accepted. They think they're helping, but I can't take it anymore. I think I need to move out. If I need to get my own place, then I will. At this point, I'm barely sleeping, feel like I'm being force-fed my meals, and I don't really feel safe after the encounter this morning in the shower."

"What happened this morning?" he growled, making parts of my body wake up.

"Um, Kurt was there."

"In your shower?" he bellowed, making me wince. "Sorry," he said calmer. "What was Kurt doing in your shower?"

"I guess he's seeing Julie. He was in her room and interrupted my shower because he had to piss." I shrugged, the whole encounter making me numb at this point.

"Okay, okay," Fletcher said, smoothing his hands over my forearms. "I want you to do something for me, Henley. I want you to focus on coaching and doing your best today. I'll take care of your roommate situation. Let me do that for you, please?"

I started to argue that I could handle it, but the twitching in my right eye, the sourness in my belly, and not getting a good night's rest all week said otherwise. Closing my eyes, I took another deep breath. The realization I'd been doing that a lot keyed me into the fact I needed something to change. It wasn't a weakness letting someone help me. If Fletcher could improve this situation, I'd be an idiot to do it alone when I was already drowning.

"Yes, okay." I nodded, opening my eyes. Fletcher smiled, lifting his thumb to wipe away a tear I hadn't realized was falling.

"Done. Now, go have breakfast, and I'll see you this afternoon. You're going to kick ass, Coach."

He kissed me, lingering a little longer this time, reminding me how good of a kisser he was. When I pulled back, my lips felt slightly puffy.

"Thanks for the lift, Fletch."

Climbing out, I gazed over at the sun that was now rising, and I promised myself to remember that no matter what happened today—it was only a game.

CHAPTER 27

Henley

WALKING INTO THE CAFETERIA, I immediately wondered whether this was a bright idea. Despite the fact it was early, several students were milling around as they waited in line for food or for their friends. A few hockey players nodded toward me discreetly, dropping eye contact once the deed was done.

It might be easier to accept me on the ice with pads, a helmet, and a jersey so they could forget I was a female. But in the cafeteria, even dressed in a hoodie and jeans, I was very much a girl.

Well, too bad, fellas. You needed to accept that I was your coach and pull the hockey stick out of your ass.

Lifting my chin higher, I headed toward the line, determined to feel comfortable. Grabbing a tray, I was surprised at the school's set up. Though, at this point, I shouldn't have been shocked. If there was one thing Lux did well, it was to provide for the people here.

Ordering an omelet from the chef, I waited while it

was prepared at the station. Folding my arms over my tray, I peered around the room as I waited for Reese.

When their brown hair came into view, floppy, as usual, I smiled, realizing how much I was missing my sibling. At home, we didn't get much time together, but we usually made an attempt at meals. Here, I saw them at practice, but since I was in coach mode, there wasn't any sibling bonding occurring.

Lifting my hand, I caught their attention just as the chef finished my omelet. Reese headed over to me, a smile on their face.

"Hey, Sis."

"I'd hug you, but I wasn't sure if that would ruin your street cred," I said when they neared.

Reese laughed, lifting their shoulder. I took my omelet, and they looked at the options before deciding on oatmeal. Together, we headed toward an empty table with our food. It was quiet as we sat, both of us eating. It felt a little awkward between us, but that could have been my imagination or lack of sleep.

"So, how's it going? Do you like the school?" I asked when Reese hadn't said anything.

"Yeah, it's not bad. My tutor seems cool. I'm still not used to spending most of my day playing hockey."

I nodded, taking a bite. "It's wild, isn't it? You're playing great, by the way. I try not to focus on you while we're on the ice, but I've noticed how much you've grown in just this week, Reese."

Reese blushed, ducking their head as they took a bite of oatmeal. "Thanks."

"How is it having a roommate? I hope yours is better than mine."

"Brianna's great. Plus, Braden is a floor above, so we all get to hang out a lot. What's going on with yours?"

I blew out a breath, chuckling. "Do you think there's such a thing as *too* nice? It's like living in a sorority house without remembering you joined a sorority. I feel like I'm going insane because it doesn't sound as bad when I say it out loud. But I'm telling you, they're sociopathic, Reese. They're breaking me down, bit by bit." I gripped the table, leaning over my tray as I peered at my sibling.

"Geesh, that sucks. Any way to change it?"

"I hope so. Fletch said he'd take care of it so I could focus on the scrimmage for today."

"Oh, *Fletch* did, did he?" Reese teased. They batted their eyelashes, placed their head on their hands, and sighed. I swatted at them, but my cheeks heated nonetheless.

"Does this mean you're with him?" they asked.

"Yes, and no. Things are still the same. I'm being open about who I want to date."

"You know, I thought it was kind of harsh to Fletcher at first." Reese ducked their eyes, playing with the spoon in their bowl. "But I think I understand more now."

"Oh?" I asked, wiping my mouth. I wondered if this had to do with the twins.

"Yeah. My tutor, Mr. Turner, is in a relationship with some of the other staff. He's only dating one girl, but from what I've witnessed, they all seem happy. If you can be that happy, I want that for you."

"I thought you were going to say you had feelings for the twins," I said, scrutinizing their face.

Reese's head jerked up, their mouth opening in shock. I couldn't tell if they were blushing from it being the truth or the fact I'd thought they were involved with both. With Reese, it could be either. Reese shook their head but was stopped when a teenage boy dropped down next to me at the table.

"If it isn't freak 1 and freak 2," Anders said, leaning back in his chair.

"Excuse me?" I asked, turning toward him, anger boiling up.

"You heard me. My dad said your days are limited. If you don't win tonight, you're gone." He sneered at me, dropping his eyes down my body again. Whoever this kid was, he was about to learn a lesson in conse-quences.

"Whether I win or not doesn't change my employ-ment here. I'm sorry you were told otherwise. But it doesn't matter, since you won't be playing tonight."

"Yeah, right," he scoffed, rolling his eyes as he

picked something off my tray. His friends had circled around the table, making Reese retreat. Anger roared up in me. These teenage boys were not only disrespecting me, but they were also activating my momma bear.

I glanced around at the others. "It seems like Rodgers, Smith, and Richardson will be joining you on the bench. Unless you want to make a different choice?" I asked, ignoring Anders as I looked at the other three. They gulped, perhaps a little shocked I knew their names.

Two of them crossed their arms, keeping silent. But one of them edged away, taking a stand. "I'm sorry for the way they've treated you. I think you're an excellent coach. In just this week, I've improved my stick-handling so much. I'd very much like to play." His eyes darted toward Reese at the table before returning to me. "And Reese is a great player, too. I'm glad they're on the team."

His friends glared at him, and I knew how difficult what he just did was. I respected him a hell of a lot for stepping away from his friends to do what was right and put his career above peer pressure.

"Thank you, Jack." I smiled before turning to face the others, my bitch mask falling into place. "The three of you, don't even bother dressing out. And if your *father* has a problem," I started, cutting off Anders, "he knows who to call. Now, Reese and I are trying to enjoy our breakfast, and you're interrupting it."

Anders started to protest, but the other two had the good sense to pull him away before he dug his grave any further. Jack gave a soft smile before heading in a different direction. I was pleased when I saw Braden pull out a chair for him, nodding at me as he took a seat. I wondered if he had gotten up to come to my defense.

I didn't need it, but it was nice to see some of the players respected me as their coach. I looked over at Reese, who had their head down.

"You okay?" I asked softly.

"Yeah." I watched them, categorizing all their movements.

"That wasn't the first time they've said something to you, was it?" I asked.

Reese shook their head before taking a deep breath and glancing back up. "No, but it doesn't matter. This is the best school I've been to, and I'm getting to play elite hockey. I'm used to bullies."

"I'm not making it easier, am I?"

"I mean... they definitely say things about you, but I don't think you not being the coach would make it easier, either. Bullies are bullies."

The cavalier way that Reese said that made my

heart hurt. I knew my journey had been fraught with bullies along the way, but I couldn't imagine it was any easier for Reese.

"People suck, but we can't let them take the things we love," I said, needing to remind myself. "We both love hockey, and we're both great at it. How's that song go, 'the haters gonna hate, hate, hate,'" I sang badly and off-key. Reese laughed, and we finished the rest of our breakfast.

"I'm glad you're here. I've missed this. Can we make sure we do this more?" Reese asked as we headed out of the cafeteria.

I threw an arm around their shoulders. "Absolutely. Maybe you could come over for dinner or something once I get my living situation figured out. I need my sibling bonding time. Plus, we can't get behind on our favorite show."

"Bake-off," we shouted together, grinning.

"That sounds perfect, Sis." I hugged them tightly, rocking back and forth.

"Have a good day, and I'll see you this afternoon."

"Okay. Try not to crush any more kid's dreams," they teased, walking off. I saw the twins waiting a few feet away, and I waved as they waited for Reese to join them.

I checked my watch and decided it was time I paid Dmitry a visit. I'd been meaning to all week, but practice and training had been taking most of my time as I settled into the routine of being a coach, needing to plan plays, and things like knowing all the players. Thankfully, that time had come in handy this morning.

Marching into the admin building, I didn't realize how angry I'd gotten on my walk until I stomped into the main office, startling the woman at the front desk.

"Oh, I'm sorry," I said, taking a breath. "I need to speak with Dmitry."

The woman eyed me but picked up the phone, pressing a button. "Mr. Aldridge, Henley Henshaw is here to see you."

This time it was me who was startled that she knew who I was. She smiled at me smugly, giving me a wink. "He'll see you now. Second office on the left."

I began down the hall, stopping when I realized how rude I was being. "I'm sorry, I didn't catch your name."

She smiled, fixing her glasses. "It's Linda."

"Nice to meet you, Linda. Sorry for the rude charge inside. Had a bit of an altercation during breakfast with some players and needed to speak to Dmitry immediately."

"Oh, yes, that Michelson boy." She nodded, and I knew his dad had already called.

"Awesome. He already knows," I sighed. I'd hoped to get in front of it before he heard the parents yelling.

"Don't worry, Coach. Dmitry hasn't been the head of a winter sports school for years without learning to manage overbearing parents."

Chuckling, I nodded, hoping she was right. Waving, I felt a little calmer and took the last few seconds to arrange my thoughts. I knocked on the partially open door, and Dmitry called me in instantly.

"Henley," he said, smiling and directing me to take a seat. "Sounds like you've had an eventful morning."

Blowing out a breath, I nodded. "Yes. I wanted to talk with you about some students. There are a few who haven't bought into me being the head coach, I'm afraid."

"Ah yes, I hear Anders Michelson is the ringleader." He steepled his fingers but didn't elaborate.

"Yes. He and two of his friends cornered Reese and me at breakfast. They called us 'freak 1 and freak 2,' stating my days were numbered. I benched him and the others for being disrespectful."

"As you should. Jack wasn't part of it?" he asked. I had a suspicion he already knew, but wanted to hear it from me.

"I gave the three other boys a chance to decide their fate. Jack was the only one who apologized and separated himself from them."

"Hmm," he said, nodding. When he didn't say anything else, I worried I'd overstepped.

"Well, I was wondering if there was anything else

to be done about them, or I don't know, if the school was going to side with them or me," I rushed out, getting to the root of my visit. I was worried I once again wouldn't be supported by the people who were meant to.

Dmitry smiled like he'd been waiting for me to ask that question. "Who's the coach of the senior hockey team, Henley?"

"I am," I said, pushing my shoulders back.

"Then, like I told Mr. Michelson earlier, I will support the person I hired to bring this team to the next level. That's you, Henley. I know you haven't always had it easy, but we believe in you here. The times that you believe in yourself as well, that's when I see magic out on the ice. I know you feel a lot of pressure on your shoulders to prove you have what it takes to get this school out of the penalty box with the other schools and the Olympic Committee. But you're not the only one. Rely on your assistant coaches and players to put all the things you've been teaching them to use."

I sat back, stunned that he'd laid it all out like that. I felt embarrassed he could tell I'd doubted myself at times. But it was nice to hear that I wasn't alone.

Thanking him, I stood and walked out of the office, a million thoughts in my head. I could admit I also felt lighter, knowing the school and Dmitry believed in me. Now, I just had to believe in myself.

"Don't let them steal your soul." Reed's words echoed again, feeling even more imminent.

A few minutes later, I headed into the hockey arena, a fire burning within.

CHAPTER 28

Reed

HENLEY BLAZED into the locker room, a fierce expression on her face. I stopped what I was doing, losing myself as I watched her. I'd been doing that more and more over the week.

Working alongside her day in and day out was beautiful torture. I got to be around her, learning more about this woman that intrigued me. But it also meant I was near her, never able to touch or feel her.

Of course, I hoped that would change soon. The flirty banter between us was so intense, I was always surprised when I walked away that a fire hadn't started from the sparks that had flown.

Fletcher had asked me what I was doing tonight and if I wanted to join him in taking Henley to the Pub for an after-game celebration. It was still odd to think about us both dating her simultaneously, but I couldn't dismiss the opportunity. Plus, I hadn't been lying when I said it helped remove the pressure to not mess things up.

Most days, I could hold off the grief while I was on

the ice and coaching, knowing I was doing what my mother asked. At night was the hardest.

Alone in my room with no one to talk to, my thoughts would overwhelm me, and the grief made itself known. In some ways, I welcomed the pain; the memories allowed me to keep her in my life.

But it was draining, and I knew I was coming to a crossroads soon. I couldn't keep drowning in the evening and pretending I was okay during the day. It was easy to ignore the pain when I was around Henley. Even Fletcher and the kids were taking some of it away, but I knew I was on a slippery slope and would need to take action soon.

Taking a deep breath, I promised myself I'd do something about it this weekend. Right now, I wanted to be there for Henley.

Walking toward her, my eyes trailed over her body, taking her in. She was beautiful in jeans and a hoodie, her dark hair pulled back into a braid. She wrote on the whiteboard, making plays in quick succession.

"Everything okay, Hen?" I asked.

She jumped, turning and holding her heart. "Hey, Reed." She smiled and laughed. The angry part of me soothed at the action.

"Sorry, didn't mean to startle you."

"It's fine. I was in a bit of a zone."

"I see that. You're changing the plays?" I asked, leaning back against the lockers.

"Yeah. Michelson, Rodgers, and Smith are all benched. So, I need to rework some things."

"Sounds like there's a story there. Want to talk about it?"

She smiled, reaching out to touch my forearm. Her hand was warm, setting off goosebumps. "They said some things while I was having breakfast with Reese. So, I reminded them who the coach was. Michelson already had his dad call."

"Dmitry better back you," I growled, standing up straight.

I instantly regretted it as her hand fell off my arm. The only consolation was it had brought me closer, her shampoo smell tickling my nose. I stared down at her, both of us going quiet as we stared at one another. She licked her lips, and I bent down, reaching for her. I could no longer hold off the need to touch her.

When our lips met, I groaned at the sensation. Her mouth pressed into mine hungrily, and I debated picking her up and pressing her up against the locker when the door slammed closed.

Stepping back, I kept my hand on her hip as I stared down at her. Her mouth parted with an "oh," causing a smile to form. I felt so carefree at that moment, having kissed the girl of my dreams. It kept all my demons at bay, back in the shadows where they belonged.

"You benched our best player?" Kurt bellowed, breaking up the moment. We turned, finding a red-faced Kurt standing a few feet from us.

"Not our best player, but if you're referring to Anders, then yes."

"You're giving this game away, much like you give it away to any hockey guy who pays you any attention. So, when's my turn? Huh?" Kurt asked, leering at Henley. I didn't have to think about my next move.

All the demons I'd been locking up emerged while I made my trek to Kurt in a few seconds. Drawing my fist back, I let it go as Henley screamed something behind me. It was too late; the anger and grief had merged, and I struck Kurt square in the nose. Everything was in slow motion as blood poured. He didn't even have time to cover it before he fell backward. I reached out and grabbed his shirt, intent on punching him again. His body was slack and time seemed to restart as I realized I'd knocked him out.

"Fuck," I yelled as sound began to return.

"It's okay, Reed. Just lay him down."

I blinked, finding her beside me. I was worried she'd look at me like I was a monster or, worse, be afraid of me. Her face was blank, though, offering me no clues.

Turning back to the dickwad in my hands, I lowered him to the ground. Once he was safely down,

Henley rushed to the medical supplies and grabbed a towel, wetting it. She returned, placing on gloves as she cleaned him up with more care than he deserved.

Kurt came to when she finished, wincing as the pain registered. She handed him an ice pack before leaving him and looking at me. She held out her hand, but I couldn't figure out what she wanted. I was in a daze as people moved around me, too worried I'd ruined everything to think about anything else.

With a soft smile, she stepped forward and took my hand. With careful touches, she cleaned my hand free of blood and then tended to my knuckles, breaking open another ice pack and placed it on them. I stared down at my hand, not registering the pain.

Soft hands bracketed my face, pulling my eyes to hers. I could hear Kurt muttering in the background, but I wasn't focused on him. I could barely register the beautiful woman in front of me.

"Come back to me, Reed. *Please.*"

Her eyes were wide as she stared at me. I didn't know why. Hadn't she just seen me hit that guy? It was the "please" that made me pause. When a tear fell, I couldn't stay in the numbness of doing nothing. My eyes shuttered as reality returned, and I pulled her close to my body.

"You're shaking," she whispered, her hot breath falling on my neck. Her hands threaded through my hair, soothing me. I inhaled her fruity shampoo smell, the act of breathing her calming me. My body slowly relaxed as the shaking stopped, the rest of the room coming into focus. There were more voices, and I knew I couldn't hide from the consequences of my actions.

Once I let her go, she stepped back, peering into my eyes. Kissing me softly on the forehead, she turned and stood. That was when I realized I'd sunken to the floor. Glancing around, I stopped on Fletcher and Oliver, curiously watching me.

"What happened?" Oliver asked, glancing between Kurt's bloody nose and my fist. I watched as Kurt opened his mouth to spout whatever lie he'd concocted when Henley cut in.

"Kurt slipped, and when Reed went to grab him, his fist hit Kurt in the process. One of those weird things," Henley said, almost convincing me, and I'd lived the actual event. "Ain't that right, Kurt?"

He glared, but Henley narrowed her eyes. "In fact, Kurt had just told me that I was doing a great job of coaching, and he was going to sit this game out to prove how superior my skills were."

Oliver looked between Henley and Kurt, understanding crossing his face. "That's very humble of you, Kurt. Perhaps you can watch the three that have been benched, so they don't get themselves suspended for the rest of the season?"

"That sounds like a great idea," Fletcher said, stepping further into the room. "You're so intuitive, Kurt."

It was hard to tell what Kurt's face looked like since it was mostly covered by an ice pack, but I could imagine he was scowling. It wasn't uncommon for hockey players to tussle, but I had a feeling if Henley went to Dmitry with what Kurt said, it would be a different story for him. Lux took sexual harassment seriously, especially after everything that occurred last year; their policy was zero tolerance.

If he wanted to keep his job, he had to go along with the story she'd shared. I didn't like it, but I didn't want to contradict her in front of everyone.

"Yep," he said. Standing, he glared at the four of us before he stormed out of the locker room. Oliver's smile dropped when the door slammed shut, and he stepped closer.

"Now that he's gone, I want the real story. I might only be here for one more week, but I'm not going to leave you with assholes, Henley."

Henley sagged, taking a seat on the bench. Fletcher immediately went to her, wrapping his arm around her. I pulled myself off the floor and sat down on the other side, hoping I was still wanted. Her hand reached out for mine, settling my nerves.

"I was reworking the plays, speaking of, close your eyes, Fletcher. I don't want to redo them for a third time," she teased. Fletcher gave a dry chuckle but nodded, keeping his head tilted the other way. Oliver smiled and walked over, flipping the board, so they weren't showing. He crossed his arms and leaned against the opposite lockers.

"Continue," he said, staring at the three of us. If I wasn't mistaken, he had a slight crinkle in his eyes as he watched us, making me curious about what it was for.

"Michelson, Rodgers, and Smith caused some issues this morning at breakfast. So, I told them they were benched. I was reworking the plays without them when Kurt stormed in, spouting how I was blowing this game, and made some remark about how I gave it up to all the coaches and wanted to know when it was his turn or something. Well, then, um, Reed—"

"His nose met my fist, is what she's trying to say."

"Good. He deserved it," Fletcher said, giving me a nod of respect.

Oliver sighed, rubbing his hand down his face. "Okay. I'm guessing you're not going to say anything so he won't report Reed?"

"Correct," Henley said.

"Bullshit. I'll take the reprimand," I said, not wanting her to be around that douche more than necessary.

"You'd be suspended too, then, leaving me all alone. Is that really the better option?" she asked, turning toward me.

Gritting my teeth, I shook my head. She had a point, but I didn't like that the guy was getting away with making a comment like that.

"It's your call, Henley. Just be sure you're making the right one. I have a feeling he'll be more careful from here on out, but don't allow him another opportunity to take a chance."

"I'm sorry, but did you just say that it was my fault he's a sexist pig?" she blurted, standing up.

Oliver, realizing his mistake, lifted his hands, shaking his head. "Sorry, I didn't mean it that way. Just that I don't want you to be alone with him."

Henley took a deep breath, sitting back down. I glared at Oliver, and he winced, realizing he'd said the wrong thing.

"Yeah, okay," Henley said. "But right now, we need to focus on the game. It's even more important now that we put our best foot forward. Sorry, Fletch, but that means you must leave." She kissed him, standing to push him out of the room.

Fletcher smiled as she shoved him, not making it easy on her. He made eye contact when he got to the door, giving me a nod.

In that one nod, it said a lot. He respected me for

standing up for Henley. That she was under my protection now. And that I was part of something.

As Henley, Oliver, and I continued to rework the plays, focusing on how to win the game, I realized the demons weren't as close as they'd been before. In fact, they were a little quieter altogether.

CHAPTER 29

Henley

PULLING ON THE SCHOOL JERSEY, I glanced in the mirror, noticing how it looked on my frame. It had been so long since I'd worn a different jersey that it threw me off for a second.

"Looks good on you," Reed said from behind me. I glanced up, catching his gaze in the mirror. His blue eyes appeared less haunted. I'd been worried about him since the punch. It had all happened so fast that I still didn't know how to feel about it.

I understood the urge to punch that creep. Even I'd taken a step forward at his words; the culmination of Dakota's hate, the league's dismissal, and the morning shenanigans had pushed me over the ledge of bullshit I was willing to take.

When Reed had stepped in, it had felt nice. Like someone was finally standing up for me. *Me.*

It had been hot in a way I'd never considered before. I wasn't a stranger to violence playing hockey, but it was usually contained to the ice. Seeing that power to defend my honor had stirred things in me. My heart had already claimed Reed, despite the fact we hadn't talked about anything and only shared a single kiss.

As far as my heart was concerned, we'd exchanged notes with the box checked yes and were now an item.

I didn't really want to disagree. Reed Cole was a beautiful man, one I'd lusted after. To have him in my life, kissing me one second and protecting my honor the next, was a fantasy come to life.

Smiling, I smoothed the material down. "Thanks. I could say the same about yours," I teased. Reed lifted the corner of his mouth, making him even more devil-ish, if that was possible.

"You ready?" he asked, placing his hands on my shoulders.

"Yep. Let's go kick Fletcher's butt," I said, grinning widely.

Reed snorted, shaking his head at me. Grabbing his hand, I smiled up at him when he peered down at the action. A rare smile formed on his lips, doing funny things to me.

My nerves grew the closer to the arena we got. The noise of a crowd was evident, the sound almost foreign to us after a week of practice in the quiet. Reed dropped my hand when we approached the door, assessing me as he placed his hand on the handle.

"No matter what, you've been amazing this week." He dropped his head, landing a kiss on my lips before pushing open the door.

The sweet words and gestures gave me the courage to step forward with my head high. This was it. The moment of truth to see if I had what it took to be a coach.

As much as I wanted to believe it was just a game, it felt more significant to me than that. Maybe I'd put too much pressure on myself, but it wasn't every day that a female coached a senior elite hockey team—high school level or not. For every woman player out there, this was their moment, too.

Skating out onto the ice, I focused on my players as they ran the warmup Oliver was putting them through. Reese smiled as I passed, making me feel better. This was a big moment for them, too. To be equal for once in a league that liked to remind us of our differences.

Looking into the stands, I took in the audience as they gathered. Most were students and other instructors who appeared excited about the first game of the year. A few parents and townsfolk lingered, supporting the school as they mixed among the crowd. It wasn't packed, but it was fuller than I'd expected for a game that didn't count.

It was tradition, though. And in a school where tradition was important, this was a big game.

Okay, time to do some more deep breathing before I psyched myself out for the thousandth time. After a few laps, I felt better once I'd stopped looking at the spectators. I caught Fletcher watching as I made my final loop.

"It's only a game," he mouthed, reminding me of my promise earlier. Nodding, I tried to convince him I still believed it.

Oliver waved me over, so I skated toward him, realizing it was time to huddle up. Blowing out a whistle, the senior team circled around me as best they could. There were a few disgruntled faces, probably hearing about their three friends who weren't playing, but I was pleased to find most were supportive, waiting for me to give my opening pep talk.

"This is it, Blizzards. Everything you learned in camp and this week will be put to the test as you go up against your classmates. The senior/junior scrimmage is the first chance you all get to show what you know. While I might be new to some of you, I've seen you all play this week, and I know the caliber of players you are. Focus on your plays, watch for your teammates, and let's score some goals! Blizzards on three. One, two, three, Blizzards!"

They joined in, to my relief, hooting as they skated to their starting positions. The rest of the team climbed into the box, waiting for their shift. The opposing team skated toward them, the referee nodding toward Fletcher and me that it was time. With a coin toss, the seniors called heads, winning it.

"It's ours," Braden said. While most of the time it

was favorable to receive first, we'd decided during our emergency practice to start off with the puck, so we had the first chance to score, setting the momentum for us to carry.

I held my breath as the referee nodded to both centers, their sticks facing one another in the center of the rink, before he tossed the puck. There was nothing like that moment as you waited for the puck to flip through the air and land. In a split-second, it was falling, and the next, Braden had it as he pushed off with his skates, flicking the puck over to the right wing.

The junior team skated close, the defensemen closing in on the right-wing. I watched as Coleman lifted his head, noticing the approaching figure, and looked for someone to pass it to. With a back flick, they passed it to Reese. My hands tightened on the railing as two defensemen closed in on them. This was the part I hated.

While I believed in Reese's ability to play as good as any of these guys, they didn't have the muscle mass as some of the other players. Some guys purposely went after them, wanting to prove a point. Reese was quick, though, and turned, skating around a player, passing the puck back to Braden. The defensive player shoved Reese, making my blood boil, but I couldn't do anything to jeopardize their place here. So, I reined it in, focusing on Braden as he closed in on the goal.

He lifted his hockey stick and struck, the puck

sailing through the air. I sucked in a breath as it flew, the goalie's mitt reaching for it. It sailed past it and dropped into the goal in a miracle of miracles. The siren blared, lighting up red as the puck bounced on the ice in the goal.

My mouth dropped open as I turned to Reed, who looked as shocked as I did. Throwing my hands up, I pumped the air as I celebrated.

From there, the game picked up, and it was a back-and-forth match. We managed to block their next goal, but they returned the favor when Jack got a shot off. It was tied 1-1 at the end of the second period. The siren blared, alerting us to the fifteen-minute break.

Heading into the locker room, I ran through all the plays I knew, trying to find one that would work. The players grabbed some water as they sat down, waiting for my direction.

"You guys are doing well. How are you feeling out there?" I asked, wanting to take inventory.

"Tired," someone said.

"I don't remember the junior team being this good," a voice in the back stated.

"Maybe we just suck," another said.

"Okay, enough." I held up my hands, stopping all conversation. "Here's what we're going to do. It's time to implement the beanstalk."

The kids sat up, looking around at one another. "Braden, you're going to enter the zone on the right side and stay close to the boards. It's their weakest. Once you cross the blue line, you'll stop quickly. Reese and Jack, you're going to be trailing him. Whoever is open will cross the blue line, and that's who you'll pass it to, Braden. The goalie will focus on you and be off-centered to their shot."

The kids nodded, looking at the board I'd drawn on. Reese looked nervous, but I believed in them and knew they could do it when it came down to the wire.

"Alright, let's get back out there and show them what the senior team is made of! Blizzards!"

The team shouted as they gathered their things and headed back to the ice. Reed gave me a nod of approval, making me feel confident this would work.

The game started, and I bounced on my skates as I passed the box. The players were tired, and the penalties began to roll in. When Braden entered the penalty box, I got nervous now that the star player was out. I watched the clock count down until Braden could re-enter the game.

The only consolation was that the junior team was playing sloppily too. We needed to work on stamina so they could be better prepared for the third period in our real games.

The buzzer went off to let Braden out, and I nodded. It was now or never for the play. He skated quickly out there, McDaniels returning to the box. The sound of sticks slapping against the ice echoed around the stadium, the crowd yelling for their favorite players. When Braden managed to break away with the puck, I jumped up, my heart in my throat as he skated closer to the boards, our play in action.

Reese and Jack followed, blocking defenders as they neared the blue line. The goalie was focused on Braden, and a defender was hot on his heels as he crossed the blue line. Just like we'd practiced, he abruptly stopped, causing the defender behind him to crash into the boards. With a quick slap of his stick, the puck flew toward Reese, who'd managed to get open.

The goalie scrambled, realizing what was happening. But it was too late as Reese lifted their stick and slapped the puck. It sailed across the ice, the stadium collectively holding its breath as we all waited to see. The goalie dove, but it wasn't necessary.

As the buzzer for the end of the third period went off, the puck hit the goal post and bounced out. We didn't score, the game ending in a tie of 1-1.

Reese hung their head, and I worried I'd put too much pressure on them. The sister part of me rose up to make sure they were okay. But I couldn't at this moment. I had to be the coach, which meant skating out and shaking hands with the other team.

Hopping over the boards, the junior and senior teams congratulated one another on a good game as they passed by in a line. Fletcher smiled when I neared, giving me a wink and a covert slap on my ass as he passed. It helped lift my mood a little, but I couldn't deny I'd wanted to win. A tie wasn't a loss, but it wasn't a win either.

The players headed off toward the locker room; the mood was more somber than it had been at the start of the game. Reed and I followed behind them. He gave me a nod, his eyes letting me know it would be okay. I took a deep breath, knowing I needed to be there for these kids in the next moment, not myself.

So, stepping into the locker room, I channeled the coach I always needed after a loss but had never had.

CHAPTER 30

Fletcher

LEANING AGAINST MY POOL STICK, I smiled at the woman who'd quickly become my heart. She was talking with Reed about the game again, discussing a different play they could've tried in order to win. It was cute how she kept forgetting I was on the opposing side.

"Baby Shaw, no more shop talk. It's Friday night. We're celebrating, and you get free drinks."

Her nose wrinkled as she eyed me. Her dark hair was pulled up into a topknot. She wore a long-sleeve thermal shirt with jeans that had more holes than it did fabric, and yet she'd never looked more beautiful.

Because she was here in this bar with me.

"I believe it was loser buys the drinks. We tied. Neither of us won, so the loser is inherently both of us."

"The fact you can say inherently without slurring means you need more to drink." I laughed, motioning for the waiter.

Sticking her tongue out at me, she lined up her pool stick and made a shot. The cue ball smacked into the solid, sending it careening for the hole. She whooped when it sunk down into the leather depths.

"Nice," I said. "Maybe you should give me some pointers," I teased.

"You just want me to put my arms around you from behind," she said.

"Busted." Chuckling, I bent over the table, preparing to line up my shot, when my ass was smacked, making my shot go off course, hitting one of her balls into the pocket.

Reed snorted, enjoying the fact that she'd gotten me. Turning my head, I eyed her up and down, enjoying taking her in. Henley posed, placing her hand on her hip, letting me.

"Fair is fair, Baby Shaw." Winking, I stood up as she gulped, going around the table to make her next shot. She kept her eyes on me as she leaned against the table, her pool cue sliding through her fingers. I didn't take my eyes off her, wanting her to feel secure in her shot.

Just as I hoped, she dropped them to look at the ball, assuming I couldn't make it across the table to her. Looking at Reed, he was already in position and poked her sides, making her jump as she hit the ball. The ball hopped before falling dead in the center of the table.

"Why, you!" She giggled, then looked between us. "I don't know if I like the two of you teaming up."

Heat flooded me at the thought, and I glanced at Reed, finding he didn't seem to mind the image either. "Hmm, well, I can think of some other things we'd be great at together."

Henley's jaw dropped as she peered between the two of us. Her face turned bright red as she seemed a bit lost for words. The waiter dropped off the pitcher, and I filled our glasses, handing one to her. She took it eagerly, downing half of it in one go.

"Alright then," I said, taking a big gulp. Reed took a cautious sip, eyeing the two of us.

"I'll be the DD," he said, making me respect him a little more. He cared about our safety, and that spoke volumes to me.

Henley giggled, making me believe she was already feeling it. Not that it was difficult to get drunk that quick when you didn't drink that often. Reed and Henley had just come out of the pros, meaning they had followed stricter diet regimens. I, on the other hand, had been out for a while. I stayed in shape and ate well, but having a beer was no longer a no-no for me.

Focusing back on the game, it quickly descended into chaos when neither of us could make a shot due to someone interfering. I soon learned that Reed was an equal opportunist and picked on me as much as he did Henley. It was a carefree side of him I hadn't seen much of, and I was glad I was getting to.

After pool, we moved to the jukebox, taking turns playing songs and singing badly at the top of our lungs as they played. By the time we'd finished the pitcher, the place was getting crowded as locals and tourists filed in for the night to find their next hookup.

Looking at Reed, I noticed for the first time the glass of water. "You good?"

He nodded, tapping the water. "It's my third water. If anything, I need to piss. I haven't had a beer in almost two hours."

I blinked, not realizing it had been that long. Henley was swaying to the music, humming to herself. I smiled as I watched her, enjoying seeing her relaxed. She'd been so anxious and stressed since she stepped foot on campus that it was nice to see her letting go with us.

"You grab her, and I'll meet you outside," Reed said as he headed toward the bathrooms.

Sliding out of the booth, I placed cash on the table for the waiter. Walking up behind her, I put my hands on her hips and rested my head on hers.

"You ready to go, baby?" I asked, the term slipping out more seductively than I'd intended.

Henley tilted her head back at me, biting her lip, staring into my eyes. My whole body heated up with a single nod, ready for action.

Linking our fingers together, I led her out of the pub, even more eager to get her back to my place now. There was still one more surprise I had to share with her. I was a little nervous since I hadn't run it past the guys yet, but if what I believed was occurring between Henley and all of us, it would make it easier. It might also be what pushed Dax out of his hole.

The night air hit my skin as soon as the door opened, and I glanced at Henley, worried she would be too cold. It wasn't extreme temperatures yet, but the night was colder than the day had been.

"Are you cold?" I asked, standing in front of her to block the wind. I started rubbing her arms, trying to generate some heat. Her head tilted up, a beautiful smile on her face.

"Not anymore."

Leaning down, I took a moment to truly kiss her like I'd wanted to all day. Each second I was with Henley, and not worshiping her luscious lips was a crime.

The taste of the beer lingered slightly as I deepened the kiss, swirling my tongue around hers. She stepped closer, her hands gripping my shirt to pull me. The world around us faded as I cherished this uninterrupted time.

I was happy for her career path, but I would be lying if I hadn't wanted to spend more time with her—jealous of the time she was coaching. Camp had been a little better because I got to see her more. Now, we were like two ships passing. One of us coming and the other going.

It made the living situation I'd sorted even better. I stepped back and peered down at her when it became apparent we needed air. She still had that smile on her face, and I took a mental picture to always remember it. That smile had been because of me.

The door behind us opened, and I glanced up, spotting Reed. I highly doubted he'd needed that long to take a leak and wondered if he'd given us a moment together. It made me believe that this type of relationship would work if we were already being considerate of one another's needs.

"Ready?" he asked.

Nodding, I turned and pulled Henley under my arm. She stopped, reaching her other hand out for Reed. He peered at it for a second before taking it, and the three of us walked toward the car together.

"This is nice," Henley said, and as odd as it was, I didn't have any reason to disagree. Because it *was* nice.

Tossing the keys to Reed, I waited until he unlocked the Jeep, and I opened the front door for Henley. She kissed my cheek as she climbed in. I waited until she had her seatbelt buckled before I closed the door and climbed in the back. It was a bit strange riding in the backseat of my own vehicle, but for safety purposes, I'd suck it up.

The drive was quiet, the streets barren, as we

returned to the house. I wasn't surprised that Dax's car was gone when we pulled in, but it made me sad. I hated seeing him hurting, but I had no intention of giving up Henley. He'd either get on board or lose out on knowing a great person.

The three of us walked into the house, and I turned on some lights, making the place feel homier.

"Oh, Henley. I talked with Dmitry, and we found a solution to your housing issue. You can move out tomorrow."

She'd sat down on the couch and, at my statement, turned, looking at me with wide eyes. "Really? Where am I going? Is it bad? Do I have to live with the students now since I couldn't hack it with the big girls?" she whined.

Reed snickered behind me as he walked around and sat down with her. He lifted her feet up into his lap, taking off her shoes.

"I hate to break it to you, but you won't be living with girls."

She nodded slowly, trying to decipher my statement. "Okay, so on my own? I hope I'm not far from you guys."

"Nope. You'll have three roommates. And I think you'll like the distance."

"Three roommates..." she said, trailing off as she tried to figure out where she was living. "Wait, does that mean?" she asked, her eyes hopeful.

"The room between Reed's and mine is all yours, Baby Shaw."

A scream erupted out of her, and she leaped up, wrapping her arms around me as she leaned over the back of the couch. Her front was plastered to Reed's face, and I chuckled as he struggled to know what to do. She let go, falling back to the couch and sighing.

"Oh, this is going to be the best. Speaking of, can someone go with me to get a car tomorrow? I'd go on my own, but they always try to oversell me, which gets on my nerves. It's just that I'm tired of walking around campus. I need some wheels," she rambled.

"I can take you," Reed offered before I could. "While we're out, I wanted to see if you'd go with me to the animal shelter. I was thinking of adopting a cat. That is, as long as no one is allergic?" he asked, looking between the two of us.

"A kitty! Yes!" Henley nodded, clutching her hands to her chest. "This is turning out to be the best evening, despite losing. I'm kind of mad at you, Fletcher, but not really because I'd never want to win if I didn't earn it, but why did you have to be so good? Huh?" she leaned up, placing her boobs in Reed's face this time as she pointed her finger at me.

Reed groaned, shifting his legs, and I knew there was only so much torture he could take. Apparently, the rest of the beer was hitting Henley, making her an amusing, touchy-feely, buzzed person.

"Time to get you to bed, Baby Shaw. Come on, before you break something of Reed's that he might need."

Reed rolled his eyes at me, punching me in the arm. "You try to control yourself," he mumbled. Then, as if he had just realized something, he smirked, patting my shoulder. "Nah, good luck."

Shaking my head, I walked around the couch and lifted Henley into my arms. She giggled at the movement as she played with my hair.

"Your hair is so soft, Fletch." Resting her head on my shoulder, I wondered if she'd even be awake by the time I got her to my bed.

Getting her to change her top into something comfortable was akin to dressing one of my nieces, and I was glad when she finally laid down. Slipping under the covers, Reed's words began to make more sense as she snuggled up close, her hands roaming me.

Yep. This was torture.

CHAPTER 31

Henley

AT SOME POINT during the night, I woke up with an intense need to pee. Crawling out of bed, I spread my hands out in front of me, hoping not to bump into anything. Fletcher's room was pitch-dark, and when I tripped over a random shoe, I vowed to make him get a nightlight and clean his room if he wanted any more overnight visits. Though, I could always just go back to my own bed.

A giddy squeal erupted out of me at the realization I was free of the Barbie Brigade and the cotton candy nightmare. Fletcher grunted behind me on the bed, and I froze, covering my mouth. I had no idea why, but it felt essential for my escape to the bathroom. There was no way I was making it across the sea of trip hazards to his bathroom. Hallway one it was.

The feel of the metal doorknob made me fist pump in the dark as I mimicked a crowd going wild at my victory. Maybe I was still a little drunk. The urge to pee reminded me of my destination, and I quickly opened the door and stumbled out into the hall. The hallway was a little brighter, a light shining from somewhere.

Finding the half bath, I almost did another celebratory cheer but decided better of it; my bladder was no longer okay with my antics.

Once I'd relieved myself, I washed my hands and stared at myself in the mirror. I was wearing a shirt of Fletcher's, so I pulled up the neck of it, inhaling his fabric softener. It smelled like him, and wearing his shirt made me feel closer to him in a weird way. Sighing, I dropped it back down and turned off the light as I opened the door.

Instead of open space, my face smacked into a naked chest. Assuming it was Fletcher coming to find me, I ran my hands up, feeling all his perfect muscles beneath my fingers. When my hands reached his neck, I felt long hair as my fingers began to tangle in it.

Hands slid around my waist, pulling me closer to the half-naked body. I gasped as my brain caught up with what my hands knew to be true. Looking up, I could vaguely make out Dax's face as he peered down at me, a light further up acting as a halo around his head.

"Mm, Petal. You're the perfect midnight snack."

"Eep!"

Dax chuckled, his hands lifting my shirt and touching the skin on my back. My brain shut down the way it always did around Dax. He was a hot guy aphrodisiac, and I was high on him.

"Henley?" a voice asked further down the hall,

breaking the spell that Dax had me under. The sound of feet moving closer had Dax finally letting go and stepping back.

"To be continued, Petal." He stepped into the bathroom, shutting the door, and left me in the hall with Fletcher.

Grimacing, I peered up slowly at Fletcher, expecting him to be upset. Instead, he watched me, an understanding look on his face.

"You good?" he asked, reaching out his hand.

Nodding, I swallowed, trying to find my words. "Yeah. I had to go to the bathroom. And your room is really dark. I tripped over something," I rambled, taking his hand and letting him lead me back to his room.

"Hmm. I guess I'll have to correct that, then. I hope to have lots of Henley sleepovers in my future."

The heat in his eyes ramped up the arousal I'd been feeling all night. In perfect harmony, our bodies moved closer to one another. The door closed, and I jumped up, wrapping my arms and legs around Fletcher. He caught me, smirking at me as he moved his head closer.

"I've been dreaming about this moment," he whispered. His eyes were full of warmth and sincerity.

Running my hands through his hair, I yanked him the last few millimeters to my mouth. Desire raced through me as his lips moved over mine. I tugged on his strands, my hands seeking more of him.

I felt us moving, but I was unaware of the direction, too consumed with his mouth on mine. Gasping, Fletcher used the moment to sweep his tongue in, gently massaging mine with his. Our faces felt fused together, the thought of separating too much to bear.

The world tilted briefly before I met the soft mattress. His warm hands moved up my body, sliding effortlessly under the shirt. I arched up, meeting them as I hooked my legs around him more. My pussy throbbed, my clit a beacon for him to touch. When the shirt made it up to my neck, I released his lips and pulled away long enough to toss it off.

Fletcher paused, blinking as he took in my naked chest.

"You okay?" I asked, slowly threading my fingers through his hair.

He nodded, dropping his mouth to my nipple. I wasn't expecting it, gasping at the contact. I'd always been self-conscious of my nipples, afraid they were too big or weird. But the way Fletcher was worshiping them had me re-evaluating my fear. The peaks were sensitive as he swirled his tongue around them, pulling back to trace his thumb around my areola.

Gasping, I bucked up into him, my head thrashing against the sheets. "Holy crap, what are you doing to me?" I asked.

"Do you want me to stop?" he asked, lifting up. His eyes bore into mine, waiting for me to answer.

"Fuck, no," I cursed, reaching to pull him back down. He chuckled, his hot breath hitting my sensitive peak as he returned to work.

My body tensed up, the pool of tension building in my stomach. Fletcher watched me, gauging my reaction as he twirled his tongue around one nipple and passed his thumb over the other. He had me wound up so quickly that I almost didn't believe what was happening.

Rocking my lower half, I gripped his hair as I began to convulse. My body was in overdrive as I came from his nipple play alone. I let out a breathy moan as I crashed back down.

Fletcher smirked, moving further down my body to grip my panties, ripping them off me before I could protest. His beard met my thighs in the next two seconds, rubbing against my flesh in the most delicious way. When his tongue licked up my core, I whimpered.

"You're so wet for me, baby."

His words made me wetter, and I realized it was what I'd always been missing from my other lovers— outside of Dax. He had a mouth so dirty it would make a porn star blush.

I didn't have time to think about Dax when Fletcher's mouth started sucking on my clit, his tongue twirling around it as he flicked it against my throbbing bundle. He demanded all of my attention, and for good reason. My thoughts left me as I melted into a puddle of goo. His fingers, mouth, and tongue paid reverence to me. Fletcher made me feel like a goddess with the adoration he bestowed upon my altar.

After a third orgasm, I lay on the bed, panting. My limbs were noodles as I tried to catch my breath. Fletcher trailed his fingers up my legs, enjoying watching me twitch with each pass. When I caught my breath, I rolled and pushed him down onto the bed.

"My turn," I demanded. Fletcher smiled, laying back with his hands behind his head.

"Do your worst."

Running my fingers over his pecs, I felt every muscle, taking my time to kiss and massage them as I straddled him. His cock was hard against my ass, which I occasionally would rock on, edging him with each tease. His moan every time was music to my ears.

When I made it down to the boxers he wore, I teased my fingers along the waistband, his breath coming fast now. I scooted down, his dick tenting the tight material. Running my hand over him, I gauged his size. Easing down his boxers, I took my time, kissing each inch I revealed. I was drawing it out, wanting him to be as desperate as I'd been.

At the first sight of his thick cock, I gave in and pulled off his boxers the rest of the way. His rigid member sprung up, ready to be out of the tight chamber.

Swallowing, I licked my lips as I stared at him, now free. Taking my hand, I gripped the base, my fingers unable to touch. Squeezing, I stroked him once, rubbing my thumb over the tip, smearing his pre-cum. Bending over, I stuck out my tongue and licked up the bead, the salty taste rolling over my tastebuds.

"You win, Henley. I. Need. You. Now."

Fletcher rose up and rolled us around, putting me back on the bottom. He reached into his bedside table and, in under five seconds, had a condom out and on. Hooking my legs into his arms, he bent down and positioned himself at my center.

Staring deep into my eyes for half a second, I felt the space of a lifetime pass between us in that moment. This wasn't a one-night stand or even a casual thing. This moment between us was something beautiful, and I couldn't sully that by calling it anything other than that.

Fletcher Cromwell was going to wreck me in the best ways.

As he pushed into me, my walls stretched to accommodate his girth. I sucked in a breath from the feeling of finally having him in me and the knowledge that this was something real.

I could feel that now. I could understand how different my experiences in the past had been from this.

We weren't just using one another to meet a need; we were expressing things only our bodies could say. I knew I'd never be able to just have sex again—not when I knew how much that emotional connection mattered.

My body eagerly accepted him, pulling him all the way in. His arms bracketed my face as he bent down. We were both still for a second, adjusting to the feeling. Fletcher raised his palm, brushing my hair back.

"You're so beautiful, Henley."

Leaning down, he kissed me. Our lips touched, and he rolled his hips forward, spearing me an inch deeper. Gasping, his tongue sought out mine as his hands threaded through my hair, tugging my head back. I struggled to focus on him as he pumped in and out, but his kisses made me dizzy. It was intoxicating, feeling this high on him—his touch, his kiss, his cock.

"Yes," I breathed before my mouth was covered by his again.

My nails ran down his back, his muscles bunching underneath my fingers as I gripped him to me. His thrusts were so powerful I could feel the bed shifting with each one. His pelvic bone hit my clit, making my toes tingle. I'd already orgasmed so many times I didn't know if it was possible again. Not to mention, I didn't tend to orgasm from only vaginal stimulation.

My body was worn out, though, every nerve ending feeling sensitive. My nipples brushed against his pecs, my clit rubbed his pelvis, and his cock hit me so deeply, I couldn't think.

Thoughts completely left me as I was overloaded by sensations, and I became a firework. Everything in my body sparkled as Fletcher thrust into me.

"Oh, God," I screamed, unable to hold it in. Part of me was aware there were two other men in the house, but I was too far gone to care. Everything in me exploded as the waves of an orgasm crashed into me. My muscles convulsed, my pussy walls tightening and squeezing him even harder.

Fletcher cursed, stalling above me as he mumbled incoherently. My mind blacked out as I continued to be bombarded with sensations. Opening my eyes, I found Fletcher leaning over me, wiping tears from my eyes.

"You okay?" he asked, concern etched in his voice.

"Mm-hmm," I mumbled, unable to form words just yet. I smiled, caressing his face with my hand.

"You passed out for a second and began to cry. It made me worried I'd broken you," he admitted. His cheeks heated, and I brushed my thumb under his eye.

"Nope, not broken. Though, I'm not sure that can ever be repeated. That was epic," I whispered.

Fletcher relaxed, his shoulders dropping, and he laid his head on my bare chest. I combed my fingers through his hair for a few seconds. I started to drift off, but forced myself up and cleaned quickly, returning to the warm bed and the man in it.

CHAPTER 32

Dax

AFTER A TORTUROUS NIGHT OUT, I'd come home to find Henley half-naked in my hallway. Again, it felt like the universe was sending me a message. I just wasn't sure what it was anymore.

By the time I emerged from the bathroom, I could already hear what they were up to behind Fletcher's door. Gripping the edge of the doorframe, I debated going to the gym and working out this aggression with the added bonus of not having to hear them.

My breathing escalated as I stood there, my heart beating rapidly. When Henley let out a breathy moan, I was incapable of leaving her. Stepping the rest of the way into my room, I quickly shut the door and locked it, not wanting anyone to bear witness to what I was about to do.

Stripping off my boxers, I lay flat on the bed, my cock already hard as a rock. From the moment I'd touched her and felt her luscious ass in my hands, I'd been ready to go. Hearing her now brought me back to that night in the club.

It didn't take much thought for me to grip my erection, squeezing the head for a second before stroking my length. Fuck, this was better than porn. Hearing Henley, I could imagine it was me as I recalled our night.

Visions of her pussy filled my mind, my hand stroking faster as I remembered how she tasted on my tongue. I had to give it to Fletcher; whatever he was doing, Henley was thoroughly enjoying it. Her moans and whimpers echoed around my room, driving me to the brink.

I pictured her spread out on that pool table and then up against the glass, the club below us. I remembered how soft her skin had felt, how I couldn't touch her enough. Her smell invaded my nostrils, intoxicating me with her scent.

Everything Henley swirled around me—the past and the present converging together. Quicker than I thought possible, I jerked up, my hand pumping quickly as I began to come. The liquid sprayed across my stomach as I stared at it in shock.

"Holy shit," I gasped, my cum still spilling out.

When my balls felt drained, I fell back on the bed as I listened more. I might not be in the room with them, but I felt like I was part of it. Something tugged at the back of my brain, but since all the blood was elsewhere, I couldn't grab hold of it.

Getting up, I took a few tissues to wipe off the cum and tossed them into the trash. Pulling on a pair of pajama pants, I stepped out into the hallway and walked toward the bathroom again. I took a minute to clean myself better, splashing water on my face. I could still hear Henley, the sound more of a welcome tune now instead of the torturous one it had been minutes before.

I didn't want to ponder why, so I quickly washed my hands and headed back to my room. As I lay in bed an hour later, the sounds of their lovemaking having ceased, I could finally pinpoint what my mind had been trying to tell me.

I hadn't been jealous.

And with that thought running circles around my brain, I fell asleep.

LEAVING THE HOUSE EARLY TO GET STARTED ON MY DAY, I'D managed to avoid everyone. I didn't have anything pressing to do, but it was more about escaping my own feelings and not wanting to think about Henley for a while.

I knew it was futile, but I was giving it my best, at least.

Snowboarding had become a passion of mine since I'd moved to Utah. It was one of those sports that I could lose myself in it, making it the perfect time waster for today. The school had an excellent course, and I was eager to blaze my way through it. Tightening my goggles, I nodded to a few of the snowboarders already on the slope as I walked over.

"Hey man," Soren Stryker, one of the best snowboarders in history, said.

"How's the powder today?" I asked, twisting my arms.

"It'll be better once we get some fresh snow. It's not too bad yet, though. You got here early," Chloe added, snapping on her board. "Catch ya at the bottom." She took off, snow flying up in her wake.

Shaking my head, I smiled, already feeling freer from being up here. Soren tapped my shoulder before descending himself, a yell of joy leaving him as he swished through the snow.

Once he was clear, I snapped on my board and rocked forward, letting my momentum take me. My board sliced through the snow as I twisted, leaning forward. A small jump loomed ahead, so I bent my knees and grabbed my board. Taking flight, I did a slight rotation before straightening and landing back on the snow. The adrenaline rush from landing had me throwing my arms up into the air.

After a few more jumps, I reached the bottom; my heart rate was quick, and my breathing was heavy, but I felt alive. I went down one more time before I moved over to the halfpipe. Chloe was still going down the main course, but a while ago, Soren had come over to the halfpipe too.

I stood back and watched him work, constantly amazed by how precise he was. Soren made it look effortless. When he finished a tricky flip, a double cork, I watched as he ran over to a guy and girl who'd been watching. He tossed off his mask and stepped out of his board, picking up the girl and kissing her. When he was done with her, he turned to the guy, laying another kiss on him. I watched them for a few seconds, realizing it was the ice-dancing couple, Rey and Sawyer. So why had Soren just kissed them both?

I didn't know the answer, so I focused on the halfpipe, working on my momentum as I went from one side to the next. Building enough to be able to get some lift, I bent my knees and held the board for as long as I could before landing. I did it a few more times before my legs burned. I checked my watch and noticed I'd been out here for a few hours. No wonder my legs felt like I'd run a marathon. Because I had—in snow.

At the lodge at the bottom of the mountain, I changed out of my wet clothes and into the ones I'd worn here. The lodge had lockers you could rent out for the season to leave all of your gear. They even had a dry-cleaning service to wash your snowsuit when needed. Considering I didn't want to deal with any of it, it was perfect for me. Low maintenance with easy access.

Heading out of the locker room, I knocked into Soren, who was coming in.

"Hey, man. You looked great out there," he said, stepping into the locker room.

I stepped back into the space, allowing the door to shut behind me. I didn't know why, but it felt important to talk to Soren more.

"Uh, yeah. It felt good to let go."

Soren nodded as he began to strip off his snowsuit. I shuffled my feet, feeling like I wanted to ask him something, but not sure how to say it.

"You okay?" he asked, shaking out his hair. It was weird watching him. I blinked, realizing I was probably throwing off some weird vibes.

"Yeah, sorry. Just something on my mind."

"Anything I can help with, Dax?" Soren stopped and turned, giving me his full attention.

My mouth moved before my brain caught up to what I wanted to know. "You're dating two people," I blurted, my cheeks red.

Soren chuckled, assessing my face as he nodded. "I am."

"And they're dating other people?" I asked, needing to know all the information.

"Not exactly." He turned that time, pulling his pants off and sitting on the bench. "We don't date anyone outside of our family. And only some of us are dating others. Sawyer, she's with all of us, Henry is with me, and Oliver and Ty are together. Three of the guys are only with Sawyer."

I blinked, trying to keep it straight in my head. Soren grinned as he changed his clothes. I sat down on the bench, my mind feeling fuzzy.

"How did you come to this type of relationship?" I asked.

"Well, I'm pansexual, and I always wanted a relationship that included a guy and a girl, so it wasn't that much of a stretch for me. Some of the other guys had a harder time, but when the option of dating Sawyer or not was presented to them, they decided to see where things led."

"Huh." I rubbed my jaw as I thought about everything. "I thought Henley was crazy for wanting to date my roommate and me, but maybe she wasn't."

"You know, if you're questioning things, you might want to speak to Rhett. He was the first to like Sawyer and bring the idea to the rest of us. He researched and wrestled with the idea, so he could probably help you better."

"Rhett." I nodded. "Okay, thanks, Soren. I didn't mean to pry into your relationship."

"No worries, Dax. Always here to lend an ear when needed. I'll catch you later." He stood, heading toward the shower, and I took that as my cue to leave.

I didn't feel ready to face Fletcher yet, so I drove around town, ending up at the coffee shop. Sitting in the back, I browsed the book section and took sips of my coffee. Nothing was catching my eye, but it helped calm my racing mind. I couldn't quit replaying last night over and over in my head.

Hearing Henley's pleasure and taking my own from it.

In the light of day, I wanted to feel grossed out about it. But it was Henley, and nothing with her felt sordid.

It was difficult for me to admit that I liked her more than I wanted to. But it was becoming even harder to deny. Could I do this type of relationship she wanted? Would it be better than being left behind?

At first, I'd been worried I wasn't good enough on my own, my old relationship scars flaring to life. I wanted to be chosen, to feel good enough to be some-one's person.

But just as I knew there were a million different ways to heal someone's body, I was beginning to accept there were multiple ways to have a relationship.

And perhaps, heal a heart.

Finishing the last of my coffee, I tossed the paper cup into the trash as a plan formed. I wasn't entirely in yet, but I was willing to offer an olive branch to see how things played out.

Crossing the street, I headed into the small grocery store to pick up a few items. I didn't know how to make a lot of meals, but my mother's lasagna was one of the things I could do well. Grabbing pasta, spices, marinara, and some garlic bread, I headed to the checkout with my items.

This felt right. This moment and change of direction was the path I was meant to take. I didn't know how I would do it just yet, but at least I felt I was finally on the right track.

"Have a good evening," the cashier said, her hand grazing mine as she handed me back my change. I smiled, not even cataloging her as I mentally worked through the steps I needed to complete when I got home.

The air outside felt more alive, the mountain air filling my lungs with a sense of purpose. I was practically skipping to my car, excited to get home and start the preparations.

A shadow stepped out from beside my car, stopping me in my tracks. Gareth loomed large in front of me with a menacing frown.

"I'm going to enjoy this," he said, stepping closer. I didn't have time to think as arms grabbed me from behind, pinning me in place.

CHAPTER 33

Henley

CURLING INTO FLETCHER'S ARMS, I heaved a sigh of relief at how nice it felt to be right where I was. His arm brushed up and down my back, and I felt an overwhelming sense of calm. Smiling against his stomach, I tilted my head up as I opened my eyes.

"Good morning, baby," he said, his voice a little deeper with sleep.

"Good morning, Fletch." I kissed the skin closest to my mouth.

"Mm, if you keep that up, it will be even better."

Giggling, I moved back and sat up, brushing my hair from my face. "As much as I would very much like to repeat everything, I have an appointment at the car dealership."

"Ah, right." Fletcher pouted, making me laugh even more. I didn't think he realized how adorable he was with his big lip sticking out.

"What are your plans today?" I asked, turning on the bed. I grabbed the first clothing item I could find and put it on. "Is cleaning your room on your list?" I teased, turning to look at him.

Fletcher gave a sheepish grin, shrugging. I could've sworn he also blushed.

"Yeah, I've been meaning to get around to that." He rubbed his jaw, shrugging.

Leaning across the bed, I pushed some of his hair out of his eyes. "I'm just teasing you. Though I did stumble on something last night, so it might be a tripping hazard until you get that night light."

"Ah, yes. Night light. I'll grab one. We can head over to your room and pack up your stuff when you get back. I want you out of there *tonight*."

"I will not fight you on that."

Kissing him, I got lost in it for a second. It was so easy to kiss Fletcher and forget everything else that was going on.

"Mm, you better go before I pull you under the covers," he purred, seriously making me question my plans.

With strength I didn't know I possessed, I pulled away and pulled on the rest of my clothes. I'd need to stop and get something new to wear. As it was, I was commando. No one wanted to wear dirty underwear twice.

Spotting one of Fletcher's hoodies, I snagged it as I finger-combed my hair. Tipping upside down, I pulled it up into a high bun before standing back up and pulling the hair tie around it.

"Whoa, that's impressive," Fletcher said from behind. Chuckling, I turned and blew him a kiss.

"Bye." I waved, opening his door and peering out into the hallway. When it was clear, I took a deep breath. I wasn't avoiding Dax, but after the grope session in the bathroom, it felt as if I was only an inch from stepping on the release valve before the whole minefield blew up in my face.

Determining it was safe, I stepped into the hall and closed the door behind me. Reed was in the kitchen, a smug smile on his face, when he spotted me.

"Hey," I said, waving. I didn't know why I was being shy all of a sudden. It had nothing to do with the fact that he probably heard me orgasm a million times.

Walking toward the coffeepot, I poured myself a cup, glad someone in this house knew how to make it. I pretended to busy myself as I prepped it, taking my time before I spun around and leaned against the counter, taking a sip.

Reed hadn't wavered in his stare, his blue eyes intense as he waited me out. My cheeks heated even more, and I finally caved.

"Um, sorry about last night. If you know, I was too loud, or whatever." I cringed, wanting to hide my face, but Reed had a way of making you hold eye contact, even if it felt uncomfortable.

"Don't be. It was the best soundtrack."

I didn't know how it was possible, but my cheeks heated even more. I sputtered as my brain tried to understand what he was saying.

"Um, so... um." I shook my head, took a few steps to the table, and fell into the chair. "I'm sorry. What are you saying?"

Reed leaned on his forearms. "Do you need me to spell it out for you, Hen? The sounds of your moans had me so rock hard that the only relief was to pleasure myself to you coming for hours."

My breath stopped as I stared at Reed. I licked my lips, debating jumping across the table and seeing what else he'd say. It was even more obvious now that I had a thing for men who knew how to get me wet with just their words.

I leaned forward, the wood of the chair creaking with the effort. Reed smiled, the act sending shivers down my spine.

"You ready to go?" he asked, slapping the table as he stood up.

I fell forward, panting, and realized what he'd done. Groaning, I tossed back the rest of the coffee, not caring that it burned my throat on the way down. I needed the pain to remind myself I couldn't jump on the men in this house at my every whim—no matter how much I wanted to. Boundaries were good for a reason.

Reed grabbed his keys, motioning for me to walk in front of him through the door. I walked by closely, brushing against him as I did. Trying to get him back for leaving me wanting a few seconds ago.

He groaned, my mission accomplished. Wearing my own smirk this time, I skipped as I walked around to the passenger side door.

I ran into Meadows and changed without alerting any of my roommates. The rest of the ride was quiet as Reed maneuvered through town, following the GPS as it navigated us toward the car dealership. When we pulled in, I turned to him with a serious expression.

"I already picked out the one I want. I just want to take a test drive and make sure it handles nicely. They have it priced four thousand over market value, so I'm hoping to get them down at least two. If they start to hassle me, that's when I'd appreciate your man stare."

"Man stare?"

"Yeah. The one that says you have a penis and therefore know more about cars than me."

Reed lifted an eyebrow, the corner of his mouth lifting up as he stared at me. "The what look?" he asked.

"That one right there," I said, pointing to his face.

Reed grunted, the corners of his mouth tilting up slightly. Giggling, I leaned over and kissed him, surprising him. Pulling back, I caught the slight blush on his cheeks, warming my insides.

"Okay, I'll be sure to remember that," he said.

Opening the door, we climbed out and walked around the car lot. I spotted the blue SUV I'd been eyeing and approached it. After a few seconds of looking at it, I felt the car salesman draw near.

"You've spotted a good one. There's a lot of horsepower behind it. Are you sure you can handle it?" he asked, giving me a lecherous look.

"Yep. This is the one I want. I'd like to take it for a drive."

He continued to stare, glancing at Reed once before returning to me. "Yeah, okay."

Rolling my eyes, I turned back to Reed. I was surprised when I found him fuming, his fists clenched tightly.

"Hey, you okay?" I asked, stepping closer.

"Do you experience men like him often?" he asked, his eyes not wavering.

"Oh, him?" I asked. "More than I'd like. It's part of being a woman. I wasn't joking about the penis comment. There are men and women who won't take you seriously, no matter what you say. It's infuriating, but if I focused on how mad it made me, I'd always be angry, and that feels like a punishment against myself and not them."

Reed continued to stare but let out a breath, closing his eyes as he nodded. "Okay. I know I can't fix this for you. So, I'll be mad on your behalf and help when I can."

Stepping closer, I pulled his shirt toward me, so he bent down, giving him a slow kiss. When I drew back, his eyes had softened, the anger dissipating slightly.

The car salesman returned shortly after, and I took the SUV out for a drive. Reed was able to intimidate him enough to let us take it without him, making the experience more enjoyable. After some haggling and one stare from Reed, I signed on the dotted line at the price I wanted. I now had my own vehicle, meaning no more walks about campus for this hockey coach!

After a quick stop back by the house, Reed dropped off his car so he could ride with me in mine, stating he wanted to spend as much time with me as possible. I couldn't argue with him about that logic.

Before we got to the animal shelter, we stopped by the pet store to pick up a cat carrier, food, and a few toys I couldn't resist. I hadn't even met the cat yet, but I knew I would love it.

"I'm not sure who's more excited about this. Me or you," Reed said as we debated over a collar.

"I've never had a pet before," I stated, looking at him. "So, I guess I'm living vicariously through you."

"Then it can be our cat," Reed said, watching me.

"Isn't that a little bit fast? Owning a pet together?"

Reed shrugged, finally deciding on a black collar

with a little bling. "I've learned this year that sometimes you have to do things your own way. If you wait for things to happen to you, then you'll miss out on them."

His eyes closed for a second, his voice a little solemn, and I wondered what had happened to him. He looked sad, and I wanted to improve it, but it seemed like something I couldn't fix with a hug.

"You're right. So, a house cat, then? We can all be its owners." I said.

"Yeah, that sounds perfect."

Checking out, we thanked the employee for their help and made our way to the animal shelter. Cats and dogs filled the space, their cries making me want to adopt them all.

"The kittens are on this side, and our older cats are on this one," a worker said, leaving us to our search.

"Do you want a kitten or an older cat?" I asked, looking in between the two areas.

"I was thinking of an older cat. One that needed a home. Everyone always goes for the kittens, and the older cats get left behind."

"I like that," I said, taking his hand and walking into the older cat sanctuary.

We peered around at the cats as they lazed on cat mounds, climbed up cat towers, and played with balls. They didn't really give us the time of day, just watching us curiously from their perches.

"Any of them calling out to you?" I asked, staring

around. It was a bit overwhelming looking at all the cats that needed homes.

"That one," he said without any hesitation. I followed his line of sight, spotting a giant gray cat that sat on top of a tower. The cat was licking its paws, not paying us any attention.

Walking closer, I slowly reached a hand out, and it stopped what it was doing. The cat watched me for a few seconds before dipping his head down, allowing me to pat it.

The fur was soft, and a loud purr erupted out of its chest. "Oh, yes, this one," I said, staring back at Reed.

The worker returned, telling us about our new cat and how she'd been at the shelter for almost a year. It made me happy that we were getting her. She needed a home as much as we did.

"What's her name?" I asked as we were led up to the counter.

"Lady Sterling," she said, the name fitting the cat.

Twenty minutes later, Reed and I walked out with Lady Sterling in the cat carrier, smiles on our faces. As we walked along the sidewalk back to the car, I stopped dead in my tracks when I spotted a body lying next to a familiar car.

CHAPTER 34

Henley

EVERYTHING STOPPED as I tried to breathe. In the next second, I took off, rushing toward the prone figure. My brain knew who it was, but my heart wasn't willing to believe it yet. Their blond hair was sprawled out across the pavement, along with a small pool of red.

"No, no, no," I screamed, dropping the bag to the ground. I kneeled on the pavement, the concrete pressing into my knees. The world slowed down in that second. My hands hovered over his head as I tried to figure out what to do. Why did basic first aid seem to leave me the moment I needed it?

Everything sped back into focus when the body moaned, and I blinked as it all rushed toward me. Bile crept up my throat, and I swallowed to keep it down. It wouldn't do well for me to get sick at this moment. I spotted Reed next to me, pressing something against the wound on his head. His eyes met mine, worry swirling in them.

"Check the rest of him to see if anything is broken," he directed, nodding toward his body.

I felt calmer having something to do, so I scanned his body and lifted his shirt to check for other injuries. There was bruising along his torso, and I worried he might have internal bleeding. My fingers lightly touched his ribs, but I felt nothing out of place. Touching his legs, I didn't find anything broken or any other bleeding. I sighed in relief, the feeling of my heartbeat returning to me.

"He might have internal bleeding, but nothing seems broken," I reported to Reed. When I glanced back at Dax's head, his eyes blinked open.

"Dax!" I moved toward him, searching his eyes. He groaned, his tongue coming out to wet his lips. "Dax, can you hear me?" I asked, leaning closer. "What were you doing? What happened?" I asked rapidly, then realized it didn't matter. He started moving, reaching out toward me, his eyes wide as he looked around.

"Don't move," I said, pressing my hands on his chest to keep him down. I brushed his hair away as I stared into his eyes. "We got you." Dax looked up, finding Reed over his head.

"Lasagna," he whispered, and I bent down to figure out what he was saying.

"Lasagna?"

"I wanted to make it for you," he whispered, reaching up to grasp my hand. Something about the statement made a tear develop in my eye.

"He must've hit his head harder than I thought. We should call 911."

"No ambulance," Dax wheezed. "Take me to campus."

Reed and I shared a look, unsure if we should listen to the possibly concussed and bleeding man or not. Shaking my head, I peered down at Dax, his hand squeezing mine.

"Please. The facility there is top-notch," Dax said again, a little stronger. "It looks worse than it is." He slowly sat up, holding his side. Reed kept the material pressed to his head, but it seemed the bleeding had stopped. I glanced toward Reed again, and he seemed as unsure as me. Deciding it was better to get him looked at, period, I would agree to go along with the center for now and let them be the bad guys if it was more serious.

"Okay, as long as you agree to go. You can't just brush this under the rug, Dax. I don't know what happened, but it's not okay. You're hurt, and something could be wrong!" I shouted, realizing how scared I was. Sucking in a breath, I tried to calm my racing thoughts.

"Petal," Dax started, his dark eyes boring into mine. I focused on how clear they were, taking note for the doctor. "I'm sorry I scared you. Can you take me to the clinic before I bleed out on the pavement?"

"Oh! Right. Okay, um, yes, right this way," I babbled, my face beginning to brighten.

Letting go, I stood, picking up the things I'd dropped. Reed helped Dax stand, trading off who was pressing against the head wound. Once Dax was steady, I took his hand and led him to my car. Internally, I winced, not wanting to get blood on the interior, but decided to keep that to myself. I couldn't be picky over some blood when he might die.

Reed picked up Lady Sterling's carrier, watching us as we walked the rest of the way toward my vehicle. Unlocking the door, I tossed the bag into the back and helped Dax into the front seat. Reed climbed into the back with Lady and buckled himself in by the time I made it around to the driver's side.

My hands shook a little as I gripped the steering wheel. I pressed the gas, but nothing happened. Reed reached up, laying his hand on my arm, stopping me from shaking.

"Take a deep breath, Henley. It's okay." Nodding, I focused on his crystal blue eyes and mimicked his breathing. Once I felt calmer, he let go and pressed the on button, something I'd forgotten to do in my haste.

I glanced over toward the passenger seat, finding Dax staring at me. His face was somber, his eyes pleading with me for something, but I couldn't figure out what it was.

Turning back to the road, I realized that I could

move the car this time as it went forward. Keeping my hands steady on the wheel, I safely made it back to campus and the clinic.

"You take him inside. I'll run back to the house to drop off Lady Sterling. Call me when you need me to pick you guys back up," Reed said.

Nodding, I kissed his cheek as I hopped out and assisted Dax to the front door. He went along willingly, making me question his injuries even more.

"I kind of miss your dark wit," I said as we ambled toward the front desk. Dax gave a small huff, but his face was more contorted in pain as he took each step.

The assistant at the front desk noticed us halfway and raced off, returning with a wheelchair. Dax and I both sighed in relief when he lowered down into it.

"He needs to see a doctor," I said, realizing I was stating the obvious.

"Right this way, Dr. Bellamy is in." The assistant pushed the wheelchair toward the first exam room, and I followed. I stopped short when we entered. It was one of the nicest exam rooms I'd ever been in, and I wondered when I'd stop being surprised by everything at Lux.

The attendant helped Dax onto the bed and helped him remove his shirt.

"Oh, do I need to leave?" I asked, suddenly feeling awkward.

"It's nothing you haven't seen, Petal," Dax huffed,

raising an eyebrow at me. My cheeks flamed, but I saw it as a sign that he wasn't on death's door.

A young guy in a white doctor coat stepped into the room, pulling the stethoscope from around his neck.

"Dax, don't tell me you did this training?" he asked, placing the metal on his chest. "Take a deep breath for me," he said as he listened.

Once he was satisfied with whatever he was checking, he moved on to the head wound. The assistant was already cleaning the gash. He performed a few tests, some I knew were concussion protocol, before stepping back and checking his lower torso.

The doctor moved over each area quickly, taking notes as he finished.

"Let's get a scan of this head wound and your abdominal area to rule out internal bleeding," he said after stepping back from him. The assistant nodded, moving Dax back to the wheelchair and taking him to a different room, leaving me with the doctor.

"Wow," I said once the room was clear. "I guess I understand why he wanted to come here."

The young doctor blushed but nodded. "We haven't met yet. I'm Milo. You're the new hockey coach, correct?"

"Yes, that's me. News sure does spread around here." I chuckled, sticking out my hand. "Most people just call me Henley." Milo shook mine, smiling at my comment.

"Ah, sorry. My girlfriend tends to know everything, being the social media coordinator, and then shares it with the rest of us. Plus, you're due for your physical next week."

"Right. Well, it's nice to meet you now, Milo."

"Likewise." He placed his hands in his pockets, rocking back on his feet. It fell quiet, and I debated if I should keep up the conversation or let it go.

"Will Dax be alright?" I asked, realizing I wanted to know.

"I need the scans to know for sure, but my preliminary guess is he has a hairline fracture on two of his ribs, will need stitches on his head wound, and possible mild internal bleeding."

"Shit. That sounds bad." I sat down, my mind going fuzzy with the news. "Should he go to the ER?"

Milo shook his head, watching me. "No. We can take care of all that here. He'll need to be monitored and on bed rest for a few days, so he doesn't agitate any of his conditions."

I snorted, picturing Dax on bed rest. "Oh, he's going to love that."

"Love what?" Dax asked as the attendant wheeled him back in.

"Nothing," I said, trying to keep it light.

"I'll be back in a second," Milo said, stepping out of

the room. The attendant left as well once Dax was back on the bed.

I moved closer; the urge to reach out and touch him was strong. "What happened?" I asked when I didn't know what else to say.

Dax sighed, closing his eyes. "It's a long story, Petal. I promise to tell you more later. Can we leave it at that for now?"

The urge to make him answer was on the tip of my tongue, but I noticed the dark circles under his eyes and remembered all the injuries the doctor mentioned. Whatever happened wasn't a good story, and I didn't need to make him stressed right now by reliving it.

"You were going to make lasagna?" I asked instead, grinning.

Dax's eyes blinked open, slowly turning to look at me. His fingers twitched on the bed, so I reached out, linking our hands together.

"Yeah. It's my go-to dish for apologies."

"Apologies?" I asked, blinking at him as I tried to figure out what he was saying.

"I've been a dick to you, Petal. I wanted to make a peace offering."

"Oh, that's really nice of you. Maybe when you're feeling better, you can still do it?"

"You want me to make you lasagna?" he asked, some of his spark returning.

"It's a meal that you want to make for me. Hell, yes, I want lasagna."

He chuckled, then grimaced, holding his side. "Don't make me laugh. It hurts too much."

"Probably because your ribs are practically broken," I said, narrowing my eyes at him. He had the good grace to look chagrined, even if he wasn't telling me why.

Milo appeared back in the room, confirming the injuries he'd expected. Dax wasn't happy with the order to stay in bed for forty-eight hours. It was only the threat of taking him to the hospital that made him relent.

"Ah, stitches. I've missed those," Milo said as he moved into position. He chuckled, rubbing his hands together, making Dax wince. The assistant numbed the area with a cotton swab, and I watched in amazement as they worked efficiently together. The bed was laid back and raised higher for Milo to be comfortable doing the stitches. Milo's hands moved quickly as he stitched the wound, making it look easy. He finished in a few minutes, stepping back and looking at his handiwork.

"It shouldn't scar too much, but I hear chicks dig scars if it does. I'll check in on you in a few days." He turned to me. "I'm counting on you to ensure he stays in bed."

Nodding, I walked behind the wheelchair a few

minutes later, remembering I needed to call Reed. When we stepped out into the waiting room, I spotted him waiting with Fletcher. They both stood at the sight of me, looking between Dax and me.

"He's okay-ish. He needs to stay in bed and take it easy," I reported to them. They both took sighs of relief, making Dax chuckle.

"I never knew you both cared so much."

Fletcher rolled his eyes, taking over the pushing of the wheelchair. "Oh, you're about to get so tired of me, Dax. Go ahead and get all of your jokes out. Get ready to be taken care of. Papa Fletcher is in the house."

Dax groaned, but I could tell he secretly liked it.

Watching Reed and Fletcher help Dax into the car, I saw a weird glimpse of the future, of this odd relationship I'd found myself in potentially working.

CHAPTER 35

Reed

ONCE WE'D GOTTEN Dax settled in his bed, Fletcher and I returned to Henley's house to help her pack, while Dax was passed out from the pain meds. I understood her reasoning for wanting to leave when I stepped into her room.

"I think this room is going to give me nightmares." My nose scrunched up, almost as if I could smell the horridness of it.

Henley chuckled dryly, packing her clothes into a suitcase. Since she'd only been here a week, she hadn't unpacked much, making it easy for us to gather her belongings. The part that took the longest was the constant interruptions.

"Oh, Henley, I just hate to see you go," a brunette said, walking into the room. She sat on the bed with an exaggerated pout, picking up the pink pillow and holding it to her chest. "I'm going to miss you so much," she sighed. Despite the girl's theatrics, she focused on me and Fletcher as we moved some of the heavier items closer to the door.

"Yeah, I can tell you're really broken up about it," Henley said, zipping a suitcase.

Picking up a few bags, I headed to walk down the stairs when I was blocked by a blonde girl. She stood in the middle, her finger twirling around her hair.

"Excuse me," I grunted, the bag's weight becoming noticeable the longer I stood stationary.

She giggled, batting her eyelashes. "You're so strong," she said, reaching out to touch me. I jerked away, almost falling down the stairs as I twisted to get by her.

Cursing with each step I took, I realized one of the reasons I liked Henley so much. She didn't fall around my feet like a puck bunny. Henley was a hockey goddess, and perhaps that was the difference, but something about that didn't feel right either. Even if Henley didn't play hockey, I couldn't believe she would throw herself at me like these girls. She didn't want to be with Reed Cole, hockey's bad boy. She wanted to be with me.

That made all the difference in the world.

Landing at the bottom, I had to bypass two more girls before I could make it out to the car to put the bags in. Fletcher was right behind me, a similar look of displeasure covering his face.

"Why did that feel like I'd entered an Old West brothel? They were all preening and posing like I would ask them to be my future wife based on their posture." Fletcher shook his head, a full-body shudder rolling through him.

Chuckling, I nodded, realizing he was spot on. "Yeah, that's exactly what it felt like."

"Imagine living with them," Henley whispered as she neared, placing her suitcase into the backseat. "Thank God I don't have more stuff. Let's roll."

She walked to the driver's side, not wasting a minute to climb in. Fletcher and I exchanged a look, quickly running to catch up. Chuckling, we fastened our seatbelts as she drove, not wasting a second to get out of there.

"Good riddance, Barbie Brigade!" Henley shouted, rolling down the window to wave as she drove off.

I looked at Fletcher, who stared at me with wide eyes, both of us laughing loudly at her statement.

"Oh, Baby Shaw, never change." He wiped his eyes before stretching his arm out behind her seat.

Henley laughed, a genuine smile on her face. "Gah, it feels nice to be free. I didn't realize how much that affected me until the knowledge I wouldn't have to return set in."

Her phone rang, and the name Demon Mother popped up on the dashboard. Henley growled, hitting a button on her steering wheel to decline the call. It was quiet for a few seconds, the mood shifting a little.

"Hopefully, you won't regret it," Fletcher said,

trying to save the mood. "You *will* be living with three guys."

"And a Lady," I interjected, hoping to make Henley smile. It seemed to work as she grinned widely, lifting her eyes to meet mine in the rearview mirror.

"I think I can handle you three," she said, taking the last turn before our house.

"Speaking of three... have things shifted with you and Dax?" Fletcher asked, attempting to hide a grin.

"Oh, um, I'm not sure. Dax is Dax." She shrugged her shoulders as she pulled into the driveway, but she couldn't hide the blush forming on her cheeks.

"Hmm," Fletcher said, opening his door. He stopped, turning to look at Henley and me. "Well, just for the record, I'm open to navigating whatever this relationship is with the four of us. But only the four of us."

"I..." Henley shook her head, dropping her eyes to the ground as she fiddled with her keys. I reached out, squeezing her shoulder.

"Henley, we're all in this for you. Because we all want to be with you."

She took a deep breath, raising her head. Wiping a tear, she looked between Fletcher and me.

"I know it was my idea, and it's what I want, but I wasn't expecting you to go along with it. So, when you laid it out like that, it just made me feel like I was being greedy. I want to be with you both. So, thank you for not making me choose."

"And Dax?" Fletcher asked, watching her closely.

"I like Dax and I have feelings for him, but I'm not sure he's ready for this. He mentioned trying to steal me away from you both. I don't know if things have changed for him or not, so I can't answer that until I talk with him. If he's on board with our unique dating arrangement, I'd like him to be included."

"Okay," I said, catching her off guard.

"Okay?" she asked, her mouth opening as she swiveled back and forth between Fletcher and I.

"Believe it or not, Baby Shaw, we've all talked about this already. We're in. So, let's go inside and get you settled into your new room. Then perhaps over dinner we can set out some ground rules. My sources tell me those are important," Fletcher said.

"Your sources," she mumbled, quickly following Fletcher and me out of the car. We carried her belongings in, finding it much easier without three flights of stairs and an army of women standing in between. Snorting, I shook my head when I got her joke.

"What?" she asked, turning to me with her brow lifted.

"I just got the Barbie Brigade comment. They were like women soldiers on the warpath for a husband."

"Yeah, I don't know if they wanted a husband or just your dick," Henley said, shocking me.

"What?" I asked, moments before Fletcher and Henley started laughing so hard they were rolling around on the bed.

"Sorry. They were horrible. I'm glad to be out of there."

Smacking her ass playfully, I went back out for the last box, smiling to myself. So this was what it felt like to have friends... and a girlfriend? I guess I needed to ask what we were later when we had our talk. For the first time, it didn't feel as scary having someone depending on me.

The breeze blew as I stepped back toward the door, the gentle smell of the rose bushes tickling my nostrils, reminding me of my mother. I wasn't sure what I believed regarding the afterlife, but it felt like she was with me at the moment. She showed me I could laugh again, and hopefully one day, love.

She'd been right about having people in my life. In just the week I'd been here, I already felt different. For the first time, I was making friendships with guys that weren't based solely on the hockey team doing well. I enjoyed working with the kids each day and seeing their progress. I look forward to each time I caught Henley's smile, heard her laugh, or felt her lips against me.

And now, I even had a cat.

The grief was still there—my mother's absence left a hole in my heart I could never forget. But I was beginning to understand that I didn't need to replace her or even forget her to move on. Grief wasn't something you got over. It was a living thing just as much as the person had been. It might change and morph as time passed, but I couldn't rid myself of the grief any more than I could have my grumpy nature.

Grief was a part of me. But it wasn't the only part. I could see that now.

My mother always was a wise woman, and she hadn't steered me wrong with her last demand, either.

"Reed?" Henley called, finding me still standing outside. "Everything okay?"

"Yeah." I swallowed, nodding. "Just thinking about my mom."

"Oh. Are you two close?" she asked.

"Yeah. We were. She died at the beginning of the summer. Cancer."

Henley's face changed, her sadness for me evident. Her arms wrapped around me, the last suitcase dropping to the ground as I pulled her closer.

"That must've been so hard. What was she like?"

Her statement and question shocked me. I'd been expecting what most people said. *"I'm so sorry for your loss."* When those words didn't cross her lips, I had to take a few seconds to register what she did say.

That must've been so hard.

Her comment didn't diminish my feelings or make me respond to her in an obligatory way. Henley acknowledged my pain. She validated me. It was beautiful and shocking all the same for such a simple sentence.

And then she went and asked about my mom. Henley didn't brush off the fact she was gone, uncomfortable with death or my grief. She opened the door and invited me to share with her my love for my mother.

"You really want to know?" I asked, still shocked.

"Absolutely. I know it's been quick, but I care for you, Reed, and if she was important to you, then I want to know about her. I'm sad I didn't get to meet her so I could tell her how amazing her son is."

Tears swelled at the corners of my eyes. Smiling, I felt some of the weight of my grief slide off. It didn't feel as heavy any longer—simply because I wasn't carrying it alone. Henley asking about my mother allowed me to share her love and memory—dividing up the responsibility of remembering her.

"Come on. Let's head inside, and I'll tell you all about her. She would've loved you."

"I have a feeling I would've loved her as well." Those simple words again seared on my heart, making me feel things I shouldn't so soon for Henley. Maybe it was the grief confusing me or my need to feel a connection, but either way, I knew I was quickly falling in love with her.

After placing her suitcase in her room, she walked

with me to mine, where we sat on the bed; Lady Sterling perched between us, and I shared some of my favorite stories of my mom and how she believed in fate.

"She sounds amazing, Reed. Thank you for sharing parts of her with me."

"I thought talking about her would make it harder, but with you, it's almost like she's here with me."

"I'm glad." She squeezed my middle, looking up at me. Halfway through talking, we'd moved up the bed until we were snuggled together. It happened so naturally, just like most things with Henley.

"I promised her I'd live my life after she died. I didn't know how to do that until I ran into you that day at the B&B. You reminded me what it felt like to feel alive. I'd come as a favor to Oliver, but I had no intention of accepting. Then I bumped into you, and I remembered my promise. I met Reese that night at the rink and everything felt like it was finally slotting into place."

"I'm glad you're here with me, but that was all you, Reed. You took the steps you needed to honor her and yourself."

"You have no idea how amazing you are, Henley. So, I guess I'll have to show you."

Bending down, I kissed her, then deepened the kiss. I rolled over, pressing her into the mattress. Her legs opened for me, her hands running through my hair. Every thought left me as her body pressed into mine. I wanted to feel every inch of her and explore her, taking my time to memorize how she looked and felt.

Lifting my head, I opened my mouth to suggest taking things further when a knock sounded at my door.

"What?" I asked, the frustration evident in my gruff voice. A chuckle left Fletcher, and I rested my head on Henley's chest. It moved up and down, and I realized she was silently laughing.

"It sounds like you're busy, but dinner is ready, and we were going to have a conversation?"

"Fine," I grumbled, rolling off Henley and staring at the ceiling. "Need to add not interrupting things," I mumbled, making Henley laugh.

Straightening our clothes, we walked out of the bedroom toward the kitchen together.

CHAPTER 36

Henley

STEPPING INTO THE KITCHEN, butterflies filled my stomach at the scene. Fletcher had set the table with cloth napkins, wine glasses, and candles. It made me believe even more how important he was taking this. There were only three plates setting out, making me miss the fourth member already.

"You know what, let me go check on Dax real quick. I won't be long," I said, kissing them both on the cheek quickly.

Pivoting on my socked feet, I hurried to Dax's door, realizing I'd never been in his room. Fletcher had gotten him set up when we'd returned home. I'd taken a quick shower to wash off the blood, and by the time I'd gotten out, Fletcher had said he was asleep.

Pausing in front of the door, I debated if I should knock. Opening it a smidge, I peeked inside. Dax was lying in bed, his eyes meeting mine in the small crack.

"You can come in," he said. Gone was the swagger and bravado. While I missed the sinful talk, I enjoyed seeing the real Dax under the heated looks.

"How are you feeling?" I asked, walking closer to the bed.

"Better, though a bit sore. I already hate this bed," he grumbled, making me smile.

"Do you think you could manage sitting at a table for dinner?"

He lifted his eyebrows, a small smile forming. "Will you be there?"

"Haven't you heard, Dax? I live here now." I wish I'd had a camera so I could've recorded his face. His brows lifted, his mouth gaping as he stared.

"Wow," he cleared his throat, something changing. "I didn't realize things had gotten that serious between you and Fletcher. If it's alright, I'll just stay here."

Dax turned his head, and I realized my mistake. "Okay, if you're not up to it, I understand. But I live here as one of your roommates, in my own room. I couldn't take the cotton candy nightmare anymore. And things are going well with Fletcher... and Reed. We were about to have a conversation about what we all wanted in this relationship. I thought you might want to be included, but I guess not. I'll bring you something later."

I stood, hoping he'd stop me. When I got to the door, I turned back against my better judgment. He was still staring at the opposite wall, his jaw ticking. Sighing, I shook my head as I headed back toward the kitchen. Pasting on a smile, I put Dax and his issues back in his room. I couldn't focus on the one boy who didn't want to be with me when two of the best guys I'd ever met were waiting for me.

"It smells so good, Fletch," I said as I entered the room. The guys both looked at me but chose not to say anything. Reed pulled out my chair, motioning for me to take a seat.

It was quiet as we ate. The chicken and potato casserole was good, but I'd zoned out, thinking about things. After a few bites, the guys spoke up, breaking the silence.

"I've always been a big believer in communication, and I think it will be even more important with this conversation. So, I'll be the first to break the seal." Fletcher placed down his fork, clearing his throat. "I'm a pretty open guy, and I'm not modest. I guess being around a lot of naked dudes in the locker room gets you used to seeing another man's junk."

Reed snorted, but nodded in agreement. "You're not wrong."

"That being said, I don't feel anything sexual for males, but I'm not opposed to being open-minded when it comes to you, Henley."

"Um, okay," I said, unsure I understood what he was saying.

"He's saying he wouldn't say no to a threesome," Dax interjected, hobbling into the room.

The three of us instantly turned toward Dax and Fletcher hopped up to help him into a chair despite his grumbling. Reed squeezed my thigh under the table, and I couldn't stop the smile from spreading. This felt right now. All three of them and me having this conversation.

"I thought…" I started, then seeing his pained face, I decided to let it go for now. "Never mind. I'm glad you're here, Dax." I reached out my hand, offering it to him. He stared at it for a few seconds before placing his hand in mine.

"So, threesome?" Reed asked, bringing the conversation back around. My cheeks heated at the openness, but I knew it was important. I shouldn't be doing it if I couldn't talk about having sex with all of them.

"Yep. I'm game." Fletch shrugged, taking a bite of his food.

"Well, okay then." I giggled, appreciating Fletcher helping to make this easier.

"From the sounds of it, alone time might be hard to come by, and I'm adventurous enough to know I have a few exhibitionist and voyeur kinks. I enjoy being watched and watching. So, that's not a detriment for me. But don't worry, Baby Shaw, these lips are all yours." He puckered up, the other guys chuckling at him.

"Your turn, Reed," Fletcher said, returning to his food.

"Oh, um, I guess I hadn't thought about the logistics." He tilted his head, almost like he was trying to envision scenarios. "I think I need more data before I can give you a true answer. So, for now, just go with I'm the same. I don't think seeing you with someone else will bother me, but my interest is only in you."

Nodding, I squeezed the hand that was still on my thigh. Clearing my throat, I looked at Dax. He was watching me, his hand still in mine.

"And you? Are you going to be part of this?"

Dax licked his lips, some of his smolder returning. "It seems I can't let you go, no matter how hard I try, Petal. So, for now, I'm going to give it a try."

"For now? That feels like you plan to leave." My heart stopped at the thought. I didn't know if I could start a relationship with him if he was always planning on leaving.

"It's not that I want to leave. I'm just a screw-up, Henley. I'll do something eventually to fuck up things."

"You can't have one foot in and one foot out, your hand on the eject button the whole time. That's not fair," I said, shaking my head. I dropped his hand, not able to keep holding it.

"I can understand your hesitation Dax," Reed started, his eyes focused on the man. "And I think it has more to do with what happened today."

"You know what happened?" I asked, turning my head to Reed.

"Dax has shared some of his history with me, but it's his story to tell."

I sucked in a breath, feeling slightly jealous he knew something I didn't. I knew it wasn't fair, so I tried to push the feeling away, wanting to focus on the conversation at hand.

"Dax?" I asked, looking back at him. Tears threatened to spill, and I held them back, not wanting to be a weeping mess.

Dax sighed, dropping his head back to stare at the ceiling. "It doesn't paint me in a good light. And I think I need to move to a more comfortable surface for this conversation."

I glanced at my food, scooping up the last few bites and shoving them into my mouth. I swallowed the glass of wine, ignoring the burn as it all traveled down.

"Come on, we can move to the couch." I stood, moving to help him. The guys stared at me, blinking for a few seconds. With a few soft chuckles, they finished their meals in a quick fashion.

"Help him to the couch. I'll grab him some more meds now that he's eaten and meet you in there," Fletcher said.

Dax leaned on me as we walked, taking small steps. "You know, when I thought I was getting a nursemaid to tend to my injuries, I thought it would be someone prettier."

"You love me, jackass," Fletcher yelled, making us both laugh. Dax groaned, the movement shifting his ribs.

"Fucking ribs," he cursed. Reed stepped in on the other side and helped carry him further into the room, placing him on the chaise lounge. Dax sank into the comfortable cushion, letting out a sigh of relief once he was settled.

I took a seat on the couch facing him. Reed sat next to me, and Fletcher joined us after handing off the water and pills to Dax. We all waited for him to take the meds, washing them down with the water. He set down the glass on the table, looking up to find the three of us watching him. Dax grunted, shifting again. It felt like this one was in an attempt to avoid the conversation for a moment longer.

"Before I came here, I got involved with some things I'm not proud of," he sighed, rubbing his hand over his forehead and pushing his hair back. "I was helping athletes and clients I trained to obtain perfor-mance-enhancing drugs."

My mind wanted to explode, but I kept quiet, not wanting Dax to think I was judging him. Either Fletcher knew this story or had a good poker face because he kept quiet as well, letting Dax continue.

"I thought I could get out of it whenever I wanted.

I was trying to save money to buy my girlfriend's engagement ring. Once I had what I needed, I tried to back out. The people I was selling to weren't as happy about that decision. In one weekend, I lost my job, my girlfriend, and almost my career. They broke a few bones then, and it took a while in PT to get back to where I was."

"And this morning?" Fletcher asked, saving me the trouble. I wanted to know about the girlfriend, but it didn't feel like the right time.

"Gareth," Dax grunted. "He showed up the other day, and Reed intervened. Today, he waited until I was alone and struck. I don't know how he found me, but he's here and wants more drugs. I told him I didn't do that anymore, which resulted in this." He waved his hand over his body, slumping at the end and looking defeated.

"Why aren't we calling the cops then?" I asked.

"It honestly didn't cross my mind. I'm so used to dealing with this on my own and hiding it."

"Dude, you can't hide this. Tomorrow morning I'll take you to the police station. I can help you identify Gareth since I saw him that day."

Dax stared at Reed in shock, his face slack as he tried to register his words.

"You'd help me?" he finally asked, the words cracking at the end.

"Of course. One, it's not right what he's doing.

Two, you're my roommate, and I care about your safety. And three, I'd like to think we're friends now. I want to help you and keep you safe."

Dax stared, assessing his words. He seemed to come to some agreement, nodding. "Thanks, man. I would appreciate your help. Maybe they'll believe me if it's not just my word."

"Is that why you don't want to commit?" I asked, unable to keep it in anymore. "You're afraid of this guy?"

"Partially. I didn't mention that my girlfriend... left me for my brother."

"What a bitch!" I exclaimed, jumping up and moving closer to Dax, sitting next to him on the chaise. Dax chuckled, patting my leg.

"Easy there, killer." He gave a soft chuckle, keeping himself from moving his ribs too much.

Taking a deep breath, I tried to put all the pieces together. He'd been hurt in the past. He was worried about his safety and maybe my own. If those were why he was one foot in and one foot out, I could deal with it. I could show him how we'd be different.

It didn't escape how I'd gone from not wanting to have a relationship and keeping it casual to suddenly having three boyfriends. But it felt right. I couldn't deny my feelings or attraction to them, and it was stupid to avoid it just because I wanted to be free. I didn't need anyone else when I had them. They already fulfilled me in ways I'd never been before. My life was quickly changing, transforming into something completely different, and I knew it was what I needed.

So, I could trust this, let fate keep showing us the way, and prove to Dax that he could also trust his feelings.

"Okay. If you need to keep one foot in and one out, for now, I can be okay with that. I want you to feel comfortable and be part of this relationship. I care about you, Dax, and I don't want to ignore that anymore." Leaning forward, I brought my lips to his, laying a gentle kiss on them. "Just promise me you'll try?"

His eyes searched mine, emotions swirling within. "This might be the pain meds talking, but I'd do anything for you, Petal."

Cupping his cheek, I smiled as I stared at him. A loud purr interrupted our moment as Lady Sterling climbed over the chaise and planted herself on the back cushion.

"Am I hallucinating? When did we get a cat?" Dax asked, sending the rest of us into a fit of giggles.

"Let's get you back to bed, stud." Reed and Fletcher helped Dax back to his room, even helping him with his nighttime duties, much to Dax's protest. Dax might think he was half in and half out, but from where I stood, it seemed like he was all in.

My heart warmed, and I kissed him again before turning out his light. Reed and Fletcher were waiting for me outside the door.

"Now, what?" I asked, glancing between the two of them. I was nowhere near ready for bed.

"Want to watch a movie?" Fletcher asked.

Nodding, I soon found myself between the two of them on the couch, a blanket covering my body. My head was perched in Fletcher's lap, my feet in Reed's.

As the movie started, I soon became distracted by what was going on under the blanket than the screen.

CHAPTER 37

Henley

HANDS ROAMED MY BODY, but I couldn't decipher who they belonged to. Both men were otherwise still, their eyes focused on the movie. But there was definitely a hand running over my bottom and thigh. It began to move higher, tickling my stomach as fingertips met my skin. My shirt lifted easily as the hand caressed the bare skin. I sucked in a breath, no longer able to keep quiet. The hand froze, lingering on my stomach.

"You all right, Baby Shaw?" Fletcher asked. I was too distracted by what was going on to determine if he was teasing or not.

"Yep. I'm fine. Completely fine," I croaked, wetting my lips as the hand began to move again.

Closing my eyes, I focused on keeping my breathing steady as the mysterious hand moved lower. Sensations increased as their fingers traced the outline of my silk panties. Shifting slightly, I tried to open my legs more, offering them better access. The finger brushed against my clit from the outside, sending shivers through my whole body. It throbbed in rhythm with my heart, the need growing with each swipe.

A second hand began to roam higher, brushing against my nipples over my shirt. I no longer cared whose hand was doing the touching. I just wanted them to keep doing it. The not knowing added a layer of mystery as well, making it feel a little more forbidden. I didn't know if they were both aware they were touching me simultaneously, either, adding to the whole illusion.

The upper hand tweaked my nipple, making me think it was Fletcher with his love of nipple play. I sucked in another breath, but no one said anything this time. I could hear the movie playing, but I didn't have it in me to check if they were still watching. Keeping my eyes closed, I could keep the fantasy alive and enjoy the touches being bestowed upon me.

Both hands began to breach beneath my clothing barrier in an oddly coordinated move. The upper hand cupped my breast, the thumb grazing across my nipple, making it plump. The lower hand trailed a finger up my pussy lips, spreading my wetness along it with the stroke. I couldn't move my legs another inch, but the need to feel more friction drove me insane.

A whimper left me, and I prayed they wouldn't stop. I needed them to keep touching me and to bring me to my peak. The finger below massaged my clit, stroking it as they pressed between my folds. The patience this person had to tease me to within an inch of my limit was impressive. If I wasn't stuck on a cliff between falling over into bliss and crashing back into reality, unfulfilled, I'd give them a round of applause.

As it was, I held my breath, waiting for them to give me more of what I needed.

In the meantime, the hand caressing my breast squeezed harder, then shifted to the other, giving that nipple some action. Part of me wanted to open my eyes and see what was going on, but the other part of me was worried it would all stop if I did.

When I couldn't take not knowing any longer, I tilted my head back, a moan escaping me as I looked up. Fletcher was staring at me, his pupils large as he took me in. The sight of him aroused had me reaching forward and finding his hard cock in his pants. At my touch, his eyes fluttered closed, his head falling back.

"Shit, Henley," he cursed. What I assumed were his hands paused on my nipples, his fingers twitching against them as I stroked him on the outside of his pants.

Glancing back, I found Reed watching, his blue eyes dark with hunger. I couldn't reach him fully at this angle, and the need to feel them both as they touched me was overwhelming. It soon didn't matter as I was turned, giving them both better access. My head fell to the cushion as my bottom half was pulled onto Reed's lap. Fletcher angled over me, his mouth going to my nipples, and my shirt pushed up toward my head.

It blocked my view, creating the same effect of not knowing who was doing what to me. I hadn't taken myself for getting off on not knowing, but it was definitely working for me now.

Reed's fingers found my entrance and plunged into my pussy, no longer inhibited by my position. My lower half was naked, the air meeting my hot skin as he concentrated on working me over. My arms were pinned above my head next, and I lost focus on what was going on as hot mouths kissed me, hands touched, and my body was wrung out like a wet washcloth.

"Ah," I screamed, feeling my legs tense as I tightened around the set of fingers. My pussy was desperate for more, not feeling satisfied with the offering.

"More," I whined, feeling powerless to make what I wanted to happen. Hands disappeared, and I instantly regretted my demand. Whimpering, I was relieved when the shirt around my neck was removed, and I could finally see both men.

Their hair was messed up, despite me not having touched it. Their pupils were blown, and their cheeks red. Both wore predatory smiles, and I didn't know who was about to eat me first.

"Henley, I need you to listen to me very carefully. We never asked you in all of our discussions about what you were comfortable with. So before we continue any further, I need to hear you say it. Are you okay with both Reed and me together? At the same time?"

"Fuck, yes," I shouted. "I'm very much on board with this idea. Hell, I'd be with all three of you if Dax was up to the task."

Fletcher chuckled, bending down to give me a kiss. "I love how confident you are about your body and sexuality. It's one of the sexiest things about you, baby."

"I need to go get condoms. I didn't really think a movie would lead to my first threesome," Reed said, moving my legs to get up.

"Wait!" I shouted, reaching out to him. It felt important to keep him here; the fear he would change his mind the instant he was away from me clawed at the back of my mind. "I haven't had my physical for the school yet, but I had one with the team right before I was placed on leave. I've only been with Fletcher and Dax since then, and we used a condom both times. I have an IUD, so I'm good on the baby front. If you don't want to use a condom, I'm cool with it, considering it will just be the three of us." I looked between the guys, worried they'd reconsider now that I'd voiced it.

Fletcher gulped, but nodded. "Yeah, I'm clean."

I glanced back to Reed, who also looked a bit shell-shocked.

"Me, too," he said, taking my hand. "Are you sure, though?"

"Yes, I trust us, and I really don't want you to leave right now."

Reed smiled, leaning forward to kiss me. I imagined he meant for it to be short and sweet, but it didn't take long for things to escalate when you were naked and aroused.

His hands pulled me closer, and I straddled his lap, my bare legs brushing up against the soft cotton of his pants.

"Whoa there, tiger, let's rearrange positions first. Get undressed and move to my spot," Fletcher directed.

Reed growled, but broke the kiss and moved me off his lap. He stood quickly, pulled his shirt over his head, and pushed down his pants and boxers in one go. His cock was hard as it jutted out from him. Licking my lips, I became hypnotized as it swayed slightly as he walked toward the front of the couch. He stared at me before glancing back toward Fletcher.

"Um, should I be sitting on it with my bare ass? Do I need a blanket or something?" Reed asked.

Fletcher rolled his eyes but waved him on. "Sure, go get one out of the closet. You're washing it though since it's your ass."

Reed glared at Fletcher, but moved to do as he said. Fletcher stepped forward, hovering over me.

"Time to get on your knees, Baby Shaw." He positioned himself at the end of the couch, motioning for me to move there. Kneeling, I turned to face where Reed would be sitting, figuring I knew what he had in mind.

Fletcher wasted no time, pulling my hips up and moving my knees to the armrest. I was at an angle, but the second I felt his tip slide in, I lost all train of thought. Gripping the cushion, I focused on breathing as he stretched me, taking his time as he opened me up. Once he was all in, he smoothed the palms of his hands over my ass and back, praising me.

"You're such a good girl, Henley. You take my fat cock so well." Whimpering, I held onto the cushion, waiting for him to plunge into me. "You like it when I talk dirty, don't you?"

Nodding, I opened my mouth to say something until the breath was stolen from my lungs when he pulled back and thrust back in, bottoming out in me. My eyes watered as stars built behind them. The couch dipped, and I felt a body near me, but I couldn't open my eyes just yet as Fletcher thrust in and out a few more times.

"Now, take Reed into your mouth and make him want you even more," Fletcher demanded, stopping only so I could open my eyes and find Reed's swollen dick in front of me. Reaching forward, I stroked the base, my hand traveling over his veins as I moved up and down. Reed's head fell back to the couch, his hands tensing as he struggled to not touch me.

After a few strokes, I placed my lips around his thick head, lightly teasing my tongue around his slit. Fletcher had been making shallow thrusts, giving me time to acquaint myself with Reed's cock. On my second swallow, Fletcher quickly pushed me more on to Reed.

I felt him tense, his hands landing on my hair as he moved it away, revealing my face to him. "God, Henley, you're so beautiful. Your pretty lips wrapped around my cock is one of the sexiest things I've ever seen."

I didn't have the chance to respond as Fletcher picked up his pace, pumping his hips into me so fast I lost my train of thought. When he came with a roar a moment later, I wondered if the whole neighborhood had heard. As soon as he pulled out, Reed grabbed me around my waist and lifted me onto his lap. My head felt faint at the sudden movement, and I fell forward, bracing myself on his shoulders.

After a few seconds, I righted myself and nodded to Reed that I was good. Positioning me over his cock, he gripped my hips as he lowered me over him. I slid on with ease, both of us moaning as we made contact. It was then I realized that I had mine and Fletcher's cum inside. I instantly worried he'd be grossed out, and I stopped, wanting to run to the bathroom to clean myself first.

"It's fine, Hen. I like it."

His words eased my worry and made me wetter at the same time. Again, the depravity of it made it feel hotter, more naughty than regular sex. I was realizing that I'd always craved more from my partners, but I'd been too embarrassed or ashamed to admit it. And quite frankly, I had no idea how to ask for some of it. But these three men had brought something out in me that had been there under the surface all along, waiting to be met.

It said something about how they made me feel and how I felt about myself when I was with them. The world wouldn't understand, but I saw the beauty of what we had, of what we were trying to create.

Tossing my head back, my hair fell down my back and brushed against my skin, sending shivers through me. Reed reached forward, twisting my nipples in his hands as he pumped up into me. Leaning forward, I ran my fingers through his hair, pulling his face closer to mine. I needed to kiss him as he moved in me, to feel that connection on every level. My whole body lit up at the sensations, my skin in overdrive as my orgasm neared.

"Fuck, Reed, so good," I moaned, taking a second to catch my breath.

His head fell to the crook of my neck, where he sucked the skin as he gripped my hips, pumping into me quicker.

"Yes, yes, yes," I chanted, no other words coming to my mind.

"You feel so good, Hen," he whispered, biting my earlobe. The little bite of pain was all it took to send me toppling over. My orgasm crashed into me, my muscles spasming out of control as I clamped down around him, pumping him for more.

"Shit," he said, holding me to him as he came with a growl.

A few minutes later, I pulled back, brushing the sweaty hair out of his face. His eyes were clear, focusing on me as he caressed my face.

"You've ruined me for anyone else, Hen. You're it for me."

The words shocked me, but I could hear the truth behind them. Kissing him, I held his face in my hands, wanting him to know I appreciated what he said, even if it scared the living daylights out of me.

"I have a shower ready for you, Baby Shaw, and then if it's okay with you both, we can all retire to your bed?"

"Sounds good to me." I beamed at the both of them, glad there wasn't any weirdness. They'd been true to their words, showing they were happy to share me, literally at the same time.

Walking toward the shower, I glanced down at Dax's door, hoping that someday soon he'd be part of it too.

CHAPTER 38

Henley

I WOKE up nestled between two hot bodies, my limbs entangled with theirs. A sense of bliss encompassed me from head to toe. I'd never felt so wanted and cherished by a man before. Having two of them here felt decadent. I wasn't one to believe I inherently deserved things; wanting to believe I earned the things I had in my life through hard work. But this... it felt as if the world was showing me the greatness it could bestow if I opened myself up to the possibilities.

And that felt deserving.

"Good morning, Hen," Reed said. Glancing up, I saw his eyes were trained on me, with no hint of regret or disgust. That tiny tendril that worried they'd change their mind in the light of day vanished.

"Morning," I whispered, a smile gracing my lips. "You sleep okay?" I asked.

Reed pulled me closer, stealing me some from Fletcher. "Mm-hmm. Even better now." He nuzzled my neck, kissing me tenderly. Every part of me warmed, and I wanted to never lose this feeling.

A phone vibrated from the nightstand, interrupting our moment.

"It's been doing that for a while," Fletcher mumbled, scooting closer and eating the space Reed had made.

"Ugh, it's probably mine," I grumbled, hiding my head in Reed's chest. "I don't wanna," I cried dramatically. Fletcher chuckled, his warm breath hitting me as his beard brushed against my skin. "You're not making it any easier," I grumbled.

Reed sighed, but moved over and reached back for the offending device. When he had it, he rolled around, shoving it between us. "Here."

Grunting, I reached up and grabbed it, opening one eye to stare at the device. There were several missed calls from my mother, one from Dakota, and a few text messages from Reese.

Sighing, I cleared the phone calls and opened my messages. It was too early to deal with either of those two or whatever nonsense they wanted.

REESE

You still want to do brunch today?

Smiling, I instantly answered them back.

ME

Yes! That sounds perfect.

Smiling, I clutched the phone to my chest, relishing the moment. It would be good to see Reese and spend some time with them.

"Time to get up, fellas!"

"You're suddenly a morning person? I think I'm rethinking this relationship," Reed mumbled, tightening his grip.

"Reese is coming over," I said, running my fingers along his ribs. He jerked and giggled, stopping suddenly. Laughing, I moved to tickle him again when he rolled out of bed and landed on the floor.

"I'm up," he shouted, jumping up to his feet and stepping further from my hands.

"I think someone is ticklish," Fletcher teased, kissing my neck before rolling off the other side and getting out of bed.

"I'll go grab some food in town. Reed, do you want to assist? You don't need to take Dax to the police station yet."

"Right, yes, that sounds good," he said as he

skirted out of the room. Laughing, I climbed out of bed, noticing how happy I was. The feeling increased as I walked into my closet, knowing this was my home. I wasn't just a visitor, but I lived here. It felt nice to be in a place I belonged.

After brushing my teeth and hair, I poked my head into Dax's room. He was sitting up, a tablet on his lap. When he spotted me, he waved me in and put it aside.

"Hey. How are you feeling today?" I asked, walking toward the bed. Dax gave me a smile that went straight to my lady parts.

"Better, but definitely sore. I'm hoping to not take as many pain pills today. I don't trust myself with them." He looked worried, so I made a mental note to tell Fletcher to help Dax monitor it.

"I'm headed to pick up Reese, and the other two went to get some food. Would you want to meet my sibling before you head to the police station?"

Dax observed my face, taking in every detail. Slowly, he reached out his hand and took mine. "I'll be honest, the thought scares the fuck out of me, but I want to be part of your life, so yes, I'd like that. Reese seems like a good kid."

"Thanks for your honesty. If you prefer, I can keep our relationship a secret. I don't want you to feel out of place. I know this is something new for you. It's new for me too."

Dax squeezed my hand, drawing my eyes up to his.

I hadn't realized I'd dropped my own until he beckoned me with his touch.

"I'm trying, Henley. I'll see how I feel. I don't want to complicate things." His face was sincere, and I saw the vulnerability brimming in his eyes.

"I know, and I'm glad," I said, kissing him. The move surprised him, and I felt his body deflate. He reached and pulled an arm around me, placing his head on my shoulder.

"You make me feel like I matter, Henley, and I'm so scared of losing that and disappointing you that it makes me keep you at arm's length."

His body shook, so I ran my hand down his back and through his hair. I'd never seen him like this, so unsure of himself.

"Dax, you don't have to worry about disappointing me. You already blew my world, remember?"

Dax snorted, pulling back to look me in the eyes. "Petal, you surprise me at every turn." He took a deep breath, his eyes fluttering open at the end. "You make bravery seem so easy."

Scoffing, I shook my head. "I'm not brave. I'm just me."

He reached up, placing a finger over my lips. "That's exactly what a brave person would say." Leaning forward, he kissed me softly, his lips moving over mine with skilled precision. "I'll steal some of yours until I have my own. I'd love to officially meet Reese."

"Yeah?" I asked, cupping his cheek.

He nodded, kissing me once more. "Now go before I decide a few broken ribs are worth being inside you again."

The heat in his eyes had me hesitating, but I needed to get Reese, and I didn't want to hurt Dax despite the temptation. Sliding off the bed, I blew him a kiss as I headed for the door. Lady Sterling snuck in as I left, and I smiled, hoping she'd keep Dax company while we were all gone.

"Nice car. I dig it," Reese said as they slid into the seat.

"Thanks. It's not my only surprise." Smiling, I pulled out of the dorm parking lot and headed back to the house. Reese glanced over throughout the drive, giving me a stare as they tried to pull it out of me. When I pulled into the driveway a minute later, they looked confused, blinking at the one-story house.

"I thought... Whose house is this?"

"Mine. Come on inside. The food should be here."

Reese jumped out of the car, barely hesitating enough to shut the door before racing toward the front. Laughing, I followed, hot on their trail, wanting to see their face when they discovered my new roommates.

"Reed? Fletcher? What?" Reese said, skidding to a halt halfway through the door. They turned to me, their mouth hanging open.

"I got a house change. Ta-da!"

Reese chuckled, turning their back to the guys. "And just what are your intentions in this house, young lady?" they asked me, smirking.

"Young lady? And aren't I the one who's supposed to question your intentions?" I asked.

"I'm a mature seventeen."

Reed and Fletcher chuckled at my sibling as I gaped at them in the doorway. A loud purr walked into the kitchen, stopping Reese again.

"Shut up! You have a cat? Can I move in too?"

"That's Lady Sterling, and you can visit whenever you want, Reese," Reed said, warming my heart.

"Anyone hungry?" Fletcher asked. He motioned to the table that had a spread of food in boxes.

Reese had gotten down onto their hands and knees, petting Lady Sterling. They perked up at the mention of food, looking at the table.

"Seriously. I'm never leaving."

Thoughts of what occurred last night filled my mind, and the fact I was glad my sibling didn't live with me. My cheeks heated, and I cleared my throat. "Well, about that. There's something I wanted to tell you. You deserve to know before the gossip around school starts."

Reese quirked an eyebrow, filling their plate with eggs, waffles, and fruit. "What's going on?" they asked, sitting down. I grabbed a plate, the guys following. Once we all had food, we sat at the table, the guys looking at me.

"Well, remember how I said I would date both Reed and Fletcher?"

"Yeah," they said, taking a bite.

"We've made it official, I guess you could say."

Reese shrugged their shoulders. "Okay. So, you're dating two people?"

"Technically, three."

Reese glanced around, looking for the third person. "Anyone I know?"

"That would be me," Dax said, ambling into the kitchen. At this rate, I was beginning to suspect he hid out in the hallway and waited for the perfect entrance.

"No shit. Damn, Sis. You're going to have all the instructors angry with you now."

Shaking my head, I ate some of my food, asking Reese about their weekend as Fletcher helped Dax get some food. When we were all sitting around the table, it felt nice and like everyone I cared about was in the same room.

"Braden and Briana invited me to their house next weekend after the away game. Is it cool if I go?"

"Oh, sure. How are you feeling about the game?"

Reese's shoulders dropped, their head hanging for the first time since they arrived. "I'm trying not to beat myself up for missing that shot. Braden and I practiced for hours yesterday. I'm ready to show my team I won't disappoint them again."

"Hey, you did amazing out there. We all have missed shots, Reese," Fletcher said, grabbing their attention.

"Yeah. It just sucks when I feel l have more to prove to the team."

"Anyone giving you a hard time?" Reed asked.

Reese shrugged, pushing the last of their food around. "Nothing I can't handle."

"That wasn't the question, Reese. Who?" I asked, placing my fork down.

"Nothing outright, but Anders has been commenting on LiveIt about how if he was playing, we wouldn't have lost, yada yada."

Rolling my eyes, I remembered to keep my cool around my sibling. I was the coach. I couldn't play favorites, no matter how much I wanted. "Keep me informed if it becomes anything more. I won't tolerate bullying."

"Yes, Coach," Reese said, looking me in the eyes.

"You can come to any of us too, Reese? Okay?" Reed offered.

Reese nodded, clearing their throat. "So, Bake-off?"

"Yeah. We can watch it in the living room. Go and get it set up. I'll be there in a second."

"Thanks for the food," Reese said before standing and placing their plate in the sink. I wanted to get after them to clean up more, but for now, I knew they needed some space from the intense conversation.

"You guys off to the police station?" I asked Reed and Dax.

"Yeah. Have fun with Reese," Reed said, kissing me before helping Dax to the door. Waving, I helped Fletcher clean up the dishes, buying myself a few seconds to calm down.

"You're doing great. Go on. I'll finish this." Kissing him on the cheek, I left him in the kitchen to join my sibling.

Reese was on their phone when I entered, tossing it down as I neared and groaning.

"What?" I asked, worried the bullying had already intensified.

"Mom won't quit calling me. I answered last night, and all she wanted to know was about the school here and how you got me in. She said she would get a reporter to do a story or something. I was so annoyed, I hung up and haven't answered since."

"Great. She's also been calling me, and I've been

ignoring her. What in the world is she up to with a reporter?" I asked, sitting down next to Reese.

"Beats me. Knowing Mom, it's for some payout. She only does things that benefit her."

It was sad to hear Reese speak that way about our mother, but they weren't wrong. Snuggling down into the couch, we watched Bake-off together, ignoring the real world for a couple of hours.

CHAPTER 39

Reed

I PULLED into the police station and turned toward Dax. His face was set in a grimace from the ride.

"You ready for this?" I asked.

"Not really, but Henley's right. I need to do it. I have nothing to hide, and I can't start a relationship with it hanging over my head."

"I'm glad to hear you admitting your feelings, man," I teased.

"Shut the fuck up, dude." He chuckled, then held his side. "Shit. Fucking douche had to go for the ribs. It's gonna feel like forever until I can be between Henley's legs again."

"So, we doing that? Talking about our time with her?" I asked, shifting slightly.

"Isn't that what we discussed?" He shook his head, talking again before I could respond. "I have no idea what I'm doing, if I'm honest. One second I'm sure I can't deal with it, and the next, it feels impossible not to."

"That's Henley for you. She makes you brave. Life doesn't feel as scary with her around."

Dax looked at me, assessing my face. When he seemed to come to some conclusion, he let out a deep breath.

"Sorry, I'm not used to people being so frank with me. And quite honestly, I expected you to punch me in the face out of jealousy. But you're exactly as you present, Reed."

I cleared my throat, his words stirring something in me.

"I wasn't always so open, you know. I lived most of my life keeping people away."

"What changed then?" Dax asked, apparently not in any rush to go inside.

"My..." I stopped and swallowed. "My mom died a few months ago from cancer."

"Shit, man. I'm sorry. I didn't mean to pry. That's some heavy shit."

I nodded, agreeing with him. "Yeah. It is. She was the only person I truly cared about. I realized how empty I'd made my life when she was gone. Her dying wish was for me to form connections. I thought she was being ridiculous, asking me to do something completely out of character."

Laughing, I shook my head and scrubbed my jaw as I thought about my words.

"Then I bumped into Henley, and she ignited a

spark in me. From there, people began to infiltrate my life one by one, showing me it wasn't as scary as I always made it seem. I guess that's why it's so easy to go along with this relationship. Henley's at the center, pulling me toward her, creating this team of genuine people around me. I haven't really ever had a family, so it's difficult for me to call it that, but a team, I understand. And that's exactly what it feels like with Henley and Fletcher. A true team. You're just as much a part of it as you let yourself be."

Dax kept staring at me, searching my eyes. Eventually, he nodded, his face relaxing. "Yeah, I'm beginning to understand that. Speaking of, I guess we should get this over with. I suddenly want to spend the day with a girl and their sibling on the couch."

The corner of his mouth lifted up only slightly, but some of the darkness he hid in his eyes was gone. The more I got to know Dax, the more I saw of the real man behind the hair and bravado.

"Let's do this then." I opened my door and met him at his. He had one leg out, his face straining as he braced against the door. "If you let me help, we'll be done quicker," I encouraged, giving him the choice.

Dax sighed, stopping his effort. "Yeah, okay."

Stepping into the door, I wrapped my arm around his waist and lifted him up. He grimaced but kept his groan to himself. I suppose there was only so much vulnerability he could show in one day.

Carefully, we made our way into the police station and walked to the front desk. The officer on duty was a middle-aged woman with short brown hair and glasses; she glanced up when she heard us approach. Immediately she stood and walked around to meet us.

"Oh dear, what's happened?" she asked, directing us to some chairs.

"I need to report an assault," Dax gritted out, panting loudly as he sank into the seat.

Over the next hour, Dax reported his encounters with Gareth at the school and in the parking lot. He had Milo send over his medical records as evidence, and I helped give a recount of what I'd overheard at the school. Once she had all the details, Officer Jenkins filled out the details for a restraining order and promised she'd be in touch once they charged Gareth.

"Rest up, Dax. We'll get him." She patted him on the arm as we walked out of the precinct.

We'd learned that Officer Jenkins was a big supporter of Lux and vowed to handle this herself. I glanced at Dax as we slowly made our way to the car. He was still in pain, but he looked lighter, some of his burden having been taken away.

"What do you think?" I asked once we were both in the car.

"It went better than I expected if I'm honest. I figured they'd hear about my past and dismiss me."

I thought about his words, feeling some familiarity with them. I'd quit believing in people after a few bad encounters, assuming everyone was the same.

"I can't attest the truthfulness of this for you, but I think in my experience, I dealt with the worst of people for so long, it was easy to only expect it. When you're looking for it, it's easy to find. It also reinforces the belief that being vulnerable isn't worth it. I spent a lot of my life believing I was the wronged party, never considering how I might not be getting the whole picture. There are bad people out there, but there's also good."

Dax scoffed, shifting his eyes to me. "Yeah, well, the bad people seem to outweigh the good."

"Maybe." I shrugged, turning on the car. "But perhaps you own some responsibility by only looking for it. If you surround yourself with vultures, you can't be surprised when they attack you. It doesn't make it right, but I think sometimes it's easier to blame others instead of admitting you put yourself around people you knew would never have your back and got upset when they didn't."

Dax's jaw tightened, and he turned his head toward the window. We drove for a few minutes in silence before he dropped his head, letting out a dark chuckle.

"Fuck. You're right. I hate it, but you are."

"It's one thing I don't relish being right about," I

admitted. "I only know because of my own experience with the same thing."

"So, I guess we're both plotting new paths?" Dax asked.

"Looks that way. I'm glad I met you, man. Even if you are a pretty boy I'd normally want to punch in the face."

Dax gasped, then chuckled, clutching his sides. "Shit, dude. I don't expect you to be funny, and then you say shit like that, and I forget it hurts to laugh." He sighed, wiping his eyes. "I hate to admit that you've been a better friend to me than any of the guys I hung out with back home. If I was going to trust anyone to be in a relationship with the same girl, it would be with you and Fletcher."

"Same, bro."

We smiled at one another before wiping our faces, realizing how sentimental we were getting in the car. I spotted a coffee shop up ahead and decided to make a detour.

"How about we pick up some coffee and treats for Henley and Reese? I'll even say it was your idea," I teased.

Dax scoffed, rolling his eyes. "Please. Like, I need help with my game. Pretty face, remember?"

Laughing, I shook my head and parked the car. "If you weren't hurt, I'd punch you in the arm."

"Fuck. I gotta remember there are three hockey

players in the house now. Your first solution is always punch first, ask questions later."

"You coming in or just want to wait?"

"I'll just wait unless you need help?"

"Nah, bro. I got it."

Opening the door, I quickly made my way into the shop, eager to return to my girl. When I realized I'd called her that, a smile graced my lips on its own, the feeling odd but not all that unpleasant.

Getting a tray for the drinks, I carefully carried them and a bag of muffins out to the car, shocked when I spotted Dax leaning against it instead of in it like I'd left him.

"What's up?" I asked, knowing something had to bring him out with the pain he was in.

"Kurt," he growled, his eyes not leaving the coach's back as he jogged off.

"Fucking asshole," I muttered, setting the drinks and muffins into the back. "Come on, you can tell me about it on the drive back to Henley."

Her name made him shift gears, and he managed to maneuver himself back into the car with only a few curses. Reaching back, I picked up the drinks and handed them to him.

"Can you manage to hold these?" I asked, wanting to shift his focus.

"Yeah, my arms aren't broken," Dax hissed, his eyes shooting up when I chuckled. When he realized what I did, he relaxed, sitting back. "Sorry. I'm just really pissed at him. I thought we were friends, but I'm realizing you were right about the people I surrounded myself with."

"Between the two of us, we've made it known he needs to stay away from Henley," I said, backing out. "Something tells me he won't get that message, though."

"Unlikely. When I told him to keep her name out of his mouth, he made a cryptic comment about getting his justice soon. I don't like it. You can't leave her alone with him. Ever."

Dax looked at me, his eyes wide as he waited for me to respond.

"I promise. I won't."

When he was satisfied, he turned back to the window, staring off in the direction Kurt had gone.

"I don't even know where he's going in that direction. There's nothing there," he mumbled.

We both looked down the alley between the coffee shop and a clothing store as we passed. Kurt's back was to us, but he was very obviously meeting with two other people. They were both blocked by his frame, but as we turned, I caught a glimpse of the one on the right.

It was a face I'd never forget—Dakota Hughes.

"Fuck, what the hell is he doing here?"

"You know who he was with?" Dax asked, swiveling toward me.

"Yeah. Henley's ex."

"What?" Dax screeched, turning back, but we were already past the alley. He turned in the other direction, his ribs protesting with the move as he peered out the back window. "I have a bad feeling about this," he whispered.

I didn't know who the other man was or why Dakota Hughes was in Oak Crest meeting with his former teammate in a dark alley, but it didn't bode well.

"Yeah." I swallowed; the bliss I'd been feeling earlier left me as a sinking pit in my stomach opened up. "Me too."

I pulled into the driveway a few minutes later and turned the car off. We sat there, neither of us ready to get out of the vehicle.

"What do we do?" I asked.

"I don't know. Do we tell Henley?" Dax asked.

"It feels like something we should tell her, but I don't want to worry her with the game coming up if it's nothing, either."

"Shit, our first relationship test, and I think we're failing. What's Fletcher always harping about?" Dax asked, lifting his eyebrow.

"We gotta tell her. Fuck. I don't want Dakota to throw her off her game."

"It would be worse, though, if we don't say anything, and then he surprises her."

"Yeah, you're right," I said. Sighing, I leaned back and grabbed the muffins before getting out of the car. I took the beverages from Dax and placed them on the hood while I helped him get out.

Together, we took the muffins and drinks in, both dreading having to tell the girl we were dating that her jackass of an ex was in town.

CHAPTER 40

Henley

BLOWING MY WHISTLE, I motioned for the team to gather around me and the other coaches. Looking at all of their faces, I was proud of the progress they'd all made. The week had flown by in a flurry of practices and training. It helped me ignore the fact that Dax and Reed had spotted my ex-boyfriend talking with Kurt.

I didn't want to assume it was to do with me, but it felt too coincidental otherwise. Since I couldn't do anything about it, I pushed it away.

Thankfully, there hadn't been any more sightings of Dax's attacker, and the police were on the lookout to arrest him when he surfaced. Dax was moving around better and had gotten the all-clear to leave bedrest. He wasn't up to par for conditioning, so he'd been observing and giving instruction when he could, but had given over the full workouts to Rhett.

Rhett was still as stoic as the first time I'd met him back at the B&B over the summer, but I couldn't deny he was a good fitness instructor. There were parts of me that were still hurting after this week under his care.

On top of everything else, Oliver had left early for pastry school, meaning it was the first week without him. I'd been on my own all week as I tried to inspire and coach these kids to be the best players they could be. Some were more willing than others.

The kids panted and skated over, removing their helmets to reveal sweaty heads beneath. Anders and his friends had been quiet, and I hoped it meant they were accepting me as their coach. It was highly unlikely, but I was going with it for now. The alternative wasn't something I wanted to entertain.

"Tomorrow, we travel to our first game. It's never easy starting the season with an away game, and you've all had a lot of changes this year. That shows me how resilient and hungry you are to win. You've fought your way to be here, beating out other kids for the chance to play. If we play as a team, we're unbeatable. So, tomorrow, who's taking the ice? You or the Blizzards?"

A few mumbles were heard, but it was too quiet to make any impact.

"I asked... who's taking the ice? You or the Blizzards?"

"The Blizzards," a few said a little louder.

"I'm sorry, I can't hear you. Reed, did you hear them?" I asked, looking at him. I ignored Kurt like I had most of the week, unless giving him a direct task. He seemed to like it better that way, too.

"Nope. All I heard were some measly mosquitos."

A handful of the kids grumbled but seemed to find their voices. Looking around at the team, I held their eyes. When I felt I'd imparted my wishes thoroughly, I tried one more time.

"I'll ask one last time, who's taking the ice tomorrow? You or the Blizzards?"

This time, a resounding "The Blizzards" echoed around the rink, sending goosebumps across my skin. Smiling, I hid the fact I'd noticed the few who hadn't joined in. I'd need to be on guard to avoid any surprises this week. The kids who'd practiced their asses off deserved to play the game they'd been preparing for. I wouldn't let anything stand in their way.

"That's more like it. Be here tomorrow after lunch. If you're not here by 1pm, the bus will leave without you. We have a schedule to keep, be respectful of everyone working to make this game happen. The final lineup will be posted in the locker room before we leave. Eat well tonight, take some time to rest, and get a good night's sleep. You're released."

The team skated off, chatter filling the space as they filtered into the locker room. I glanced at Kurt, knowing I couldn't escape the next part. At least Reed would be with me.

"Meet in conference room A in twenty minutes." I offered no room for argument, skating off toward the staff locker room, figuring he'd follow or he wouldn't. If he chose this moment to take a stand, then I'd have something to go to Dmitry about.

A hand reached out for mine when I entered the hallway, and I calmed, knowing it was Reed's. Looking up, I took in his confident smile and his reassuring eyes. They instantly relaxed me, and I knew he was here with me no matter what.

The urge to express my appreciation to him was strong, but the heavy footfalls behind us reminded me Kurt was near. Entering the locker room, we separated toward our lockers. It was quiet as we changed. I debated hopping into the shower, but the knowledge of Kurt being near made me decide to wait. I didn't need him interrupting another one.

Reed apparently had the same thought and met me as I laced up my shoes. Together, we headed to the conference room.

"How you feeling?" he asked once we were away from the locker room.

"Pretty good. Nervous about my first game. Worried something bad will happen. But I'm confident in the team and trying to focus on that. Winning is important, but it's not the only thing. I want to instill that in them. I was never given that message."

We walked into the conference room, and Reed

stopped, locking the door. He placed his hands on my face. His blue eyes were fierce as he gazed into mine. His thumbs delicately traced over my cheeks.

"No matter what, Henley. You've done an amazing job. Even I've learned how to be a better player from watching you coach. Remember what I said to you that day in the parking lot?"

"Don't let them steal my soul," I whispered.

"It still applies. You have this light that shines, drawing others near. You're a force to be reckoned with, Henley."

Reed bent down and sealed his lips to mine. The kiss was deep and made my toes curl. Just as it started to heat up, he pulled back and motioned me toward the head of the table. Unlocking the door, he moved to the other end. Two seconds later, the door opened, and Kurt looked at us suspiciously.

"Alright, let's get down to business. Who's making the final roster?"

FLETCHER KISSED ME ONCE MORE BEFORE PULLING AWAY AND handing me a hydro flask. He smiled at me, tucking a piece of hair behind my ear.

"I hate that I can't go," he sighed, crossing his arms.

"You have a game tomorrow. Your team needs you

more than I do." Stepping forward, I wrapped my arms around him. "It's sweet you want to go, though. Text me?"

"Oh, I will." He seemed to lighten up at that, making me wonder what he had up his sleeve.

Shaking my head, I drew back and walked over to Dax. He lifted a brow as I approached, but opened his arms as I neared. We were still figuring things out between us, but it was getting better each day. I knew he was in this with me, so I was taking it slow.

"You can text me too, you know," I said, stepping back to kiss his cheek.

A smirk appeared, and he nodded, kissing my forehead gently. "You might regret that, Petal."

The heat in his words had my body shuddering. Clearing my throat, I grabbed my bag and headed out the door with Reed. The two remaining waved, giving Reed a nod.

The drive to the campus was quiet. I was too in my head going over plays to make conversation. Reed seemed to perceive this and let me be. It was something I appreciated about him. His understanding of the need for quiet at times.

When we pulled up to the rink, the school's charter bus was already parked out front. Placing our gear bags underneath, I climbed onto the bus and took the front seat, pulling out my clipboard to check off the students as they climbed aboard. Reed took the seat next to me, making me smile to myself.

"What?" he asked, catching me.

"Nothing." I shook my head, the smile not wanting to leave.

"Would you prefer I sat in the back of the bus?"

"Nope. I'm glad you want to sit with me. It's cute. I never had someone to share seats with before."

"Me either," he said. This time, the look between us was heated. The sound of feet stomping up the steps broke the moment, and I turned, finding the driver.

After going over the travel details, Reed left to help the kids get their belongings placed underneath. Slowly, they trickled in. Most of them had smiles on their faces, eager for the game.

Anders and his friends ignored me as they passed. Their disrespect irritated me, but I let it go, wanting to focus on the game. I wasn't going to change their opinion of me by getting angry. In fact, it would play into their hands, responding the way they wanted me to. Years of playing professional hockey had taught me how to notice the difference.

With ten minutes left until departure, I was happy to report that all of the team was present. Reese smiled at me from midway back, sharing a seat with Braden. Despite the jerks they were dealing with, I was glad they'd managed to make some true friendships.

"Alright, team, we have a two-hour drive ahead of us. Take this time to focus on the plays and push everything else out of your head. This first game will show the other schools that we're still the best. It's time we got out of the penalty box and reminded them why we're to be revered."

"Go, Blizzards!" someone yelled back, riling everyone.

"Blizzards!"

The team kept up the chant as the driver pulled out of the school parking lot. Sitting back down, I turned to Reed, finding him watching me.

"You were great," he whispered. He took my hand, keeping it between our seats and out of view of the players. We weren't hiding our relationship from them; we just didn't want it to be the team's focus. Dmitry was aware, and that was all that mattered, in my opinion.

My phone buzzed again, and my mother's name appeared on the caller ID. Rolling my eyes, I shoved the phone back into my bag.

"She still calling you?" he asked.

"Yep. She's planning something, and I don't trust her. My mother has never been on my side. She only knows hers. Reese said she was talking to a reporter, so I can only imagine what she's cooked up this time."

Reed cringed, nodding in understanding. "My father was like that at the beginning of my career. He hadn't been around my whole life, leaving my mom and me when I was small. My mom became a single mother, taking me to every practice and working extra shifts so I could go to camps. She was the only person who deserved anything when I made it big, and she didn't want any of it." Reed smiled at the memory, and I turned, blocking off anyone from noticing us.

"Your mom was an amazing woman. I wish I could've met her."

"I wish that too. She would've loved you and Reese."

"Yeah?" I asked. We stared at one another; the feeling of everything else fading away was intense as we became lost in one another's eyes.

"Yeah," he said eventually, clearing his throat. "My dad, though, was the opposite. I was hopeful at first. I believed he was back because he was proud of me, that I'd finally proven I was worthy." He sucked in a breath before letting it out slowly, shaking his head once. "But the only worthy thing was my bank account. I initially gave him some money, just happy to have him around. Eventually, I realized he was only here because of the cash, and I cut off all communication with him."

I squeezed his hand, angry on his behalf, but also recognizing the hurt he felt. My thumb moved of its own accord, brushing against his.

"Once I was in the league, I kept my mom at arm's

length. I didn't go home as much, avoiding dealing with her. It wasn't until I realized how much her behavior was affecting Reese that I stepped in. Eventually, my mom couldn't deal with having a non-binary child, and her displeasure came out in the form of emotional abuse and using pills. I petitioned the courts for guardianship and was granted it last year. Of course, our mother pretends that didn't happen. She acts like she chose to have Reese come and live with me."

I shook my head, the disgust heavy. Reed squeezed my hand this time, his thumb brushing against my palm now.

"That was a brave thing to do. I don't know many twenty-somethings in the prime of their career who would take in a teenager."

"Yeah, well." I shrugged. I didn't have words. "Reese is family, and I hate myself for not realizing sooner they needed me."

"Do you ever just take a compliment, Hen?" Reed asked, his eyes crinkling a little, showing me he was teasing.

Smiling, I sat back. "It's not in my nature. But I'm trying to learn to accept them more. So, thank you. Just don't let me get a big head like you," I joked.

Reed scoffed, almost choking on his laughter. "Me?"

"Yeah. That was one of the reasons Dakota hated you."

"Hughes," Reed sneered, rolling his eyes. "He hated me because I was better at hockey than him."

"You're right. You're so modest." I nodded, my eyes wide, a giggle threatening to escape.

Reed lifted one shoulder. "There's acknowledging your talent and being proud of it and then being an ass and flaunting it in front of everyone. Hughes does the latter because he's too worried people will actually notice he's not as good as he thinks he is if he quits talking and bashing others."

"You know, that's pretty accurate. I think he was intimidated by me as well. He used to always put me down. I didn't realize it until we broke up, but I see that now. He'd gaslighted me into believing I was less than him."

Reed growled, the sound catching me off guard. I turned my head, finding him struggling to control his anger. "If I ever see him again, his pretty face will be having a chat with my fist."

"Your fist is much more talkative than your mouth," I joked.

Reed's mouth fell open, then shut, silence descending into our little bubble. I giggled, and he turned more toward me, smiling. "You might be right. It's always been easier to settle things that way. I guess that isn't the most mature way. Dax even mentioned it."

Scrunching my nose, I shook my head. "No. Not really. I get it, though. Especially when it comes to Dakota."

Reed took a deep breath, closing his eyes. It was a few minutes later before he opened them. "I won't promise, because I'll fail if I do. But I will try to keep my fists to myself regarding Dakota."

Looking around, I noticed everyone was asleep or focused on their phones, so I leaned over and kissed his cheek. "That's incredibly sexy."

His eyebrow lifted. "Yeah?" he asked, his chest puffing out a little.

"Yep." Giggling, I sat back, happy to share this experience with him.

We spent the rest of the trip on lighter topics and played games on Reed's iPad. It had been precisely what I needed to decompress before the game, get myself ready to coach, and hopefully lead my team to their first victory.

When the bus pulled into the parking lot of the opposing team's arena, I wasn't prepared for the media frenzy we encountered. It made me even more grateful for the time we'd had together to relax. Glancing at Reed, we both nodded, ready to help the kids through this.

"Alright, Blizzards. Don't let the media distract

you. We're going to try to go around them, but they're crowding most of the parking lot, so we might be unable to avoid them. Remember your training and hold all comments until after the game. Put in your earbuds or whatever you need to tune them out. We're here to play ice hockey. Let's remind them of that."

The team nodded, some taking my advice and putting earbuds or headphones on as they gathered their belongings. Reed stepped off the bus first, helping to shield us from some of the reporters. As the kids descended, I had a sinking suspicion I knew who was behind all of this. I just prayed for Reese's sake, I was wrong.

CHAPTER 41

Henley

I WATCHED as Reed directed kids and shielded them from reporters as best he could. Kurt ignored my attempts to catch his attention, shuffling past me as he arranged something in his bag. I rolled my eyes and waited until the last of the kids were off, spotting Reese and Braden at the end.

"Is this normal?" Reese asked, nervously biting their lip.

"No," Braden said before I could.

"Yeah, I didn't think so," Reese sighed.

"It will be okay," I assured them, rubbing their shoulders. "Come on. Let's get it over with. We can't win any hockey games from inside the bus."

Nodding, they both lifted their bags and headed down the steps. Gathering the last of my courage, I followed them. I hadn't encountered the media since my scandal, so their presence brought up numerous memories I'd wanted to forget. Their shouts grew louder as we descended, their true reason for being here becoming clearer.

"Reese! Over here!"

"Henley, what's it like coaching a boys' team?"

"Who did you sleep with to get this gig?"

"Aren't you worried about getting hurt playing with the boys?"

"You don't belong here."

The statements were hurled at us, cameras and phones pushed in front of us, and I worried about our safety as people pulled and tugged me. I caught a glimpse of someone who looked familiar toward the front, but they were gone when I glanced back, as too many other people crowded my view. It was only Reed coming back and shielding Reese and me that allowed us to push through to the door into the arena.

"What the fuck?" I screeched; panting as I tried to suck in some air. I bent at my knees, squeezing my eyes shut. That had been horrible. When my breathing was controlled, I searched for Reese, needing to know they were okay.

"I'm okay," they said shakily. Walking over, I hugged them, holding them tightly to me. I felt Reese relax, and in turn, it helped me as well.

"I'm so sorry," I said. I didn't know what I was apologizing for, but it felt warranted.

"You have nothing to apologize for, Henley," Reed seethed. I started to protest, but Reese cut me off.

"He's right, and I don't want it to affect our game. Let's just focus on winning."

"Spoken like a true athlete," I said, smiling.

I walked with Reese to a separate room the school had set up for us to use. As much as I hated being excluded due to gender, I understood the need with minor children present. It was safer this way and kept both schools away from a lawsuit. At least Reese and I were together. That made it marginally better.

Once we were dressed, we walked to the boys' locker room and knocked on the door. Reed opened it a moment later, giving me a strained look as he directed us in. The team was gathered around Kurt as he led them with a speech.

"This is our moment. We're not going to let any interlopers take it—" He stopped short when I came into view, and I halted, crossing my arms.

"Oh, please, continue. You were saying something about interlopers?"

He cleared his throat, his eyes boring into mine. Hatred was evident on his face as he stared me down. Gritting his teeth, he kept eye contact as he spoke. "Just getting them ready for you, *Coach*."

There was no mistake in how he said coach that he detested me. I caught Reed glaring, his fists twitching at his sides. It wouldn't look good if we forfeited the first game because the coaches got into a brawl. The kids were already traumatized enough by the reporters; we didn't need to add this.

"Aren't you the sweetest?" I said so sugary sweet I was bound to have a cavity. "It's so nice when the old staff makes it so welcoming for the new. You've handled it well and accepted you weren't cut out for the task. You know, considering they had to ask two professional hockey players. It's been years since you played in the league, after all."

His face grew redder, and I suspected he was about to explode. I slightly regretted my barb, but he'd undermined and ribbed me all week. This team couldn't afford to be divided, which meant he either had to get on board now or walk away. There wasn't another option that I could see. And him getting on board was seeming less likely by the minute.

"Alright, who's ready to beat the Bears?" Reed asked, stepping up next to me. "Hit the ice. It's time for warmups."

The team filtered out, and I followed, not wanting to give Kurt any more of my attention. The kids needed me now. It was time for me to be their coach.

The opposing team watched us as we warmed up, whispers filtering to us every now and then. They were all curious about me being the head coach, and a few were trying to figure out which number Reese was. I'd need to watch that they weren't targeting my sibling. Motioning for the team to gather around, I ignored Kurt while giving my last huddle.

"Now's the time. Let's show them what Lux is made of. Go, Blizzards!"

"Blizzards!" they cheered, filling me with school pride.

The five starters skated to the center as the rest filed into the box. Reed headed for the coach's box that gave a view of the whole ice. He'd be able to call plays and help me determine any players to watch. Kurt stood by the penalty box, since regulations only allowed one coach inside the team box during regular gameplay. As much as I missed Reed, I was glad to have Kurt away from me.

The whistle blew as the coin was tossed, the game starting as the crowd cheered. The stadium was packed, the fans loud on both sides of the boards. For one second, I let myself close my eyes and sink into the feeling of the crowd, the sound of blades on ice, the puck hitting sticks, and the players' grunts. I'd never thought about coaching before, but as I stood there, my team on the ice, I knew this was where I was meant to be. My career had taken a skid in a different direction, and for once, I was excited about where it was leading.

Exhaling, I opened my eyes, and the world returned as the season's first game began.

IT WAS THE END OF THE SECOND PERIOD, AND WE WERE down by two goals. The team sat around the locker room, sweaty, tired, and defeated. The Bears were more formidable than I'd expected and seemed to anticipate every play we had before we even attempted it. It was beyond frustrating, to the point I was becoming paranoid, worried they knew our entire playbook.

"I know it's been tough out there—"

"We're getting our asses kicked," Anders yelled, cutting me off. His eyes flashed with anger as he glared at me.

Ignoring him, I focused on the other kids.

"They're a good team, but so are we. Now, we need to try that new play we've been working on. Reese, you'll..." I scribbled on the board, reminding them of the moves. The five that were involved nodded. Reese swallowed, their eyes fierce as they memorized the play.

"It's our time to shine, Blizzards."

Leading the team out onto the ice, I watched as they warmed up, hope spreading in my chest. We could do this. Jack hobbled over, motioning toward his skate.

"My laces broke. I have an extra set in my locker."

"Go and hurry," I ushered, looking at the clock. Jack raced off as best he could with one skate loose. As the clock ticked down for the last period to start, I grew nervous that Jack wasn't going to make it. When I didn't notice Kurt on the ice, I motioned for Reed.

"I'm going to check on Jack. Something feels off."

"Let me go," he said. "I don't want you alone with him."

"I'll be quick and avoid him. Plus I don't trust Kurt not to use this as a way to step in again. I only trust you to coach these kids if I'm not here."

Reed debated in his head, his eyes scanning me. I patted his hand, not having time for him to run through different scenarios. Moving toward the break in the boards, I headed to the locker room. The room that Reese and I had used was open as I passed, and I stopped, looking in.

All of our belongings had been pulled out of our bags and thrown across the room. Slurs covered the wall in spray paint, and it looked like most of our clothes had shared the same fate.

Tears welled up in my eyes, that feeling of failing to protect my sibling emerging as I imagined them witnessing this. Before I could think about it, voices carried down the hallway. Leaning against the door, I waited to see if I could figure out who was behind this.

"I need an answer. I've given you everything that you asked for. I can't take being around her much longer," Kurt seethed. The amount of hatred in his voice shocked me.

"Everything's in motion. You've done an excellent job under the circumstances, Kurt. The team will be yours to coach by the end of the week. The Society will be in touch."

I sucked in a breath, knowing that voice—Dakota. What was he doing here? And what were he and Kurt up to? Was this connected to what the guys had seen? And better yet, what was this Society?

There were too many questions, and I wouldn't find them hiding in this room. Turning the handle, I didn't understand why the door wasn't opening. Throwing my shoulder into it, I grunted as I hit the door, but nothing budged.

Shit. This couldn't be good. Was this part of their plan? Lure me off the ice, so I missed the game?

The buzzer sounded for the period to begin, my anxiety ramping up at what it could mean for me. I started to beat my palms against the door, hoping someone would hear me, despite knowing everyone was in the noisy ice rink.

Fear twisted in my gut, and I slid down the door, my breathing becoming labored. No. This wasn't going to be how I remembered my first game.

Determination rose up in me, and I stood searching for my phone. When I couldn't find it, I narrowed my eyes at the door. Fine, I could do this the hard way.

Sucking in a breath, I moved forward, my shoulder turned to ram into the door, hoping to break through this time. As I smacked into the wood, the door flew open, a sharp pain radiating in my shoulder.

"What the hell, Henley!" Reed shouted, leaning down to lift me up. "What happened?"

"Someone vandalized my and Reese's stuff, and then I got locked in."

"No, someone barricaded you in," he said, his eyes wide as he stared at me.

"Huh?" I didn't understand what he was saying. I spotted a janitor's cart pushed off to the side. "That?" I asked, my voice going high-pitched at the end.

"Yeah." Reed nodded, his hands trailing over my face, his eyes searching for any signs of injury.

"I'm okay," I said when I realized how worried he'd been. He pulled me to his chest, his heart racing against my ear as he held me.

Thoughts began to trickle back through, and I realized if he was here, there wasn't anyone coaching.

"Wait, how are you here? Who's coaching?"

Reed pulled back, a grimace on his face. "Jack returned, and I asked him if he saw you. When he hadn't, I got nervous. Kurt arrived right then, volunteering to take over. I'm sorry, Hen. I know you wanted me to stay, but I got so worried something had happened."

I sighed as disappointment filled my gut. I didn't blame Reed for what he decided, and I'd probably have made the same choice if he'd been the one missing, but it felt too much like Kurt had won something, and I didn't like that.

"Let's see if there is a janitor or someone to report the vandalism to. We can at least get ahead of it before Reese sees it."

Reed pulled me up, and we walked toward the locker room, not knowing where to start. Opening the doors to the main lobby, I was instantly surrounded by reporters as flashing lights began to go off around me.

"Henley, why did you choose to leave the middle of the game?"

"Was it too much for you to handle?"

"You don't belong here."

"Henley, does this mean you're done coaching?"

"Unable to hack it after all?"

"Henley, what will you do next?"

"Boys need a role model. Not a model."

I shoved them away, not paying attention as Reed and I searched for a different exit. Moving toward a door to the left, we were almost through when a question stopped me in my tracks.

"Congrats on the engagement, Henley. It's so good to see you and Dakota back together after everything. How does he feel about the recent rumors you sent that video to your new boss to get the job?"

Anxiety, fear, and adrenaline overwhelmed me at their words and the realization that someone was actively out to hurt me. My heart raced, my breathing increased, and I tilted sideways as the world shifted. It was all too much.

Glancing at Reed, I feared he looked at me the way Dakota always had. Blue eyes stared at me, making them the last thing I saw before the world went black.

Maybe I wasn't cut out for this after all.

CHAPTER 42

The Society

FROM MY DARK CORNER, I watched as Dakota Hughes introduced his newest recruit to the other Society members. They all slapped one another's backs, sharing stories from their glory days on the ice. The postulating was a bit ridiculous, but I'd come to expect it when a group of men gathered together.

Especially hockey players.

Something about the accepted violence in the game made them more arrogant and domineering. A dangerous combination, if not harnessed correctly.

Fortunately, The Society had learned the secret formula to keep them in line.

The Council had tried to copy it but had gotten lost in their grab for power and greed. It wasn't a shock to anyone in The Society that they'd finally been uncovered and outed to the world.

For a secret society, they'd been too obnoxious and overt to ever stay truly hidden.

Not like us. The Society was one of the world's oldest and most secret clubs. We weren't after power or hell-bent on taking over the world, meaning other groups like The Order left us alone, soon forgetting about us altogether.

For The Society, we were after one thing and one thing only.

Looking around the room at the individuals gathered, both old and young, I stared proudly at what we'd accomplished so far, knowing it was just the beginning.

Standing, I stepped into the light; the others quieted as they watched me approach.

"Gentlemen, should we begin?"

As they gathered around the oval table, excitement built in my chest at what the future promised.

And as I smacked the gavel down onto the table, I knew this next vote had the potential to make us stronger or tear us apart.

"Henley Henshaw. Where do we stand?"

To be continued...

Henley has been one of my favorite characters to write. She's strong and soft in all the best ways. She loves her sibling with all her heart, is passionate about her friends, and tries so hard to be what the world tells her to be... Until the world turns on her, and she finds her own voice. I think that is something we all probably can identify with in a way, so I hope Henley's story resonates with you and reminds you to be whoever the fuck you want.

I plan to have this series completed and released by the end of June, so there won't be too long between books to sink your teeth into the next one and find out how it all plays out.

This book wouldn't have been possible without a few people. First, I always thank the stars for the day I met my bestie and was blessed with a permanent cheerleader. Emma, you always know how to cheer me on, support me, and love my characters. So, thank you for being there with me through another book.

Megan and Heather, thank you for your laughs and comments, for always being ready to read the next chapter, and fighting over who licks who first. You help to push me through the times when I second guess everything. I appreciate you more than you know!

Lindsay and Kayla, you both bring your A-game and give me all the support and help to make the final product the best it can be. Thank you for your love of my words and commitment.

To all my ARC readers, thank you for spreading the word and getting my book in front of people. You make this job so fun, and I love every mention, like, video, and edit you create.

And to the person reading this far, thank you for giving a new series a chance. I hope you found something you loved between the pages.

Also By

For the most up to date look at my releases. Check out all my books here: https://authorkrisbutler.com/my-books

LUX BRUMALIS

Penalty Box

Dead Lift

Breakaway

THE COUNCIL SERIES

(completed series)

Damaged Dreams

Shattered Secrets

Fractured Futures

Bosh Bells & Epic Fails

The Council Boxset

THE ORDER DUET (COUNCIL SPINOFF)

Stiletto Sins

Lipstick Lies

DRESSED TO KILL SHARED WORLD (STANDALONE)

Raven

F*CK STEAL KILL

F*ck Steal Kill

DARK CONFESSIONS

Dangerous Truths

Dangerous Lies

Dangerous Vows

Reckless (Cami's Novella)

Relentless (Nat's Novella)

Dangerous Love

TATTOOED HEARTS DUET

Tattooed Hearts Completed Duet

Riddled Deceit (Part 1)

Smudged Lines (Part 2)

MUSIC CITY DIARIES

Beautiful Agony

VACATION ROMCOM

Vibing

SINNERS FAIRYTALES

(standalone)

Pride

Kris Butler writes under a pen name to have some separation from her everyday life. Never expecting to write a book, she was surprised when an author friend encouraged her to give it a try and how much she enjoyed it. Having an extensive background in mental health, Kris hopes to normalize mental health issues and the importance of talking about them with her characters and books. Kris is a southern girl at heart but lives with her husband and adorable furbaby somewhere in the Midwest. Kris is an avid fan of Reverse Harem and hopes to add a quirky and new perspective to the emerging genre. If you enjoyed her book, please consider leaving a review. You can contact her the following ways and follow Kris's journey as an author on social media.

www.ingramcontent.com/pod-product-compliance
Lightning Source LLC
Chambersburg PA
CBHW051311190726
48290CB00001B/98